Dust Jacket, Paperback, and Ebook cover by Julia Rohwedder. (www. lunaryxdesign.com)

❀ Created with Vellum

THIS ECLIPSED CROWN

THE ELYSIAN SAGA BOOK ONE

LINA C. AMAREGO

SILVER WHEEL PRESS
FANTASY WORLDS OTHER STORIES

THE ELYSIAN SAGA 1

THIS
ECLIPSED
CROWN

LINA C. AMAREGO

To Armand,
For that car ride to New Hampshire where we stumbled into this world
together.
I will always be by your side. Step for step.

And to the rest of my family...
don't read this one.

CONTENT WARNING

This book includes the following warnings: gore, sexually explicit content (all with consent), depictions of anxiety, depictions of chronic illness, adult language, mentions of torture, mentions of parental abuse, death, murder, thoughts of suicide, depictions of strained or toxic relationships, manipulation, war, and other potentially difficult material. Reader discretion is advised.

GLOSSARY OF TERMS

Terms

Skia: Shadow Magic from Inferni that created the Shadowborne.

Shadowborne: A race of monsters born from corrupted elven souls.

Zo'is: An organically occurring dust that fuels magic

Skialogo: Shadow Horses from the Inferni plane.

Vinculum: A magical bond that unites a pair in energy and emotion.

Vassilla: King of Erebus.

Diavolos: An extinct race of demons that used to inhabit the Inferni Plane

Inferni: The dark plane where Erebus is.

Lux: The prominent empire of the Elysian Continent

Erebus: The kingdom of outcast elves living in Erebus

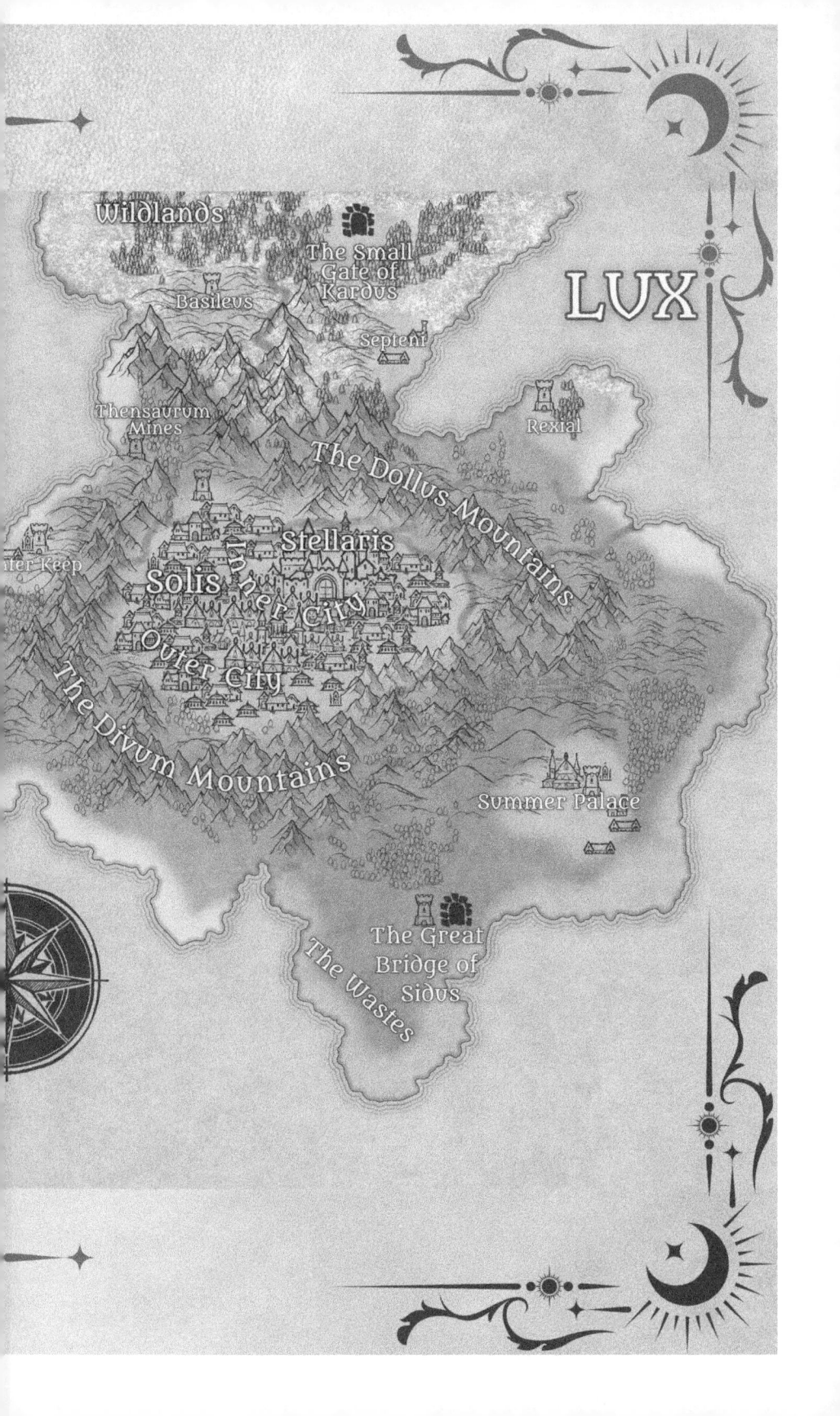

Wildlands

The Small Gate of Kardus

Basileus

Septeni

LUX

Thensaurum Mines

Rexial

The Dollus Mountains

Stellaris

Solis

Inner City

...er Keep

Outer City

The Divum Mountains

Summer Palace

The Wastes

The Great Bridge of Sidus

PROLOGUE

A babe sleeps in an ornate cradle, his mother rocking him gently.

He does not yet know the world. Does not yet know himself.

But he knows the sound of his mother's voice, gently cooing him back to bed. Knows the comfort of her fingers trailing through his tiny wisps of white-gold hair.

The world is dark. Night presses close, swaddling the babe in soft reprieve. A light flicks on, bathing the babe in luminous blue. Shadows pause in the corners, holding their breath. Waiting.

A man's gruff voice echoes, "He is so small. But one day, the whole world will fit in his palm."

The baby wakes, crying out into the world. The man's nose wrinkles. He does not understand how a creature so small can be so terrifying.

The mother stays silent. Her voicelessness is her weapon, her secrets her ammunition. She paints on a pacifying smile—one she'll teach the babe when he's older. When he, too, knows his place . . . and his weakness.

But it does not stop the thought from banging against her skull, a thunderous war-cry.

He is so small. But one day, his fist will crush the whole world.

A child sits on her father's knee, bouncing happily.

She does not yet know pain. Does not know fear.

But she knows the steadiness of her father's presence, softly patting her back. Knows the firmness of his tone as he chides her with a smile.

The world is dark. Night dwells and lingers, scratching at the door to get in. A knock sounds—the father stills. The shadows writhe and dance, breathing the child in. Anticipating.

A woman's voice shakes on the other side of the door. "She is too young. The darkness will consume her."

The father remains quiet. His silence is an escape, his omission a portal. He adjusts his crown—one he'll pass on to the child when she's older. When she, too, knows her strength . . . and her breaking point.

But it does not stop the protest from surging to his lips, banging against his teeth to break free—just once.

"She is too young. But she will devour the dark."

A girl lays awake on a threadbare blanket, listening to the song of her mother's soft snores.

She does not yet know loneliness. Does not know cold.

But she knows the warmth of a shared bed. Knows the heat of the sun, of a hug, of Mother's soup simmering on the hearth.

The world is dark. Night stretches thin, longing for daybreak. A door creaks—the mother startles. The shadows whisper, warning the girl of the dangers ahead. Hiding.

A broken growl rumbles through the small room. "Run. Before it is too late."

The mother swallows her cries. Her silence is a shield; her love, her strength. She places a hand over the girl's heart—one that will break, over and over again. When she, too, learns to love . . . and to lose.

But it does not stop her from rising from the bed, her last words a goodbye.

"Run. It's never too late."

CHAPTER
ONE

"There is nothing more powerful—and fragile—than the pride of a king." –An excerpt from Queen Glorianna's letter to the Elysian people, circa 2 A.G.W. (After the Great War).

THERA

No one warned me how heavy my father's crown would be.

If I were in a meeker condition, my neck might've snapped beneath the cold weight of the ornate diadem, made of the finest Tygian iron in the world. My father had made it look light as a feather, his strong, bearded chin never dipping an inch. Then again, Appa had made many great and terrible things look easy.

Head high, Thera. A king bows to no one.

Despite the force, I tilted my chin up, meeting Minister Stavros's inky eyes. The soupy darkness of the throne room hid the finer details of the old man's expression, but I caught the corner of his mouth bending upward. The flickering candlelight danced lethargically across his pale skin, the good old-fashioned fire-power our only option left.

We'd burned through the last of our *Zo'is* to light the floating lamps during Appa's funeral. To fulfill the last wish of a dying monarch.

It was worth wasting the precious magic dust to see my father's face one last time before sending him to hell.

Where he belonged.

Stavros stepped back on the dais, disappearing into the deep darkness once more to grab Appa's scepter. Then, venturing back into the dim pool of firelight, he knelt before me, holding the iron staff high. The dull metal gleamed in the glow, like the first hesitant rays of dawn; the daybreak of a new era over my shadow-cursed land.

The sun did not shine in Erebus. It had not since the start of the Great War, since the Mad King Alixsander cast my people into Inferni: into the land of shadows and darkness, the realm of *diavolous* and hellbeasts. Since he used his power to seal us away behind the portal, separating our kingdom from the main continent—and all light.

Two thousand years ago.

Forever, even for Elven lifetimes.

My advisor grinned ear-to-ear as I took the scepter, and my chest threatened to burst open. How brightly might Minister Stavros smile once we'd re-emerged into the sunlight? I swore to myself—to *my* new crown—I would see it happen.

Stavros had waited for this moment as long as I had, if not longer. If it hadn't been for my Minister of Laws' careful instruction since my girlhood, I wouldn't have the strength to even look at the throne, never mind dare to sit upon it. He and the rest of Erebus depended on me now.

Such was the burden of a king.

"Stand now, *Mi Vassilla*." Stavros' airy voice caressed my new title. I shoved up from where I knelt at his feet, turning away from my friend and advisor, instead looking over the small crowd amassed to celebrate the Crowning. Hundreds of coal-black eyes watched me, the glowing whites of their gazes the only other source of light in the dark room. They crammed into the crowded space, young and old, perfectly silent in their pregnant expectation.

So different from the apathetic silence of this morning's funeral, where no one shed a single tear. Where no mouth muttered the parting prayers. Even my father's most loyal followers didn't cry his name.

No use wasting words on the dead. We'd lost too many to care anymore.

Such was life in Erebus.

Finally, Stavros lifted my arm to the sky with a triumphant thrust. "All hail Thera Dymitria Umbrus. *King* of Erebus."

The word rattled through me, clanging against my ribs in time with my heartbeat.

King. Not Queen. Not consort. But King, as my power and lineage deserved. The youngest king in Erebushi history, taking my throne two years before my fortieth name day, nearly two decades earlier than my father had.

But my people did not scorn me for my relative youth. Old age was a luxury most of Erebus couldn't afford.

Riotous applause shattered the stillness, breathing life into the room for the first time in decades. A bright, burning tingle ran down my spine, almost as euphoric and potent as a draft of *Zo'is*.

This was the true power in this world. Not *Zo'is*, the fine dust that powered our magic and technology, nor the caustic shadow magic we'd learned since our exile. Not fire or food or any of the other precious resources we'd fought to the death over for the last several centuries.

7

But belief. Belief would build our new kingdom.

I inhaled deeply, savoring the scent of candle wax and kicked-up dust—the smells of life being *lived* again—and squinted into the room, making out the shapes and silhouettes of my advisors and subjects. My chosen people. My father's crown—no, *my* crown—felt lighter.

"Today, Erebus closes one chapter and begins anew," I called out, and the crowd hushed at the sound of my voice. "My father gave his life to defend Erebus, and leaves behind a legacy of greatness, one I will dedicate my life to upholding and expanding."

It was strange how sweet the lie tasted on my tongue, but I'd practiced this part over and over since I was a girl. Still, the crowd devoured the words, eyes all glowing brighter. I fidgeted with the cold ring on my pinky—Amma's ring—letting it ground me to the rocky floor.

My next words were not lies but promises. "I swear to you all, on my life and on the crown of Erebus, that our kingdom will not die with my father. Instead, we will thrive, and I will lead us into a new era of prosperity and life. We will taste the sunlight once more."

It was a heavy vow. One nearly every King before me had made and *broken*. But I did not break.

I turned and exited the dais without warning, no longer a princess waiting to be dismissed, but a king. The cheers erupted, so loud that maybe even the upworlders on Lux could hear it. If they didn't now, I would make sure they did soon.

I swept into the adorning room designated as the Select Council chambers; Stavros' footsteps followed close behind. The air was stale, stagnated by centuries of tradition. But the candlelight reached farther across the small space, illuminating the round, wooden table and half-a-dozen high-backed chairs at the center. Soon, people who demanded more than a pretty speech would fill them. Here was where my plans would become more than promises. Where they'd test my worth as king, just as my father was.

I looked at his portrait, framed in the same iron as my crown. It still hung behind the northernmost chair. His pale skin and black hair matched mine, his cheeks just as gaunt. But even in art, his stare brimmed with cold contempt, the Dark King's aura a shadow lingering long after his body decayed.

The door clicked behind me, dimming the continued cheering.

"You were excellent, *Mi Vassillas*." Stavros clapped me on the shoulder, and I relaxed under the warmth of his grip, tearing my eyes from my father's. Stavros' wrinkled face broke into an unfiltered smile.

"Thank you, old friend." I returned his grin but knew it didn't meet my eyes. "But it is easy to charm the people. Charming the snakes in this room might prove far greater a challenge."

The door on the far side of the room burst open, one that led to the east wing of the palace where the court lived.

"Who are you calling a snake?" Stavros jumped at the nymph's unexpected entrance, but I didn't; I knew she'd be the first to come.

"Careful, Nyxia, you'll give the old man a heart attack." My tone was sharp, but my smile was warm.

Nyxia floated into the room, cropped black hair swishing against her chin, her frame lithe as it was little. Her eyes—a shade of light gray uncommon in the shadowlands—burned with mischief as she sized up the old councilman. "This cockroach would survive even if I did."

"I survive by knowing my place," Stavros grunted. "Speaking of which, you are now in the presence of the King. It would be wise of you to address her properly."

"Ah, yes, *Mi Vassilla*." Nyxia rolled her eyes and bowed to me. "Should I fawn over you like the rest of Erebus? Ooh, the new king is so kind, so well spoken, so beautiful . . . " She mocked the high-pitched squeal of many of the court lords and ladies, placing a hand over her forehead. "The King has such enchanting eyes, and her ass is especially round—"

I masked her mouth with my hand, forcing her to swallow back her next insult. Despite her expert training as a spy and her second-to-none stealth, she'd never learned when to sheathe her wicked tongue in the decades I'd known her. When we were girls training in my mother's legion, it'd often meant she had to run each exercise twice as a punishment for her mouth. Which, as her only friend, meant I had to, also. Punished by proximity.

Though now, I was glad for the extra work and the strength it had brought us both.

Strength we'd need in the coming weeks.

"The *King*," I teased, lowering my hand from her mouth before she could decide to bite it, "also knows how to wield her sword rather well and isn't afraid to plunge it into your heart."

Lips curled in a twisted smirk. "Is that a threat, or an invitation?"

A laugh escaped the prison of my chest, rare and real. Nyxia might never have learned the practiced science of silence, but she'd mastered the art of mischief and humor. The only friend I could still count on for a good laugh.

Stavros, much less amused, folded his arms across his chest. "Stop giggling and let the king prepare."

"Shadows and shite, Stavros, loosen up. This is a celebration, isn't it?" Nyxia clicked her tongue, sitting on the edge of the council table instead of in a proper seat. "We have a new king, and I've been promoted from lowly spy to the new Mistress of Shadows. *I* deserve a party."

"All that shiny new title means is more work for you, Nyxia. We cannot afford to celebrate. Not yet," I interjected with a sigh, falling into the seat at the northernmost point of the table—my father's former perch. I pressed my back into the hardwood, letting it fortify me. "The old man is right. This will not be an easy battle."

"For a mere man, perhaps." Nyxia shot me another one of her terrifying smiles. "For you? Child's play."

Yesterday, Nyxia's words might have been all I needed to feel lighter. But the weight of the diadem on my head would not be carried by niceties.

The sun did not shine in Erebus. Darkness instead crawled in every corner, in every heart. Including mine. My people may have learned the language of shadows, but that did not mean we were immune to its effects.

A fact the hordes of Shadowborne lurking in the Deadlands would not soon let me forget.

I faked a grin for my friend, hoping to hide the darkness swirling in my head. "Your loyalty would warm my heart if I didn't think you were full of shit."

"*Mi Vassilla.*" The door from the council chambers opened once more, in walking another man with shadows on his heels. Nyxia jumped from the table and slid into the seat to my right, the air in the room souring in an instant. With a few powerful strides, the man's long, dark robes swept across the wood floor. He fell into a deep bow in front of me, exposing the top of his head, his cropped silver hair so short I could see the bald patch at the crown. "Rousing speech you gave out there. Your father would be proud."

Shadows gripped my chest at the mention of my father, and I was glad he could not see as I refashioned my instinctive grimace into a smile. I fiddled with Amma's ring again.

"Thank you, Commander Kappas." I donned a disinterested tone, one I used to save only for my father. The man stood again; soil-brown eyes hard as the steel he wielded. "Please sit."

Kappas complied, sitting to my right, next to Nyxia. My friend stiffened in her chair, her expression hard as stone. She might have been the only one in all of Erebus to dislike Commander Kappas more than I did, though she had fair reasons.

Like all dark places, Erebus had its share of monsters. Some bore fangs and claws and scales, feeding indiscriminately on flesh and bone to satiate their carnal appetites. Others used their titles and troops to feed their monstrous parts, instead stealing hope and choice from the weak and innocent.

Kappas was a creature of *both* kinds, much like the king he'd once served. When he'd taken command after my mother, there had been no more room for joking or teasing among his ranks, and Nyxia no longer paid for her comments in sweat—but in blood.

He seemed not to notice Nyxia's glare, his dark gaze instead fixed on me. "I look forward to seeing what other skills you've learned from the late king."

I bit my cheek so hard that the hot taste of blood filled my mouth. If only Kappas and the rest of Erebus knew all the dark tricks my father had taught me.

Two more figures waltzed through the open door, saving me from speech and bringing with them a wave of relief.

"Yes, I agree, your words today were inspired," the taller man said in greeting, nodding his head quickly in a short bow before rounding the table. His movement matched his speech, both brisk and bouncing. "Though having known your father, I can't imagine it was his doing at all. Your mother, perhaps . . . "

It took all my effort to hold back the chuckle that threatened to unleash itself from my mouth. Commander Kappas might have been the military leader, but his boldness paled compared to Minister Agyros. The handsome Minister of Medicine was the youngest elf to sit on the Select Council, and he'd earned his position with his sheer wit and unceasing energy. It also helped that his wavy brown hair and soft smile eased many lonely hearts, his talent for befriending people of every faction second to none. Even my father, who often failed to see accomplishments outside the battlefield, could acknowledge his talent and tenacity.

Agyros offered one of those winning smiles as he took his seat, and the pit in my center heated at the warmth.

The stubbier of the two men—Minister Hasapis, the Minister of Finance—waddled in after his companion, sitting adjacent to

Kappas with a frown that emphasized every cavernous wrinkle on his face. "Our late king has not been in the River of Souls for more than a few hours, Agyros. Let's not yet sully his name."

The wind did not blow in Erebus, but I could've sworn a cool gust swept down my spine at his words. No time or distance would ever dull the memory of my father's funeral. The freezing water of the River Stygia had seeped into my very soul, sweeping a part of me away with my father's burning pyre.

"It would be better if we kept our focus on the task at hand, and on the *new* king's agenda." Stavros saved me yet again, his voice pulling me from the phantom river's clutches.

"Thank you, Stavros." I cleared my throat and straightened in my seat, shaking off the remnants of the memory. I drank in the faces around the table, at the Select Council I'd mostly inherited from my father. Of all the battles I might face in the weeks ahead, this would be the most important one. Without their support, a king was nothing in Erebus, no matter how many shadows she commanded.

A truth my father learned far too late.

I would not make the same mistake. "Now that you all are here, I am eager to disclose my plans for the wellness of our shared home."

Hasapis and Kappas donned twin scowls and shifted in their seats. I raised a hand, and Stavros stood and fetched the scrolls I'd ordered drawn from one of the bookshelves. He set them in front of me, dipping his head so it never raised higher than my own. I offered a small smile before gesturing to his seat. "Our first order of business—"

"*Mi Vassilla*, with all due respect, this meeting is more of a formality . . . " Hasapis said, lounging back into his chair. The old elf loved few things more than money; namely the drinks and women one could buy with it. His greedy gaze darted to the door, the one that led back to the throne room. While Erebus did not have the resources for true luxury, the revelry beyond the oak door was palpable. There were many wicked pleasures that people could conjure in the comforting privacy of the dark. Hasapis licked his thin lips. "You should enjoy your coronation, let us Ministers reflect on policy and plans, and we will reconvene after—"

"This meeting is whatever I say it is." I chuckled, the sound a sharp edge, one I intended to strike with. "I trust you do not mind the work? If it is too cumbersome, perhaps I can nominate your replacement with haste."

The threat was empty—I had no intention of dismissing my father's court. Aside from Stavros and Nyxia, they were all snakes and liars who would dance gleefully around my pyre if given the opportunity. But I needed them to respect my sovereignty if I would truly unite Erebus to my cause. Needed them close so I could watch them.

But Hasapis didn't know that.

Head high, Thera. A king bows to no one.

I would not bow on the battlefield, and I certainly wouldn't to Minister Hasapis, of all fools. No longer a princess, but a king, I had no time for games. *Erebus* had no time.

"*Mi Vassilla*—" Hasapis stuttered, round face reddening. The other Ministers dipped their heads, each avoiding my gaze, not risking my contempt. Except Nyxia, who fought to hide a smirk.

I was less chuffed. This was my opening.

Years of careful planning. Years of secret meetings with Nyxia and her band of spies in the dead of night. Years of risking my life in the Deadlands for answers; of training and preparation that left deep scars—physical and emotional.

Of deception and betrayal that would haunt my final breath.

All for this. We were out of *Zo'is*. Out of luck. Out of time. It was my duty to fix it.

No one told me how heavy my father's crown would be. But I knew all along, and I'd planned for its price long before I seized it.

I would seize this moment all the same.

"By week's end, I will be back in Lux."

Silence filled the small space, thick with tension. All five sets of eyes snapped to me, some with horror, others glee.

"*Mi Vassilla,* I support this effort," Commander Kappas blurted first, a glib smile spreading across his face. He leaned back in his chair, puffing his chest out. "Your father and I had been readying the first and second legions for months, and I can have them prepared in two days to depart—"

"Thank you, Commander Kappas." I kept my voice low. I knew exactly what my father and the old commander had planned for Lux. I'd been their favorite weapon for decades, and I had no interest in their scheming. "But I only require a small personal escort on this trip. This is not a military endeavor."

Kappas' brow knotted. "*Mi Vassilla—*"

"Truly, it seems you are all content to wear out my new title with protests," I scoffed. "We go to Lux to make peace, not war."

Kappas took the bait, his face falling as his volume increased. "You'll surrender? When we have come so close?"

"No, not surrender. Bargain." I stood and unfurled the top scroll with a flourish, a second draft of the very proposal I'd already sent to Lux a week ago when news of my father's death had first reached the people. I smoothed out the parchment, laying clear to my council the fruits of years of labor. "It is not unknown that we need *Zo'is.* Our people live in darkness, and while many of us have learned to accommodate, the threat of the Shadowborne grows larger every day. Magic is life for the elves, and we've been half-dead for too long. And while I'm sure the first and second legions are prepared to help contain them, I have reservations about fighting a war on two fronts, and letting our people die to a disease that is avoidable."

At the mention of the Shadowborne, both Agyros and Hasapis paled while Kappas simmered in his rage. No one, not even Kappas, needed a reminder of the horrors one undead bloodsucker could conjure. Not after they'd all seen my father's body themselves. Not after the hundreds of bodies that had come before him, torn to shreds by the Shadowborne's vicious appetite, or worse . . . *turned.*

The sickness started several centuries ago as an unforeseen consequence of using shadow magic instead of *Zo'is*. All magic had a price, and most elves could only cultivate the smallest bit of darkness before the mind and body were both forever changed by it. Even the brightest of souls could be corrupted by the shadows, bodies distorted and ruined as they transformed into beasts, hungry for power. For *life*. But even then, we did not know how deep the consequences would run—that a single bite from a Shadowborne's fangs could turn a soul black, no matter how innocent.

The spread had been worse in the last few decades. Now, the Shadowborne pushed from the Deadlands, invading our borders almost weekly. And somehow, they'd even populated the upworld, too. Shadowborne nests littered the darkest corners and caves of the Divum mountain ranges.

Agyros swallowed hard, his light eyes burning brighter in the dim room. "I share your worries, *Mi Vassilla*, but what makes you think Lux will agree to truce after centuries of war?"

A question I'd asked myself hundreds of times in the last few years, if not thousands. A question I pondered every time a new body showed up in the coroner's office, drained of blood and sunken in. A question I repeated every time my father still sent me and the other soldiers through the portal border to Lux, starving and afraid, making us face strange weapons that could eviscerate ten men with a single shot.

One I finally had an answer for. I pushed the parchment forward toward Agyros with a single finger. "I plan on making them an excellent offer."

Kappas' hold on his temper frayed, the man practically vibrating with his anger. "Lux has taken *everything* from us. Our freedom, our *Zo'is*, our way of life." He grit through clenched teeth, the vein in his forehead threatening to pop. "What could we possibly offer them?"

I shrugged, sinking back into my chair with a practiced smirk. "Me."

"Someone thinks highly of herself!" Kappas thundered as he shot from his seat like it bit him in the ass.

Hasapis blinked in abundance, the numbers crunching in his tiny head. "I—I don't quite understand your meaning, *Mi Vassilla*."

Nyxia leaned forward, the little nymph no longer content to contain her gloating. This plan was just as much hers as it was mine, so much of our information won by the blood and effort of her band of spies. "King Kato is in search of a bride for his heir. The man is old, and the late *Vassillo's* death has reminded quite a few kings of their mortality."

Kato had sat on his throne nearly as long as my father had. And while the Luxian medics had far more *Zo'is* to keep him healthy, four centuries was a long time to lead.

Hasapis looked down his nose at her, his voice coming out in a preening whine. "You of all people should know, dear Mistress of Shadows, that there have been rumors of Kato petitioning the outer kingdoms and lesser lords for a suitable marriage for his son."

I fought back a snort. Those rumors Nyxia herself had planted months ago to stir the pot just enough for us to sneak our ingredients into the recipe.

Nyxia grinned, folding her arms across her chest. "And you must know, dear Minister, that no one will enter that contract, even with Lux's wealth and strength. Not while they are still at war with us. Not while we have the *Sykagos*."

Hasapis silenced, cheeks reddening with all the insults he swallowed. I kicked Nyxia's leg under the table, willing her to play nice.

"Moreover, Lux is running out of land," Stavros spoke, unraveling another scroll for me, this one a map of the two territories. Even in drawing, the Luxian landscape looked cramped and suffocated, trapped within the borders of the Divum and Dollus Mountains. The downside of stealing and hoarding resources, it seemed, was a flourishing population. And with the Shadowborne corralling the outer limits of the continent, the upworlders would have to get creative. "The other kingdoms know that if they agree to share a bed with the Luxians, they will invite them to run amok on their land."

Agyros stiffened, eyes fixed on the map. "You plan to offer up ours?"

My gut clenched, knowing all too well this was the hardest part of the plan to swallow. None of them cared about me or who I married, and if my hand—or head—was all that we needed to secure some precious *Zo'is*, it was an easy price to pay. But while Inferni was little better than a wasteland, the lightless expanse of our territory both barren and brutal, it was still all we had. Still home. Giving up even an inch of our land would require compensation.

I crafted a mask of indifference instead, unwilling to expose my worry to their scrutiny. A king bowed to no one, nor did she cry to them. "We have plenty of land, Agyros. Imagine how nice it might look decorated with Luxian *Zo'is* instead of the carcasses the Shadowborne leave behind."

I knew my words would strike true before they registered on the Minister's face, but I felt my shoulders relax as they did. His brows flew up, hope burning like coal in the black of his pupils.

Not that I blamed him. If anyone wanted to see the death rate of our people decrease more than me, it was our Minister of Medicine. He didn't need me to paint the gruesome picture for him—he lived and breathed it every day.

"You want to marry a Luxian?" Kappas slammed his fist on the table, knocking over two of the scrolls. "Let him fuck you like a common whore? To give *them* all of Erebus? If your father were here —he'd—"

"He is not here," I spat back at Kappas, reminding him exactly which parts of myself I'd inherited from my father. The shadows across the room stirred, swirling toward me in a misty haze, and

Kappas blanched. "A Shadowborne killed him. We buried him this morning, if you recall."

The shadows crept closer; the heat draining from the room as my magic grew. Fear and sweat turned the air, the rest of the Ministers keeping their gazes low.

A pinch bit my thigh beneath the table, Nyxia daring a look at me from under her thick lashes. I exhaled, releasing the tension building in my gut as the shadows crept back to their fixed places on the walls.

The room stayed silent, but I felt them all exhale.

"My father's death has reminded me of my mortality as well. Of the mortality of our people." I kept my voice gentle, reminding myself of the king I wanted to be. "How many bodies will we flush down the great river in the name of a war neither kingdom can win?"

A king bows to no one.

Neither did death. Nor grief.

"How many Luxians have you personally sent to their deaths?"

It was Agyros that set the challenge, his stare unwavering.

A deep pang of regret echoed through me, the ghosts haunting my crown whispering in the recesses of my mind. Before I was King of Erebus, I had another far less flattering title, one that many elves uttered as their last words.

Sykagos.

Soul Eater.

After a long moment, I did not hide the quiver from my voice. "Far too many to count. I was my father's favorite weapon, after all."

Agyros nodded in somber understanding. He was only a decade my senior, but he'd already been the head medic during the many mornings I spent in his office, tending to wounds I'd earned for and *from* my father.

Hasapis broke his silence, his voice as shaky as his trembling chin. "And if the Luxians can't overlook your past? If they refuse your offer?"

"Well, I imagine they'd probably send this *thing* back," I said and slid the crown from my head and let the full weight of it dangle from my littlest finger, "along with my head, and you can all fight over who wears it next."

The Ministers—even Kappas—watched the crown swing from its perch for a moment, enchanted eyes tracking the movement like hawks. Such was the curse of powerful men; they always craved *more*. Like Shadowborne, always hungry, they thirsted for it enough to risk everything.

I was counting on their gluttony to see this plan through.

I flipped the crown in my hand and returned its weight to my head, breaking the trance I had them under.

"Your plan is both risky and visionary, *Mi Vassilla.*" Stavros emphasized my title as a reminder to the other Ministers. "I stand by you."

"As do I," Agyros echoed, warm stare still fixed on the diadem. Then, it shifted to me, trained on my mouth. "Perhaps with Lux in our pocket, we could not just stop the Shadowborne from spreading, but maybe we could find a cure."

"At the very least, maybe we could *see* them better." Hapasis sighed and rubbed his eyes, resigned as a slave to his greed. "I wouldn't mind a little *Zo'is.*"

Kappas shoved to his feet, the volcano finally ready to blow. "I will not stand for this treason!"

"Then you may sit here and pout all you'd like, Kappas." I pushed back from the table and stood slowly, staring over Nyxia's head to meet his gaze. Kappas was far taller and broader than I was, but we'd fought on countless battlefields together, and he knew I was not just king in title, but in power. I ran my tongue over my teeth once as a reminder, the taste of shadows on my tongue. "But I am not my father, and I will not stand for your insubordination. Do I make myself clear?"

Kappas stared back, defiance dancing in his eyes, but did not reply, jaw clenched too tight to utter a sound. Instead, he stomped from the room, slamming the door behind him as he fled to lick his wounds in private.

I straightened my skirts, my expression neutral as I turned to the other Ministers, daring them to follow Kappas with a glare. "You are all dismissed for today. Nyxia, send a messenger to Lux, one you trust with the job."

Nyxia leapt from her chair, a feral smile on her sharp features. "Of course, *Mi Vassilla.*"

"Send my future groom a gift. Something impressive," I ordered loudly before leaning down to whisper in my friend's ear. "Perhaps a drawing of my especially round ass."

Nyxia winked once before exiting, my spy master and best friend off to seal the fate of our kingdom.

Relishing the delicious weight of the crown, I held my head high and crossed the room in a few long strides, not caring to see if the others followed. I was King of Erebus now. I waited for no one. Bowed to no one.

And I had a kingdom to conquer.

The stairs down to the Pool of Souls were barely wide enough for my slim frame to march down. Stavros insisted on following me, the man's broad shoulders bumping against the damp stones as we wound round and round, deeper and deeper, into my father's personal playpen.

The chill crept further up my spine for every step I descended, a reflection of the frost in my heart. A coldness that would never thaw, born of years without sunshine, without the warmth of a mother's love.

But I'd stopped wishing for those things decades ago. The dark and cold were all I knew, and I'd made them mine.

We crept toward the bottom of the pit, the air now cold enough to mist our breaths.

"Your Majesty, is this . . . is this necessary? The king is gone, he can't force you . . ." Stavros' voice ricocheted off the walls, splitting through my head like metal pinging against glass.

I halted and spun on my advisor so quickly he nearly tumbled into me. He caught himself on the stairs before he could send us both toppling down into the abyss. I exhaled a shaky breath, ignoring the way the shadows inched closer, their dark energy beating against my turned back. I fidgeted with my ring, raising my chin to meet my advisor's worried gaze.

"It's more necessary now than ever. My people are counting on me." I broke his gaze before my expression could betray my fear, the gurgling pit festering in my gut. Instead, I looked toward the dark pool, just a few steps away now. From here, I could hear its whispers. "Now go. I'd like to be alone for a while, Stavros."

Alone, with the magic that sent most elves into madness. That turned men into beasts.

Alone, as the only elf alive to use the shadows and *survive.*

Stavros squeezed my shoulder, a pity-soaked smile curling his lips. He took a step backward up the stairs, back toward the echo of bright revelry. "Come now. There is a party. You deserve to enjoy this victory with your people."

I swallowed back the ball of emotion that lodged itself in my throat. I wanted—desperately, *achingly*—to run myself all the way back up the dozens of stairs to the world waiting above. To launch myself into drink and sex and merriment, to let it strip me of every horrible memory my father left me with. Just one night, a moment of bliss and serenity with my people—in my home—before I had to crawl into bed with a spoiled Luxian prince.

But kings did not follow their wants and whims. Kings led.

And in order to drag Erebus from the darkness and into the light, I had to swim with the shadows first.

I turned my back on my advisor and made my way down the

final steps to The Pit of Lost Souls. "You're dismissed, Stavros. Go have some fun."

He lingered for a moment, his breath held, as if waiting for me to change my mind. To choose myself first, for once in my life.

He knew I would not.

I shut my eyes. Shut him out. After a few long moments, his diminishing footsteps signaled his retreat.

When my eyes opened again, they adjusted naturally to the impossible darkness of the pit. The floor was smooth black obsidian, my reflection staring back at me from the inky surface. My father used to say this place was a relic of the *diavolos* race that'd inhabited Inferni before Alixsander pushed them out, and the otherworldly craftsmanship made the legend almost believable. Walls of dark, uncrafted stone created a cavern, the low ceiling a natural cage of coarse rock and jagged stalactites. They reached down toward the polished floor in stark contrast, like teeth waiting to swallow me whole.

But in the center of the room, the true beast waited. A gaping hole in the obsidian floor, a pool of pure *Skia,* waited.

Shadow magic.

Without the warmth of another body, the playpen dropped even colder, the frigid air nipping at my skin. But I relished the bite, the pain an anchor to my body as I stripped every article of clothing away.

It was strange to lay myself bare like this without an audience. Without the heat of my father's stare at my back, or the stern click of his tongue as he appraised my form. Without the sharp sigh that signaled his disappointment, his harsh hand—or lash—stinging against my cold skin until it scarred.

But I was not alone. Not entirely. The shadows called from the murky pool at the center of the room, a beckoning. The grumble of fear gave way to numbness as the tug in the center of my gut pulled me to the ledge of the pool, to the precipice of sanity itself.

I'd been eight years old when I first felt the shadows' claws rake against my flesh. When my father first pushed me in, to *eradicate the weakness from my womanhood.* To forge me into his favored weapon.

And no matter how many thousands of times I'd been in since, the pain never lessened. But blades needed to stay sharp to remain useful. The kingdom was mine to protect now, and I would not allow myself to become dull and useless.

With one last breath, I sank into that numbness and dove into the pit.

Where I truly belonged, the King of Shadows.

CHAPTER
TWO

CAELUM

My mother used to say books were portals to other worlds. She'd read for hours in her favorite chair, one poised next to the largest window in the castle so she could drink in as much of the warm sunlight as she could, lost in a story. Whenever my condition flared up, she'd tuck me into her soothing embrace. Her fingers running through my hair, her lilting voice carried me and my sickly body into Elysium, paragraph by paragraph.

I sat in the library listening to Mistress Grotchkin drone on and on about the Great War, wishing my mother was right almost as deeply as I wished her alive. Wished I could hop through a book, straight into another world, far from this one. Perhaps one where someone had already turned Grotchkin into the toad she was. Or, perhaps, one where Mama was still there, still tucked into her favorite chair with a cup of blueberry tea and a story—and just enough room for me in her lap.

Wishes were for silly little princes. Not for the heir to the Sunkissed Throne.

"Your Highness, are you listening?" Mistress Grotchkin's voice snared me back from my thoughts to where she peered over her ovular glasses, lips pursed in a fine line that emphasized the valleys of her wrinkled mouth.

I forced myself to look away from the fuzzy mustache growing across the landscape of her upper lip, instead meeting her beady black eyes.

"Of course, Mistress." I flashed a fake smile, one to rival even the brightest *Zo'is* lamps flickering against the walls.

Grotchkin remained unimpressed. She sat as rigid as the back of her wrought-iron chair, the collar of her high-necked, starched white dress pinching her loose neck skin. "If you were listening so intently, *little prince*, what did I say?"

I winced at the slight insult, wishing I could throttle her by her turkey neck. Grotchkin had been my history tutor since I was twelve, and even though I translated the King Alixsander's Commandments by the time I was thirteen—in the original Old Elysian, might I add—the old hag never failed to instruct me on just how young and naive I was. Even after I'd celebrated my quarter-century mark last year, she still equated my youth with a lack of potential. *"Still but a babe in Elven years,"* she'd tsk under her breath whenever I got an answer wrong.

But I was not a child, not anymore. Not with Erebus breathing down the front gates of the kingdom I would inherit. Not with Shadowborne monsters lurking in our territory now, thanks to the *Sykagos's* magic. Not with my father's condition worsening by the day, his age showing in the wrinkles adorning his proud forehead like a crown.

And I no longer needed a tutor. I had learned nothing from the hag in the last five years, my own studies far more advanced than her shriveled raisin of a brain could comprehend.

My smile did not falter as I recounted the history to perfection, not even glancing at the open textbook in front of me, each word a thorn in her brittle old side. "In the days before the Great War, the Elven lands were united under one kingdom, the great Elysia. We lived peacefully, but King Alixsander's first wife, Glorianna, was hungry for power. She betrayed the king by breeding with a *diavolos* from the Inferni realm, a Shadow Demon named Dymitrius."

Grotchkin sucked her teeth, hollowing out her already sunken cheeks. "And then?"

I fought to hide my smile, triumph lighting beneath my skin as I successfully burrowed beneath hers. "You didn't tell me that part of the story yet."

"This isn't a story, this is Luxian history." Grotchkin huffed a proud breath, smugness twisted in the corner of her mouth that twitched upward. "*Your* history, little prince."

I rolled my eyes, lounging further into the biting metal chair. My body ill-suited for hard surfaces, I'd suffer for this later, but I wouldn't give Grotchkin the satisfaction of grabbing a cushion.

A deep breath blew past my lips. "King Alixsander was heartbroken and tried to reason with his wife to come home. But it was too late. Already pregnant with the first half-breed, she'd lost her mind to the shadows, and she would not return to the Stellaris Palace. So Alixsander sealed the portal to the shadowlands, casting her and the other lesser-elves into the darkness where they belong, protecting his chosen people."

I knew I'd recited the work to perfection by the displeased frown that graced her deflated features, but her dismissive scoff left no room for incorrect assumptions. "Don't be so impressed with yourself, boy. Even children know this story."

"It's not a story, it's history." I threw her words back in her face, my tone cool as the metal biting my back. I was not a child, but the crown prince to the most successful empire in the world. And she was my subject before all else.

"And this is not a game." She ground out, her jaw clenched so tightly, I thought her brittle old teeth would snap beneath the force. Still, despite her previous claim, Grotchkin had not yet finished toying with my patience. A snide grin devoured her face. "Tell me, oh wise prince, how *did* Alixsander seal the portal?"

I returned her grin tenfold. "He used a vast amount of *Zo'is*, which he discovered was magic during his Westward Expansion campaign of 153 B.G.S.'"

A brow raised—a taunt. "And how did he make the *Zo'is* work?"

This answer was less common, the question meant to test—or trap—me. *Zo'is* was everywhere in Lux, but in its abundance, it became mundane. Very few elves paid attention to *how* it worked, much like how birds rarely questioned why they flew. It was just a truth of our society, as commonplace as leaves to a tree. But I wasn't just a scholar of history. Aside from my personal studies— including the tomes of medical journals I'd read one summer when it was too hot for me to be outside and I was particularly bored— I'd lived among soldiers and healers my whole life. The *how* mattered to those that needed it to survive.

"*Zo'is* is an organic compound that responds and adapts to the energy source applied to it." I sat taller in my seat. "If set on fire, it becomes a potent burn or explosive. If electrified, it can power an entire city with just a few purified grams. Alixsander used the energy in his body—his very blood—to activate the locking magic. It's the same way *Vinculum* soldiers use it now to strengthen them-selves and enhance their senses."

"It is *not* the same. Alixsander did not need a second body to channel such power." Grotchkin scoffed—displeased that I'd bested her at her own game. Her glare raked over my body—over the fragile, easily bruised skin, over the fluttering, weak pulse in my neck—and frowned. "He alone was strong enough."

I didn't need her to spell it out for me.

Strong.

Unlike me.

"How wonderful for him. Maybe we should build yet another statue in his honor!" Sarcasm dripped from my tone in thick droplets.

Grotchkin swallowed, the insult at her precious deity's expense a blow she would not tolerate.

"The great war is not yet won," she continued, her voice wobbling with her neck. "And now that the Erebushi scum can control the Shadowborne, now that the *Sykagos* can use enough magic to open the portal and manipulate those awful things at will, we need a *strong* leader to keep us safe." Emotion choking her, she slammed her gnarled fist on the large glass table, sending a wave of dust from the open books sparkling into the air. "We *must* heed King Alixsander's will and sacrifice."

"*We* don't need to heed anything, Hylda." My voice dropped to an icy low. "*I* will sit on the Sunkissed throne, not you. And when I do, I doubt a king that's been dead for two thousand years or a priestess who hasn't left the walls of Stellaris in four centuries will be the ones to help me understand what my people need."

If her jaw clenched any tighter, smoke would billow out of her ears. "His Majesty will hear about this."

"Don't worry, I'll tell him myself." My iron chair ground against the polished white marble floor as I pushed out of it. Her mouth fell open, but I slammed my book shut and turned on her before she could blubber another word. "Lessons are over for today. See you in the morning, Crotchkin."

Her croaked insults followed me as I wove through the rows and rows of book stacks, my edged laughter breaking the comfortable silence of the grand library. If Rory were here, the nickname would've had her doubled over with that obnoxious laugh of hers.

The mere thought brought on another wave of laughter. More of the white-robed, stiff-lipped librarians hushed me as I bolted out through the tall, ornately crafted doors, stumbling over myself into the hallway. I threw one last flippant gesture over my shoulder before shutting the doors behind me, my shoulders shaking as I fought to catch my breath.

My head spun, my heart beating way too fast, and metallic saliva pooled behind my teeth. I lowered my head, leaning against the doorframe for support as I waited for the wave of fatigue to pass. Running like that was a poor choice for someone in my condition. But it had been worth it to see the look on Crotchkin's face.

"Do I even want to know?" The deep voice behind me sobered me immediately. I shot upright, scanning myself for imperfections. I tucked the errant fabric of my light blue tunic back into my cream-colored trousers, the colors helping my complexion look less sickly. Sucking down a deep breath that burned my lungs like a hot fireplace poker, I turned and made direct eye contact with my father.

While my soft features favored my mother's lineage, my father could've been my twin in coloring. A trademark of the Borealis line, his white hair cascaded down his back like seafoam, stark against the dark hue of his sun-warmed skin. Luminescent blue eyes—so light they tinged violet—narrowed at me, awaiting an answer.

Our resemblance stopped there. I'd earned none of his gravitas, his purposeful stare. The strong set of his chin and confident posture, nor the deep bass of his commanding voice.

I lowered my head in deference, mostly to hide the shame and exhaustion reddening my cheeks in blotchy patches. So much for the well-picked outfit. I ran my hand through my white hair, only at my chin, to smooth it. I hadn't earned the right to wear it longer. That was a warrior's reward, not that of a spoiled, sheltered little prince. "I—"

"Grotchkin got your goat?" The king cut me off before I could incriminate myself further. Slowly, I raised my head again, greeted by a small smirk tugging at the corner of his mouth.

"She's the worst." My shoulders eased as I offered him a shy grin in return. I was not a warrior or a leader, not yet. But I was my father's favorite son. Even if I was his only.

My father clapped me on the shoulder, leaning in to whisper in my ear. "I remember. She was my tutor, too, you know. Older than dirt."

His light eyes glimmered with long-forgotten boyhood, but he expelled a heavy sigh. "But she knows the histories well—Sun and Stars, she was *alive* for half of them. Learn what you can from people, even if you don't like them. A good king takes in the words of all the people he meets, not just the ones who align with him politically."

I swallowed hard, my breath steadying. "Yes, Father."

He patted my shoulder again, jerking his chin to the open hallway. "Walk with me, Cael."

I nodded, following in his footsteps as I had since boyhood.

He led me through the too-warm east wing. The afternoon sunlight poured through the rows of stained-glass windows, bouncing off the pure white marble and creating a greenhouse. My pearl tunic clung to the sweaty small of my back by the time we worked our way through the massive gold doors to the grounds outside. The cool air of the eastern gardens washed over my skin in a welcome respite, damp earth and fragrant flowers smelling like candy.

We kept walking, through the gardens and up the hill, and even though my heart rate jumped again, even though my breath drew short, I didn't mind.

When my father finally paused at the edge of Stellaris' territory, right where the grounds butt up against the Dollus Mountains, I exhaled in relief.

The golden sunlight filtered green through the breezy willow branches, reverence settling in my stomach. The willow grove was the most sacred space in this kingdom.

Here, the sunlight did not burn or bleach, but it gently kissed the shrubbery, nourishing every hungry leaf, helping them grow. The tall grass swayed in small pools of shade, the only place in Lux that allowed the quiet comfort of soft shadows.

I stepped out of the direct sunlight and nestled myself on one of the plain wooden benches beneath the tallest willow, enjoying the dim shelter of the leafy canopy. This place was simple, and it paled compared to the ornate fountains and hedges that littered the carefully plotted Southern and Western gardens. But I loved this grove, unadorned as it was, more than anywhere else in all of Lux.

I leaned back against the tree, running my finger over my mother's initials carved there. Her favorite, too, once. It was the only real decoration in the uncultivated beauty of the willow park, and it never failed to bring a smile to my face and an ache to my heart.

My father sighed as he sat on the bench next to me, his bright eyes misting as he took in the embossed letters in the rough bark. "You know, when your mother and I first married, we snuck to this tree often in the middle of the night to talk."

"Really? That's romantic." I fixed my gaze on the swirling knots in the wooden bench, memorizing the pattern. Had my mother done the same once? Had she too struggled to meet my father's gaze, the weight of his stare burning into her cheek?

His scoff surprised me, as did the smirk that cleaved his face. "Hardly. It was survival. We knew nothing about each other when our parents wed us. I was a young, headstrong prince, and she was a sheltered lady from outer-circle nobles that had never been in the city. She would come here because the *Zo'is* made it too bright to sleep."

The pain in my chest sharpened to a knifepoint. *Zo'is* was life itself, the source of all magic and progress in this world. The raw material mined from the mountains had more applications than trees had leaves—from medicine to power sources to machinery. But the harsh neon-blue brightness of the substance stung my sensitive eyes just as it did hers. Another piece of her I kept even after she was gone. "She never liked the afterglow. Always preferred actual sunlight."

And *shade*, though she rarely voiced that opinion aloud.

"She had good taste, if I say so myself." My father chuckled, his voice a deep rumble that shook his shoulders. "Though when we first met, I thought she was a bore with no personality. Sure, she was lovely, but I nearly throttled my father for making me marry such a dull woman."

Anger flashed through my veins brighter than *Zo'is*. "Mama wasn't—"

"No, she wasn't. But it took me a while to understand that," he said, his voice strained with an unnamed ache.

My shoulders relaxed. I knew my father loved my mother more than there were stars in the sky.

"Before I knew it, I was in love with her. Her sharp mind, her quiet strength," he continued, that pained smile still stretched thin across his aging face.

Something twisted in my gut, instinct churning around the words he wouldn't say, the hidden meaning beneath the softness of his tone. He rarely spoke of her these days, his grief a gag. I narrowed my eyes. "You're nostalgic today. What's gotten into you?"

"I married for duty, as most in our station do, but I also won love through that bond. I wish I could offer you that same opportunity, my boy."

He patted my knee; the action laced with strange comfort. My father and I were close, not just my idol, but a true mentor my whole life. Everything I knew, I learned from his example. He did his best to teach me despite the ways my illness held me back; protected me when I couldn't do so for myself. But he was rarely this affectionate, this . . . well, this much like Mama.

My stomach flopped again, anxiety prickling through my veins. "But?"

Papa turned away, his eyes fixed on the outline of Stellaris in the distance. Even in the quiet shade of the willow grove, the opalescent palace glittered and blinded. The pride of Lux, and the symbol of the duty Father carried in the weight of his crown—the same crown he'd one day pass to me.

"We received a missive from the Tygian Castle this morning," he finally said, voice just as cold and sharp as the palace walls. "The King of Erebus is dead, and his daughter Thera has taken his throne."

The twisting thing in my gut snapped straight, a bow suddenly pulled taught and ready to fire.

Theron Umbrus of Erebus was dead. The Dark King, gone.

A victory for the people of Lux, perhaps the signal to the end of the war, if not for the even darker monster lurking in his expansive shadow.

The Soul Eater.

A threat not to just Lux, but to Elvenkind as a whole. The most powerful, lethal creature to blacken this world. Some said she was not really Theron's daughter, but a *diavolos* disguised as an elf, her horns and leather wings hidden by glamours. Others said that she was just born cruel, her thirst for blood born of a sick, twisted mind.

Without her master to hold the leash, what unspeakable atrocities would she commit?

I leapt from the bench, hands shaking at my side. "Father, what are we doing? We must ready the troops—surely the Soul Eater will be here soon with more of those Shadowborne monsters."

My father stood, blocking my path before I could begin pacing. His bright eyes stared through mine to my very essence. The whirling in my head quieted as he shook his head slowly.

"On the contrary, Thera has proposed a truce. A surrender." His lips formed that thin line again, this time slimmer than a single blade of grass. "You know I wouldn't ask anything of you I wouldn't offer freely myself, son."

Realization exploded through me with the force of *Zo'is* bomb. In its wake, a black hole formed in the center of my chest, sucking out all the hope from my heart.

The sharp undercurrent to my father's nostalgic rant finally rose to the surface, those unspoken words thundering in my head.

"You want me to marry her."

I waited for his denial, for him to shake his head again. For my father to absolve me of the duty to my people, to put his responsibility as a father before his commitment as King.

Instead, he nodded. "I want you to protect the people of Lux, in whatever way we can."

To protect Lux, the most wonderful, marvelous place in all Elven history. My mother's homeland, my birthright.

My people, who'd suffered at the *Sykagos'* hands for too long. Whose fear scented the air of the lower town whenever I rode among them. Whose sorrow clouded the sunshine.

I swallowed my apprehension, shoving it all deep, deep down, as I did when Mama died. "This could be a trap."

But my father shook his head.

"Perhaps. But this could end the war." The phrase, though his tone undecorated, glittered in front of me like a jewel. A single, sparkling kernel of hope against that darkness that threatened to consume me from within. "I'll give you time to think it over."

My gut clenched.

An end to the war. Or at the very least, a pause, to give us time to find a new way to save our people.

Perhaps the *Sykagos* was a devil in disguise, or just a twisted perversion of nature. Perhaps the new king had sharper fangs than the Dark King before her, or maybe Erebus was truly out of options and ready to surrender.

But her intentions—her nature—did not matter.

Mine did. And if I would make my father—and Mama—proud, I would have to make my name in this world.

Caelum Borealis, consort and conqueror of the *Sykagos*. Not just a little prince, but a king to be respected. A savior of the people.

"I don't need time. Send your fastest messenger." I broke my father's gaze, instead staring at my mother's favorite tree. She may have favored the shade, but even she stepped into the sunlight every day, her duty more important than her wants and wishes. She would've given her life to protect Lux. In many ways, she had.

And even though I longed to linger in the shade a little longer, even as I wished I could jump into one of Mama's books and disappear into a different world . . .

I lifted my chin with painted-on confidence, practice for when I'd one day wear my father's crown. "Tell the staff to plan the wedding."

My lungs struggled to suck in air, each breath scraping in and out faster than the last.

I'd held it in through my goodbyes to my father this afternoon, all the way back into the palace, up the stairs, and down the long hall to the west wing, passing dozens of servants and guards with curt nods and tight smiles. But in the safety of my quarters, I let myself unravel. The moment I burst through the door to my chambers, the whirlwind crashed into me like an oncoming storm, hot bile rising in my throat and into the porcelain sink.

I'd been prepared to marry for duty my whole life. It was my job as the future king, to ensure the Luxian line stayed strong, to marry another Sunkissed Noble and continue the line of power for another generation. As the one and only heir to my father's blood rite, it was of even greater importance. My seed was the only chance we had to live on, to keep our people happy and whole as we had for centuries.

It was why my father never let me join him and the others on the front lines of battle. Sure, I'd sat in on every strategy meeting and war council since I turned ten, absorbing every ounce of information I could amongst Father and his generals. And sure, despite my illness, I'd learned some swordsmanship and combat strategies with the occasional defense exercises Rory put me through, those alone enough to have me panting.

But my protection was not just for my sake—it was for the sake of the kingdom, for Lux itself. My life was not only mine. It belonged to the people and their children and their children's children. And I would willingly lay it down at the foot of whatever girl my father chose for me if it meant keeping that legacy strong. Father had inquired quietly for a few months now that I'd reached adulthood, ready to secure more heirs in case anything ever happened to him or I. The threat had grown even greater in recent years, with the Soul Eater and her dark, lethal abilities bringing the war closer and closer to our doorstep.

I just never imagined it would be *her* I'd share a marriage bed with.

The air thinned even further. The thought of her cold, shadowed claws closing around my neck sent shivers down my spine. I'd never seen her myself, but every report from the warfront said the same thing.

A monster, shrouded in pure darkness, a creature vicious enough to rival the Shadowborne, but without their unthinking bloodlust. She'd felled entire legions with her power alone, a force of unholy nature to be feared by even the most seasoned warriors.

Thera Umbrus. *Sykagos*. The Soul Eater.

My future wife. My *queen*.

The knock at the door kept time with the pounding beat of my heart slamming against my ribs.

"Caelum? Are you in there?" A raspy whisper from the other side, one I knew as well as my own.

I wiped my mouth, voice shaking as I called out, "Not now,

37

Rory."

Normally, my guard's presence was a welcome warmth, her fire and friendship all I typically needed to right my mood.

But I knew the worry that would wait in her liquid-gold gaze, the unspoken disappointment that would slump her shoulders once I told her . . .

No, I couldn't handle that right now. Not on top of the soul-crushing loss I already felt, having signed my life away to satisfy the Soul Eater's insatiable hunger.

A scoff from the other side of the door, then the creak of the hinges as it opened. "Put your cock away, I'm coming in."

I whipped around, a growl at the back of my throat. "Sun and stars, I said—"

"What's wrong?" Rory cut me off with an efficiency that matched her swordsmanship, quick and brutal. She stood in the archway between my sitting room and my washroom, platinum armor bright against her deep bronze skin. Her stare burned with questions as they quickly swept over me, my trusted guard and dearest friend assessing me with clinical scrutiny.

Her brutal beauty always caught me off guard, her sharp cheekbones and strong jaw, the sapphire tattoo that wound up her arm and across her neck and face, her long golden hair the color of the sunlight that glinted off the opal palace . . .

Even the jagged scar that covered her left eye, pink and raised even after the few years that had passed. Somehow, it completed her, a mark of the hardships she'd endured and overcome. She'd been pretty when we were little, but as an adult and a soldier . . .

Power and danger incarnate, a woman forged into a sword. Not just any blade, but *my* blade, my guard, my right hand.

Would I get to keep her by my side after I married the *Sykagos?*

That would be selfish. *Spoiled.*

I cleared my throat and hid my shaking hands behind my back, standing upright. "Nothing. I'm fine."

She sank into her hip, tongue pressing against her cheek.

Aurora Bellatore had the uncanny ability to see through bullshit like it was clear as glass. Specifically, my bullshit. "Liar. I know you. What's wrong?"

"For starters?" I pushed past her so she couldn't read the lie in my eyes, walking from the marble washroom into the carpeted comfort of the adjacent bedroom. The plush creme-and-caramel furnishings warmed the space but did nothing to clear the chill that'd settled in my soul. I tinged my voice with a veil of sarcasm, keeping my back to Rory. "I have to put up with a nosy guard that doesn't listen and infringes on my privacy even when she's not wanted."

A full pause, a moment of stagnant silence as the insult struck. Rory had confided in me before. What it had been like for her to be discarded, abandoned by the people who were supposed to love her most as a child . . .

"If you needed a moment for a wank, you could've just said that," she fired back before the quiet could stretch too long, before old hurts could resurface. Quick footsteps sounded her attack as she scurried past me and plopped onto the edge of my bed, her armor clinking and dirtying my duvet cover, a wry smirk twisting her scarred face. "I'd wait thirty-seven seconds outside until you finished."

"Listening in and getting your own rocks off, I assume." I tried to rearrange my grimace to a smile, tried to play along like I always did. This was how it was with Rory and I. Teasing, light. *Real.* A jab one moment and a caring gesture the next. Julius might have been her bonded *Vinculum*, their matching tattoos brandishing that unity on their skin, but our connection went soul-deep.

It would hurt like all hell if I had to lose her.

"Someone woke up on the wrong side of his princess bed." Rory's eyes narrowed as she patted the too-fluffy mattress, bouncing on the edge in a motion that toppled three of the half-a-dozen pillows to the floor. "Are you going to tell me what's wrong, or do I have to go ask the kitchen staff?"

"I haven't even seen them today." I waved her off, flopping onto the mattress next to her, staring at the ceiling. At least this way she couldn't see the worry in my gaze, even if her excellent hearing could still detect the shifts in my heartbeat.

"So it was Grotchkin?" She poked my ribs hard enough to bruise, and I twisted away from her. "Wow, she must have been in rare form to get under your skin this much."

"Aurora," I ground out her full name, my stomach still tied in expert knots. I couldn't manage this facade much longer, already the familiar sting of budding tears pricking at the back of my eyes.

Rory leaned over me to pinch my other side. Golden hair swayed like willow branches as it dangled in front of my face, offering the same soothing shade. "You know I hate that name."

"Rory," I pleaded in a whimper, my feeble facade cracking entirely with her so close. "Please."

She stilled, the unnatural, focused stillness of a warrior. A predator. Rory sat back slowly, like a great cat crouching just before it pounced.

"Caelum Arturus Borealis. I have known you your whole life," she said, her voice as soft as the downy pillows lining my bed, despite the lethal, killing power that lined every inch of her frame. "And I have been your best friend just about that long, too. I've seen you shit your own pants, and I held your hand when you cried for sixty-seven hours straight when your mom passed. If you can't tell me what's wrong, who can you tell?"

The dam holding back my traitorous tears broke under the caress of her raspy voice, the first dewdrops of warm liquid budding on my lower lashes, blurring my vision. "You won't like it."

Her hand found mine, warm and calloused and firm. "I don't have to. I just need to be your friend."

My friend, as she had been since I was six and she was ten, when Mama took her in after she'd lost hers, knowing how desperately I needed a playmate. My friend, as she had been through our awkward teenage years, when she painstakingly corrected my form in the training pits even when I could barely hold a sword, my long, gangly limbs getting in my way. My friend, when at twenty, I was reduced to a mere child, my tears a never-ending current as they watered my mother's newly packed grave.

Fuck, she wasn't just my friend. She was my home. My light in the darkest of hours, my shade against the too-bright lights of my position.

A long-abandoned daydream slithered into my mind's eye; an image that'd kept me warm through the longest winter nights. Just an idea—a snapshot of a different life, where I was not an heir and her not a guard. Where we were just people, citizens living in the city, perhaps merchants or farmers or bakers. Where we were friends before all else. Friends . . . or more.

Daydreams were for silly little princes. Not for the heir to the Sunkissed Throne.

I pulled my hand from her grasp, letting go of that vision before it could drag me to hell. I rolled on my side—facing her head on. "I'm getting married."

"Oh." Her mouth parted over the single syllable, full lips round with the action, but I hated the way her strong shoulders fell ever so slightly. Like she'd been wishing on that daydream too, waiting for never-after to come along. But she recovered faster than I did, a nonchalant shrug to dismiss whatever disappointment lingered. "I mean, I guess that is tough, not being able to choose, but we knew it was coming one day."

"I know. Getting married was always on the table, I'm not opposed to that. It's just—" I shook my head, dread pooling in my center. If only I *could've* seen this coming. Could've prepared her, prepared myself . . .

"Who is it?" Rory flicked my knee, positioning herself to sit directly in front of me. "Is it that ugly one, what's her name— Oreatta? Oreanna?"

"I wish." I pictured the bull-faced troll of an elf from the outer

41

city. Only a few years my senior, not yet in her fifth decade, but the pushed-in nose and too-thick brows did little to suggest her youth and vitality. On my twenty-first name day celebration, she'd followed me around like a lost pup, earning the nickname The Dreadwolf from Rory that night.

I'd take her to wife in a heartbeat if I could go back to that night and change my fate.

"Who is worse than The Dreadwolf?" Rory wrinkled her button nose—her daintiest feature, cute even when contorted. "Are you marrying Crotchkin?"

A dry laugh blew from my lungs, but there was no humor in it. No mirth, not even in our favorite punchline. No, the *Sykagos* had stolen all laughter from my world when she proposed the one thing that could save it.

No more delaying, no more dwelling in old daydreams and jokes. We weren't little kids, not anymore, and we didn't live in a world where we could be just Cae and Rory. She was the Captain of the Prince's Guard, and I was the Crown Prince of the Luxian empire. She had to know—and she deserved to hear it from me. From her future king.

From the future consort to hell itself.

"The King of Erebus has died, and Thera has taken the throne. Her first official act was to send a peace offering to the Luxian guard with a message to my father."

A beat, and Rory pushed back as if my words hit her harder than any blow she'd endured as a soldier. As they cut deeper than even her most gruesome scar.

A scar she'd gotten from the *Sykagos* herself.

"Caelum, no." She stood, fists tight at her side, her voice a strained wobble. "*No.*"

But her denial would not change my duty. I lifted my chin, looked the woman I loved dead in the eye, and said, "I'm to marry the King of Erebus. The war can finally end."

42

CHAPTER

THREE

> *"A soldier's greatest duty is to protect the crown at all costs. All other rules become null if and when they interfere with this most sacred commitment." –Rule Twelve of the Luxian Soldier's Codex, written by King Alixsander the 1st, 3 A.G.W, Updated by Commander General Atlas Tiberius, 1989 A.G.W.*

RORY

The Luxian sun had been my dearest friend since girlhood, its warm rays as comforting as a lover's caress.

But now, as the sun reached its apex in the open training field, I recognized it as the burning, life-draining opponent it was. It drank the water straight from my flesh with the thirst of a Shadowborne, my sweat beading across my brow and back, feeding the sun's gluttonous appetite.

Still, I moved through my exercises until the old wound in my side ached in protest, until I had no water left to give, no air in my lungs.

Funny how the thing that fueled life could also drain it.

I punched the poor sandbag over and over again until it drew blood from my knuckles. There was no fighting the sun and its envious blaze, but this training dummy would be my prey until the deeper ache subsided.

I'm to marry the King of Erebus. The war can finally end.

I hit the sandbag again and again until there was no tan left on the canvas sack, my blood painting it crimson instead. With each punch, I blotted away more and more of the training pitch, ignoring the sounds of sandals on sand and the grunts that followed steel blades twanging together. Hit after hit, I shut out the smell of sweat and blood and the resin used to shine the bowstrings. Closed off my senses to the burning ball of fire glaring down my back.

All that's left was my opponent. My enemy. The sting of my knuckles and the fury of my fists.

"Someone's worked up today." Jules snorted by way of a greeting, leaning against the nearest column in the circular arena. His long honeycomb hair fell out of his braid and in front of his face, a product of his sparring efforts. I hadn't even noticed his presence in the arena earlier, but judging by the sweat that dripped in rivulets from his brow, he'd finished his workout already.

Normally, the mere presence of my *Vinculum* would've tempered me. After all, we bonded warriors fought all evils together. The tattoo laced with *Zo'is* we both shared wasn't just decorative, but a promise, bound in our blood and flesh, to fight at each other's side.

My tattoo itched, as if to remind me of just that.

Breathe, Rory. Promise.

Today, promises lost all meaning. Even the strongest of bonds could be burdensome.

It's my duty.

Jules rubbed at his mark—stretched across his broad, tanned chest—and I knew he could feel the rage pulsing through it like it was his own. In the ten years since we both accepted the bond, I'd tried to temper my own emotions, as not to add more weight to Jules' strong shoulders. But for once, I didn't care.

"Not in the mood, Jules." I continued my reps, hitting the sandbag dummy with renewed force. A part of my mind wandered, wondering if the King of Erebus' slimy, pale flesh would yield beneath my fist just as easily. My next punch packed the weight of an anvil, even though my knuckles groaned. A woman could only hope.

A towel smacked the side of my face.

"I bet I'd be a better match for you than that sad little bag." Julius crossed his massive arms across his chest, accentuating the deep blue lines that marked his clay skin. A jolt of amusement—*his amusement, edged with worry*—ran down my spine as a sly smirk crawled across his face. "Who knows, maybe today is my chance to take down the great Aurora Bellatore in battle."

My breath scraped like rusted steel through my lungs, my old injuries not nearly as sore as my aching heart. "I said I wasn't in the mood."

Jules was my best friend since I entered the core at fifteen—the only other trainee in my year who took me seriously from the start. While all the other recruits sneered or gawked at me, either disgusted by a woman's presence, or lusting after it, Jules had treated me like a *person*. A worthy adversary. He'd never pulled his punches or underestimated me because of my sex. And when I ranked first in our recruit class, outpacing the three dozen other cocky pricks, it was Jules standing at my side in second.

Just as he had been during the battle of the Great Bridge of Sidus. When we stood strong against nearly a thousand of Erebus' most elite soldiers and four dozen Shadowborne; when the Soul Eater strode in, cloaked in shadows, and unleashed her killing gift across the fields, leveling an entire legion of elves.

45

When he'd packed my resulting wounds with his own clothes, flimsy bandages against a tide of gore. When he strapped my mutilated body to his back to drag me to the medics.

We made the *Vinculum* pact that night; the medics implanting the *Zo'is* into our skin that let us share our energy. Had I not been able to draw on his strength, his very *life*, I would've died there, another victim of the Sykagos' wrath.

I shook the hazy memory of that night away, letting my breath steady me.

Breathe, Rory. Promise.

But today, for the first time in a long time, I didn't want my friend's strength or support. I wanted to sit and stew in my sweat and rage, wanted to beat myself up for not being able to do my one duty.

Protect the prince.

Jules wasn't having any of that. He leaned in, waggling his brows like some of the other guards did before I introduced them to my fist. "Should I romance you first, perhaps buy you dinner?"

Anger rolled down my back in waves, just as hot and oppressive as the sunshine. I knew it was a joke; in all our time together, even with the *Zo'is* connecting us emotionally, neither of us had ever made a real pass at each other. Many other *Vinculum* had that kind of arrangement, but we had written our bond in blood, a necessity for survival, not a symbol of devotion.

But I wasn't in the mood for his jokes, no matter the fact I owed him my life. I ducked under his arm—a benefit of only coming up to the gargantuan man's chest—ready to put my friend and this awful fucking day far behind me.

But Jules didn't take well to being left behind. Stupid *Vinculum* bond made him harder to shake than an imprinted duckling.

"No, you're saving yourself for the prince, I forgot," he called— loud enough for other guards and a few First Legion soldiers—to turn their heads from their own workouts. Loud enough to make my blood boil beyond my body's limits.

I swiveled on my heels, light flaring from the *Zo'is*-laced gauntlets that decorated both wrists.

"Shut your mouth," I ground all three words out in sharp, staggered syllables, my fangs gnashing together as I wished I could sink them into my friend's flesh. He could tease me all he liked, but Caelum . . . Caelum was . . .

I'm to marry the King of Erebus.

I swung at my friend, the rage all-consuming.

"There you are, sunshine." Julius grinned as he dodged easily, my form messy with passion. A wince flashed across his face, a signal of the internal pain he felt soul deep. *My* pain. My rage. He dropped into a ready stance, egging me on with a wave of his hand. "Come on, let's brawl, and then you can tell me what's bugging you."

"Fine, but I warned you ahead of time." I cracked my neck and mirrored his posture, my heart slamming against my ribs in an all-too-familiar ache that told me I was near my limit. But I ignored it, relishing the pain, *savoring* it.

A breath in. A promise of vengeance.

This time, when I lashed out with a foot aimed for Jules' ribs, I didn't miss. His block came down a moment too late—his elbow to my ankle reduced my force by a fraction, but the shot landed.

I danced out of reach of his counter-jab and struck again with an elbow to his opposite side. Julius grunted, but he flashed a toothy smile as he jumped back, rubbing the sore spot. "Ouch, that almost hurt."

My heartbeat in my ears deafened the rest of the training arena . . . and the vicious thoughts swirling in my head. A proud, selfish part of me hated that Julius was right. Hated how I needed this blind violence and sharp pain to manage my emotions.

But I was not proud enough to deny myself that easy medicine, my fists up and ready for another round. "Again."

As he always did, my *Vinculum* happily provided.

We moved with the speed and ferocity of the tigers the king

kept in his fighting pit: two feral, hungry creatures attacking and defending with uninhibited instinct. Pure Elven violence; my chosen partner never did me the dishonor of holding back, his attacks quick and hard. Nor did he run from my wrathful blows, taking the full brunt of my rage head-on with each strike and parry. But through each brutal hit and scratch, through each ragged breath and bone-deep bruise, I could feel the knot in my heart unraveling. Could feel the fog of fear and doubt in my head recede.

The new King of Erebus could play whatever games she wanted. She would never hurt Caelum.

Julius and I would not allow it.

When we were both too worn out to properly stand, our swings sloppy as we tried to move our leadened arms, I fell back, signaling my defeat. Julius mimicked the posture, both of us collapsing to the ground, covered in sweat and gasping for even a breath of air.

"Thank you for that." I smiled at Jules between pants, my face muscles finally remembering how to form the expression. "I needed it."

Jules matched my grin and leaned forward, his head between his knees as he recovered, sweat dripping from his brow. "How's the eye today?"

"My eye?" My hand instinctively flew to the old scar that claimed my face. Aware of it as I normally was, today the ugly spot that stole what once might have been beautiful was the least of my worries. No, the pain I felt today traveled deeper than even my most gruesome scarring. "Fine. It's my chest that's sore, but I'll be okay."

"Ahh, the toil of heartache. You moved well despite it," he said, grabbing the nearby jug of water, holding it out to me for the first drink. "So what is on your mind, sunshine?"

I took the peace offering but couldn't bring it to my lips. Instead, I squinted again at the greedy sun, its brightness blinding. "What do you think about the war with Erebus? What would you give for it to end?"

"As much as I'm loathe to say it, *anything*," he responded quickly, and I didn't need our shared tattoo to understand the truth of his words. He'd lost just as much as any of us—his mother and sister both dead after the first time the Sykagos attacked the outer city. Not to mention the countless good soldiers we'd buried together—or burned. Julius sighed. "We aren't fighting people anymore, not really. The Shadowborne attack before we get the chance, and when the Sykagos comes topside, she can take out legions of us with a single strike before we can even make headway. It's a drain on all of us, and I'm tired of losing good elves to beasts. I'd give my life and then some if it made a difference."

I tilted my head back further, letting the sun burn the tender, raised flesh of my scar. I'd sacrificed much already to the Soul Eater's appetite. My blood, my sweat. My beauty as a woman, my future as a soldier. I loved being Captain of the Prince's Guard, but I'd be on track to claim Knighthood had the Sykagos not nearly ripped me in half.

But I'd give more, too, if it meant peace in Lux. Give everything, my life, my soul in the world after. Every soldier in the kingdom would, our loyalty to the crown, our life's blood.

Caelum was not a soldier.

But he would sacrifice all the same. And as his loyal subject, as his friend, I owed him the opportunity to do so.

I sheathed my face from the sun's envious stare with a hand to my brow, turning to my *Vinculum* again, ready to face the truth I could not beat away, no matter how many punches I threw. "Caelum is going to marry King Thera as a peace bargain."

Despite his exhaustion, Julius straightened, a soldier ready for war whenever it called his name. "Sun and fucking stars, are you serious?"

"Serious as a Shadowborne bite."

"I'm sorry, Rory." His shoulders went slack, surrender in his stance. He placed a hand over his chest, rubbing at our shared tattoo. "I know how you feel about him."

So did everyone, it seemed, aside from the prince himself. The soul-deep ache pulsed again in my ribs, my love for the prince just as burning and all-consuming as the sun today.

But much like the ball of fire hanging aloof in the sky, I could never climb high enough to touch him. I had learned to live contented by the warmth of his distant rays. Learned to squint at his brightness from afar, always in sight but forever out of reach.

"My feelings have never mattered," I reminded my friend, and myself, for good measure. "I'm a guard now, not a knight. I have no title, no land. It doesn't matter if I've known him my whole life, I never would've had a chance. But to see him married off to the King of Erebus, to the *Sykagos* . . . "

Her title tasted like poison on my tongue, just as she'd ruined and rotted all thoughts of peace in Lux since the day she crossed the Great Bridge and unleashed her festering curse on Elvenkind.

To imagine her on the Sunkissed throne next to my sun and stars, my bright, beautiful Caelum . . .

"Good thing he'll have you there to protect him, then." Julius' voice dropped low, a promise in his stone-edged tone. He stood, offering a hand out to help me up. Always the one person who elevated me, who I could count on to raise me and fight with me, no matter the shadows that threatened us. "He'll have all of us. No fight endured alone, remember?"

Something other than rage choked my voice this time, something hotter. Brighter. My *Zo'is* bracelets glowed again.

Let the Sykagos offer her pretend peace. We Luxians had something potent enough to chase away even the darkest of shadows.

I took my friend's hand and stood, that loyalty and love offering me the strength of a thousand elves. And I saw it mirrored in his open expression, too. Felt it flare through our tattoos.

Breathe, Rory. Promise.

"Captain Bellatore?" A familiar bellow called from across the training field, its tone laced with nearly two centuries of authority.

Julius and I snapped to attention on instinct as the Commander of the Imperial Army strut across the sandy stadium, his imposing presence bringing all the morning's machinations to an abrupt, submissive halt. I cleared my throat, bowing my head as he approached. "Yes, Commander Tiberius, sire."

The old elf was built like a *Zo'is*-fueled tank, his pristine gold armor glistening like a giant star come down to earth. But his expression held no luster, his strong jaw tense and cold as stone.

He turned the full gravity of his empty stare on me. "You've been summoned to the King's chambers. Hurry up."

I blinked twice, perhaps too much sunshine or exertion clouding my brain. "I—the king? What does he want with me?"

The commander shot me a look that could've doused out the sun. "I don't know, kid, but if I were you, I'd put my ass in gear to go find out."

From the top of King's Tower, one could see all of Solis. The golden city sparkled in the sunlight, like a trove of jewels in the storybooks Caelum always carried on about. I lost myself counting the turquoise and bronze rooftops of the vast city, like stars forged into homesteads. Cae always fantasized about escaping, but I never understood. Who would want to live anywhere else, when the entire world bowed before the Stellaris Palace and its splendor?

What would I give to save this majesty from war? Julius was right. We'd kept the fighting in Erebus' territory for ages, but now the Soul Eater knocked at our doorstep once a month with fresh Shadowborne on her heels. What good was a beautiful city if we all died to keep it safe?

As a soldier, I'd offered my life as sacrifice time and time again. And I would keep offering it, no matter how many times the god of death rejected my soul.

I just didn't think I'd ever have to offer my heart instead.

"The king will see you now." The butler called from the giant crystal-carved double doors that framed his chambers, his monotone voice pulling me from my melancholy. I tore my eyes from the window, from the city I sold my soul for.

I followed him through the doors, breathing in my surroundings. Even in the safest room in all of Solis, I couldn't help but rely on my training and instinct, assessing the space for threats. The King's office was drenched in the same sun-dappled brilliance as the rest of the palace, jewel-toned fabric and gold-and-opal accents framing the room, but there was a worked-in feel to it I admired. Old strategy books and ledgers, lined in worn-out leather, stacked high on the floor-to-ceiling bookshelves, and maps dotted with troop markers and supply routes occupied the other unadorned walls.

It spoke of the elf that dwelled in it—a warrior, not just a king. A leader, willing to bargain anything for the sake of his people.

Even his son's happiness.

"You summoned me, Your Majesty?" I struggled to keep my voice deferent, the offense I felt on Caelum's behalf almost as intense as my awe for the ruler before me.

Almost.

The King sat on a golden chair behind a wide glass desk, parchment strewn about in attempts at piles. He leaned his elbows on the surface, his pearl-colored shirt unbuttoned at the top and the sleeves rolled up, his fine gold vest hanging off the back of his chair.

He was handsome, even in his advanced years, his white-blond hair long and soft, his frame corded with muscle from centuries of battle and training. But in the quiet of the barracks, all the guards had been whispering lately—his age showed. In his slightly lopsided gait, in the wrinkles around his eyes that seemed to sink deeper and deeper every day. Of course, it made sense. He was nearly as old as Grotchkin, but powerful elves like him could live for centuries. Millenia, even. The blood coursing through his veins came directly from Alixsander's line. To see the beginnings of a great king's Fade . . . It had us all on a knife's edge, especially with Erebus encroaching deeper and deeper into our borders.

Especially now that they had a new king—a monster.

The *Sykagos.*

Fresh rage sizzled in my veins without Jules here to quell it.

Caelum's *betrothed.*

The King's violet-blue eyes snapped up as I entered, knocking me off my center with their force. They were nearly identical to Caelum's, but there was an edge to them that gleamed like freshly sharpened steel—harsh, cutting, unforgiving.

He leaned back in his chair and gestured to the identical one opposite him. "Please sit, Captain Bellatore."

"Yes, Your Majesty." I bowed low again, my sweat-matted hair falling forward, before scurrying to the seat. The cool metal iced my back, so foreign from the creaky benches in the barracks or the too-plush outfitting of Caelum's quarters. I let my weight settle, and the backs of my thighs stuck to the seat with a disgusting squelch. I hadn't even thought to be embarrassed at my appearance as I made my way up here, but I realized too late that my bloody knuckles and sweaty, smelly training linens were probably not the most appropriate choices for an audience with the king. My cheeks warmed.

The King chuckled, the deep sound reverberating through the small space. Gently, he reached across the desk, patting my shoulder in an unexpectedly soft gesture. "Enough with the formalities. I've known you since you were in your mother's womb, girl. She was a good friend to my wife. You're like family."

My cheeks flared hotter still as I stammered. As a warrior and a guard, it was rare for me to feel so unnerved and unsure of my footing. I'd known the King since girlhood, that much was true—my mother had been the queen's favorite maid, and despite her rank, the late monarch had been generous with her kindness and attention.

It had earned me an easy life in the castle, playing with Caelum when we were kids, though the King would occasionally interrupt to collect his son for princely lessons. He'd never been unkind either, but my station was still that of a servant. An expendable, untitled extra in the Luxian puzzle. I tried to keep the suspicion from my voice as I found my tongue amid my surprise. "You honor me highly, Your Maj—*my king*."

"Your honor is your own, I've heard." The King eyed me with similar scrutiny, his battle-tested stare sizing up the specimen before him. I tried to keep my back straight under the heat. "The youngest member of the First Legion in Luxian history, a hero at the battle of the Great Bridge of Sidus, injured on the frontlines, and now the youngest Captain of the Prince's Guard."

Despite their truth, his words did little to flatter. I knew my place, my worth.

My failures.

Still, I offered a respectful nod. "My accomplishments are all a product of your generosity and the mastery of my teachers."

The King laughed again, waving me off with his hand. "Humble too, just as Caelum said. He speaks most highly of you. No wonder why."

A different heat bubbled within. The Prince and I were close friends. But to speak of me with the King . . .

Dangerous, delusional wishes dangled in my mind's eye, forbidden carrots on a string. I pinched my thigh beneath the king's desk, commanding my attention back to the reality at hand instead, clearing my throat. "The Prince is known for his generosity and kindness. I am grateful that he extends it to my name."

The King leaned forward, his muscular arms flexing with the casual action. My instincts prickled—there was no doubt that this elf had been the one to unify the upper kingdoms, his power just as potent and tangible as the *Zo'is* that fueled our technology.

"Give yourself some credit, child. You've proven yourself more worthy than even some of the most seasoned soldiers in the legions. You have a gift; true loyalty." My gaze shot to his, surprised to hear my earlier thoughts echoed on his lips. His voice dipped low, a question and an answer in it. "And that's why I have a very special assignment for you."

"I accept it graciously, Your Majesty," I fired back—too fast— my loyalty to this empire unwavering.

He raised a brow, a smirk playing on his mouth. "You haven't heard what it is."

I crossed my hand to my heart, our most honored salute—and the only save for my blunder. "It is an honor to serve Lux, no matter the task."

The King paused for a long moment, staring at me as if he read my very thoughts. I swallowed hard, the first droplets of fear beading across my brow. What could the King of all Lux want with *me*? Especially when he had generals like Tiberius at his disposal, a battle-tried elf with cunning and steadfast loyalty.

He stood and paced around the desk, his purposeful steps taking him to the large, circular window at the east wall of his study. "I'm sure you've heard by now, but by week's end, we will meet with the new King of Erebus to strike a peace accord, born through my son's union to the King."

I leapt to my feet, my head still lowered—mostly so he couldn't see my jaw work as I chewed over the odious words. "I—yes. I was told."

To my advantage, his endless gaze did not falter from the wide window, a conqueror staring down at his reward.

"I'm loath to admit it, but Lux needs this agreement to happen just as much as Erebus does. I'm sure I don't have to tell you what the Shadowborne are doing to our people, or how desperate we are to expand the magic and power of Lux beyond our current borders." A century-old sadness laced his voice. He nodded out the window to the vast, cramped city beyond. "We're doing so well that things are getting a bit overcrowded, wouldn't you agree?"

"Yes, Your Majesty. . ." I didn't follow, nerves settling in an uncomfortable knot in my stomach. "And I will do whatever it takes to make sure this goes smoothly and to protect the Prince, as my charge commands."

"Good." He nodded. "Because I need you to kill the Soul Eater."

"Excuse me?" I sputtered, forgetting all formalities as shock snipped the last threads of my sanity.

"Your assignment is to assassinate the King of Erebus *after* the wedding," he drawled, putting his back to the window and offering a tight-lipped smile. "Once we have secured the treaty, you will end her life. Preferably in a way that looks natural."

I stared at him, my mouth agape, for a moment too long, unanswerable questions churning over themselves in my gut. Kill the Sykagos? *How?* If it were that easy, I'd have done it a thousand times over.

One question rose above the others, tainted in doubt and dismay.

Why me?

"Your Majesty, I—" I struggled to tame my tongue into words, my whole body numb. "I am a soldier, not a spy."

"No, my child, you are a guard." He stepped closer, and even though he was only a few inches taller, I felt smaller than a babe as he looked down his nose at me. "And the only way to protect both Lux and Caelum is to wait until the deal is sealed, and then the plague that is Thera Umbrus can end."

The whirlwind in my head paused; instead, a soldier's focus latched on to the last delicious word.

End.

It could all *end.*

I wanted Thera of Erebus dead and burned, her shadowy curse eradicated from existence, her name struck from the history books.

I wanted Caelum safe, wanted his brightness undimmed by the darkness of Erebus, wanted him to choose for himself and live in Luxian peace for the rest of his many days.

But dread still crept along my spine, worry knotting my shoulders. Even if I could manage the impossible and end her . . . My oath was to protect, not to murder. And though I'd killed on the battlefield many times before, though I had taken lives in defense of my prince, there was an honor in those deaths. A code.

Then again, the *Sykagos* didn't discriminate between which souls she devoured.

"I have many concerns."

The king exhaled, looking me up and down, as if he too were deciding whether I was truly worthy of his request. "I'm sure you do. This is not a small task. And should you complete this mission, it would not just be worthy of praise and laud."

His stare bore holes in my face, like he could drill straight into my head and mine my thoughts like Zo'is from the eastern mountains.

"When we take Erebus once and for all, there will be plenty of land. Land that will need Ladies and Duchesses and Countesses to govern and rehabilitate it. That will need knights to protect it. *Titled* positions. And who better to earn such a merit than the elf that saved the heart of Lux?"

My stomach dropped, a new dread overtaking me. I didn't care if I was a countess or a kitchen wench. But I couldn't imagine forsaking my vows to the core, giving up my position as Captain to live out my days in some distant country estate, wearing silly dresses and lording over Erebushi peasants. Away from my *Vinculum* and the position that gave me purpose. Far from the city —and the man—I loved. No, I'd rather die on the battlefield with my honor and my heart intact. My voice was quiet, but it did not waver for the first time since entering the king's quarters. "I care not for my station, Your Imperial Majesty. I am content in my current standing."

The king tucked his hands behind him and walked to the window again, dismissing my response entirely. "Then, when it is time to look for a proper Queen Consort for my son, one to help him shape the New World and mend his wounded heart . . ." He looked over his shoulder, his next words intentional and slow.

"Well, all single, *titled* females would be eligible. Do you understand?"

The words he *didn't* say glittered in front of me like *Zo'is*, just as bright and powerful and dangerous.

Kill the King of Erebus and win the one thing I'd always wanted more than anything else. The one forbidden wish I rarely voiced, even in the privacy of my mind.

Kill the *Sykagos*.

Marry my prince.

No, that was a selfish, ugly thought. Of course, I wanted him. Loved him, even if he never saw me the same way. But an ill feeling rolled through my gut, that secret wish now tainted by the king's implications.

But my wants and daydreams never mattered. Caelum's did.

And if this was my chance to help make them come true, I had to take it. Had to honor my highest code, my most important duty.

Protect the prince.

Including his heart.

Before I could think it through, before I could second-guess or let my gilded honor get in my way, the words tumbled from my lips, hastened by a foolish hope. "I'll do it."

"Then we have an accord." The king clapped, the sound booming through the crowded office. Bounding across the room in two long strides, he gripped my shoulders, his hands cold. But a warm smile spread across his handsome face. "I see why my son is so taken with you."

I gnawed my lower lip, wondering what Caelum would say about this. Would he fault me for stealing his duty, for robbing him of the opportunity to right the world? Would he judge me for what I had yet to do?

"Does he know?" I asked, one last moment of hesitation before I surrendered myself fully to the task.

The king sighed again, the weight of the empire in the breath. "No, nor will he. You know how he is—so kind, even to the lowest of beasts. He cried for a week when we had to put the old dog down after it bit his scullery maid. Imagine how he'd react to this news, even if the *Sykagos* is a *diavolous* made flesh. Caelum is good-natured. He'd feel responsible if we let him know of our plans." The king stepped away, his brows drawn tightly together, casting his light eyes in shadow. "And we can't have the *Sykagos* finding out, either. You are to tell no one of your assignment, not even your *Vinculum*. This palace has ears, and I do not trust that word would not get back to Caelum somehow. I do not want to break his heart until it's necessary."

He was right, even though the thought of keeping a secret from both Julius and Caelum made me physically itchy, my skin too tight. Caelum's heart already worked too hard, the beat faster than anyone else's. It was a birth defect; one he'd inherited from his mother . . . and the same one that'd eventually ended her.

No, I would not risk his well-being with too harsh truths. I just hoped my friends would forgive me. Even if Caelum picked some other lucky girl at the end of all this, even if his daydreams included abandoning me, I could give us a chance. Give *him* the chance to choose.

All was left was my opponent. My enemy. The sting of my knuckles and the fury of my fists.

My blade, and the end of the *Sykagos*.

I swallowed the lump of fear that rose to my throat, nodding once. "Yes, Your Majesty, I understand."

CHAPTER
FOUR

"But what is a king without his throne, but a fool standing all alone?" –From "A King's Folly," by Luxian Poet Obilos Hammon, 832 A.G.W

THERA

The best way to tell a person's true nature was to bed them.

A tool I'd learned too young, but it hadn't failed me yet. Seduction was a battle, and I'd mastered it. Each partner I'd taken revealed far more to me than I ever conceded to them. They could feel and touch my body, could pillage and plunder and fuck. But I'd dig my claws deep into their mind, into their soul, each kiss and caress giving me a taste of their very essence. Of their strengths and weaknesses, information I'd exploit when necessary.

I'd lost count of how many partners I'd bed across the years.

Most of them members of my father's legions or among his dissenters, all eager to bed the heir like it gave them an advantage.

It never did. I always walked away victorious, as I had in every other kind of battle, too.

Kings did not fail.

Minister Agyros fucked like he tried to conquer. Like there was something to take, a war to be won between my legs and beneath my silk sheets. Like with every meager thrust of his pretty cock, he'd get closer and closer to my heart. My *crown*. He gripped my hips with the ambition he tried desperately to mask behind his role as the courteous medic. No hiding that greed as he pounded into me from below.

But I did not concede, a fact that both thrilled and frustrated the Minister as I rode atop him, a king on her throne. His breathing went ragged as he climbed higher and higher, closer to the edge of his blissful oblivion.

I fought an eyeroll as I moaned and whimpered with him, this song both familiar and faked. There was pleasure to be had in winning, though not the kind I craved tonight. I'd have to chase my release after Agyros left, as usual, careful not to rupture the handsome man's ego. For an elf so well versed in anatomy, it was a wonder how he always missed the cues mine gave him. A wonder how easily he bought the lie.

"Oh, Kristos, yes!" I dug my fingers into his fuzzy chest, crying out his given name like it meant something for an even more dramatic effect, ready to be done with this chore.

On cue, Agyros offered one last strangled grunt before his hot seed spilled inside of me, a satisfied glaze overtaking his face.

As my personal medic, he was one of the few people that knew it was safe to do so. Knew that the union I offered the prince was built on a lie, my body unsuited for childbearing.

He took advantage of that fact every time we met this way, always leaving me sticky and annoyed.

Before he could even finish his contented sigh, I rolled off him, flopping onto the bed. Perhaps if I pretended to fall asleep, he'd scamper off and I could finish my last morning in Erebus with a bit of pleasure.

To my dismay, he rolled over, snaking his arm around my waist and pulling me close. He nuzzled his face into my neck, sighing into my hair and sending an unwanted tickle down my spine. "I'm going to miss this, Thera. Miss *you*."

I laid still, staring at the dark ceiling and ignoring the shadows creeping along my fingers that begged for their own release. "You know I will too."

I lifted his errant limb off me, sliding quickly to the edge of the bed. His long fingers caged my wrist, halting me. A frown tugged his pretty face. "Don't go. We can find other routes to peace. I could help more, could take care of you—"

"Do you want to be my queen, Kristos?" I winked at him, my tone teasing, but my shadows curled around my hands; a hidden threat. I liked the Minister well enough, his cleverness easy to connect with and his handsome face a lovely perk. But I would not sacrifice my ambitions for him. Would not let myself be swayed into submission by someone who fucked like an overly excited pup humping a leg. "What would your other patients say?"

He offered me his loveliest grin, but his eyes narrowed at my whirling power. "You know you're always my favorite."

I let the shadows recede. "You're mine, too. That's why I keep you around." *Despite the pitiful sex.*

The hall clock chimed outside, the metal contraption clanging through my skull, and disappointment settled in my lowest parts. There'd be no time for me to finish myself off, then. I suppose I'd have to walk into Lux tightly wound.

This rendezvous hadn't just been one last romp with Agyros to secure his alliance further. In truth, I'd needed this for myself. An escape, before all the plans I'd laid came to fruition, before my life as a single woman—and my father's war—came to their bitter ends.

But disappointment was a language I spoke fluently. And though this moment hadn't scratched the deepest itch, it had been a temporary respite. I sighed, snatching my black dress from the floor and tugging it over my head. "Button me up."

The creaking of the large bed behind me signaled his obedience. A moment later, his long fingers trailed down my spine as he wrangled the half-dozen buttons of the garment closed. "I mean it. I'm getting close to figuring out a cure for the Shadowborne, and once I do, we won't have to resort to living in fear. We can take your inventions and expand westward, back into the mountains where the resources are plentiful. We can—"

"Perhaps you should've mentioned all of this at the Select Council meeting." I ignored the chill that raced down my spine. There was no cure for the Shadowborne. No way to uproot the darkness once it took hold.

I would know.

I turned to Agyros, my chin high to meet his gaze. "My mind is made up. Your place as my bedfellow does not earn you an extra vote."

He winced as my boundary smacked him, but his hands lingered on my waist, brow knotting. "Thera—"

"*Mi Vassilla*," I corrected, stepping out of his reach. With purposeful, slow steps, I walked to the dresser of the small room and grabbed my crown from where it rested.

Agyros fucked like an invader—but I was unconquerable. My father's favorite weapon. King in both name and power. I offered him my prettiest smile, one showing all of my battle-sharpened teeth.

Agyros went still, his heartbeat thumping faster in his neck, fear and arousal dousing his scent. "Yes, Mi *Vassilla*."

"That's better." I stroked his cheek, shadows sprinting to my fingertips as I enjoyed the texture of the light stubble that marked his skin—and gently reminded him of the killing curse that rested beneath mine. But I kept my voice sweet when I spoke again.

"Don't give up on me just yet, Kristos. I need you here, in Erebus, keeping our people healthy and settled while I take care of my business in the bright lands. I'll be back in a few months with a new title and all the resources we need. Sure, I might have a silly pup for a husband in tow, but that doesn't mean I won't have time for our . . . very important . . . " I placed a light kiss on his chin. "Our very *confidential* meetings."

His pupils flared again with desire, his ambition stoked once more. This was the benefit of our unsatisfying bed play: information. Access. I knew what made him tick, and exactly how to use it to my advantage. An advantage I would need if I were to survive the coming storm.

"Be careful, *Mi Vassilla*." Agyros took a brave step further, burying his face against my shoulder and murmuring kisses against the hollow of my throat. "Think of me when he disappoints you, hmm?"

I simply chuckled in return before unwinding myself from his embrace and walking out the door.

"You need to be careful. The whole top floor heard that." Stavros waited in the dark hallway, his face twisted in a frown that emphasized his age. But it was pure concern that laced his low whisper.

Still, despite his admonishment, I couldn't help but smile. Of all the men my father had employed, Stavros was the only one that never thought of what he might gain from me—only how he could give. And though he'd made it clear over the years how he disapproved of my bedroom escapades, he'd also never once tried to stop me, never tried to convince me out of my mind.

An exception to the rule, I didn't need to bed him to understand his true nature. He clearly wrote it in his every good deed. My shadows receded in his presence, the eternal chill warming ever so slightly under the safety of his watchful eye.

It was a kindness I'd miss desperately in Lux. I took my advisor's arm, leading him down the hall.

"You know, I wanted them to hear." I nudged his ribs, unable to withhold from teasing him one last time. My chest ached. Another thing I'd miss. "Let them think Agyros has my ear."

Stavros' frown was immovable. "And other parts."

"And other parts." I winked at him, and the left corner of his mouth twitched upward—a battle conceded and won. I continued, letting my most trusted servant in on my secret. "It'll keep the people in line while I'm gone. You know I don't like leaving this soon after my coronation. But I have to hope I've made a strong enough impression already, and that you and Agyros can help keep the other idiots contained while I'm gone."

"All will be well." Stavros squeezed my arm, his voice catching. "You better get moving. The sooner you leave, the sooner you can come home."

I sighed, dragging my feet as the end of the corridor neared, wishing I could have one more moment of this easiness before I turned the world on its head. Beyond the tall black doors, my escorts waited for their king. The people of Lux gathered along the main passage to the Gates of Sidus, ready to see us off. Ready for us to bring the long-awaited peace I'd promised.

Such was the burden of the king.

Head high, Thera.

Kings did not fail.

I pressed a chaste kiss to Stavros' cheek, my last allowance of vulnerability before I built my shields, stronger and harder than even the rocky cavern of the Pool of Souls. "I'll be back, Stavros. I promise."

The entrance to the Great Bridge of Sidus wasn't a gate, but a portal between realms.

Right where the dried, cracked plains of the Deadlands met the stagnant edge of the Black Sea, it yawned open like the festering, reeking mouth of a great beast. Its locking magic seeped into the air, the rotted, stomach-churning stench making it hard to swallow back the saliva that choked me.

The Mad King Alixsander's last act of cruelty against Erebus: the swirling vortex of wind and darkness separated the downworld —Inferni—from the realm above, blocking us not only from the sun's precious rays, but from all other resources as well. From the *Zo'is* mined in the foothills and mountains of Lux and the food that grew in excess across the verdant pastures of the Outer-Limits.

From life itself, leaving us with only the shadows to keep us company.

Shadows that corrupted our minds. Shadows that helped us survive.

Those same shadows—*my* shadows—had allowed us to pass through to Lux without sacrifice in the last few decades. Before I'd offered my talents, soldiers would sacrifice their lives to open the gates, the portal's cursed magic sucking them dry of their very essence.

But my father had a different plan. With me at his side, he could take the fight to the upworlders.

Now, they'd *invited* us.

Nyxia sat beside me atop her *Skialogo*, the skeletal beast huffing from its mighty snout at the smell. Death and despair wafted from the portal, rotted and stomach-churning. Even the Death Stallions knew to fear Alixsander's dark gate. Nyxia worried her bottom lip between her teeth. "Eyes ahead, *Mi Vassilla*. We don't know what's greeting us on the other side of that gate."

I patted the scaly neck of my steed—a young, mischievous colt named Asteri—trying not to focus on the cold sweat that lined the back of my knees. "Hopefully, a better smell and my future consort."

"And potentially dozens of Luxian murderers," Commander Kappas snarled from his mount behind us, his stare boring holes into the back of my head. "This could be a trap."

The Luxians had responded, clear and concise—they'd accept my bargain, on the condition I brought only two escorts and a single wagon of supplies with me. This time, they'd open the portal themselves, rather than allow me to use my *Skia* magic. I was more than happy to let them do the heavy lifting with the gate. Though I possessed the power at my fingertips, I'd rather not ruin the nice dress I'd picked for myself.

But when Kappas insisted on accompanying us instead of Stavros, my irritation knew no bounds. It was better to keep him close, where Nyxia and I could keep him pressed tightly under our thumbs, but...

"Thank you, Commander Kappas, for your very interesting opinion." I twirled Amma's ring to steady my nerves, forcing a half-cocked grin to my face. "But don't worry, the Luxians are like spiders. More afraid of us than we are of them."

Despite the Luxians outnumbering us one-thousand-to-one, despite their resources, technology, and advantage of territory...

The last few decades had proven fruitful for my father's war. For his fear campaign, headed by his leash tied around my neck.

I hoped to make a better impression this time around.

Kappas, the buzzed-cut idiot, seemed to forget our mission and his station, his lips pulling back in a snarl. "This is not a game, *child*. Your father gave his life to save Erebus from these monsters."

Killing him for insubordination wasn't an option—not yet, anyway—without scattering my army in the process. But I'd find sleep easily tonight, even in the sunny planes of Lux, imagining his death in vivid color.

I cocked my head to the side, flattening him with a bored look. "And I'm about to make sure he didn't die in vain." I squeezed my heels into Asteri's side, nudging him forward as I called over my shoulder, "Smile, Kappas. Maybe you'll make some friends."

As my colt surged closer, a deep groan echoed through the open plain, shaking the ground beneath us hard enough to bounce the pebbles lining the splintered soil.

I drew my steed to a stop, cooing at him as the ear-splitting screeching drowned out his frantic whinnies.

The Gate had been opened.

Nyxia moved closer to me, her face twisting in a grimace that matched mine. It was time. I straightened up on Asteri, shoving the last of my nerves back into the Pit of Shadows inside me, where they belonged. After a too-long moment, my head pounding as the noise clanged through it, the first specks of bright blue light dappled through the endless darkness.

Zo'is.

A crackling, zapping sound as the magic cleaved through the spell work. And then—

The portal sucked us in, drawing my stomach to my throat with the abrupt speed.

My eyes squeezed shut on their own command, the blinding, brilliant light painting the inside of my eyelids bright crimson.

Sun.

I blindly slid off Asteri's back, finding my legs beneath me. Something tickled my ankles—*grass*—a cool breeze blowing the hair back from my face.

And oh, moon and mist, the *warmth.*

My eyes still watering and shut, I tilted my head back so my pale cheeks could savor the welcome sting of the rays feverish embrace.

Lux.

"Halt!" a male voice hollered nearby, and I blinked rapidly, covering my brow as my eyes struggled to orient themselves in the too-bright day.

Day.

I'd been to Lux before on my father's errands, but in the past, I'd been cloaked in layer after layer of my own shadows, so thick and twisting not even a single glorious ray could penetrate their shielding force.

This was different. This was rapture.

For all the ways we were different, I understood why the upworlders were so protective of their territory.

My gaze finally focused through budding tears, the image of a man taking shape in the blur. The light glinted off his heavy gold-plated armor, still masking his face, but the edge of his tone was clear enough to convey his high opinion of me.

As were the three dozen elves behind him, all clad in similar battle-attire, their glowing, *Zo'is* encrusted spears drawn and pointed at me.

"You must wait here until further orders are given," he said in his own tongue, not bothering to speak my language as he stepped closer to Asteri. The prideful beast snorted at him, and the guard flinched.

I stroked the colt's black mane before responding in perfect Luxian. "Don't worry, he's friendly. As am I. I appreciate your assistance, but we'd much rather—"

The guard positioned his spear at my throat. "My orders were to allow you to pass through the Gate. Not to let you travel further."

The swish of metal behind me signaled that both Kappas and Nyxia had drawn their blades, but I held up a hand to stop them.

I sucked at my teeth, tightening my internal grip on my magic as it bubbled in my gut. My father had raised me as a weapon, but Stavros had tutored me in the art of politics, too. Fear and force were not the only weapons in my arsenal.

I nodded to the guard, lifting both of my hands high, my palms exposed in surrender. "How diligent of you. But I must remind you, we've been invited."

"Sykagos!"

"Murderer!"

"Monster!"

The soldiers cried over each other from the pack before the commanding officer shushed them with a stern glare. On instinct, I scanned their ranks, but their golden helmets hid the culprits' faces. Another wave of discomfort crashed through me, the hairs at the back of my neck standing straight. My shadows rumbled, threatened vipers twisting and hissing in my veins.

"Where is the royal delegation?" Nyxia whispered in Erebushi as she slinked closer to my side. The guard's eyes flicked between the two of us, as if suddenly aware that I was not the only threat that made it through from Inferni.

"We must be early." I smiled broadly, still translating for the guard, tapping the tip of his spear with a finger. "Be patient, Nyxia."

"This is a trap," Kappas ground out in broken Luxian, shifting his weight into a defensive stance. My irritation prickled. Kappas didn't command my killing power, but if he went unchecked, he could do serious damage, even outnumbered. "I told you—"

"Hush," I commanded as I allowed a single shadow free, one small enough to gag the commander unnoticed. He opened his mouth, but only a labored wheeze escaped. I fought a smirk as I turned to the guard again, jerking my head at Kappas. "My companion doesn't know much of your language, I'm afraid. I would highly suggest you let us pass, sir, before we have a miscommunication on our hands."

The guard shook where he stood, the first semblance of fear finally flooding his features. But even with wobbling knees, he shoved his spear closer, drawing a single drop of crimson from my fingertip. "I don't take threats from Inferni scum."

Harsh words surged and died on my tongue, a loud fizz thankfully interrupting with a flash of bright blue light. Stupid fucking *Zo'is*. I covered my eyes against it, hissing as forms materialized amid the brightness.

Three elves astride pale horses.

The royal delegation.

"No, but you do take orders from your king," the elf in front of the pack boomed, sitting atop a pure white stallion, his back straight. He wore unadorned, neutral riding clothes, and his white-blonde hair sported no crown, but the proud tilt of his chin spoke of the regality that laced his ancient bones. "Come now, Officer Parlus, that's no way to treat our guest of honor."

The soldiers—including their leader—all bowed deeply to the King of Lux. He waved at them once before they all fell back into casual readiness.

I lowered my hands and stood tall, an aloof smile painted across my face. The Luxian bastards had been here the whole time, using the *Zo'is* to cloak themselves from view.

A test. A *taunt*.

Good thing I had a sense of humor.

My shadows sniffed out the threats of the three males. The massive gold-armored, stone-faced elf to the King's left seemed the most formidable, the *Zo'is* imbued longsword dangling from his hip a hint of his power. The other male was much smaller, his robes cloaking what looked like a soft, round frame, his thinning brown hair dancing in the wind, but his sharp blue eyes narrowed as they watched me in return. An advisor, not a warrior, but an opponent all the same.

But the King himself made my shadows twitch in discomfort, his placid expression and cutting gaze a contradiction of themes. I tucked my hands behind my back—mostly so he couldn't see me fiddle with my ring.

"Bastards," Nyxia grumbled in Erebushi, and I was tempted to translate for our audience.

"Your Majesty," I said instead as King Kato Borealis of Lux dismounted his steed, dipping my chin once.

"I apologize for the unfriendly first impression." King Kato strode closer, white teeth exposed in a wide grin. "We were simply waiting to make sure things were . . . safe."

Making sure the Sykagos wasn't hungry.

He stopped a mere four feet away from me, both a show of trust and an insult, as if he'd measured my worth already and found me wanting without my shadows to hide my slim form.

Not that I cared. Appa always said it was better to be underestimated than overconfident.

And I wouldn't make the mistake of brushing the king off, no matter how pleasantly he presented himself.

Staring into the King of Lux's eyes, they met me with a darkness that matched my own.

"Old habits die hard." I shrugged, sinking into my hip, letting him think I was conceding dominance. "As did my father. I plan on putting both behind us. We come with peace and forgiveness as our flags, King Kato."

"Forgiveness?" Officer Parlus balked, his face heating bright red.

I sucked my teeth, biting back shadows, but the King of Lux's head snapped to the guard first.

"Another word, Parlus, and you'll be stripped of your rank." His frigid voice sucked the heat from the air, the onlookers going silent as death.

Despite the warmth of the sun still shining too bright, a chill ran down my spine.

Appa used to tell stories of Kato, Alixsander's heir, and of the atrocities he'd committed in the name of peace. My ledger ran red with my moral transgressions, the burden of my power, but at least I wore my crown of shadows with sincerity.

Perhaps monsters dwelled in the land of light, too.

King Kato turned to me again, his silken smile a thin veil for the devil he hid beneath. "King Thera, this is my commander of the First Legion, General Tiberius, and my most trusted advisor, Lord Laris Pall."

He gestured to the men behind him, confirming my earlier assessments. Tiberius grunted by way of greeting, his jaw working hard to contain the rage that reddened his face, but Lord Pall didn't even bother looking my way, instead picking Zo'is dust from his horse's mane.

I ignored both in return, gesturing to my escorts. "This is

Commander Atticus Kappas and my personal advisor, Lady Nyxia Drakos. They will be my attendants for the duration of this trip."

Kappas hummed a single syllable, all he could manage, still gagged by my shadow, while Nyxia, untamable as always, blew the Luxian Commander a kiss.

"We meet again," she said in perfect Luxian, her accent imperceptible from a native speaker.

General Tiberius tightened his grip on his reins, knuckles turning whiter than King Kato's hair.

We'd all met before, of course. On open fields much like this one.

Fields watered in blood. Fields filled with the discordant, screaming song of the dying.

Fields torn to bits by my shadows.

"How charming." The King wrinkled his nose at Nyxia before taking a small step back. As if for the first time since his arrival, he stopped to remember just how wrong this treatise could go if we desired it.

Smart man.

Not that I'd let it come to that. Kings did not fail, and I was on a mission greater than any personal pettiness. All ledgers were wiped clean the day my father died and I inherited his crown. I wouldn't write in the same blood-red ink he had.

Kato cleared his throat. "Well, we meet today on much happier terms. This is a delegation of peace and mutual benefit. Without further ado, I am happy to introduce you to your betrothed, my son and heir, Prince Caelum Arturus Borealius."

With another disorienting zap of light—a cocky show of both needless wealth and power—two more bodies took shape.

To my surprise, a female in full armor appeared first, sprawling tattoos and vicious scars covering half of her face, a slick honey-gold braid running down her back. Only an inch or two taller than me, her light eyes narrowed my way immediately, sharper and harsher than the sun that burned my cheeks. A guard—I presumed by the way she stood angled in front of the other newcomer—who'd most likely earned her injuries in my father's war.

Oops.

I nodded to her, earning an incredulous scowl, before turning my attention to the tall, willowy male next to her.

Wintry hair matched the ivory-embroidered waistcoat he wore, both framing the deep bronze of his skin. But despite his coloring, he was all opposites to the elf that sired him, all soft warmth instead of harsh cold.

The Crown Prince of Lux.

He stared at me with a delightful mixture of fear and awe, violet-blue eyes blown wider than a full moon, his pink lips parted on an exhale.

Delight chased away the shadows from my mind, the pretty pup a pleasant surprise. If this was the price of peace, it seemed I received the easy end of the deal.

And I certainly didn't need to bed him to note his true nature. It was written plain as day across his unguarded expression, written in a naivety I hadn't seen in decades. In my lifetime, perhaps.

How refreshing.

"Prince Caelum." I offered him a full curtsy, my gaze drinking him in. "It's my pleasure to finally meet you. Even the ladies in Erebus speak of the Elysian beauty of the Sunkissed prince. I now see that perhaps, with their poor eyesight, they have not nearly done you justice."

"Hi," he took a single, hesitant step forward. He extended a trembling hand. "You're—you too."

I reached for his offer, but the guard dog blocked my path with a sidestep, a growl low in her throat.

"Stand back, My Prince," she commanded, and the prince's expression fell as he obeyed. The guard kept her gaze glued to me as she addressed her king. "Your Majesty, might I suggest we continue this affair back at the Summer Palace, where it is more secure?"

I scoffed, sharing a quick glance with Nyxia, whose smirk matched my own. We both looked at the pair again in unison.

The first weak link in the chain.

We'd come to make plans, not wage war. But even peace required a certain amount of . . . *pressure*. And now I knew exactly where to apply it.

I met the guard's glare, reading every emotion in it like a story penned just for me.

My future husband had himself an admirer.

"Captain Bellatore is right, wouldn't you agree?" King Kato clapped the woman on the shoulder, breaking our silent stand-off. "Come, let us gather and celebrate."

I breathed in, tilting my head back to face the sun one more time, relishing the prickling, tingling smolder. If all of Lux was this interesting, perhaps I could make myself at home here, after all.

Without further prompting, I hopped back onto Asteri's back, staring down my nose at my future subjects. "Lead the way."

CHAPTER
FIVE

"The lesson of the Swan Princess, as always, is that love can transform—and destroy." —Queen Dellia's recovered letters to her son, Prince Caelum, circa 2096, A.G.W

CAELUM

Monsters in Mama's stories always had sharp teeth and claws. Gruesome, garish creatures that stole babies from cribs and killed with sick glee. Ugly, vicious beasts that matched the darkness that made them. At night, in the twilight of my bedroom, those terrible monsters would come to life, my imagination distorting the blackened world into startling shapes and nightmares. So much so that Mama had given me a *Zo'is* nightlight that never went out to help 'protect me' from the beasties.

The *Sykagos* didn't look like the beasts I read and dreamed about. Didn't look like a beast at all.

Thera of Erebus was possibly the most delicate, beautiful elf I'd ever seen. Like the dark swan princess in Mama's favorite tale, her every movement was both fluid and sorrowful.

From where Rory and I waited, hidden by *Zo'is* glamours, I watched closely as the portal spat her and her companions out like a dark monster spitting black fire from its jaws. The two elves with her had instantly hissed and covered their faces, crouching against their terrible steeds, cockroaches that ran from the light.

But the *Sykagos* did not shy from the sun's burning rays.

Arms outstretched, she'd stood there in that field, long, dark hair a veil whispering in the breeze, her angular face turned *toward* the sun, gentle tears streaking across her pale skin.

She didn't look like a monster come to steal and kill. She looked *saved*.

And then when she spoke, her voice clear and bright, the way her slight accent smoothed over her sharp words like melted butter.

It's my pleasure to finally meet you.

The moment replayed in my head over and over for the entire afternoon trip back to the Summer Palace, and I couldn't help but steal glances at her.

She hadn't looked at me since, her back straight on her steed as she rode at the front.

The ride had been thankfully quick, the small, breezy summer castle located just along the outskirts of where the Divum and Dollus Mountain ranges met. We hadn't come here in over a decade, the war too close to its borders, making the location unsafe for summer holidays. But it was the perfect way-station for us to stop at before we made the week-long trek back over the Dollus Mountains on our way to Solis.

We'd arrived at our meeting spot via airship, the fastest way to travel the continent . . . but my father's advisors had hesitations about floating thousands of feet above the ground with the *Sykagos* in tow. If she turned on us, a crash would mean a swift death for the entire future of Lux.

Which meant tomorrow we'd begin the grueling trek journey to Solis by land. The first leg would be manageable—the tanks were noisy, but the vehicles were smooth over the open planes of the countryside. But once we hit the mountains, we'd have to go a decent portion on horseback, which I dreaded immensely.

It would be a test of how much my body could withstand. How far I could push myself without suffering another flare up, which would leave me groaning in bed for weeks.

Yet tonight, the Summer Palace would have life breathed back into it, our first dinner as potential allies on the agenda.

While it wouldn't be much by Luxian standards, it was an important first impression for our guests. My father had clarified that he wanted to present as both pleasant and powerful—a difficult balance to maintain. I was required to show up in my best. Quintin, my attendant, stood with me in my chambers, helping me lace the unruly sleeves of the fancy tunic I wore as I prepared for the dinner. It was a silly gold color, the family crest—a dawning sun over mountains—stitched into the front like a glorified flag. But it made a statement.

Quintin was only a few years my senior, the son of a wealthy merchant, but he was the only man I knew in all of Lux that could tie the stupid, overly complicated ties correctly. "Your Highness, other arm, please."

"Hurry, Quin," I grumbled, tired of being dressed like a doll. I understood the importance of appearances, but my gut rolled at the thought of being presented before the King of Erebus like a fluffed peacock. It made me look young and silly. *Weak.*

Meanwhile, even in a plain riding dress, her hair unbound, even after being hurtled through the portal, Thera had looked . . .

Well, if my father wanted an example of regality, I had a subject in mind. Next to her, I was a boy in the shadow of a deity.

"Poor thing, this must all be such a fright for you." Quintin mistook my quiet for a different discomfort as he finished my laces. He wrinkled his nose as he flattened out the sleeves for me. "Pale as ghosts, those Erebushi beasts are. I nearly jumped out of my skin seein 'em."

I clenched my hands at my side, a misplaced annoyance scratching across my back. "The only thing frightening right now is how you insist on droning on."

"I—" Quintin's eyes blew wide. "My apologies, Your Highness. I spoke out of turn. You must be sad enough as is without my comments."

The itch deepened, burrowing beneath my skin. "Sad?"

Quintin shrugged, a frown pulling his features. "Well, I mean . . . You have to marry that *thing*."

That thing.

The *Sykagos*.

My bride.

"The King of Erebus, you mean," I corrected—both him, and myself.

Quintin nodded, a pitying smile replacing his frown. He leaned closer. "I . . . I know it's unconventional, but my cousin knows this courtesan in the outer city who sometimes takes a pill to help herself relax during . . . difficult clients." He cleared his throat. "I could get her information, if it would help."

I stiffened. "And why would I need that?"

"Well, My Prince. Perhaps she can provide you with some of the substance to help you withstand your wedding night." Quintin patted my arm—like one would pat a toddler on the head—and winked. "Or she could provide you with some company."

Something lit up my veins, hotter than a fever, but my stomach sank.

This was how they saw me, then. Not as a monarch, making a noble attempt at peace. Not as a ruler with a head for strategy or compassion.

But as fodder to be served up on a plate to the King of Erebus, a roast pig with an apple in its mouth, ready to be devoured. Or as a sickly, cuckolded little prince that couldn't even find his own companionship to cheat on his soon-to-be wife.

"Another word out of your mouth about my personal relations, and I'll have you fired and blacklisted," I snapped, rare venom lining my fangs. "And the only thing you'll need from your courtesan friend is a job in her establishment. Unless, of course, you have a friend that cleans sewers you'd rather shovel shit with instead."

Quintin's jaw snapped shut, a vein appearing in his forehead. But even as anger brimmed in his gaze, he fell into a deep bow. "Yes, Your Majesty."

I swallowed the lump of regret that rose from my gut, a deep-seated guilt snaring my chest like the tight laces around my wrists. "No, I'm sorry, it's been a long day."

Quintin offered a nod before scurrying out, likely to tell the other servants how I'd truly lost my mind.

I rubbed the back of my neck, but the tightness lingered. Quintin's prejudice was not unfounded. After all the war and bloodshed, we Luxians had every right to be afraid of Erebus. And his words were not just his—I'd uttered them myself not even yesterday, my perception created and clouded by the stories I'd heard of the *Sykagos* and her despicable kingdom.

Perhaps if Quintin had seen what I had today, he might understand. Maybe that was what Lux and Erebus both needed—a chance to shine the light and open our eyes to look at the monsters we thought crawled around in the dark. To see that their fangs and claws were really mirages, crafted by unchecked shadows and vivid imaginations.

And even if I couldn't get him or the others to *see* Thera differently, I would change their image of me. Would prove I wasn't an impotent prince, but a tactful king.

"Cae, are you ready?" Rory knocked on my door before entering, and her presence eased the knot forming in my gut. She wore her dress uniform tonight—a high-necked, sky-blue, two-piece silk suit that cinched at the waist with a gold belt, dozens of matching opal and gold medallions lining her shoulders. Both sleek and stylish, it accentuated the hard muscle and lithe lines of her, while also speaking of finery that befitted the great kingdom of Lux. Even her long curls had been slicked back in a tight bun, giving her the impression of a natural gemstone, freshly mined and polished by the eroding winds of a wild tempest.

I frowned, fiddling again with my overly complicated attire. "How do I look?"

Still, Rory offered a kind smile, her gaze sweeping over me in one polite pass. "Incredible."

"Is it too much?" I tugged at the collar, the frilly, tight cravat choking me.

"Are you trying to impress her?" Rory raised a brow, but her voice dipped low.

The threads in my chest tangled again, forming lines I could not cross. My fears were all just nightmares, all smoke and shadows in a world where it was easy to invite in light. But Rory had seen darkness firsthand. Had fought it tooth and nail and sword. Had almost died because of it.

I tried not to let my eyes linger on her scar, the only unpolished piece of her tonight. A mark that no fine clothes or jewels could erase.

And yet, I couldn't school my tongue into submission, couldn't bring myself to give Rory the answer she wanted; the afterimage of Thera's face still burned in my mind's eye.

It's my pleasure to finally meet you.

"Is that so wrong? I thought we were making peace." I cleared my throat, turning to look at myself in the mirror—if only to avoid seeing the disappointment on Rory's face. "She's my future wife, and the key to ending a war."

Rory shifted, her gaze meeting mine in the reflection, filled to the brim with unanswered wishes and untempered accusations. "She's the *Sykagos.*"

As always, I made out the words she didn't say.

Traitor.

I shoved the guilty thoughts down, binding the threads like the laces that cut off my circulation, starving them of any air. If I wanted to survive this and do my duty, I had to lock away the errant dreams—and nightmares—that still clung to my mind. Had to see the *Sykagos* as more than a monster.

And had to see Rory as no more than a friend.

My grin did little to mask my sorrow. "She doesn't look nearly as bad as you all made her out to be."

She swallowed down the words she wanted to hurl at me. The walls went back up behind her gaze, the molten gold hardening to cold, unfeeling indifference.

She'd do what she needed to survive, too. Even if it meant ending our friendship.

"Perhaps you're only seeing what she wants you to." With a small bow, she turned to go, purposeful strides leaving me in her wake.

Panic surged through me, hot as the midday sun. I should've let her go, should've let her protect herself in all the ways she needed. But I needed my friend more than anything. And I was selfish enough to ask her to stay.

"Rory, I don't want to fight." I stumbled behind her and reached for her arm, gently catching it around the elbow. "I need a friend. I'm so ... "

Confused. Curious.

Frightened.

Frightened, not of the *Sykagos,* but of my reaction. Of the pull I felt toward her, of the doubt clouding my mind. But I had no uncertainty about my feelings toward Rory. Inappropriate and unachievable as they were, I loved my friend no matter what happened. And

I needed that certainty to brace myself against the chaos that'd blown in with Thera of Erebus.

Rory's tongue poked at her cheek, but then her expression softened. She covered my hand with hers, her palm warm. "I know, and I'm sorry. I'm here to protect you, no matter what."

I winced. If only she didn't see me as some spoiled little prince that needed protecting, then maybe I could see myself as something else, too.

"You're doing an excellent job at smothering me." I rolled my eyes—mostly to dispel the tears budding in their corners.

Rory nudged my side, a well-missed warmth returning to her features. "Come on, you don't want to be late for your date."

Settling into step beside her, I lifted my chin, ready to face the evening with whatever shreds of bravery I could manage.

The Summer Palace was sparsely decorated in its disuse, the style throughout a decade out of fashion. Yet as I walked into the formal dining hall, I was surprised by what the servants had pulled together on such short notice. The floor-to-ceiling glass windows framed by garlands teeming with fresh wildflowers, *Zo'is* luminaries woven throughout to provide a soft, ambient light. The large white-oak table matched the rest of the room, crystal glasses and opalescent ceramic plates stationed in front of every seat. It wasn't the overflowing finery of Stellaris, but the whimsical charm still spoke of Luxian beauty.

Drawn away from the decor, I focused solely on the most radiant jewel in the space.

Seated in the high-backed gold chair, Thera's dress shone deep ruby instead of black, the off-the-shoulder cut emphasizing every sharp corner of her pale neck and collarbones. Her dark hair swept up in a loose bun, giving her a softness that seemed discontent with the power radiating in her stare.

A stare—I realized as I approached—that didn't quite match, now that she wasn't squinting. Heat flushed to my face as it settled on me, one eye the color of grass, the other ice. Ice that chilled to the core, that froze and trapped.

Ice that sparkled in the sunlight, so desperate to feel its warmth, it risked melting. And soft green, like light filtering through a willow's branches.

My heart stuttered, and I nearly tripped over myself.

"Caelum, my boy, come sit. Dinner is almost served," my father called from the head of the table, gesturing to my seat at his right —directly between him and Thera.

Rory squeezed my arm once before she dropped it, moving to her seat further down the table between Lord Pall and Julius. I swallowed down the fear that rose to my throat, instantly missing Rory's warmth at my side. I kept my steps slow and deliberate as I journeyed to my seat, passing the other two Erebushi delegates— both watching me like hungry hawks—with my head down. I offered a polite wave to Commander Tiberius and Lord Pall, both sitting at my father's left, before taking my chair.

"Good evening, Father." I bowed my head once to him, and then to my right, doing my very best to remain composed and regal. "Queen Thera."

Thera's lips twitched. "*King.*"

The small delegate next to her—Nyxia—snorted.

I blinked twice before catching my blunder.

"I'm sorry, I—" I blubbered, waving my hands as I fumbled through an apology. Women were not kings in Lux, no matter the circumstance. "It was a slip of the tongue. I truly meant no offense."

"Do you always blush when you're embarrassed?" she asked quietly, the corner of her mouth lifting. "It's rather charming."

I opened my mouth—and closed it again, all language fleeing the empty walnut I called a brain. As a habit, I looked to my father for aid. He cleared his throat, patting my shoulder with a proud smile. "You must forgive him, he's—"

"That actually brings up a good point." She relaxed back in her chair. His eyes blew wide—as did mine—in utter disbelief. But Thera pressed on, tapping the edge of the ceramic plate with a long fingernail. Drawing looks her way like a king well versed in commanding attention. "King Kato, when Caelum and I wed, how shall we address the issue of titles? I certainly do not fancy myself a queen."

The Luxian crest was white, blue, and gold, but in this moment, my father's face matched the color of Thera's dress. I gripped the arms of my chair, readying myself for whatever fury the King of Erebus had stoked with her rudeness.

"I'm sure we'll think of something," my father said with a terse smile, but his eyes narrowed to sword-tips.

Thera leaned forward, her elbows on the table as she looked my father dead in the eye. "And as far as our trade agreement . . . we'll have to start with infrastructure and *Zo'is* in Erebus before we can have Luxian settlers. I've built aqueducts, and we have a fairly sophisticated irrigation system, but—"

"Ah, that will be settled." Lord Pall grimaced, his gaze flicking from Thera to my father's ever-reddening face. "I have already presented His Majesty with proposals for that."

My father nodded to Lord Pall and opened his mouth, as if to speak.

"Lord Pall," Thera said, her wicked tongue faster, "I had no idea you were an expert in Erebushi infrastructure." Her look could melt flesh, but then she dismissed the advisor with a wave, instead turning to my father like Pall had not spoken at all. "And will we have access to Luxian technology, too, or just raw *Zo'is*? I'd love to look at one of those airships, to see how they use the powder to fly —"

My father slammed a fist on the table, a tight-lipped smile a thin cover for his rage. "Let's save talk of business for a more appropriate time, shall we?"

I clenched my own fists beneath the table, head down, daring only to glance at the others through my lashes. No one ever spoke over him or pushed past his boundaries. No one dared.

A fact that everyone at the table instantly *felt*, all of them shifting in their seats. The Erebushi General's fists turned white as he clutched his goblet, and Tiberius watched him without blinking. Lord Pall stifled a grin, and Ambassador Nyxia clutched her fork like she planned on sticking it in his eye. Julius stared at his plate, like he was inspecting it, and Rory tensed for a fight next to him, her whole form taut like a bowstring waiting to snap.

Thera might have been a king, but my father was, too. To most Luxians, he was a *god*.

I knew him well enough to know how long his memory lasted. My father did not easily forget.

I squirmed in my seat, hating myself for starting things off on such a sour note. Perhaps, had I not misspoken, she wouldn't have overstepped, wouldn't have angered Papa—

"Ah, the first course! Delightful." My father clapped as a long line of servants marched through the kitchen doors, each carrying heavy gold platters of decadent food and washing away the palpable tension. My stomach grumbled, the scent of rosemary and citrus and pepper hitting me all at once, saliva coating my tongue. The ache in my chest eased.

Mama always said full bellies softened most jagged moods, and shared supper could make friends of foes.

The servants set nearly a dozen platters before us, each more decadent than the last. Roasted duck and lamb chops, both seasoned with an elegant blend of spices and wrapped in slabs of thick-cut bacon, all likely slaughtered this morning. Two kinds of whole-cooked fish over a bed of multicolored potatoes and a wide bowl of seafood-topped pasta, courtesy of the nearby coast. Two big pots of hearty venison stew, three loaves of fresh baked bread, and an assortment of cheeses from all over the region.

Father certainly knew how to put on a show, even if the remote castle had much less to work with.

I looked at the three Erebushis to my left, their expressions a rainbow of mixed emotion. Nyxia looked like she was about to jump out of her seat and dive face first into the bowl of pasta, her eyes wide and hungry, whereas the broad, grouchy general on her left wore a frown and narrowed eyes—likely wary the food had been poisoned. I stifled a laugh by biting the inside of my cheek.

But it was Thera that was the hardest to read, her face crafted in pure apathy, all amusement and ferocity from the moments before gone. Except in her mismatched eyes—both of which had impossibly darkened despite the warm lighting.

I grabbed the crystal pitcher of blood-red wine placed before me, pouring a serving in my goblet before holding it out to her like a peace offering. "Would you like some wine?"

Her attention snapped my way, her head tilted. "Unless you prefer I drink your blood."

I nearly dropped the pitcher, just barely saving it and resting it back on the table. Thera's lips curved into a full smile again, some of that amusement reigniting her features, but my gut clenched.

"Ah, is that . . . " I coughed, my hands shaking as I took a sip of my wine, wishing it would wash away the bile that surged to the back of my throat. It didn't. I did my best to keep my voice level—casual—but it was another failed endeavor. "Is that something you will require frequently?"

"She's teasing you, Caelum." My father forced out a laugh, before I could shove yet another foot in my big mouth. He stabbed a hunk of meat from the platter before him and lopped it onto his plate, not breaking eye contact with Erebus' King for a moment. "Our guest has a wonderful sense of humor."

"I wouldn't dare tease." To her credit, Thera didn't cower beneath my father's presence. She chuckled, sitting back and staring at the length of the table with vague distaste. Her accented voice drawled over her slow, deliberate words, and in that moment, I wanted nothing more than to hear her speak her native tongue.

87

"King Kato, this spread is rather . . . impressive. How generous of you to go to such lengths for us."

She forked a single potato, plopping it straight into her mouth, not waiting for permission to enjoy like the rest of us did. I couldn't help but watch, fixated on her lips.

"This meager arrangement?" Father scoffed, breaking off the duck's drumstick with his bare hands. "Just wait until you see the food at the Stellaris Palace when we arrive next week. We will throw the celebration of the millennia."

She chewed her food slowly. "I can hardly wait." Her tone, bored; her response delayed.

I glanced sidelong at Rory, who shrugged. At least I wasn't the only one lost in this battle of flowered words and silk-wrapped insults.

"Let's eat." My father raised his goblet and uttered the one command that Erebus and Lux could mutually obey without hesitation.

The minutes stretched on in quiet, the scrape of forks against plates and the chorus of chewing only interrupted by the occasional placid, bland attempt at conversation, sentences like, "Is the weather always so lovely here?" and "Did your travels go smoothly?" or "This stew is delicious." awkwardly peppered throughout the evening, all met with equally monotonous responses. No one wanted to tempt the fury of the two kings again with talk of anything more substantial. But at least mouths were fed, even the surly Commander Kappas eventually surrendering his doubt and tucked into the lamb chops with fervor.

Everyone stuffed themselves but Thera, who'd eaten a few potatoes and some pasta, but had pushed the seafood around her plate in an artful attempt to make it look less uneaten. I'd done it plenty of times as a child, always trying to bargain my way out of finishing dinner so I could skip straight to dessert.

I leaned closer to her, my voice low. "Is everything all right? You've hardly eaten."

She blinked up at me like I'd caught her off guard before she sat straighter, placing a hand on her flat, hollowed stomach like it was full. "Ah yes, I've always had a poor appetite."

"She really has," Nyxia chimed in, still chewing her fifth plate of food, while sliding the rest of the King's portion closer to her with a gleeful grin. "Don't worry, I'll finish for her."

Surprise lifted my brows at how comfortable she was with her king, but I turned back to Thera, a strange worry still rumbling in my own overstuffed stomach. I'd never gone to bed hungry in my life, and I'd rather die than ever succumb to such torture. "Are you sure you're all right? Would you prefer something else?"

"I suppose she prefers live game," Lord Pall chuckled, and the room went silent. Pall jerked his head up from his plate, as if he hadn't meant to say it out loud. But the twisted grin on his face showed his message was as intended.

"Would you like to test that theory?" Thera cocked her head, but my father's advisor twirled his fork through his fingers, unashamed and undeterred from his challenge.

All the eyes in the room locked onto the exchange, backs straight and expressions drawn, old enemies ready for someone to yell charge so the battle could begin.

"I suppose I'm too old for your liking," Pall bit back, his cheeks rosy and bold with the two goblets of wine he'd managed. Still, his slurred speech managed a menacing edge. "I hear you prefer to snatch Luxian babies from their cribs."

Thera's smile was all teeth—stained red with her own libations. "I've been known to enjoy a good *vintage* from time to time."

A chill shuddered up my spine, and my father's glare darkened. "There is that winning humor again. Is everything so laughable in Erebus?"

Thera flinched—just a slight tick of her jaw—but her smile didn't waver.

"There is very little laughter for those cast in the dark," General

Kappas answered, his gruff voice a low rumble, like thunder warning of more lightning.

I braced in my seat, hair standing on my arms like the air itself had turned electric, the static building in the room, ready to snap.

But my father had commanded us to make a peaceful, pleasant first impression, and I wouldn't fuck up any more than I already had today.

"I'll say, I'm exhausted from the day," I blurted, noisily rubbing my hands together like I'd seen my father do countless times when he wanted to create a distraction. I smacked a broad smile across my face, pretending to be utterly oblivious to the hair-raising tightness in the room—and dismissing Pall and the General in the same breath. I turned to my father before the Lord could reclaim the reins. "Your Majesty, would it be too much trouble to call our evening short? Everyone should likely get rest before we set out tomorrow evening. You know I don't do well without a good night's sleep."

It was an easy ploy to use my illness as an excuse. It was the one advantage my weak immune system offered me, and Sun above, I needed to use any tools I had.

My father laid his full attention on me, the faintest hint of surprised pride lifting his brows. My heart swelled as he nodded. "As much as I'd love to stay and chat more, I suppose you're right." With a contented sigh, he stood, and the scrape of chairs clamored through the hall as the rest of the assembly followed suit. "Good evening, everyone. Dessert will be brought to your rooms if you wish."

"I'll escort you, My Prince." Rory cleared her throat, dismissing herself from the table with a deep bow to my father before coming to my side.

"I'll depart too, then." Thera stood last, brushing off her skirts. She turned fully to me and then curtsied—her back to King Kato. I couldn't help the rapid beat of my heart as she blinked up at me through thick, dark lashes. "Goodnight, Prince Caelum. I'll see you in the morning."

She didn't wait for a response before sauntering away from the table, her general and advisor quickly scurrying after her flowing crimson train.

"Goodnight, Your Majesty," I called after her, ignoring the way my cheeks heated. She paused, turning to look at me over her slender shoulder. I struggled to keep my chin high beneath the weight of her emerald-and-ice stare. "Sweet dreams."

She said nothing else, but the long, appraising gaze she left me with would haunt my own dreams that night.

Thera of Erebus did not look like a monster. She looked like a daydream, a fantasy turned flesh.

And for the first time since I met her, I wondered if that was exactly what made her so dangerous.

CHAPTER
SIX

"A soldier's life is forfeit the day they enter the core, offered to their fellow warriors as sacrifice. But fear not—a soldier can only give one life, but they receive infinitely more in return, mutual obedience a gift." –Rule Nine of the Luxian Soldier's Codex, written by King Alixsander the 1st, 3 A.G.W, Updated by Commander General Atlas Tiberius, 1989 A.G.W.

RORY

The mark of true partnership was mutual obedience.

One of the first lessons taught in the First Legion— the most important objective before we could take our oaths as *Vinculum*. If we could not obey each other's needs, if we could not sacrifice the whims of self to further the success of our partner, we had no place in the core. Some said the magic of the *Vinculum* ceremony wouldn't take for those that didn't adhere to the principle. There were records of soldiers' bodies rejecting the Zo'is entirely, their bond breaking before it could even take hold.

It was a vow I took seriously—with both Julius and Caelum. I would always deny myself to better their worlds. As would they for me.

But watching the King of Erebus at dinner had confirmed my suspicion; she knew nothing of respect and loyalty. Her only objective had been to disarm and distract both the king and the prince, to worm under their skins with pretty smiles and vicious words until they squirmed. Until all of Lux crumbled.

She didn't come to Lux for peace or mutual obedience. She came to fell the empire from the inside.

The night stretched on as I stood outside of Caelum's chambers for the first guard shift, planning all the ways I'd stop the *Sykagos* in her tracks. She'd already laid bare a few of her weaknesses; ones I would test.

One, she took her reputation seriously. Her emotions betrayed her insecurity. She'd cracked her own jokes, hiding behind her steel-sharp wit, but as soon as Pall hinted at the Soul Eater's appetite, her hackles went up like a wolf scenting blood. And two, without her shadows to surround her, she looked rather frail, rail-thin and pale as she was. She'd barely touched her food, not eating a single bite of protein. If there was a way to suppress her magic, I'd have an easy enough time taking her on in combat.

But the most important weakness I'd noted was how alone she was. The commander she'd brought looked just about as ready to rip her head off as I was; the glares he shot at her throughout the first meeting and the meal just as dark as the ones he leveled the Luxians with. Perhaps her ascent to the throne hadn't been smooth as she wanted to pretend it was. On the other hand, the crude ambassador, Nyxia, seemed to be a little more attentive to her king, but she never intervened on her behalf; a follower, not a leader or partner.

The King of Erebus had no partner. No *Vinculum* to protect her back.

And that's exactly where I'd one day plunge my sword.

If I could find the strength.

The door creaked behind me. I spun on my heel, unsheathing my weapon in the same fluid motion. Steel sang in the otherwise empty space.

Caelum's bright eyes shone in the blue glow of the *Zo'is* luminaries that lined the hallway. "Stand down, it's just me."

I sheathed my sword once more and smacked him on the arm. Hard. "You shouldn't sneak up on me. I thought you were a threat."

"Coming from *inside* my chambers?" He waggled his brows at me while rubbing the tender spot where I'd hit him. He'd bruise like a peach, but a sick part of me loved leaving little marks on him. Everyone else treated him like he was fragile, but he was stronger than the doctors let on.

He stepped closer, looking down his nose at me. "I know that look. You were daydreaming on the job. Tell me, Captain Aurora, where is your head tonight?"

If, by daydreaming, he meant planning ways to assassinate his future wife, he'd be right. My gaze fell to the floor, his expression too warm and lovely to stare at directly.

Would he hate me for what I had to do? He was already eating out of the King's pale hands, his attention undivided from her for most of the ride to the castle and throughout dinner. Of course, it was natural to be curious about shiny new things, and I knew Caelum was desperate for novelty. He'd spent so much of his life locked up in the castle, it was understandable that he found the Sykagos . . . interesting.

It still didn't quell the jealousy that burned ulcers into my gut. Or the shame that sat like a stone in it, either.

"I'm tired, that's all. I shouldn't have eaten so much dinner," I lied, hating I couldn't tell him exactly where my head was. This wasn't what partnership looked like, not what my oaths upheld.

We'd never let deception sit at our table before, and it burned me up to invite it to dine with us now.

He sighed, like he could smell the mistruths on my breath; but if he could, he didn't offend me by voicing it aloud. Instead, he gnawed at his bottom lip, a telltale sign of the prince considering one of his famous mischiefs. "Wanna get in some trouble?"

"Absolutely not."

"Fine, then." He folded his arms across his chest, leaning back onto his doorway. He'd changed into casual clothes, a loose, plain tunic and soft cotton pants signaling that he'd been in bed—or at least, had gotten ready to—but he still wore boots despite the late hour. He grinned like the cat that had just caught the mouse. "Want to protect me while *I* get in trouble?"

I pinched the bridge of my nose. Despite his lack of combat experience, Caelum knew exactly how to pick apart my weaknesses. I sighed. "Do I have a choice?"

"No." He pushed off the doorway and strutted down the long hallway at a pace that would leave him breathless.

Someone was in a hurry.

Against my better judgment, I followed; a loyal dog after its master.

"Where are we going?" I asked once we moved through the east corridor on quiet feet and headed down the first level of stone steps, away from the personal chambers and into the section of the castle designated for common rooms.

"Kitchens." I should've known before he answered; his smile was brighter than the luminaries lighting the corridor.

A laugh bubbled out of me. "You're not stuffed to the gills?"

He shrugged, upping his pace. We half-ran through the entrance hall and toward the expansive galley. "You know me."

I did. Caelum had a sweet tooth that could single-handedly keep all the candy and pastry shops in Solis in business. It was a miracle he wasn't three times his size with the amount of sugar he guzzled down, but I supposed he was blessed with a fast metabolism as well as his good looks.

Lucky bastard. I exercised my body to its limits day in and day out, my form sculpted by years of hard work into a brutal weapon of its own. Yet, if I even *looked* at a pie, it would find a way to pad my hips and thighs.

Perhaps one day I'd let myself indulge, plump and happy on some farm.

Perhaps I'd learn to let go.

I sped up to outrun that particularly painful train of thought, surpassing Caelum entirely and winning our undeclared race.

He wheezed by the time we arrived, his face flushed, not just with exhaustion, but exhilaration. He never complained when I pushed him, enjoying every moment—even though he'd usually pay for it the next day, his heart racing or his stomach cramping.

I shoved down my protective instincts, instead focusing on the Prince's sacred mission for sweets.

The kitchens were luckily unattended, the surfaces of the marble countertops wiped clean and the fires burning low. Despite how quickly the staff had thrown together the feast, my guess was they'd all tucked away for the night, conserving energy before packing up and shipping off with us tomorrow. Caelum flicked on the switch next to the entrance, the luminaries in the room buzzing on in an instant to light our way.

Catching his breath, he grabbed a wicker basket—likely intended for tomorrow's trip—from the cupboards before scurrying about, headed first to inspect the tall pantry that housed dry goods.

"Can you grab me a bunch of those cheeses and berries from the icebox?" he said, his head sheathed inside the store closet as he rustled around. "Carrots, too, if they have them."

"Since when do you eat carrots?" I snorted, dutifully retrieving the produce, placing it on the table. "You only like vegetables when they're baked with sugar and made into a cake."

"Not true." Cae popped out from the cupboard, glowering at me with his arms full of three loaves of bread and an unopened jar of jam. "I love a good carrot in savory meat pie, too."

I fought an eye roll.

He frantically assembled the assortment into the basket, his tongue poking out of the corner of his mouth as he concentrated.

"Caelum, where are we taking this?" I bit the inside of my cheek, suspicion truly sinking in when he passed over a container of cookies—his favorite snack—and instead grabbed the bundle of bananas behind them.

He didn't answer my question, lifting another jar from the counter and scrutinizing it. "Oh good, there are nuts too." He finally looked at me. "Those have protein, right?"

I crossed my arms firmly across my chest, my stomach sinking to my toes. "Caelum, tell me what you're up to, or I'll go right to your father."

He set the nuts down, hurt flashing across his face. "Did you just threaten to tattle on me? To my *father?*"

"Do I need to?" I asked quietly. Regret twisted its way down my already-rigid back, but I held firm. Caelum hated being treated like a child, but I wouldn't entertain anything putting him further in harm's way. A difference between pushing his boundaries and lowering my guard; I was his protector before I was his friend.

Caelum pursed his lips then crossed the kitchen floor and grabbed my hand. His warm grip unknotted the tension in my shoulders, but his brilliant stare stirred a different tightness within me. "Do you trust me?"

I swallowed. Breathed. "Always."

"I think the King's a vegetarian." Caelum sighed, like that was a terrible diagnosis to live with. He let go of my hand to finish the basket as I stood still, missing the heat of him. "She barely ate. We have a long journey tomorrow, and I doubt it will be pleasant. She should eat before we go."

Something vicious and cruel writhed in my veins, something

that begged for vengeance. Fragmented memories—the iron stench of blood and the throaty screams of the dying—flashed through me. I ground my teeth together to keep the horrors at bay.

No, the *Sykagos* wasn't some fragile damsel in need of a prince and a picnic basket. She was the devil, the King of Monsters, the Soul Eater.

And to see Caelum take care of her, to see him *worry* . . .

"Or Pall is right, and her appetite is more suited to Elven souls." The insult somehow slid through my clenched jaw.

Caelum's eyes glazed over with an emotion I hated almost more than I hated the Soul Eater.

Disappointment.

The vicious thing slithering through me scurried back to the dark chambers it came from, shame driving it away.

"If you won't come with me, I'm going alone." Caelum nudged the basket, voice rigid. A line in the sand.

I tilted my head back, begging the Sun and Stars to deliver swift mercy on my soul.

The *Sykagos* was a monster, but Caelum was my true adversary tonight. His ability to sweetly manipulate and his blindness to his own talent for finding trouble a deadly mix for us both.

"Fine. We can drop it off to her chambers, and then we go," I grumbled before my rational parts could take over. Snatching the basket, I pointed a stern finger at Cae. "Five minutes. You need rest, too, or this coming week will be hell for you, and Julius has the second guard shift."

I rubbed at my tattoo, secretly hoping that Jules could feel my apprehension and would come rescue me.

But the eye-crinkling smile that splashed itself across Caelum's mouth could make airships float. "You're the best."

"I know," I lied. Sun and stars, it would shatter him when I had to end her. Already, he'd attached himself, the fool ill-versed in self-preservation.

Luckily, killing the *Sykagos* would also give me the chance to remain at his side; his protector until my last breath, ready to obey his every need. At least, that was the lie I'd tell myself to help me sleep.

And while the mere thought of this errand made me regret how much I ate earlier, I knew better than to pass up a reconnaissance opportunity. Knowledge was a soldier's sharpest weapon, and if I was to find a crack in the *Sykagos'* armor in time, I'd have to take a closer look.

I fell into step beside him, and he led us back through the castle to the west wing, where our guests stayed. With any other visitor, it would've been silly to house them in a separate wing with as few servants as there were in the Summer Palace, but no one would've slept well with the *Sykagos* across the hall.

Sick dread grew in my gut with each step up the stairs and down the long path. The dusty paintings hanging on the wall cast in the eerie glow of the *Zo'is* luminaries highlighted the sinking feeling. No wing could be far enough away for me to feel safe as long as she was in Lux.

We stopped in front of her unguarded door, the silver knocker an ominous threat looming before me. I'd agreed to this, and yet, doubt leadened my steps. Letting Caelum come with me tonight was a mistake. Seeking the *Sykagos* out in the middle of the night, where there was little sunlight to combat her shadows . . .

An egregious misstep.

But before I could vocalize my worry, without hesitation, Caelum banged the knocker twice, the sound echoing through the hall like a death knell.

"This is madness," I said in a low whisper. A chill raced up my back, and I grabbed his arm. A soldier's second-greatest tool was their ability to know when to sound retreat, and we were not quite past the point of no return. "Let's go."

Caelum tore from my grip, gaze burning with the thrill of another one of his mischiefs. "Maybe I should knock again."

"Caelum, this is a bad idea, we should—"

The door creaking open silenced all protests on my tongue, the useless muscle drying up like sand in the sun.

The *Sykagos* stood in the doorway, wrapped in a floor-length, black silk dressing gown that pooled around her ankles in fluid shadows. She raised a single brow, amusement dancing across her jagged features. "Well, I certainly didn't expect you two to trouble me so late at night, but I can't say I'm disappointed."

She eyed us, a predator ready to stalk its prey. Every hair on my body stood at attention. Next to me, Caelum burned bright red, his mouth hanging open like her very presence rendered him both dumb and mute.

Her grin went feral, and in that moment, I absolved myself of any qualms about ending her. "What, Shadowborne got your tongues? Come on in."

CHAPTER
SEVEN

"*The diavolos are brutal creatures, but there is an honesty to their desire. Elves are too blinded by their greed and gluttony to even begin to see the truth.*" *—An excerpt from Queen Glorianna's letter to the Elysian people, circa 2 A.G.W.*

THERA

R age sizzled in my middle, sloshing around in the empty, hollow pit of my gut. Barely eating the night before a long journey had never bode me well and yet, I couldn't stomach a single bite.

And for once, it wasn't even about my aversion to meat, though it didn't help that nearly every dish had a face still intact.

No; it was the excess. The *privilege*. It was sprinkled through every dish like the cook's signature seasoning.

The unnecessary show of it all. The *waste*. There'd been less than ten mouths at the table, and the first course alone could've fed an entire Erebushi village. Moon and mist, there would've been *leftovers.*

King Kato had piled his plate high, sampling bite after bite of the poor, innocent creatures slaughtered to feed his gluttony before discarding it all like scraps. It was the behavior of a man that had never known hunger; that'd never watched his people die in the streets, clutching their swollen, empty bellies, their chapped lips bleeding as they parted over whispered pleas.

Pleas that would go unanswered. Mouths that went unfed.

A clear display of power. A ploy to rub the Luxian wealth and prosperity in my face, to goad us into an unfavorable deal so that we might sacrifice our position to taste such indulgence, too.

It'd only infuriated me. Resolved me to my task.

I paced through the large receiving room of my chambers, the movement dispelling a layer of deep-seated dust. They hadn't bothered to clean before shoving me in the far side of the castle. Another power move, but one I'd use to my advantage. It meant fewer ears to listen in as I mulled over my disquiet with Nyxia— still careful not to let Kappas in the next room hear.

"The King thinks he has the upper hand."

"He does." She shrugged from where she had sprawled across a tall-backed, cream-colored chair, her black boots dangling over an arm. "Isn't that why we're doing this?"

"No, he doesn't." I halted my steps, taking a deep, grounding breath, fighting off the shadows nipping at my ankles. "Do you know what I saw tonight, aside from a bunch of pigs stuffing their faces?"

Nyxia shot up in the seat and crossed her arms with a pretend scowl. "Hey, I resent that. I prefer the term *hog*, thank you."

The moment of humor did wonders to ease the tension from my back. I plopped down on the golden chaise next to her, nudging her knee with my heel. "My mistake, your swine-li-ness."

Nyxia leaned forward, expression softening. "What did you see, *Mi Vassilla*?"

"I saw a king that has gotten far too comfortable. That would not know how to survive if suddenly his resources ran dry." I kept my voice low, even though no one would hear. But my words were not unfounded.

The King had once been formidable, and his wealth made him dangerous, yet he had never known survivalism like Erebus did. We'd had to live like insects for the last few hundred years, but it had strengthened us. Foragers and hunters scurrying for scraps in the darkness, willing to do whatever it took to keep ourselves alive.

Cushy palaces made for soft asses.

And softer heirs. Prince Caelum wasn't just shocked during our first meeting, as I'd initially suspected. No, the boy with stars in his eyes was awestruck; not just by me, but by life. By everything new and novel his gaze could drink in. He had the tact and efficiency of someone that had never lived past the palace walls . . . and it showed. "And I saw an untested boy about to inherit his title. He doesn't trust his son, not yet. He's too soft."

Nyxia shrugged, and she sipped the tea she'd made. "I think he's sweet."

Sweet—like berries so ripe, they were almost rotten. The boy had a big heart, that much was clear—its beat uncommonly fast, though it could have been nerves. To be twenty-five and not have a mind of his own spelled trouble for Lux down the line. If they didn't properly teach him, that sweetness would give way easily to corruption and ruin, would ferment in him and spoil any potential he had.

Still, a strange hope stirred in my center, my chest clenching around it.

Sweet dreams, he'd said. And he'd meant it.

No one had ever wished I dreamt well. No one believed it possible, not even my closest friends, knowing what they did about my life. My past.

About the shadows that lunged for my mind every time I shut my eyes.

103

But the Prince of Lux in his ignorance—or hopefulness, I didn't know—still believed the *Sykagos* capable of dreaming.

"I think he's sweet, too," I finally answered Nyxia, my cheeks warm at the thought. Fools and dreamers made the best visionaries in a system where doubt and disbelief had ruled for far too long. Maybe sweet was exactly what both Lux and Erebus needed after lifetimes of sour disappointment and pain. "Kindness is a different luxury in this world."

Nyxia quirked a brow, like she could smell the curiosity wetting the tip of my tongue; my spymaster and strategist never strayed too far from the mark. "What I don't understand is—"

Her head swiveled to the door like a dog that caught the rabbit's scent.

"What?" I whispered, urgency thumping in my ribs like a thunderstorm.

Then I heard it, too.

A wry smirk curled her mouth. "You have a guest." She jerked her head to the door at the same time knocks sounded against it. "Two."

I raised a brow, quietly floating over to the door. My hand grazed the cold knob, but two bickering voices on the other side stilled me.

"Maybe I should knock again," a bright tenor whispered.

The Prince.

And of course, accompanied by who else but his devoted guard. "Caelum, this is a bad idea, we should—"

I swung the door wide, amusing myself as the guard dog jumped.

"Well, I certainly didn't expect you two to trouble me so late at night, but I can't say I'm disappointed." I looked them over, assessing the nature of the visit. Captain Bellatore had re-donned her chain-mail uniform, abandoning the pretty silk pantsuit she'd worn for dinner. A shame, too, since it did wonders to soften the scowl she never seemed to drop around me. But the Prince wore what looked like bed clothes, aside from hastily laced boots and a large wicker basket.

This had not been on my agenda tonight, but a thrill raced through me. King Kato could make his power-grabs all he wanted.

His son already came straight to me.

I stepped back, gesturing toward the receiving room. "What, Shadowborne got your tongue? Come on in."

Caelum nodded, taking a brave step closer, but the captain jutted her hand out, blocking his path. She grabbed the basket from him—albeit a little gentler—before thrusting it at me. "We are only here for a delivery."

"So, you're Captain of the Prince's Guard and a delivery service?" Nyxia snagged the basket from her grip and dangled it before her. I hadn't even heard her sneak up behind me, the little devil. "How quaint."

The captain looked like she was ready to blow; her face red and shaking, but Prince Caelum pointed to the basket and then to me. "You're a vegetarian."

I blinked at him, another fresh dose of surprise satiating my empty stomach.

He was naive, yes, but that didn't make him a fool. His observational skills could prove useful if they were sharpened with experience.

A stone sat heavy in my stomach. Perhaps he hadn't come here on his own whim, after all. He could just be his father's most discreet spy, his unassuming smile the perfect mask.

But the hope shining in his admittedly pretty eyes made even my jaded heart want to believe.

"How kind of you to notice." I swallowed the strange lump of emotion that balled in my throat. Even if this was a mission in espionage, it meant I would have a decent meal and some much-needed company. I turned and sauntered into the room, hoping he'd follow. "Nyxia and I were just enjoying some tea, and I suspect whatever you have in that basket will go well with it."

Unsure footsteps followed, and I smiled to myself as the Prince entered the receiving room. It was his castle, yet his gaze darted around to take in the space, shifting his weight between his feet like an uncomfortable guest.

The captain hesitated in the door, her fists clenched at her side. "I don't think it's appropriate—"

"Well, good thing the prince has a big, strong guard like you to protect him." I waved my hand. I didn't take kindly to guards giving me orders.

Though, something thrilling wormed in my lowest parts as she glowered at me, the daggers in her eyes sharp enough to cut. If I had to guess, Captain Bellatore fucked like a true warrior. Disciplined, aggressive . . . and with unparalleled stamina.

"This thing is heavy," Nyxia whined as she dropped the basket onto the dusty table in the center of the room, rattling the teacups that sat on it. Without hesitation, she opened the top, prowling through like the forager she was.

I came up beside her, pulling out the assortment carefully, leaving Captain Bellatore in the doorway. Several loaves of bread, a jar of nuts, several types of cheese, a few carrots, and a bushel of particularly ripe berries. While at least this time it was all items that favored a vegetarian palette, there was still far more than the four of us could eat, even with Nyxia present to make a considerable dent.

The prince gnawed his lower lip. "I didn't know what you liked, so I got a variety. But whatever you don't eat, don't worry, we'll pack it up for the trip tomorrow."

Another strange tug to parts long forgotten. I looked up at the Prince. If he was just a ruse to tempt me, it was working. His conscientiousness for wasteful behavior fed exactly into the hungriest parts of me. Not just physical parts.

"Please sit." I gestured to one of the high-backed chairs before sprawling onto the gold chaise myself. I plucked a ripe blackberry, squeezing it gently between my fingers before popping it into my mouth. Sweet juice coated my tongue as I stared at Prince Caelum, waiting for him to take his seat. With a sigh, I relinquished a truth —a show of peace. "Berries are one of the few things that grow easily in Erebus."

He finally sat right at the edge of his seat, back rigid. From her post at the door, the captain let out a huff and stalked into the room, standing directly behind his chair, arms crossed securely. The prince nodded to her before turning back to the food, his eyes burning with a curiosity I recognized in myself as he stared at the berries. "How do you grow food there? Don't plants need sunlight?"

I glanced at Nyxia, worry churning in my gut. The sun did not shine in Erebus, but we'd made our own light. Though peace was my priority, I didn't want to sacrifice all my people's secrets to the prince before I'd earned his trust.

But Nyxia nodded—my spymaster's sixth sense for sniffing out liars and cheats unparalleled. The Prince was neither.

I cleared my throat, offering an admission as an olive branch. "We've worked very hard to make water flow intentionally with aqueducts, and we rotate soil. We also choose crops that do well with little light, like spinach, beets, carrots, cabbages . . . and we've been able to use the little *Zo'is* and firepower we have to create artificial heat lamps for some of the produce."

Caelum smiled, leaning his elbows on his knees as he sat forward. "That's genius. Who came up with it?"

My lips twitched, a smile of mine begging to answer his.

Nyxia ripped off a large hunk of bread, stuffing her face with it. "Her Majesty. Before her, we were all hunting whatever terrible creatures haunted the mountains and foraging for bugs," she said, her mouth full.

Caelum's gaze flicked to me as he let loose a sigh. "Incredible."

I leaned back into the chaise, the soft fabric enveloping me. Of all the things I imagined I'd find in Lux, this starry-eyed prince was not one of them. "Thank you. You're not what I expected, Prince Caelum."

He tilted his head to the side, his gaze narrowed like he couldn't fit the puzzle pieces together in his head. "Neither are you."

Behind him, the captain scoffed, disgust twisting her full lips into a considerable frown.

The admirer was jealous, it seemed.

How exciting.

"Ah yes, I left my fangs and bat wings at home." I laughed, the sound low in my chest, and the Prince's eyes widened—confirming which stories he'd heard about me.

"Funny," the captain finally interjected with an eye roll, her foot tapping against the wood floor. She swiveled, putting her back to Nyxia and I like it meant we couldn't hear her. "We've stayed too long. Julius will be looking for us if we don't move soon. Let's go, Caelum."

I stilled in my seat.

Caelum.

If only the guard knew exactly how much she gave away with her interactions with him. If she was so obtuse in front of me, in front of someone she clearly saw as an enemy . . . I wondered how her carelessness could endanger him in front of those that might do him harm.

And I cared. Not just because I needed the prince for my people, but . . .

Kindness was a luxury I hadn't indulged in for a long time.

"Do all of your subjects address you so casually, *Your Highness*?" My tone was sharp. I snagged another berry from the pile, piercing it with my long fingernail so the deep maroon liquid stained my skin in streaks of red.

The captain turned, a moment of realization flashing across her face before it settled back into stone.

Caelum swallowed, his throat bobbing with the action as he faked a laugh. "Don't mind Rory. We've been friends for ages."

The way his tenor voice smoothed over the word *friend* awakened a stinging envy in my veins I didn't quite want to address.

Captain Bellatore's admiration was not one-sided, as I previously assumed. The Prince had his heartstrings tied up in this messy knot, too, and if he wasn't careful, they'd both get caught in the snare.

Lucky for him, I had a penchant for making yarn of tangled messes.

"*Rory*. What a cute nickname," I crooned, tugging at the childhood moniker with a voice sweet enough to make the captain nauseous. On cue, she opened her mouth as if she'd fumble an excuse, but I saved her the trouble, turning to my right. "Nyxia and I are the same, aren't we?"

She pointed a carrot at me like it was a saber before chomping the end off with a vicious crunch. "Sure. You let me eat your food, I make sure you don't piss anyone off too much with that mouth of yours."

Silver eyes blared the signal of retreat, Nyxia's coded warning clear. I was in dangerous territory, provoking the captain. If her and the prince were as close as they seemed, if she had a piece of his heart . . . well, then she likely had his ear, too. And I couldn't afford for the songs she sang about me to turn personal. It was one thing to speak of my reputation as the *Sykagos*. It was another to let them see King Thera as the villain.

I looked at the captain again, at the lithe form of her stuck in that rigid stance, at those pretty gold eyes narrowed in contempt. Her crush on the prince was still a weakness I could exploit, but perhaps she could be a tool to further my agenda as well. Win her over, and there'd be no obstacles to an easy transition of power. I nodded to her, conceding this battle so I might win the war. "Prince Caelum, wouldn't your father be displeased if he found out you were here?"

I swore the Prince looked disappointed, his shoulders slumping as he deflated. "I think he'd be chuffed we're getting along."

Perhaps it was low blood sugar or the long journey, but my

heart skipped a beat. My smile was not faked. "Is that what we're doing?"

"It's late. Your father would not be happy to see you about the night before a journey. You of all people, need rest." The captain struck quickly, not missing the opportunity I'd given her. She squeezed the Prince's shoulder with a gentle grasp; an act of dominance masked by an affectionate gesture.

Curiosity piqued within me at another mention of the Prince's poor condition. Perhaps the rapid heartbeat wasn't just his nerves getting the best of him, but an underlying illness—invisible, but still enough to keep him restrained.

It would be a question for another night.

"Yes, it's past my bedtime, too." I faked a yawn, stretching further onto the chaise. My robe spilled open ever so slightly, my left thigh peeking out from beneath the dark fabric. To my surprise —and delight—*both* of their eyes scanned the action, pupils blown wide. *Desire* . . . or at least curiosity. More potential tools for me to tinker with. A cry of victory tore through my insides, but I kept my voice level as I covered my leg again. "Perhaps your chaperone is right. Time to turn in."

Screams outside of my chambers cracked through the banter like a hammer through glass, all four of us jumping to attention. Shadows quickly snared in my chest, coiled vipers ready to strike. Nyxia threw me a terse glance; she didn't know what was happening.

"What was that?" Captain Bellatore snarled, her weapon already drawn.

Ice ran through my veins.

Not to her knowledge, either. Not good.

Heavy footsteps barreled down the hallway, and I took an instinctive step closer to the door—in front of the prince and Nyxia —ready for whatever came through it.

A massive elf burst through the door, not bothering to knock as he practically tore it off the hinges. His blonde hair was a mess of tangles, like he had roused too early from sleep, and his bronze face devoid of the same russet color it'd had this evening at dinner as an unnamed horror plagued him.

But I did not strike, the face familiar enough even though we'd only had one encounter.

Lieutenant Julius Fortis, the captain's *Vinculum*.

His worried eyes landed first on Prince Caelum—then on the captain. "Your Highness, Captain, are you both . . ." His gaze trailed to Nyxia and I. "Are you secure?"

Captain Bellatore didn't sheath her weapon, but she did lower it, her *Vinculum's* presence washing away the stress that knotted her brow—despite the streaks of dark blood that painted his. "Jules, what's going on?"

I'd heard of the *Vinculum* bond, the soul marks that the Luxians dabbled in. Tricky business, that much trust. But it was clearly reciprocated, the giant elf's shoulders slackening as he stepped into the room, glad to see his captain and prince safe.

I felt anything but.

His gaze finally narrowed at me. His sword hand twitched, and I returned his stare, the *Zo'is* in the hilt glowing brighter as his emotions flared. "A Shadowborne was loose in the castle. There was an attack." He bowed his head to the prince, the final words stuck in his teeth. "Quinton Vender is dead."

The room went entirely still; the words settling in. Then, all at once, movement. The Prince, in his shock, fell into his seat, the blood running from his face. My shadows swirled at my feet, whispering the promise of a larger threat as Nyxia danced closer to my side, twin daggers drawn.

Another drove of loud footsteps silenced us before any of us could speak, before we could even understand.

Flanked by five or six guards, Commander Tiberius of the Luxian Army stormed the threshold first, one hand holding a bloodied sword, the other . . .

The other gripping a Shadowborne's decapitated head by its

matted hair, its twisted, gray-skinned face frozen in a permanent roar, long fangs dripping red blood.

Unseeing ruby eyes stared at me as the commander raised it high, his sword pointed to my throat.

"You," he snarled, dangling the head like it was proof of my treachery. "What have you done?"

CHAPTER
EIGHT

> "But what is a soldier without his sword, but a puppet to a general's word?" –From "A Soldier's Dilemma," by Luxian Poet Obilos Hammon, 836 A.G.W.

RORY

It would've been so easy to let Thera of Erebus die by Commander Tiberius' outstretched sword. Easy to let her take the fall for Quinton's murder, to end this madness before it even began. King Kato would've had to adjust—instead of a peace treaty, we'd have to take Erebus by force, but without the *Sykagos* alive, we'd have much better odds.

But for reasons I could not name, reasons I dared not explore . . .

I stepped in front of Thera, Tiberius' sword now pointed squarely at my throat. The muscle bobbed on instinct, a dry swallow scraping down my gullet.

"Commander Tiberius, sir, there has to be a mistake." The

words tasted like poison on my tongue, but I spat them out anyway.

"Stand down, Captain Bellatore, or I will find you in obstruction of due justice and will offer you just punishment." The commander's stone face betrayed no emotion, his rocky voice booming commands like rolling thunder.

He didn't need to spell that out further for me to understand it meant my head would soon adorn a spike through it if I did not abide his order. I raised my hands in surrender, and I watched Julius go utterly still, his panic strumming through my tattoos like a feverish song.

"Sword down now, Commander." Caelum found his voice, spurring from his seat on wobbling legs to stand at my side. He rose to his full height, tall but slender, next to the commander's armored mass. Still, he did not balk, and my heart clamored in awe of him.

"All due respect, Your Highness, but I answer to the King." The commander ground his teeth together. His guards behind him stood in a staggered line, all ready to deliver swift justice at his command. His gaze darted between the prince, Thera behind me, and the dismembered, gory head still hanging from his fist. "This vile creature just allowed one of her beasts into the castle, and now a servant is dead. On our soil, under our roof."

A whine from behind me sent goosebumps skittering down my back.

"I did no such thing." Thera's movements were like a dance, the slender woman warping around me in a spin that would've been dizzying had I not been standing perfectly still. Nyxia was at her side in another swift motion, two small daggers drawn from some hidden sheath, her movements impossibly quiet.

I'd have to pay more attention to them—the skills they easily flaunted unexpected from a frail king that relied on dark magic and her 'advisor.'

Thera tapped the end of Tiberius's sword, the metal singing as her long fingernail pinged against it. "But as the King of Erebus, I warn you that if you threaten me, my *betrothed*, or his guard again, I will take it as a declaration of treason and see you hanged as my personal wedding present."

The commander's face went a deep crimson, though his expression remained unchanged. The most emotion I'd ever seen from the man in the decade I'd worked beneath him. But he paused, assessing Thera's threat for the true tipping point it was. One more step, and he'd be declaring war. He grimaced before thrusting the rotted head closer; the stench choking me. "Then explain this."

Thera's nose wrinkled, but she didn't give ground. "That's a Shadowborne head, Commander. Keep up."

A dark, traitorous part of me might have laughed if the most powerful commander in history didn't hold a sword within slicing range of my throat.

Tiberius wasn't just built like a tank—he was one of the few elves that could handle as much *Zo'is* as one, his ability to channel the substance unmatched.

I squashed that part like a bug beneath my boot, rooting myself to solid ground again.

The commander was less amused as he threw the head at Thera's feet. Dark blood splashing across her robe and melting into its deep hue. "You dare mock me, you vile—"

"Stand down, Tiberius." A voice that sent chills through my veins sounded as he rounded through the doorway, the King's indomitable presence silencing all other noises in the room. Light eyes scanned the scene like a soldier would—quick, decisive, efficient—before a sigh lowered his shoulders. "Is everyone here all right?"

I stood at attention, heart hammering in my chest.

"Yes, Pa—Your Majesty. We only just heard about . . . Quinton." He took a step closer to his father, the tension unwinding from his frame.

I forced myself to look away as his lower lip wobbled on the last word, pity spearing through my heart. Caelum was too good for this world. Too kind.

Quinton Vender didn't deserve death by Shadowborne attack, but he was a gossiping, haughty twit that had always rubbed me the wrong way. Yet Caelum would mourn his loss like a brother. Like a martyr.

King Kato's sharp glare flicked from his son's grief to me. And to Thera of Erebus, who still stood at my left, like we were in the same category. "Do you two have anything to say for yourselves?"

I might have responded if my tongue hadn't turned to lead in my mouth, heavy and useless. Shame coiled around my chest, making the air too thin to breathe. I'd failed the King, failed my post as a guard . . .

Thera crossed her arms, like the King's wrath was no more bothersome than a gnat buzzing around her head. "I know how this looks, but I swear I simply enjoyed a fine indoor picnic with your son and his guard before your untamed hound came poking his sword and his nose where it doesn't belong, hurling accusations at me I couldn't possibly be responsible for."

Commander Tiberius' sword trembled with the rage shaking his frame.

"Captain Bellatore?"

I inhaled as deeply as my fear-struck lungs would allow, drawing on my *Vinculum's* presence for comfort. Julius winced where he stood, my concern flooding him, but I relished the battle-calm that cleared the misty confusion from my mind.

The *Sykagos* was many things. A monster. A disgrace to all elves. A trickster. A wolf dressed in silk and beauty to mask her deceptive darkness.

But she did not murder Quinton Vender. She couldn't have. At least, not by herself.

I cleared my throat before uttering words I would've named treason just yesterday. "Caelum and I have been here for the last twenty minutes, and before that, we were in the kitchens. We would've heard the Shadowborne if it was already in the building at that point. There is no way the *Sy*—King Thera could've let it in."

I braced myself for accusations of treason, for the King to strike me down for siding with Erebus over Lux. Something settled in King Kato's brilliant glare, a shift that answered just as many questions as it asked of me.

"She could've used her unholy *Skia* magic, Your Majesty," Tiberius said.

The King stayed quiet, staring at me, making sweat settle and pool on my neck despite the chill of the room.

"Or Commander Kappas was behind it," Tiberius droned on, oblivious to the king's disinterest.

"Commander Kappas has been . . . " The King grimaced, finally releasing me from the snare of his stare and addressing the room, "indisposed in the toilets since dinnertime. Several servants have mentioned checking in on his condition and finding it . . . incapacitating."

Much to my surprise, Nyxia snorted, and a hint of a grin played across Thera's face, and she dropped her arms to her side.

"Luxian food must be too rich for his stomach." She shrugged before kicking the Shadowborne head away, face wrinkling in disgust. "Though I must admit, I'm feeling rather queasy myself with that thing in the room."

It stopped in front of one of Tiberius's guards, who looked about ready to shit himself as he stared at the monster's massacred face.

It was a disgrace that the thing had made it into the castle walls at all. I'd have to discuss it with the commander and other guards. How we could've let something so dangerous slip through our ranks, how we could've been so blind to a threat.

But one thing was clear—the threat was not from Erebus. Not unless they had some way to compel the Shadowborne from a distance and without words.

I flicked my eyes toward King Thera, wondering if the *Sykagos* was capable of that. But if she were, why enter this treaty at all? Why ever enter the battlefield herself? Why not just send droves of Shadowborne to do her work for her while she sat comfortably on her dark throne?

As loath as I was to admit it, it seemed unlikely that she possessed that power. She'd just been whining to Cae about the struggle to grow crops in Erebus, and none of her body language then had hinted at deception. It seemed almost uncomfortable for her to make such admissions, her lithe frame stiff and shrinking in on itself as she'd parted with that truth.

If her and her people really were on the brink of starvation, and she'd possessed the power to flatten us without having to lift a finger of her own . . .

She'd have taken the chance. She'd have had no choice.

Which meant that for once in my life, the *Sykagos* was not the singular source of all my problems.

I stood straighter, clearing my voice of the previous discomfort I'd harbored. I had a job to do, one I would not fail twice in one night. "Commander Tiberius, I ask that you give Julius and I permission to investigate the true culprit of this heinous crime, though I must insist that King Thera had no involvement."

Thera's head whipped to me, her dainty brows lifting. She bowed her head to me—an offering of respect that heated my blood. "Glad we agree, Captain Bellatore."

The commander offered me a look that might have flayed the skin from my bones. "I did not expect you to be so easily swayed, Captain."

"Permission granted, Bellatore." The King clapped, as if this had just been a simple afternoon business meeting, not a midnight murder interrogation with the potential to have started a full-on battle between the *Sykagos* and the most powerful Luxian Commander in history. King Kato spun to my *Vinculum*, acknowledging his presence in the room for the first time since his arrival. "Lieutenant Fortis, please take my son to his rooms."

Julius puffed out his chest before lowering his head in a deep bow. "Yes, Your Majesty."

Then King Kato turned back to the other regent in the room, their gazes clashing like thunderclouds. "King Thera and Ambassador Nyxia, I ask that you stay put here until further notice. Guards will be stationed outside of your rooms for protection."

Thera fiddled with the strange ring on her skeletal finger, the only external sign of her discomfort. "I could also help find the culprit. I have a good sense for these things."

I froze, blood pooling like anchors in my toes. What a suggestion that was, the *Sykagos* offering to help bring justice to a Luxian instead of delivering the killing blow herself.

But whether it was a genuine attempt or a ploy for power, it didn't matter. Thera of Erebus would come nowhere near this investigation if I had any say. She wasn't responsible for this murder, but the blood of thousands still caked her pale skin.

Only a fool would trust her.

"That won't be necessary." King Kato's lips pressed in a thin line of dismissal, echoing my sentiment.

Thera's gaze darkened, but for once, she kept her mouth shut. A gift to us all.

The King's icy glare darted to me again, and all heat fled from the room. "Captain Bellatore, come with me."

Fear clattered through my ribcage. Thera of Erebus was innocent in this matter, but someone would have to pay for Quinton's death.

Caelum shifted uncomfortably at my side. "Father, this was my —"

"Yes, Your Majesty." I would not let my charge take my place on the chopping block. Whether tonight had been Caelum's idea, it was my job to keep him safe and organize patrols of the grounds. My affection for Caelum had clouded my judgement. I'd let mischief and daydreams carry me away from the one duty I'd sworn to never abandon. I'd betrayed my post.

119

This failure—Quinton's death—was on my head just as much as it was the Shadowborne's.

The King nodded once before leaving the room, the unspoken command for me to follow trailing in his wake. I didn't hesitate, scurrying to keep up with King Kato's long strides. If I headed to my just punishment, I might as well be snappy about it.

I felt both Caelum and Thera's stares follow me, boring different-sized holes into the back of my uniform, but I did not let myself turn.

"Make sure he gets some rest, Jules." I patted his shoulder as I passed, my last tether to duty I hadn't shredded. My *Vinculum's* fear flashed through me, but I tampered it down, my fists clenched to my sides.

The King was already halfway down the corridor by the time I caught up, the monarch not slowing his pace for the likes of me. But despite the feverish gallop of his steps, his expression relaxed, chasing away most of the tempered cold it'd sported in King Thera's chambers.

"Eventful night, I take it?" His boots echoed against the stone floor.

My head spun, struggling to find center. "Your Majesty, I apologize for leaving my post tonight. Caelum wanted to see the King, and I misjudged—"

"You did wonderfully." He nudged me with his elbow, the action so unexpected it nearly knocked me on my ass. I stumbled to regain my footing.

"Getting closer to the King is a smart move," King Katos continued, pride lining the tone of his deep voice. "She'll get used to you, let her guard down . . . it's perfect. Well done, Captain."

I chewed the inside of my cheek, his praise soured by my failure. I didn't deserve to be commended when the pungent scent of tragedy hung so fresh in the air around us. "You're not . . . you're not upset?"

King Kato raised an eyebrow at me like I'd asked the stupidest question in Elven history. "Why would I be?"

I swallowed hard, my throat constricting around the truth. "A man is dead. Caelum could've gotten hurt, there was a Shadowborne—"

"Oh, that?" He clicked his tongue. "A tragedy, what happened to Quinton, but we must move on and use it to our advantage. This will make it easier to accomplish our mission."

"*What?*" I halted and glanced over my shoulder, making sure we weren't being followed. It was strange that the King felt so comfortable to speak plainly in the middle of a hallway, especially while there was a potential traitor on the loose.

King Kato slowed, face unreadable. He tucked his hands behind his back. "Quinton's death is horrible, but it is important we do not let him die in vain."

Words slammed against my skull with the force of a ton of bricks, banging together senselessly as I tried to shield myself to no avail. A person died, his body not even cold yet, and the King worried about how it gave him an advantage?

I clenched my hands at my side, fear creeping through my veins.

"I appreciate your concern, Captain, but we have other things to discuss." His tone held no room for argument. Undeterred, his eyes set forward as they brimmed with plans and plots as he resumed his breakneck pace, knowing I'd still follow. "She's quite charming, isn't she?"

The change of topic struck me like whiplash, but I recovered quickly.

Thera.

"Yes." I grimaced, loath to admit the truth that had walked through the portal. The *Sykagos* had other disguises outside of her shadows, one being the witty, delicate-looking king that lounged about with a pretty smile. And while I knew it was merely a mask, it was effective. Even I had been drawn to it, like a poisonous flower enchanting unassuming prey.

Then again, we all wore ill-fitting masks these days. I was supposed to be a guard, a protector, and here I was playing spy and assassin.

"But people must also remember she is dangerous. Even if she didn't orchestrate this attack, her history with the Shadowborne is well known," the King continued as if he spoke of the weather. "When you kill her, you need to make it look like an accident, or that it was her own doing. This attack will make it easier to frame her down the line."

"I understand, Your Majesty," I said, though the thought tangled around thorns in my mind. It had been easy to imagine killing the *Sykagos* when she was the monster from the battlefield I still had nightmares about. But now, she was an elf, with a face and a name. Though I wasn't fond of either, it made it harder to betray my oaths of honor.

I shook away the distracted, traitorous thoughts before they could consume me.

"But your intervention tonight in her rooms was a boon as well. It makes her depend on my magnanimity and grace." He came to a full stop in front of his chamber doors, somehow already halfway across the castle. A darkness crept across his brow despite the glow of the *Zo'is* lamps. "I could've let Tiberius end her tonight, and everyone in Lux would've thanked me for it. She knows that. She'll be careful not to displease me."

He spoke of Thera, but I heard the underlying reminder for what it was. I was only as valuable as my usefulness to his mission.

King Kato was a strategist—a soldier used to leading men to war and weighing the cost of it. And he wanted Thera dead.

Either I could be the weapon he wielded or dismissed from his trust.

"I see." I nodded, but a fresh worry still gnawed at my nerves, fraying them to bits. "But this still doesn't make sense. The Shadowborne shouldn't have breached our perimeter without our knowing."

A deep frown carved his face as he patted me on the arm. "I didn't mention this earlier because I didn't want to sully the dead's name. But I believe Quinton himself let the Shadowborne in."

My feet went lame beneath me as shock rattled my core. "*What?*"

"According to one of my informants, he talked all night to the other servants. Complaining about Caelum and saying the King bewitched him." Kato laughed, but the sound held no mirth, only a sharp edge that twisted my insides. "He made threats as well that he'd 'uncover the Prince's true loyalties' and 'let him deal with the real monsters.' It seems his plan backfired."

Rage exploded through my veins, and every ounce of my being wanted to curse the pissant's name to Inferni and back.

Quinton was a piece of shit, and while Shadowborne's fangs brought a harrowing form of justice, Caelum had been loyal to the attendant. Quinton didn't deserve to even speak Cae's name, never mind sully it with vicious rumors and an even more insidious assassination attempt. A sick part of me relished Quinton wouldn't have further use of his tongue and could no longer threaten the Prince's safety.

"Understood, Your Majesty." I bowed low so he could not see the wrath that splayed across my face in red blotches. "Thank you, for, erm, explaining."

"Don't tell Caelum. He was fond of Quinton, and it will hurt him." He ruffled my hair like I was a loyal hound, and another flare of warning went through me. "Keep up the good work, Bellatore. I knew you were the right one for the job."

I straighten, finding my backbone for the first time that night. "Your Majesty?"

"Yes, Captain?"

I wrestled with the words I knew I had to share, not for my benefit, but for my ward. No matter what happened to me, my duty was to protect him—and his heart most preciously. But if servants already talked, perhaps his good intentions would be his undoing.

"Caelum believes . . . " I hesitated, but the king ushered for me to continue, and I spat the words out before my senses could stop me. "Caelum seems to think King Thera truly wants peace. That she isn't as terrible as she seems."

The King's answering smile was sweet enough to make my stomach uneasy.

"Oh, I'm sure there is much more to her than meets the eyes." He opened the door to his chambers, the conversation over. "Find out what, Captain. Report back when you do."

The echo of the door slammed in my face sounded like the final nail hammered into a coffin.

I spent a good hour looking over the horrible crime scene, Quinton's body mutilated beyond recognition. He'd been alone, halfway between the servants' back entrance and Caelum's quarters, like he'd purposefully been drawing the Shadowborne there. It was a good plan—the guards paid far less attention to protecting the servants' passages, especially when we were this understaffed.

I sighed. All evidence seemed to corroborate the King's assumption.

It still sat like a stone in my stomach.

Caelum had trusted Quinton. I had, too.

When I returned to Caelum's quarters, worried and worn out, I found the Prince awake in his bed, tears tracking down his face in rivers. He clutched the plain duvet to his frame, knuckles white where his hands fisted in the fabric.

Julius leaned against the doorframe, and a strange pity wafted through the tattoo—mixed with exhaustion of his own—but I ignored my *Vinculum*, adrenaline focusing in on the crying prince.

Despite the fatigue that deadened my limbs, I sprang forward to his side, kneeling next to him on the mattress and inspecting him for harm.

When no bodily ailment presented itself, I looked over Cae's shoulder to Jules, frustration seeping into my bloodstream. I'd only been gone for an hour, and I'd needed my partner to take care of my ward, not let him unravel at the seams.

Then again, none of us were doing a very good job of holding the world together right now.

"What happened?" I asked neither of them specifically, the question intended for both in different ways.

"See you in the morning, Rory," Julius rubbed a tired hand across his face before dragging himself across the room. Answers from him would wait until dawn, but it didn't stop him from sending a prickle of annoyance and a boatload of concern down the bond.

His hand lingered on the brass doorknob for a long moment, like he wanted to say something else but couldn't muster the energy.

"We'll talk tomorrow."

I bit my tongue as he exited, shoving down errant thoughts. The benefit of the bond let us always know each other's mind; let us rely on each other to steady us both even in the roughest storms. But conversely, when both of us were tired and pissed, it took double the effort to shut it out.

It didn't help that I couldn't even tell him why I was so far past my limit. Why my mind buzzed with unanswered questions and my heart ached worse than any physical blow I'd ever felt.

No, this was my duty and pain to bear all on my own.

Find out what, Captain. Report back when you do.

Dragging Jules into this would only result in both of our necks beneath the executioner's blade.

"I was cruel to him today," Caelum sniffled, voice shaking as he quieted his tears.

I blinked, struggling to understand his meaning. Had Cae been rude to Julius? Was that why my partner was so sour?

Caelum rubbed his eyes with the back of his sleeve. "He'd always been a good worker, and kind, too, and I was mean to him today."

"Who, Quinton?" Realization settled over me like the itchy blankets we soldiers received in the barracks. In all my fretting over my conversation with the King, I'd forgotten to think of how Caelum might take this.

King Kato had been right—he was devastated even without the knowledge of Quinton's betrayal.

Cae stared off into the distance, eyes bloodshot and glassy. "He didn't deserve to die, and it's my fault."

Guilt churned through me, the secrets I had to keep like bile at the back of my throat. But instead of spewing them all to him, I gripped his hand tightly. "How on earth is this your fault?"

Caelum collapsed into me, his head nestling across my lap. For a moment, I stiffened at the contact before relaxing into it, hating the way I loved it. *Loved him.*

"The other servants said that he looked for me," he murmured into my thigh. "Because he wanted to say sorry for earlier . . . when he . . ."

Another sob racked through him, his tears staining the fabric of my trousers. But a warmth spread through my chest, chasing away all the worry and the ache. Of course, I knew Quinton hadn't been sorry, nor had he done Caelum any favors. The blame for his death laid squarely on his own dismembered head, the boy a fool for thinking he could manipulate a Shadowborne.

And he likely hadn't been alone.

Perhaps there was more unrest brewing amongst the staff and civilians now that the *Sykagos* had been invited into our home with open arms. I'd have to warn the other guards to be on high alert for talks of rebellion. Nothing was right in this world anymore.

And yet, Caelum's kindness was somehow the cure. If the rest of us were all liars and cheats, all monsters in masks, he was the only authentic elf left. And one day, perhaps he'd be the one to lead us out of this dark mess.

"Hey, look at me." I gently lifted him by his shoulders, sitting him upright. I stroked his cheek, wiping away the saltwater evidence of his tears. His eyes met mine, pupils somehow brighter in the low light. "This is not your fault. None of this. You are so good and kind and brave. You see the best in everyone. This is not on you."

Caelum gave me a smile, but it didn't capture his whole face in the way I knew it did when it was real. He laced his long fingers through mine, and the heat spread through my whole body.

"Stay with me tonight?" His voice was feeble—not a prince, but a boy begging for a friend. "Please?"

I should've said no. I'd already shirked my duties once tonight, and it had landed us both in a steaming pile of shit with a stink that would follow us for weeks to come. Plus, I didn't deserve his friendship, this boy who cried for those who wronged him. This prince in title and in heart. He was goodness embodied, and I was lying to his face, playing treacherous games in the shadows.

I should've said no.

Instead, I said, "Move over."

And when my head hit his pillow, our hands still intertwined, I realized two truths.

One; that I was no better than the *Sykagos*. I would lie, cheat, murder, and steal to further my cause.

And two; neither Thera of Erebus nor I would survive this game of kings.

CHAPTER
NINE

"Peace is a fairytale written by elves that do not know what it is to suffer. Do not fall for their lies." –Excerpt from a letter from King Theron Umbrus of Erebus to General Danae, circa 1773 A.G.W.

THERA

A king bowed to no one, but with Luxian guards posted outside of my door, there was little I could do but pace my quarters and think.

Shadows whispered warnings unheeded and blurred the edges of my vision. It'd take less than a thought to disarm the guards outside, but I'd had enough excitement for one evening. Being accused of one murder was enough.

Luckily, Nyxia didn't need doors.

The little devil strapped the sack of food to her back—a repurposed gift from the prince—before climbing out the window, ready to scale down the four-story stone wall. She grinned, this small mission child's play for my Mistress of Shadows. "If I'm not back in an hour, sound the alarm."

"Be careful." I pressed a quick kiss to the top of her head before she descended, her fluid form blending in with the misty night air.

I inhaled a steadying breath, hoping the moonlight-scented fog could help chase away the shadows that waited for me.

But with her gone, little stimulus distracted the hungry beasts that dwelled in the back of my mind, ready to take a bite out of it.

I stretched across the chaise again, snatching another berry the prince had brought—one of the few things I insisted Nyxia left behind—and tossed it into my mouth.

As I fed myself, savoring the sweetness, the thoughts I'd held at bay surged to the surface, demanding to be properly examined.

It would be foolish to think the Prince's presence tonight wasn't a smartly planted distraction. But whether he was in on the gag was to be discovered. The Prince could've been just as in the dark as I was, his kindness exploited by those who'd wield it as a weapon. Mist and moonlight, I didn't even know that there *was* a murder. I hadn't seen a body, only the evidence of a Shadowborne. Perhaps the whole scene had been a devised performance to paint the Prince as an ally I could trust.

And to remind me of my place in the King's 'good graces.'

I let my head relax, glaring at the ceiling above me, but my fists clenched, the thought of Kato enough to set me on a knife's edge. The blustering, self-important prick had entered right on time, a reminder that he always watched me like some self-appointed god, and that he held the leashes to all of his hounds.

Well, almost all of them. It was stranger still that the captain chose to stand in front of me and defy her commanding officer, to *speak in my favor* in front of King Kato. Was it honor and honesty that bolstered her, or did she have her orders—her part to play too?

Maybe her defiance was also an act, her attempt to get me to trust her just as I had tried to appease her.

The berry went sour in my mouth, and I fought the urge to spit it out.

If there was an actual murder, as Nyxia would soon know for sure, things were even messier. Who had let a Shadowborne into the palace? Who would risk it? Had Kappas been involved, despite his convenient alibi, to undermine my reign? Had the boy in question not died, it would've been an outbreak, and it would've turned everyone before dawn's first rays.

A shiver ran up my spine. I was well-versed in the dark language of shadows, their voices still seducing me in the land of the light. But even I wouldn't chance using a Shadowborne as a method of murder.

Not again, at least. They were too unpredictable, too lawless to trust.

Nyxia somersaulted through the open window, sparing me from my guilt. The curtains swished as she brushed through them, the only notice of her arrival.

Not a single hair out of place on her head, her clothes immaculate despite her arduous trek; yet the dark expression she wore matched the rolling pit of worry in my gut. "Our suspicions were correct."

I pinched my nose, leaning my head back against the stiff arm of the chaise. So there had been a murder, then. "An inside job. But who?"

Nyxia flitted across the room, checking all entrances, pausing only to listen to the door and the guards beyond it. When she heard enough to be satisfied they wouldn't interrupt or overhear us, she collapsed into the chair next to me, gray eyes narrowed. "The servants don't know. The chain of command is off. They just know that Vender was grumbling complaints about the Prince all night until he received a message from Caelum saying he wanted to speak with him near his chambers. The servant went and was ambushed exactly there. The body was torn to shreds, but it was him. A guard that knew him found him and ended the Shadowborne."

I fiddled with Amma's ring, but for the first time since my father's death, I wished he were here. King Theron Umbrus knew exactly how to preen rotten weeds from his ranks.

At least, all except for the one that ended him.

I shook off all thoughts of my father. Terrible and tactical as he was, he had no way of helping me from beyond the veil. In this, it was just Nyxia and I. I turned to my friend, trying to piece together the puzzle she'd presented me. "But we know Caelum didn't send the letter. Unless he's a part of the plan, but it strikes me as unlikely."

Nyxia nodded, and something unknotted in my chest. No, if Caelum had a part to play, he was just as unwitting as I was. Nyxia's approval confirmed that enough—no one had a better read on people than my Mistress of Shadows.

I just didn't know why it mattered to me.

I shifted the subject, my head still snagging on the thorny answers that evaded me. "So then who? Tiberius?"

Even as I suggested it, it felt off, like shoes a size too small. The massive commander had a deadpan expression that was hard to crack, but even in that, I could smell his fear. Could see his rage and utter terror mixing in the cold soup of his stony gaze. That kind of shock was hard to fake.

And the commander struck me as someone that fucked and fought like a machine. Everything about him was strategic, practiced, predictable. *Boring.* He struck with a longsword right to the throat for all to witness; not with a Shadowborne bite in the dead of night, shrouded by shadows in some lonely corridor.

"Not likely." Nyxia shrugged. She twirled a dagger between her fingers. She was stumped too, a rare occurrence for a spy of her caliber. "What about the captain? She's hiding something, but I don't know what."

Discomfort settled across my shoulders like a heavy shroud. The captain was a puzzle all to herself, a rare contradiction of uninhibited instinct and calculated cunning. Capable and incautious.

Lovely, with her sunshine hair and twilight eyes.

Lonely too, perhaps, with that desperate, determined gaze toward the prince.

Perilous if I let myself look too long.

I cleared my throat. "Bellatore is tricky. I agree there is something off, but then again, she's a terrible liar. She can barely contain her emotions around the prince. I think a murder is above her pay grade."

Nyxia huffed in agreement, but sucked her bottom lip, still toiling with the dilemma. "But there is something. Something she's even hiding from the Prince."

Of course, Nyxia was right. She'd been quick to run off after the encounter, with the King no less. She didn't even offer Caelum one of her pretty, wistful parting glances, instead bolting from the room as fast as she could.

Bad liars made good runners, and Aurora Bellatore was running from something.

But the real question was, how did it all relate back to the events of the evening?

A question I intended to answer. "I love poking a good sore spot to find the underlying affliction."

Nyxia finally relaxed, snagging the last of my berries and shoving them all into her mouth at once, staining her lips blood-red.

"King Kato also seemed to hold her trust," she mused, her mouth full. "Could he be behind this?"

The shadows surged at that, greedy little bastards begging to take a bite out of me. The king was another strange case, my future father-in-law, both the least likely and most unpredictable suspect.

But to assume King Kato had ordered and orchestrated a Shadowborne attack on his own people was madness. He'd never put the whole Summer Palace at risk, his *son* . . . for what? To kill some poor idiot servant? No, a former soldier like him would not be so reckless and unhinged.

I sighed. "It could be anyone, but I can't get a read on the king either. He's weak in ways he doesn't even see, but his presence is intimidating."

"We'll keep our eyes on him too, then."

"Well, at least one thing is clear." I stood, cracking my stiff neck. "We trust no one."

Nyxia paused, an uncharacteristic sadness swimming in her silver stare. "Now you sound like your father."

Phantom pain clattered through my broken-and-mended bones at the mention of him. I was Appa's greatest weapon, but I'd come too far to still be his tool. I'd sacrificed too much of my soul.

But the price of peace was even steeper, and a frightened part of me I pretended to ignore wondered how long it would be until I paid with my life. I shot Nyxia a dark look. "Perhaps he wasn't so wrong after all."

Nyxia matched my stare, and we stayed like that for a long moment, air thicker than blood between us. We'd both spilled our share of it, and done all we could to rinse our hands clean.

She wiped the edges of her mouth and stood, then smacked my cheek lightly. "Get some sleep. You're waxing dramatic."

She didn't need further dismissal as she crossed the sitting room and entered the smaller bedroom that would be hers, shutting the door with a firm click.

A part of me ached at her absence, the shadows plummeting the room to frigid without her presence. I wished it was like when we were girls again—wished I could ask her to stay with me for the night, to stay up far too late telling scary stories and discussing our dreams for the future.

But we were past the age of wishes. Now, all we had were plans, carefully laid and executed. And I was no longer a girl, but King. My father had seen to that, eradicating any last whimsy from my soul via beatings and bloodlettings.

And Nyxia was no longer just my friend. She was my advisor, my subject.

So with only the shadows to keep me company, I went to bed, my mind another battlefield to war with.

CHAPTER
TEN

"The Luxian miracle is that of civility. We alone understand that true power is maintained through order, etiquette, and fealty to our rulers. Without those tenets, we would be as lawless as them."
—The Commandments of King Alixsander Borealis the 1st, 4 A.G.W.

CAELUM

Rory was gone when morning came.

Which was for the best. I was the Prince of Pricks for asking her to stay at all. My intentions had been innocent enough, and it wasn't the first time Rory had fallen asleep at my side, the comforting white noise of my dearest friend's gentle breathing easing the ache in my chest. With Quinton's death, the urge to hold my loved ones closer itched at the back of every thought, like somehow if I just kept everyone within arm's reach, they'd all be safe. But there were lines we could no longer cross—lines that had already blurred too far.

I was an engaged man now. And even if I had the freedom to choose, Rory loved her work as Captain. I couldn't undermine her position by painting her as the Prince's whore, even if it was the farthest thing from the truth.

And it would cause even more trouble for King Thera, something I was not eager to make a habit of. Though it seemed I'd been little more than that to her so far, a fly buzzing around her head and bringing shit residue with me wherever I went.

Still, when I turned over and reached for Rory on instinct and found the bed empty on her side, my stomach plummeted. Light streamed through the dusty curtains as I blinked awake, my shame laid bare in the morning sunlight.

I sat up and rubbed my face, my back sore and my skin flushed —a bad sign that my crying and staying up too late would do me no favors today. But I didn't have the option to stay in bed or soak in the bath all day.

Sun and stars, I needed to get myself together. I was the Prince, my father's heir, and it was time I started acting like it.

Love and leadership were so much easier in the romance novels the servants passed around, the tales I read under the covers by *Zo'is* light. Good intentions and a full heart were all anyone needed to cure all conflicts and overcome all obstacles.

But reality didn't paint its monsters or lovers in black and white. More and more, I saw the shades of shadowed gray that laid in each elf, me included. I'd need more than honorable intentions to rule, and I'd have to do better on all accounts if I'd be a half-decent husband, too.

Before I could manage a plan on what that actually looked like, I had to get up. I stretched, my back cracking in three places, the tunic I'd fallen asleep in static-clinging to my abdomen and tickling me.

Julius burst through the heavy door, and I almost fell out of bed. Already dressed in his gray travel uniform and chain-mail, he kept his gaze fixed on the wall, not looking at me as he dipped his head in a cordial bow.

A different embarrassment squeezed my sides, my face heating. I straightened my wrinkled, clingy tunic. Julius had been here last night for my meltdown, and though he didn't say a word about it, I could read the judgment in his amber stare.

I was a silly, sensitive boy compared to a capable, battle-fed elf like him. No wonder Rory trusted him the way she did.

It stung that she'd never see me that way, as a rock to rely on instead of a child to coddle.

Julius saluted me. A formality, not a true show of respect. "Good morning, Prince Caelum. I've been instructed to collect you. Get comfortable clothes on and drink your tea, we're leaving in an hour."

"So soon?" I flung back my blankets, shooting from the bed in a too-quick motion that left me dizzy. "I thought we weren't going until tonight."

"King Kato thought it best to leave as soon as possible with the current threat to this castle."

My head spun. I tried to justify the sudden change in plans, but another problem swam back to the surface, more urgent than medicinal tea or travel plans, and my stomach flipped.

Quinton.

"But what about the investigation into . . . into Quinton's murder?" I clenched my fists at my side. Sun and stars, I was the King of Asshats. Not only had I gotten a man killed in my cruelty, but then I'd sat here feeling sorry for myself instead of doing something about it this morning. And now, I was running out of time.

Julius shifted his weight between his feet as he looked to the floor. "It's been ruled an accident. Understaffing and the wrong place, wrong time."

Panic and rage battled in my blood, both boiling to the surface in a violent wave. Quinton deserved better than how I'd treated him, and he deserved justice. I would not let his murder go unsolved, would not let the traitor who let the Shadowborne in strike again.

My teeth ground together. "That makes no sense. Who made such a hasty call?"

A pained expression crossed Julius's face that mirrored the bone-deep agony that yanked at me, too. "Captain Bellatore, Your Highness."

My jaw dropped in shock, the floor bottoming out beneath me.

"Rory wouldn't—"

Words evaded me. Rory wouldn't *what?* I trusted my guard's judgment more than anyone else in the world, but the pieces didn't add up. Perhaps she'd found something that could somehow explain all of this, and I just had to hunt her down and ask. "Nevermind. I'll talk to her myself."

Julius nodded, his mouth a thin, grave line. "You can discuss it on the road. We leave shortly."

I shook away the last of my trepidation, finally propelling into action. This was my chance to prove myself capable, to act like a future ruler and not a coward for once. I marched to my dresser, pulling out riding clothes with determination.

"You're dismissed, Julius."

But the guard did not move; a deep sigh rattled his frame. "If I might, Your Highness . . . She was in a poor mood this morning. Please be gentle with her, for my sake."

A jealous, ugly part of me I hated squirmed down my spine, raising the hairs on the back of my neck. Whether he'd spoken with Rory or just felt it through their bond, I wouldn't know. It was a festering wound being scraped that I'd never be that person for her. Never be the one she went to when she was upset or hurting, never the one who could ease her mind. Instead, I'd always be the selfish, spoiled child who cried to her and begged her to make it better, even at the risk of her personal happiness.

My fingernails carved crescents into the fabric of the shirt I held. "Thank you, Julius. I'll keep that in mind."

The caravans were packed by the time I washed, downed my disgusting *Zo'is* tea, dressed, and made it out to the front gates of the castle. The envoy of guards and servants already busied themselves with departing.

My father's delegation had left a few minutes ahead of time, his armored vehicle and Commander Tiberius' men leading the charge. It was safer for us to split up so that the current king and the Sunkissed Heir were never together on the road. A necessary precaution to preserve our line, in case of bandits or Shadowborne or other unseen threats. Still, I wished I'd had time to discuss our predicament with my father before we abandoned the Summer Palace and all evidence of Quinton's murder.

But I set my sights on the other person I desperately needed answers from, not giving up yet.

Rory stood among the remaining guards, her hair slicked back in a tight braid, dressed in her uniform and light armor as she dictated her garrison's orders to them. Her expression was carved from stone this morning, all but the deep blue bags beneath her eyes.

I had a sinking feeling both were my fault.

I cleared my throat and tried to paint on a smile as I approached. "Good morning Captain Bellatore, how did you—"

"Good, you're awake." Rory didn't turn to meet my gaze before she sauntered off toward the large tank I'd be riding in.

"Let's get moving, we're wasting daylight!" she bellowed to all gathered.

I'd have preferred it if she smacked me in the face, my cheeks heating instead. I deserved her scorn, but I thought we were close enough to at least talk about it. Shutting me out hurt far worse. But

I swallowed my pride as I followed her, grateful that my long strides let me keep up with her faster, shorter ones. She didn't make it easy, her pace brutal as she marched toward her steed, my breath dragging behind.

"Everything all right?" I tried again, my tone as gentle as silk.

"Fine." She reached the massive tank, its engine humming loudly as the *Zo'is* flowed through it, the bronze and titanium exterior glowing. Rory opened the passenger door and finally turned to face me, but her expression remained cold. "Please step inside, *Your Highness*."

My title, not my name.

Again, I'd have preferred if she called me an ass and been done with it. I tried not to let the hurt register on my face, though I couldn't help the stinging sensation at the back of my eyes.

If she didn't want to talk to me about where things stood between us, fine. Perhaps the sappy, tear-filled reconciliation I wanted also only existed in a romance book. But I had other pressing questions that demanded immediate attention. I crossed my arms, compressing all my other feelings into a tight ball in my chest. "Rory, we need to talk about Quinton's death."

Rory stood at attention, unmovable. "It was an accident."

I waited for more, for the tidbit of information I'd been hoping for that would clear the storm clouds of worry and mistrust from my mind. But she simply maintained that unfeeling, metallic stare, her jaw clenched.

I stepped closer, peering down my nose to see her as I tried to keep my tone low, frustration rising in me like the sun climbing higher above the far-off mountains. "You think Quinton's death was an accident? Commander Tiberius said himself—"

"Commander Tiberius is a soldier that is trained to look for foul play in every interaction. But I did my due diligence. This was just an accident." Rory's voice held no inflection, an emotionless drove of monotone information that only incensed me further. "The Shadowborne must have come through the portal after we left, and because we were all distracted by dinner and there are so few of us, it managed to get through."

My head ached at the poor explanation. Even if that *was* what really happened, that so many unlikely factors and oversights matched up, there was a tug in my gut that 'ifs' and 'buts' wouldn't satiate.

Maybe easy answers only thrived in my daydreams and stories, too. I ran a hand through my hair, trying to untangle this mess of a puzzle. "Don't we have *Zo'is* fences to help us keep intruders out even when soldiers are short staffed?"

Blinking eyes flicked to me, like I'd somehow caught her off guard. But before I could press on, she reapplied her mask in broad strokes of stern disinterest. "Not in the Summer Palace. It's been ten years since we've been here. We should've updated the tech beforehand. It was an oversight."

"This isn't fair. Quinton—"

"We will honor Quinton in the capitol, but he wasn't the first to die by such unfortunate circumstances, and he will not be the last." Rory shut down all arguments, her facade made of impenetrable steel. She looked away again, past me, like I was nothing more than one of her underlings that she could dismiss at will. "I have buried far too many good soldiers for you to lecture me on *fair*."

Wicked, vile parts of me twisted around my heart, locking it away. I'd made a mistake last night, asking her to stay, an infraction I'd own up to. But I wasn't a spoiled prince making a big deal out of nothing. And though I'd never known the pain of seeing soldiers die in front of me, grief was an old friend. *Quinton* was a friend. His, and each and every Luxian death, weighed heavy on my head, the price of the crown I'd one day inherit.

I straightened my spine, rising to my full height. My frame cast a shadow over Rory's face.

I could've chosen kind words, could've tried to apologize my way around my friend's ironclad barriers. But kings did not submit to insubordination, even from people they loved. *Especially* not from those they cared for most, if my father's legacy meant anything.

If I would rule one day, I'd have to think like a king, not a boy.

Or at least, that was the excuse I offered myself.

I stepped back, leaning against the vibrating metal of the tank like this exchange was beneath me, and let the cruel words fly from my mouth like venom. "Yes, he will be the last friend either of us bury, thanks to *your* oversight. Lux and Erebus will be united in squashing this threat. When I marry Thera."

Finally, a crack ran through Rory's armor, her throat bobbing. "Cae—"

The engine's guttural hum drowned out all other sounds.

"A lover's spat so early in the morning?"

Thera twirled from behind us with a smirk on her pretty face. Rory and I both startled.

My tongue tied itself in a knot. "That's not—"

"I'm teasing, Caelum." Thera patted me on the cheek, her touch cool. I shuddered as ice ran down my spine. "Though I'd love to hear more about your plans for the world once we marry. Care to ride with me?"

She gestured over her shoulder, where the other two Erebushis waited with a few tall, skeletal demon horses that made my stomach clench.

I opened my mouth to refuse, but Rory cut in. Her hand gripped the hilt of her sword, and her glare glinted off Thera. "That's not advised. As we cross through the plains to the mountain pass, he should stay in the tank, as should you, for his protection and yours —"

"Oh, come on, Caelum," Thera blinked her long, ebony lashes at me, a dangerous, delicious mischief simmering beneath them. "Ditch the babysitter and let's make this fun."

My heart picked up its beat, dancing a furious jig in my breast. I hated riding as it was, and the thought of bouncing atop one of those *Skialogo* made my meager breakfast threaten a return. But spending this journey with Thera . . .

"Why don't you ride with me in the caravan instead?"

I knocked on the side of the car, the metal pinging as my knuckles rapped it.

Rory's face went bright red, but I ignored her, the hurts between us too fresh to face.

Thera tucked her hands behind her back, emphasizing the way her dark black riding tunic and trousers hugged her form. The heel of her boot dug into the dirt. "No thank you. It's been too long since I've enjoyed the sunlight, Caelum. I prefer to ride."

My heart sank, another disappointment obscuring the bright day.

Rory cleared her throat, her hand finding my back like she still had a claim to it. Like she hadn't iced me out minutes ago. "Your Majesty, please get into the—"

"You know what?" I stepped from her reach, a rare rebellion flaring through me. This was not some book, and I didn't have to play the part of a prissy prince. I offered Thera my brightest smile. "That sounds lovely."

Thera's smirk went feral, and a heat ran through my core. "Excellent."

It was not, in fact, excellent.

Instant punishment for my pride; sitting atop a horse that galloped full speed to keep up with the tanks a torture in itself.

Nyxia had gladly offered me her steed, opting to ride in one of the servant's cars instead, which I now realized was pure cruelty from the small devil. After the first hour of riding, I could hardly feel my backside and legs, every muscle wrapped in thick bands of numb ache. My knuckles turned white, my grip on the rains unrelenting, in my effort to stay on. There was very little room for any conversation with the King, leaving me alone with my wounded thoughts and impossibly sore ass.

I nearly kissed the ground when we took our first break at the edge of the foothills, sliding off the *Skialogo* on wobbly legs.

A firm hand caught me—delicate, bony fingers wrapping around my elbow.

"Steady there." Thera laughed, her grip strong as I righted myself. She cocked her head, her hair falling over her shoulder in silken strands, not a single bead of sweat on her.

Meanwhile, my trousers stuck uncomfortably to my damp skin, an itch I'd never dare to scratch in public stirring as things chafed.

Thera smirked like she could read my every thought. "Don't take this the wrong way, but you look foul today."

I straightened out my tunic. "I had a rough night."

"The dead boy . . . he was your personal attendant?"

I blinked at her, the candor disarming, especially after my conversation with Rory this morning. "Yes."

Mismatched eyes studied my face with a scrutiny that felt like peeling dead skin off a sunburn. "I know the pain of losing friends. If I can help uncover what happened, I will gladly offer my help. Though it will be difficult while fleeing the scene of the crime."

I swallowed back the lump that rose to my throat, my hands shaking. Strange, to have such kindness from someone who was supposed to be my enemy, when my friends couldn't be bothered to treat me with such respect. Yet Thera was a king, willing to honor the death of a servant.

A stranger willing to offer me support.

I cleared my throat, staring at the *Skialogo's* dark hide instead, unable to meet Thera's all-seeing gaze. "His death has been ruled an accident."

"An accident?" Her nose scrunched like she smelled foul play.

Her understanding lit the wick beneath my ass, the fire spurring me into action, but I stamped it out, too disheartened and unwell to have this fight twice today.

"Because we're understaffed in the castle," I regurgitated the poor excuse I'd been fed, the whole affair tasting like crap. I glanced over my shoulder to where Rory stood next to the tanks, discussing something with Julius as they both shared a canteen of water. I wondered if she offered him the truth, or if she'd given him the same paltry dish of lies I'd had to withstand.

"Very odd," Thera said before mounting her steed again, and I didn't know if she meant Quinton's death, or the rift that had opened up beneath my world, separating me and Rory farther than we'd ever been.

I didn't linger on either thought as I climbed the *Skialogo* again, for once in my long history relishing the pain my body felt, letting it drown out the heartache.

We crept through the foothills, the tanks navigating the twists and hills at a much slower pace than before. By nightfall, we'd reach the base of the mountains and have to abandon the tanks entirely for horseback and a few wagons. The tanks would go around the long way with the servants in tow. My body shuddered at the mere idea of the next four days—riding on uneven terrain, camping on hard ground.

"You know, I told you a bit about Erebus last night." Thera rode beside me, this pace much more manageable for conversation. She stroked the neck of her steed aimlessly, eyes straight ahead. "Why don't you tell me what I should anticipate in Lux?"

Somehow, the gesture loosened my sore muscles, relief spreading through my taut back. My mother used to say I talked too much for my own good, a sentiment Grotchkin would stand stalwart by, but I was in too much pain to pass up such a distraction.

I smiled, my first genuine one of the day, as I pictured Stellaris glittering in the sun. I'd be home in a few days, and everything would be right then. "Solis is beautiful. The castle is massive, and everything is crafted in a way that makes it all feel like magic.

Whole hallways made of windows and opals that reflect the sunlight..."

I glanced at Thera and imagined her beauty amidst the sparkling city, imagined her soaking in the sunlight like she had that first moment out of the portal. "You'll love it."

Thera's expression offered no tells, but she pressed on. Another gift to my gossiping mouth. "And what of the people?"

My back tensed again, knowing what the initial response to her presence would be. Rory and the commander were not the only ones in Lux who held hatred for the *Sykagos*. Most servants, like Quinton, had only heard the horror stories, could only see through their own experiences...

It would be an adjustment. But I'd see to it that she'd be welcomed eventually, and that no one else had to spill blood on either side of this treaty. I'd meant what I'd said to Rory—Quinton would be the last.

I exhaled, giving Thera a truth instead of a placation. "The servants might not be so friendly at first, but they're all extremely hard workers. I'm sure they will come around once they get to know you, like I did. And the nobles that are closest to my father are kind to me—"

"I meant the people of the city." Thera slowed her steed's pace. "What is the general attitude toward royalty?"

"Oh, I—" The question disarmed me, and I thought of the times we'd rode through the city for parades and name day celebrations. The commoners always lined up along the streets, tossing flowers in our path, crying with joy, shouting our names. Though I only spoke to those that worked in the castle, the festivities were indication enough of their agreeableness. "Well, they love us, I suppose."

Thera pursed her lips, and my stomach clenched. I didn't know what I was missing, but my ignorance clearly left a sour taste on her tongue.

She gracefully pivoted before I could stick another foot in my mouth, tossing her long hair over her shoulder and clearing the tension. "What's your favorite place in the city?"

"The castle library or the Willow Grove." I adjusted myself in the saddle, trying to sit taller, to fit the role of King I'd one day carry. The jolt of pain up my back vehemently disagreed. "They are the best places in Stellaris to curl up with a book."

As long as Grotchkin wasn't in either, of course. But a quiet part of me was eager to see Thera flay Crotchkin with her sharp wit. Or to see her sitting on my mother's favorite bench, the willows blanketing her in soothing shadow, reading something new . . .

"You read?" Thera's voice pitched high with curiosity, and she tugged on her steed's reins, slowing.

Hooves crushed over the dry grass, and I held my breath, unsure as I approached the topic. I'd been teased relentlessly for my taste in novels, even the servants who'd lent me their favorites snickering whenever I'd turn up crying at the end of a sappy read.

Of course, a classical education was an important part of my upbringing, and I was a talented scholar, much to Grotchkin's chagrin. And though I'd read heavy tome after heavy tome by all the best historians, strategists, and philosophers, and though I could write in three languages, none of that made me who I *was*. None of that held my heart and taught it compassion, or soothed my spirit and molded it into its shape.

If I let Thera read between those lines, would she accept the subtext of my identity? Or would she, like Rory and the others, taunt and prod and tell me it made me less? *Lacking*?

A horse's urgent trot stamped out my thoughts before I could even attempt to voice them. Rory wrangled her steed's reins, knuckles white as bone, wedging between us and matching our pace.

"Please stay quiet, Your Highness." Rory scanned the sparse trees. "The foothills are known for Shadowborne activity, and the elves that live in these parts can be jumpy about it."

Thera clicked her heels, urging her *Skialogo* ahead. "If you wanted your chance to talk to me, Captain, you just had to ask."

Rory huffed and whipped the reins, her horse keeping pace with Thera's. "King Thera, I must ask you to cooperate."

Unease settled in my gut as her voice pitched higher, real urgency lancing its normally even timbre.

Thera's head swiveled on a swift wind, her light eyes darkening with a challenge as she stared at Rory.

"It's fine, Captain Bellatore," I called after, her title foreign on my tongue as I did my best to command authority, to manage the tentative peace of the day. Rory didn't spook easily, and I couldn't help but wonder if this was an attempt to twist the knife further into my gut from before.

But Rory was above such petty squabs, and hurt flashed across her face, lips a tight line. "I am trying my best to protect you, Prince Caelum. Please do not make my job harder."

My stomach dropped, apprehension settling in it like a stone. Rory *was* spooked, her fear and hurt rare, but true. My friend was bullheaded and stubborn, but she was also the bravest person I'd ever met, and before all else, good at her job.

It was my responsibility to heed her warning, whether or not I agreed. I shoved down lingering pride and hurt as I nodded to Rory, our unspoken alliance repaired through need. "King Thera, perhaps we should . . . "

A front guard's panicked cry shattered the quiet tension, fear snapping like a bowstring in my belly as the voice carried. "Captain, there is something ahead—"

Everything slowed and sped up all at once.

Thera was the first to move, yanking the reins of her *Skialogo*, barreling around—

Toward me, mismatched eyes wide with panic as they met mine—

No, as they looked *past* me.

I turned around just as Rory shouted; her scream tearing from her throat in a hoarse burst. "Caelum, get down!"

But I could barely hear it over the deafening roar that flooded my ears as my sights set on an elf clad in a suit of leaves, their face covered in a mask, the tip of their cocked arrow pointed straight at me.

The world stopped turning as they let go.

But before I could shut my eyes and brace, before I could even inhale a full breath—

A shadow clouded my vision, faster than a bullet from a gun, whizzing in front of me—no, *leaping*. Not a shadow, but a dark, lithe body, shadows hugging her form like she was made from them . . .

My heart threatened to stop when the arrow pierced King Thera's shoulder.

CHAPTER
ELEVEN

"In every instance of Skia magic, the body bears a price, some more severe than others. But the magic cannot inhabit a vessel that has not been destroyed—and rebuilt." –A Study of the Effects of Shadow Magic, Minister Kristos Agyros, 2079 A.G.W.

THERA

The shadows came from where they slumbered; from beneath the trees, black pools at their rooted feet. From the tiny pebbles of darkness beneath my steeds' hooves; from the sheets of lightlessness beneath the tanks. From the minuscule gaps between the soldiers' teeth. Wherever there was light, shadows dwelled, hiding, *waiting* for me to command them.

It was as easy as breathing.

Easier still to mold them to my will.

Shadows swarmed to my fingertips, vicious beasts ready to claw their way through the world, ready to do my bidding. Pain pulsed in my shoulder, but it only fueled my shadows' fury, their misty hands wrapping me in bandages of darkness.

I stared at the elf with the bow—the bastard that shot me—and noted seventeen other distinct scents that drifted on the back of the wind, their arrival somehow sneaking beneath my radar.

But I had them now.

With another thought—less than a thought, really, but a more unshaped, instinctive want—I lashed out, my shadows a black whip of energy. They cracked against a nearby branch, toppling three of the hidden fiends to the ground. Two moaned when they hit the floor, stumbling back to their feet. But one fell wrong—his neck hitting first, a sick snap echoing through the clearing . . .

And then madness followed.

Arrows flew, raining down like storm clouds opening and creating a chaotic symphony.

"Caelum, get to cover!" A golden flash next to me, and Rory hurtled forward, her sword slicing the first elf's head clean off his shoulders. It hit the ground, mouth still forming a shocked O.

"Everyone else, defensive positions!" the captain cried out.

I held off my next attack, waiting as the others scurried into position. The Luxian soldiers leapt to action, huddling together in a tight circle, swords and shields at the ready, their captain's firm command resonating through the air like a bell's toll.

Nyxia twirled around, slicing the throats of the two elves that'd toppled from the trees, their blood watering the underbrush. But the remaining thirteen enemies had the high ground, several of them shooting crossbows from the trees like birds of prey striking down field mice. Three dove straight for the captain, hatchets and daggers drawn to strike.

"Captain, watch out!" Lieutenant Fortis screamed from the soldier's huddle.

I was faster.

Shadows snared around their throats, vines pouring into their mouths and robbing the air from their lungs. They choked and convulsed as my dark magic shriveled them like raisins in sunlight. Their final breaths soured the air. The frenzied buzzing in my chest grew, victory pulsing through my veins in time with my heartbeat.

Their husks dropped to the ground with lifeless thumps. I met eyes with the captain. Her mouth hung open, eyes blown wide— with fear or awe, I couldn't decipher. Either made my stomach crawl.

"Go to the Prince," I panted, my breath short as the magic coiled through me, snakes still rattling their tails, ready to strike again. To invite the shadows was as easy as breathing, but it was another task entirely to banish them. Like forgetting how to breathe; like fighting the most basic instinct of survival.

Another arrow whizzed by, but I sidestepped it this time, my shadows now nearly at full tilt. They threaded closer, forming an exoskeleton around me, a dark armor that lived on my rage and intent. I could finish this myself, but the leash I kept around my curse wavered, pulled too tight and about to snap. And if Rory and the Caelum didn't get out of my way—

I would not entertain the thought. This ended here.

My father's favorite weapon did not concede battles.

"Captain, the Prince," I repeated through grit teeth before the shadows could mask me entirely, setting my sights on the elves still hidden in the trees.

Ten enemies left.

"What—" Bellatore stumbled forward, like I'd turned the world upside down.

"*Now.*"

Thank the mist and moon, she snapped back into action, barreling for Prince Caelum, who crouched next to Asteri as the colt whinnied in distress.

I swiveled away, confident that my steed and the captain could keep the Prince safe. It was, after all, her only job. Now I just needed the other Luxians out of my way. The building pressure pounded against my head, seeking release. I caught my people huddled next to the tank, weapons drawn and ready for orders. Relief washed through me as I called out to them, "Nyxia and Commander Kappas, protect the Luxian guard."

Kappas grimaced. "Why should I risk my ass to save them from their own?"

But Nyxia nodded once, catapulting over the tank despite the fire of crossbows and landing next to the Luxian formation. "Get behind the tanks *now*, you old ass!"

I didn't wait to see if they followed orders, the whistle of more arrows calling my darkest parts forward.

The assailants would not get the chance to reload.

With the rest of my allies safe, I exploded.

Darkness blanketed the clearing, blotting out the sun as I moved, body and shadows in perfect synchronicity.

This is what I was: blackness incarnate, the absence of life and light itself.

They didn't see me coming as I shot into the branches, my extremities lengthened by dark limbs of power only bolstering my strength. I snagged four more assailants from the tallest treetops.

Their bodies smashed into the ground, their screams cut off in abrupt cracks. My shadows finished them in slashes of pure night.

Six left.

Another exhale, and I flew for two more, their scents only three trees away. This time, they knew I was coming, shooting blindly into the darkness. Another arrow grazed my arm, but as it sizzled in pain, my shadows latched onto both elves' life forces, withering them in an instant, their choking sobs the last sounds they'd ever make.

Four more.

I smelled them retreating, their scents drifting away through the trees, back toward the mountain.

But they couldn't regroup, couldn't gather reinforcements. I wouldn't let them.

Freeing myself entirely, my shadows snaked through the tree

153

line faster than lightning strikes. My focus sharpened; three blades of darkness became skewers, piercing through their hearts.

But the last shadow lassoed itself around the final prey, dragging him back in a cocoon of darkness. Night closed around him, and his shrieking screams crescendoed.

I laughed at the heady high surging through my veins, the predator in me roaring with victory.

This is what I was: a monster, a creature of control and chaos. A beast of blood and carnage.

The Soul Eater.

The *Sykagos*.

My shadows dropped the final elf at my feet, his bruised and battered form splatting against the mossy earth. I snarled as I straddled him, the scent of piss fouling the air as he trembled beneath me, the snot and tears running down his face smudging the green and brown camouflage paint.

The darkness around me peeled back, my face visible once more.

I smiled, exposing all of my teeth. "You now have the pleasure of being our prisoner."

"Please," he whimpered, a coward's final words as he shielded his face. "Please don't hurt me. Please just kill me."

Power crackled in my veins, ready to grant him his wish.

"*Mi Vassilla—*" Nyxia's voice cut through the shadows' dark whispers. Then, a hand on my arm, tugging me back to my body, back to the light. "Thera, stop! Come back!"

Come back, Dymi. Come home.

"Sorry, I—" I blinked, darkness clearing from my vision in blurry spots. My legs went lame beneath me as the energy rushed back into the tight ball I stored in my chest, the world bottoming out.

The mist and smoke released me from their cage, running away as the threat receded. The captive's head lolled back as he passed out, his black chains evaporating into thin air—or more accurately, retreating to their proper places.

Lieutenant Fortis bounded forward, binding the prisoner in rope, as Captain Bellatore sounded another command for her soldiers to survey the damage.

But I could barely hear it, the throbbing mallet banging against the inside of my head with the force of a thousand Elven miners.

My knees struck the ground, the world shimmering as a haze clouded my eyesight.

"You *saved* me." A face floated before me, short white strands of hair swaying in the breeze. I smiled, the color like pure light; blinding and beautiful. But his brows pulled tight, wrinkling his bronze forehead. "You're wounded."

The words called forth the deep, pulsing ache in my shoulder. The wound suddenly spurred to painful life. I squeezed my eyes shut, trying to blot out the searing heat, trying to steady my spinning head—

"She needs medical attention immediately."

"We need to keep moving, there could be more—" an urgent voice ground out, but it was so far away, the darkness calling me to sleep . . .

Come back, Dymi. Come home.

Darkness swallowed me whole.

———

My seat jolted beneath me, practically vibrating, the beast that'd eaten me whole *breathing* as it bumbled over the terrain.

I shot up in a start before falling right back on my ass, my balance wavering. I blinked as the world came to focus.

No, not a beast.

A tank, rolling clumsily over rocks. A metallic engine, buzzing with *Zo'is*, humming through my bones.

And the deep, festering chill that racked through my body in the shadows' absence.

The withdrawal.

I groaned, my tongue a chapped, useless thing in my mouth.

Nyxia sat across from me, the only other elf with me, sprawled over the opposite bench. She skinned an apple with a dagger, a basket of ripe fruit next to her.

"Good, you're awake," she said, not looking up from her craft.

I ran a hand over my face, pinching my nose where the headache was sharpest. But a fresh wound clawed at my heart, a shame I hadn't yet mastered. I kept my voice low so the elf driving the tank couldn't hear me through the thin divider that separated the cabin from the driver's hutch. "How bad was it?"

Nyxia shrugged, finishing her carving. "Not the worst. You passed out before any real damage happened."

"How long was I out for?"

"Only a few hours." Nyxia chunked off a piece of the apple and extended it to me, a generous remedy for the hollowness eating me from the inside. Worried eyes finally met mine. "The arrows were dipped in poison. We can blame it on that."

I snagged the apple piece and bit into it, greedy for the juice as it coated my dry tongue. The sugar instantly revived some of the energy I'd zapped, but my shoulder still throbbed, an indication that Nyxia's assessment was unfortunately correct.

But injured or not, today's attack was two things:

One, a demonstration that Lux was more divided than we'd originally assumed, and it'd be harder to decipher between friends and foes. The assailant had encountered my fury, but his target had been the *Prince*, not me. And how many more of his kind lurked in these waiting mountains was still to be determined.

And two, most regrettably, a sign that I wasn't as in control of my power here as I wanted to be—another disadvantage. The shadows had been mine since girlhood, but it was a battle I had to fight every waking day. I'd gotten good at it over the years, a result of my father's tutelage.

But what had happened today was not the product of a well-sharpened weapon, not a master wielding a fine-made blade.

Today was messy. *Vicious.* One shade of darkness shy of a berserker on a rampage.

Sighing, my head fell back and hit the steel siding with a thunk. "I've been away from the Pool too long."

Nyxia, graciously, did not do me the disservice of denying it. "You're just going to have to learn to control it a different way. But perhaps you take it easy. Last resort only."

Taking it easy was a luxury I did not have. A king did not rest while her subjects starved. And though I was amiable to learn Luxian customs, I wouldn't adopt King Kato's taste for waste and complacency.

I had to remaster my shadows before they dominated me.

I took another bite of the apple, letting it fuel me anew. There was work to be done. I stretched, nudging Nyxia's knee with my foot. "Stop being such a worrywart. I need you sharp, too."

She snorted at me, the unspoken understanding that she was nothing *but* sharp, and pointed her dagger at my shoulder. "I did a cheap field stitch on the wound, but when we make proper camp tonight, you'll need to get that healed with *Zo'is.*"

I groaned, my hand covering the mark. I needed my strength for the battles that remained. But I'd rather eat Shadowborne shit for breakfast than let the glowing goo inside of my body.

I hated the way it set all my nerves aflame, like I was suckling the teat of a lightning storm. Hated the maddening euphoria that blew through my bloodstream, and the subsequent crash after the magic settled. And though I knew they'd proven it to be both medically and magically useful by the best Elven healers, there was something *wrong* about it in my mind. I was not a lamp, nor a Luxian war tank. The same substance that fueled engines and built cities should not mend me.

"Why didn't you do that already?" *While I was unconscious, preferably.* At least then, I wouldn't feel the desperate rush.

"No clue how to properly use the stuff." Nyxia shrugged once more, and I sighed again.

Erebus hadn't had a steady stream of *Zo'is* in ages, so only a dwindling, pitifully small number of us had any experience with making it work. And even then, we often distributed it toward our infrastructure and defense plans.

Nyxia waved a hand, the little devil just as uncomfortable with the substance as I was. "I'm sure one of the Luxians will be better with it."

A new shame crept along my spine, realization settling heavy on my shoulders. "Great, I'm sure they're all just *dying* to help me after what they saw. The *Sykagos*, reigning terror on Luxian elves."

Elves that had attacked their prince.

But elves that shared their customs, their laws. Elves that deserved to be punished by their standards, not mine.

The divider pushed open, a grinning face peering through. "Don't mind me eaves-dropping, but I thought you were pretty badass. When we stop, I'd be happy to look at that shoulder."

I stiffened despite protesting muscles, a practiced, political smile on my face. "Thank you, Lieutenant Fortis."

The broad elf flicked a few strange buttons in the hutch, letting the machine guide itself for a moment, shifting so he could lean himself fully through the opening. Warm eyes burned with a gratitude that couldn't be faked.

"You saved two people that are very important to me. You're *good* in my book." He crossed his hand over his chest—a Luxian salute of honor, a soldier's highest compliment. My stomach constricted, a strange pride squeezing tight. But the Lieutenant waved his hands, dispelling the tension like it'd never been there at all. "And there is a part of me that would love to learn whatever the hell kind of magic that was."

My lips twitched of their own volition, a soft chuckle escaping. "Maybe I'll teach you."

It was an absolute lie. I would never let another soul learn the dark truth of *Skia* magic, useful or not. But the overall sentiment was true. I wouldn't mind fighting with an honorable elf like Fortis.

Nyxia leaned forward, sheathing her dagger, a comfortable familiarity somehow relaxing her stance. "What happened to the prisoner?"

Fortis' genial demeanor evaporated, a new disquiet sucking the air from the wagon.

Gold eyes flicked to me. "Captain Bellatore has him. He's messed up, but you kept him alive."

At that, a new fire lit in my belly. I was the *Sykagos*, a creature of destruction and ruin. My father's daughter. But I was also King, a political servant to my people, and I had more than my claws in my arsenal.

I sat straighter, this time righteousness ironing out my spine. "Have there been attacks like this before?"

The Lieutenant frowned, leaning back into the hutch. "That's, um . . . " He scratched at his chest absentmindedly. "I don't know that my *Vinculum* would be too happy if I told you."

I clutched my shoulder with half-faked dramatics. "Yes, but if a king is going to take arrows while you guards stand around, I'd like to understand what I'm up against."

At that, the Lieutenant grinned, and he stopped itching. "Fine. Fair enough."

He pointed at the basket of apples, nodding to Nyxia, and the imp graciously tossed him one. He examined the red-skinned fruit, polishing it twice against his uniform, before sinking his teeth into it.

I waited, fighting the urge to tap my foot, my patience thin.

"Did you know the late queen was actually from a lesser house in the outer city?" he asked, still chewing.

"I'd heard." I'd be the worst king in Erebushi history if I didn't know *that* much about my enemy. "Does this have anything to do with the rebellion?"

Lieutenant Fortis took another bite of his apple, dangling the fruit in his hand. "Sort of. Queen Dellia was well-loved by the people. Coming from a no-name family made commoners feel . . . more seen. Hopeful. Like if she could be royalty, maybe they could improve their sorry lot in life, too." He rolled his eyes, the gesture undercut by a smile he couldn't hide. "Hells, my sister and my mom used to celebrate her birthday every year."

I didn't miss the specificity of that sentence.

Used to.

"They stopped?"

The Lieutenant stilled, gripping the apple tighter. A darkness I knew too well clouded his face. "They . . . well, they lived in an outer village since it was cheaper than the city. Out near the Divum Mountains . . ."

Tension sucked the air from the already cramped compartment, the words he left unsaid crowding us further.

The Divum Mountains were on the far coast of the continent . . . and had been a Shadowborne haven for the last two hundred years. The Luxians had practically forsaken the territory.

Nyxia peeled another apple, not looking up, but her voice softened slightly, its usual knife's edge dulled with kindness. "Shadowborne?"

The Lieutenant blinked, shadows clearing from his gaze.

"While I was gathering supplies." The formidable column of his throat worked as he swallowed. "I joined the core the next day."

"I'm sorry for your loss," I offered, and I meant it. While the nobility in Lux were vultures and greedy fiends, the common folk in the small villages were almost as poorly off as my people. No wonder they'd clung so tightly to the People's Queen, their only source of hope—of *light*—in an otherwise dark world.

They, too, would be a priority when I married Caelum.

As mercifully as I could, I redirected the subject. "Did the queen pass soon after?"

Fortis nodded; hands again animated. "Yeah, a few years ago. She'd been ill for a long time, so everyone had fears, but one day her body just decided it'd had enough. It was a shock to those who knew her personally . . . .but the people lost something that day, too."

I nodded, the all-too-familiar feeling lodged in my chest. When Amma had passed—the most loved general in Erebushi history—it'd been all too easy for so many of my people to fall into my father's desperate hands. Too easy for them to believe in the reality of bloodshed instead of the fantasy of something better.

Myself included.

"The rebellion started after that?"

Julius shrugged. "Rebellion is a strong word. It was more a small faction of dissenters. Loud-mouthed extremists that never went past hosting rallies in the town squares and in pubs. They have gotten bolder over the years . . . a few stolen *Zo'is* shipments, a couple of protests where soldiers and guards were attacked . . . " He clutched his apple hard enough to bruise the skin, his knuckles white. "But there has never been anything this . . . organized."

I sat back in my seat, exhaustion settling in again.

Even in Lux, where the sun shined and plants grew and life flourished, there was a similar festering lack that had plagued Erebus, too.

People didn't just need resources. They needed leadership.

Hope.

And in its absence, darkness would spring up and take root.

"They were hoping Caelum would marry another people's princess." I sighed, rubbing the bridge of my nose. "And they got me instead."

Nyxia gnawed at her bottom lip. "But they didn't shoot at *you*. They aimed at him."

Julius shrugged, settling back into the driver's hutch. "Out of the two of them, which one would you target if you were trying to stop the wedding?"

The Sunkissed Prince or the *Sykagos?*

An easy choice.

Still, unease churned through me like the few bites of my apple had gone rotten in my gut. This clarified the motive and target, but not how they'd known the caravan moved through that area. The rebels might've been born from the unrest in the underbelly of the Empire, but they were being fed by someone with more power. More organized resources.

"Thank you for your story, Lieutenant." I forced myself to eat another sliver. I'd need my strength for the game to come. "But it's a good thing the prisoner lived. I have questions."

CHAPTER
TWELVE

"Zo'is tastes like life and hits like death, but so does my wife, and she costs less." —From "Blue Gold" by Luxian Poet Obilos Hammon, 857 A.G.W.

RORY

Nightfall brought a sense of cold quiet as we reached the base of the mountains, making camp before the morning saw a new, grueling leg of the journey.

But even with the tanks surrounding our enclosure, their last stand before they would drive the long way around the mountain range to the city in the morning, we were all on high alert, the day's attack leaving my soldiers shaken.

Not just the fear of the rebellious elves, potentially more of them with unclear allegiances lurking in the night beyond. But of the things we housed *in* our tents, the dark, brutal creature that'd *saved* us.

She'd requested my presence twice already—the demanding king used to giving orders—but I'd put it off, busying myself with the preparations for the evening, and then questioning the prisoner. To my dismay, he'd given me very little, the poor elf so horrified he could barely string a coherent sentence together. But though I had plenty on my plate to bite into, there were also parts of me dreading the king's tent. Avoiding what I'd have to face in there.

The *Sykagos*, crafted in shadow and flesh. A monster who sucked life from elves with less than a thought.

A shudder racked my spine. Terrifying, to see it up close. To watch the shadows heed her call, to witness them turn from simple pools of shade to moving, living weapons and shields. To see her transform as the darkness built itself around her, her lithe form slipping beneath the dark waves as the massive, hulking beast of her own design swallowed her up.

My *savior.*

The moon was almost at her apex by the time I finally mustered up my courage, armoring myself with humility and duty. I was Captain of the Prince's Guard, and she had assisted my men in our time of distress. I was not afraid.

"You summoned me?" I pushed through the King's tent-flap, my fists clenched at my side as I rallied my bravest parts.

But when my eyes latched onto King Thera's bare back, I stilled, all sensible, brave thoughts dashing from my mind.

She sat on a pile of thick blankets in front of the small *Zo'is*-fueled heater, long legs crossed beneath her. Turning to face me, her dark hair swished over her shoulder. Red, bloody bandages across her breasts and the wound just beneath her collarbone barely covered her. She leaned back, the glow of the *Zo'is* casting shadows across the bare, bony mountains and valleys of her protruding ribs. A smirk danced across her face. "Did you forget how to knock?"

"I'm sorry, I—"

My tongue went lame in my mouth, dry and heavy and useless. I gulped down my discomfort, internally bashing myself. Nudity was not uncommon as a soldier, the barracks unfriendly to modesty, and I'd seen plenty of bodies on display before—male and female and non-identifying alike.

But something about seeing this king—this terrifying, power-ful, captivating monarch and monster—laid bare, *vulnerable,* made my gut flip in ways I dared not explore. I forced my gaze to stick to her wound, the bandages there the deepest crimson. "That's likely to get infected if you don't heal with *Zo'is.*"

I convinced myself my concern was honor-bound. She'd saved us, Caelum and my men, from danger today. Saved me from burying more true Luxian elves. It was only proper that I saw her healed from a wound she'd received in my prince's defense.

"I'll manage." She waved me off and closed her eyes, stretching out across the blankets like she was about to take a nap, the long lines of her frame on an even greater show. Her trousers hugged her thin legs as she kicked them out from under her, the waistband dipping low enough to emphasize the slight curve of her hips, and a new shyness crawled along my spine. One eye—the lighter one—popped open, staring directly at me. "Would you like a drawing, Captain? It'll last longer."

"No one offered to heal that for you?" I fought the embarrass-ment that flooded my cheeks with heat, pointing to her shoulder like that drew my focus. A lie to both her and myself. "I thought Jul —Lieutenant Fortis would've—"

"Oh, he offered several times." She groaned as she sat back up, her hand covering the mark. But despite the casual confidence in her tone, her lips pulled tight, eyes darting toward the floor. "I just don't see the necessity."

A wave of understanding settled over me, the air in the tent suddenly less dense and suffocating. Slowly, I prowled deeper, crouching down in front of Thera. Both of her incongruent eyes flicked to me, warnings stewing in their depths.

165

But from this angle, she looked a far cry from the shadow beast I'd seen devouring a forest full of men today.

In the lowlight of the small, warm tent, she just looked like a girl. A young, underfed, wounded thing afraid of magic she did not understand.

Perhaps here, that was all either of us were.

I let loose a sigh, the tension I'd felt all night finally dispelling. "I hate the Zo'is, too. The feeling is . . . strange. But fleeting."

I lifted the hem of my tunic, exposing the sprawling, winding scar across my side. Even now, it still twinged sometimes with the memory of what it'd felt like, to be ripped apart by death itself and sewn back together by powdered, unnatural lightning. To ride the line between unending pain and otherworldly pleasure. I covered myself again, instead tapping the scar on my eye. "It's worth the results. Trust me."

Something I refused to name settled in her expression, an honesty we probably would both deny if ever questioned. She moved her hand away from the wound; the blood coating her fingertips in scarlet. "I don't know how to use it properly."

The admission was the only invitation I needed. I sat down, crossing my legs beneath me as I rolled back my sleeves. "Fine. Let me."

Thera scooted back. "That's not necessary, Captain—"

"Listen up." I grabbed her wrist before she could wriggle further away, determination and authority lacing my tone like I was talking to one of my underlings, not the King of fucking Erebus. But she halted, and I pressed on before the window of opportunity closed. "The next six days will be grueling. The ride is not friendly; the terrain begs to consume us. And there could be more of those rebels waiting. We don't have many dissenters to the throne in Lux, but especially this far from the city, we see small bands of them. And that's not considering how they—and the Shadowborne—might be incensed by your presence here. You need your strength, or you'll slow us all down."

Silence stretched for a long breath. This close, I could hear her heartbeat, a fast jaunt thrumming through the pulse in her wrist. But her face betrayed nothing, an unwavering wall of nonchalance.

"I thought you, of all people, would be glad to see me wounded."

I let go of her, words slamming into me.

Words that were true as of this morning. Words I'd said myself.

I wanted Thera dead. It was my personal mission to see the next arrow through her skull. I should be disappointed that the free elves hadn't done it for me, should be plotting how to let her infected wound kill her slowly instead.

But in the liminal escape of this tent, the night outside a veil of shadow, nothing was clear. Here, she wasn't King, wasn't my target or my enemy. And I wasn't her would-be assassin, or Captain of the Guard.

She was the girl who'd saved the boy I loved today. Who'd corrected the mistake I'd let slip through my security unnoticed.

"You saved him." I blew out a breath. "You took a poisonous arrow to the shoulder for a boy you barely know."

Thera shrugged, but her gaze wavered. "He's my betrothed. It was in my best interest."

The reminder stung exposed parts of me, but I let my gratitude wash away the hurt.

"Still," I hedged, unsure of why I let such truths tumble from my tongue. Dark memories clouded the edge of my consciousness. "I've seen what war can do to people. When the survival instinct kicks in, they all save themselves first. You could have done the same."

Thera looked at me for a long moment, her own mask discarded. "Is that what happened to you?"

The soft sincerity of her voice threw me off my center.

Of course, she had no memory of what I'd suffered at *her* hands. I was just another nameless, faceless elf, a soldier to be mowed down by the same dark wisps of energy she'd used today. Sliced open like the dead elves we'd left to rot in the forest.

No, the *Sykagos'* one good deed today didn't clean her hands of the blood of the countless. It wouldn't save her from the justice she deserved. Wouldn't remove her head from my chopping block.

But it bought her time. A temporary truce, until after the wedding. A respite earned.

"Stop moving," I ground out, shoving back the last remnants of my sour vengeance. "Bandage off."

Thera smirked as she sat forward, her chest sticking out. "Usually elves will try to woo me first before asking to see my—"

"Either you peel it off, or I will."

"Fine." She rolled her eyes, but complied, peeling off the bandages from her shoulder and chest with a hiss.

An angry, vicious cut stretched from beneath her collarbone to the top of her left breast, like the arrow had jostled in the fight, or ripped out poorly afterward. But the uneven black threads that dotted her pale skin in jagged lines looked even more painful, the stitch work shoddy.

"Who the hell stitched you up?" I ran a finger over the raised mark.

Thera shivered under my touch, and I jerked my hand back. She exhaled. "Nyxia."

"Your ambassador is either blind as a bat or cruel."

"Both, maybe." She snorted, but her smile did little to hide the pain, the expression bordering on a wince. "Well, show me your advanced skills, then."

I fought another sharp retort as I fiddled for the tiny glass vial of *Zo'is* in the small satchel tied around my waist. The concentrated, bright blue inside giving off its own light as I drew it out.

Like I had a dozen times before, I popped open the metal lid, the metallic scent hitting the air. From the same bag, I removed the syringe, carefully drawing just enough of the potent powder into the barrel, twirling it to mix with the liquid solvent already waiting inside.

I squeezed the plunger just enough to force the air bubbles out of the tube before setting my sights on the festering wound.

"Hold your breath." I cleaned off the skin just above her breast. "And maybe hold on to something. Some elves pass out when the *Zo'is* first hits their bloodstream, especially if it's been a while."

Thera rolled her eyes. "I'll be all right—ahhh!"

I plunged the needle just beneath the skin, pressing the *Zo'is* into her veins, and her words pitched high into a heady moan. Her entire frame shook, eyes rolling in the back of her head as she bit her bottom lip, as if waves of pleasure cascaded over her.

I swallowed, knowing the feeling all too well, the rushing, buzzing rapture that seized her by the throat. My heartbeat increased, the sensation almost contagious as goosebumps flecked over me.

Her hand clamped around my thigh, fingernails digging into the flesh, sending a ripple of desire through my body. She squeezed her legs tightly together, the ecstatic power thrumming through her, her exposed nipples beading to sharp points.

I looked down, but did not push her off me, my voice tight, caught in the unintended intimacy of the moment. Instinctively, I covered her hand in mine. "Shh, breathe through it."

Her grip went slack, and her back arched, another cry piercing the quiet; shudders racking her frame before she went limp.

"Mmm." She groaned, her voice hoarse. She hid her face in her hands, pulling away from me. "Thank you."

Thank you.

The phrase rattled around in my skull, knocking loose thoughts I didn't want to face.

"No, thank you." I stood fast, stuffing my supplies back into my satchel, falling back into my role of Captain, not makeshift healer. I cleared my throat. "We're settled now."

She folded her arms across her chest, caving in on herself like

169

she'd finally remembered to be shy. But she raised her head, her gaze still sharp enough to cut steel, her chin tilted high. "I want to see the prisoner."

Right, the prisoner. The reason she'd summoned me.

The elf currently losing his mind, a victim of the *Sykagos'* indomitable power.

A warning of what would happen if I stayed too long.

"You won't get any answers." I grunted as I moved to go, the tent suddenly suffocatingly small as reality crashed around me, my duties calling from the night beyond.

"I tried not to—"

The urgency in Thera's voice gave me pause, tugging on a bleeding heartstring I didn't know I had. I turned to face her, the grave expression she wore a sobering contrast to her normally caustic smirk or the unguarded desire I'd witnessed just before. She wrapped a blanket around her, the thick cloth making her look small. Her voice was just as diminished. "The psychological effects should wear off in a few days. We should keep him with us. My questions can wait until then."

My fingernails carved deep cuts into my palms as I clenched my fists, desperate to hold on to my truths.

There was no part of me that had sympathy for the *Sykagos*. No part that offered her any gratitude or admiration. My debt was paid with a healed arrow-wound and a few kind pleasantries. And when the opportunity came, I'd be the one to end her reign of terror.

Despite how desperately I held on to them, my convictions slipped through my fingers like sand, just as soft words breathed from my lips. "Of course. Sleep well, Your Majesty."

I pushed through the tent flaps and into the night air before I could concede anything further.

CHAPTER
THIRTEEN

"She came for my mind first, a thief in the night. And when I awoke, my heart was hers, too." —Quote from "A Tale of Forgotten Love," A Luxian Epic Romance written by Madea Thisbe, circa 1867 A.G.W.

CAELUM

The world was indescribably, irrevocably changed when morning came.

Sleep evaded me better than wind slipping through a net, our first night at camp a festival-for-one of tossing and turning and stewing on my bed pallet.

I told myself it was a symptom of the element I was in. The firm ground was a far cry from my luxuriously soft bedroom at the palace, the skin of the tent a thin membrane between me and the wild night beyond.

But my heart was too heavy to find respite, my mind a whirlwind of thoughts and worries that would not quiet, much like the howling zephyr that slapped against my accommodations.

Growing up in Lux, trapped in my father's impressive shadow, I thought I'd seen power. Thought I'd stared at its face every waking moment, thought it glistened like the opal and glass facets of Stellaris's glorious exterior.

But the image of Thera's shadow-clad form flying through the trees, the scent of the elves's blood and piss drenching the soil, the screams that tore through the forest and sent birds scattering . . .

The image of an arrow piercing her shoulder, of the whites of her eyes as they fluttered closed. Her small, skeletal form crumpled on the ground, her face serene in unconsciousness . . .

That power was the stuff of nightmares and daydreams alike.

Both plagued me, even as the first prodding rays of dawn painted my tent purple, then pink, then gold. Even as I washed and dressed, pulling on a soft tunic and thick riding trousers. Even as I picked at the rations of bread, boiled eggs, and soft cheeses offered for breakfast. Even as I downed the *Zo'is* tea that kept my symptoms at bay, the putrid flavor less noticeable this morning.

Thera of Erebus might have been the *Sykagos,* but she was my savior, both in mind and body.

With that truth, there would be no returning to the world I thought I knew.

But this new world was far more dangerous than I could've possibly imagined from my ivory tower. The elves that attacked us in the woods, the Shadowborne attack at the Summer Palace, Quinton's death, Thera's power . . . too many threats that I knew an uncomfortable little about, and not enough solutions that didn't involve my future bride throwing herself in front of me like a corporeal shield.

When the sun climbed high enough, the sounds of guards rustling outside my tent finally breaking the morning quiet, I decided to take today into my own hands.

We had a long journey in front of us to the capital.

But I had an even longer journey from spoiled prince to someone that would be a good leader one day. And in the restless pre-dawn, I'd decided it would be a voyage I'd start today.

Soldiers were eager to pack down my tent immediately after I exited it, like they were desperate for a task . . . and as I walked deeper into the camp, it was clear why.

King Thera stood with Nyxia and her commander, her arm held in a sling, plain black riding clothes hugging her form. But despite the simpleness of her attire and her apparent injury, she stood with the authority afforded to her station, her head high and her smile expertly intact.

My fellow Luxians gave her a wide berth, nearly ten feet between her retinue and the gold-clad garrison.

I passed them without a word.

"Good morning, Your Majesty," I cleared my throat, my hands tucked behind my back to settle their shaking. Nyxia smirked, and the balding Commander skewered me with a dark glare, but I did not balk beneath it. "Are you feeling better?"

Thera spun, light eyes warm in the early morning gold, green and blue tinted in rainbow shades.

"Much better now." She smiled, an assessing look sweeping over me. A wrinkle formed between her brows. "You look like you haven't slept."

Warmth rose to my cheeks. "I was worried."

The commander scoffed like that was the most ridiculous thing ever said, crossing his arms over his dark armor. But Thera's lips pursed.

"Everyone, listen up!" A familiar voice tore through the din, authority dripping from her commands.

Rory stood on a small block, giving her a bird's-eye view of the nearly collapsed camp. The soldiers fell silent, even the horses holding back their whinnies as she addressed us.

It took all I had not to sigh her name in sheer awe, her strength always striking at something deep in my chest. Maybe it was admiration. Maybe it was more.

I dared not name it.

"Here we go," Commander Kappas mumbled under his breath, the only one among us brave—or disgruntled—enough to utter a sound. My gaze darted to Thera, waiting for her to join in with a witty retort.

But Thera clicked her tongue, nudging her commander with her good arm. "Hush, Kappas."

I titled my head, staring wide-eyed at the king. At the way she looked *up* at Rory, her signature smirk nowhere to be found, instead a professional respect gracing her high cheekbones.

What was *that* about?

"The next few days will be rough," Rory spoke on, her cadence a steady drumbeat, "and we still don't know how safe we are in these parts. We sent a scout ahead, and a messenger to King Kato's retinue, so we can combine defensive strategies, but until we receive word, everyone is on high alert."

"Yes, Captain," the soldiers all responded in clipped unison, her garrison's loyalty unwavering.

But she shifted her weight, the slightest hint of indecision unbalancing her normally rigid frame. Her gaze fell on where Thera and I stood, her mouth a tight line. "However, King Thera's injured, and will likely struggle to ride her own horse. So we will need volunteers to ride with her."

Disgruntled murmurs soured the air, the soldiers all casting their eyes down or away, like schoolchildren nervous to be called on.

Thera kept her head high, their fear glancing off her like she was made of stone, but the corners of her mouth twitched downward in the slightest hint of a frown. "Oh, that won't be necessary, I'm feeling much better already."

Yet her body spoke a different story—one I knew too well—her arm held close to her chest, her stance favoring her uninjured side.

Even if she'd used *Zo'is* and she no longer bled, sometimes the medicine's aftereffects were even worse. Rory had told me stories of how the drug had been potent enough to keep her awake all night after her injuries. And as someone who took a steady, prescribed dose, I knew firsthand how the body's natural response sometimes left one's muscles tired and sore for days.

An idea roared to life in my mind, my fingers stretching at my side. I'd never be the best with a sword or shield, but I was not useless. Not anymore. I took a step; the first in my personal growth journey. "I'll ride with her."

Another wave of curious—*fearful*—whispers slithered through the guards. Rory's brows flew toward her hairline like they were trying to reunite.

"You're not a guard, My Prince—"

"Right, but doesn't having both of us closer together help you manage patrol patterns?" I spit back words I'd heard her use, pretending I was confident enough to understand their meaning. Rory often grumbled about how much more difficult it was when Father and I were separated, and I intended to manipulate that knowledge to my advantage. "That way you're not pulling away anyone from the defense or scouting teams?"

"That's actually not the worst idea, Captain." Julius raised a tentative hand, giving me a respectful nod. Victory blared through me like a trumpet at his casual validation. "It consolidates potential targets." He shrugged, addressing Rory directly. "But it frees us up and makes it easier to focus on one weak spot to protect instead of two."

"We Erebushi can handle her on our own." Commander Kappas' hand flew to the weapon at his side, lip curling.

Nyxia stepped in front of him, rolling her eyes. A feral smirk twisted her mouth. "The King has never needed protection. You saw yesterday what she can do."

The garrison's whispers rose to a feverish pitch, several of them stepping further away from the King like she was contagious. Like her shadows might just snap out and swallow them whole at a moment's notice.

"Enough." Thera stamped her foot with a huff, the most child-like display I'd ever seen from her. Maybe the *Zo'is* altered her brain, too. "I'd like to offer my—"

"Respectfully, no." Rory cut her down with the brutal efficiency I expected from her, but there was a novelty in the way she scanned the king—not with reproach, but *concern,* written in the deep lines between her brows. "You have already demonstrated an unwilling-ness to seek proper treatment, so I do not trust that you are being fully honest in your recovery."

I blinked.

The world changed this morning. There would be no return to the world of yesterday.

I did not know what'd inspired the shift in my best friend, but I wouldn't waste the opportunity to further my agenda. I plastered on my widest smile as I looked between them both. "We can ride your horse if that's more comfortable."

My body would hate me for it at the end of this journey.

Right now, I didn't care.

Both, thank the sun and stars, swallowed any last retorts, their battle of wills ending in a surprising truce that signaled my victory.

"Fine, fine." Thera pouted. "But I will not be putting up with this the whole way. Just for today."

The strong set of Rory's jaw said that was highly unlikely, but no one argued further. The soldiers dismissed to their stations a moment later, and the urgent call of yesterday's danger setting our brisk pace for the day.

I followed Thera over to the horses with my chest puffed out, triumph a song in my heart.

A song that was short-lived when we got *on* the horse.

Thera leapt up first, somehow still graceful one-handed, her *Skialogo* expelling a friendly neigh as she mounted.

But as I scooted on behind her—my thighs still sore from the day before, my heart rate high after a sleepless night—nerves replaced all other thoughts in my head.

Even though the *Skialogo* was two hands taller than a normal stallion, and Thera a great deal slimmer than I, in my attempts at chivalry, I'd *greatly* underestimated how close our quarters would be.

I kept my arms extended as they wrapped around her, careful not to touch her as I grabbed the reins, but there was no escaping the way my chest brushed against her back with the action, other, *lower* parts settling closer by command of the saddle's structure.

Heat burned in my cheeks and down my back, and even though the morning was cool, sweat clammed my skin.

Only minutes later, the caravan rolled out, Rory signaling us forward. But the waiting felt like a lifetime, my breath uncomfortably held, my lungs already arguing with me, as the promise of a whole day of this proximity had my blood near a boiling point.

Thera clicked her tongue, and the *Skialogo* lurched forward, sending her knocking back into me again.

Sun and stars.

The mountain pass was uneven, but relatively wide, enough for eight or nine riders across. It'd narrow the deeper we went, but for now, the soldiers rode around us in a circular formation, Rory leading the charge, Julius and the two other Erebushis covering the rear. With Thera and I at the center, it was hard to talk to any of them, the clomping of hooves and the clinking of armor creating a bubble of sound around us.

I cleared the lump from my throat, trying not to notice how floral and sweet her hair smelled. "Sorry if this is uncomfortable for you, King Thera."

A laugh blew from her, the sound vibrating through the places where we connected. "On the contrary, you seem to be the one . . . out of sorts." She turned, our faces only inches away. But her smile held a sadness to it despite the warmth in her voice, twisting my heartstrings. "I'm sorry if what you saw yesterday frightened you, but I promise, I would never harm you."

"I know that!" I exclaimed too quickly, too emphatically. "You saved me. You were *incredible.*"

Some clouds dissipated from her expression, and her good hand left the pommel of the saddle to settle on my knee. I jerked back as a reflex; the touch sending a shiver through me.

Her smile sank. "Then why do you flinch whenever we touch?"

"I'm—" My face heated to a temperature only the Sun could hope to master. "Well, you're a lady, and I—"

Several endings to that sentence danced on the tip of my tongue, but the mere thought of each one of them signaled *other* bits of me that were far too compromised right now to risk.

Oh sun above, I was in trouble.

Thera's eyes widened as if she could smell my thoughts, or perhaps hear the way my heartbeat kicked in double-time.

"*Oh.* I'm so sorry." She shifted forward in the saddle, biting her full lip to suppress a laugh. "I didn't realize . . . have you never touched a woman? Or a man, I suppose."

Shame crawled over me, and my chest deflated.

"It's not funny," I grumbled, like I'd used to when Grotchkin had caught me stealing books from the adult section of the library. Just like I had then, I kept my voice low, insisting on a maturity I hadn't yet captured. "Of course I've touched women."

Not in the way she asked about, but she didn't need to know that.

"I mean . . . " Thera laughed again, darker this time. Deeper. Her hand found my knee again, lightning zapping through the spot. "I mean, have you ever fucked, *My Prince?*"

My Prince.

The way she casually caressed my title made my head spin, and all the blood in my body pooled low. My doctor would call this *an ill-advised stressor.* I swallowed hard, a different, headier heat flaring through me.

"Sun and stars." I gulped, wrangling my tongue to form words, doing my very best not to spill the dozens of dirty thoughts that entered my head. "When you put it like that—"

Thera turned over her shoulder again, eyes hooded as she leaned back into me. "So, no?"

Searing, delicious heat spread where her back arched into my chest. It took all my remaining willpower not to answer with both *'no'* and *'please.'* Instead, I croaked, "Have you?"

Her finger traced a gentle, hypnotic circle over my kneecap. "Does it displease you that I have?"

Before I could regain control, my overactive imagination flared to life.

Thera, in every position I'd ever read about, her head thrown back in ecstasy, her sweet voice crying out . . .

Displeasure was far from the word.

Envy, perhaps.

Desire.

"No. No, it does not."

The *Skialogo* sped up as my fists unconsciously tightened around the reins. Thera chuckled, clicking her tongue to tame the creature, but it did nothing to slow my rapid, demanding heartbeat.

The soldiers grumbled around us, annoyed at the briefly broken formation, but I barely registered a single word of their complaints, my thoughts trained on the places Thera pressed into me, on the floral scent of her hair, on the insinuations this conversation toyed with . . .

Sun and stars. Ours would be a marriage of necessity, but perhaps that did not mean it would be pleasureless.

The thought excited me far more than it should've.

Again, like she read straight out of a manual on how I operated, Thera shifted, her backside firmly rubbing against the current channel of all of my blood flow.

Embarrassment stayed me for a moment, but it evaporated

when her voice went so low that only I'd hear, "I promise that when the time comes for us to consummate things, I'll let you decide when it's right, and what *you* like." Her hand firmly squeezed higher up my thigh, the gesture equal parts comforting and unnerving. "It's a shame that your first experience will be one of duty, but I will do my best to make it a pleasurable encounter."

The rope I had tied around my self-control frayed and snapped. One of my hands covered hers, rooting it in place on my leg.

"I'm not completely daft, you know." Pride bubbled from me as I breathed into her long hair, my heart beating so fast I was sure she could feel it through her back. "I . . . read."

A teasing sigh had all my muscles tightening. "You mentioned. Does the castle library have a good section on Elven biology?"

"Better." I laughed, my voice so dark I barely sounded like myself. "Romance novels."

"Oh?"

The things I'd do to coax that single syllable from her mouth in a much more intimate setting.

My head spun, dizzied and frenzied by this glorious creature's simple, effortless seduction.

A brave, bold instinct inside of me reared to the surface and took over, and I gladly gave it the reins to my body. I was no longer some naive, virginal prince, but the leading love interest in my favorite steamy book, one I'd read in the privacy of my bath time and time again. My fingers threaded through hers, and I leaned closer, my mouth just barely brushing against the delicate shell of her pointed ear as I whispered, "Some of them are extremely descriptive about what pleasure can look like."

"I see." She shuddered against me, and a primal part roared with elated achievement. But Thera was a king, and she would not be won easily. No, she would not be conquered at all, an evident fact as she whipped around to face me again, those sharp eyes scalding a fever across my skin. Her gaze watched my mouth, and my tongue darted out to lick my lips before I could think. She noted the action with predatory focus, holding every muscle in my body in rapt attention. "Then what kind of pleasure, *exactly*, do you like to read about?"

What did I like?

Her.

Whatever pathetic scraps of attention she'd bless me with.

"Everything," I said instead, and it was true. The library had gorgeous romances, courtesy of my mother and some of her ladies-in-waiting, but the books the servants had lent me from town . . . dark, filthy, *wonderful* tales, some of them so base and vulgar, their very titles brought a welcome heat to my cheeks. Others, so vivid and vibrant in their detail, it was like I was there, writhing and moaning alongside the characters, sometimes with their *multiple* partners all at once . . .

For a prince who'd never strayed outside of the palace walls unattended, I'd lived and breathed and loved through thousands of stories.

And for the first time in a very long time, I ached to be present in my own.

I fought for control of my wild imagination, shaking my head to free myself from the drunken fog her presence had put me under. But there was no hiding my arousal as it crowded the minimal space between us. Her scent had changed, too, floral notes tangling with a sweet musk, an unspoken call and response . . .

"Lend me some favorites, then." Her voice dipped husky; *wanting.*

An invitation. I cleared my throat. "I could tell you about a few of my favorites."

A nod. Lonely; *welcoming.*

So I did.

And as I did, the rest of the world faded around me, my duties and titles falling away. I was not the Prince of Lux and the heir to the Sunkissed Throne. She was not the King of Erebus, the *Sykagos*.

We were Caelum and Thera, two flirts dancing on the cusp of

more, and all that existed was the delicious heat of her palm massaging my thigh, the glorious pressure of her back to my chest, the mingling scent of our desire forming a bubble around us.

The easy cadence of my voice as I recounted tales I'd memorized—stories of love, pleasure, betrayal, joy. The soft pulse of her breath as it hitched and caught at all the right moments.

And all worldly notions like embarrassment and shame and regret and pain evaporated like I'd never known them at all.

Somehow, despite the rocky terrain and bumpy ride, I didn't notice as the sun had reached its climax in the sky, hot and bright as it pounded down on us. It nearly blinded me as we crested over the first short peak and onto a plateau, the path yawning open into a small clearing, a few trees lingering around the edges.

"Your Majesty, Your Highness." A curt command broke me from my trance as the soldiers' formation shifted, Rory trotting through. "We're going to dismount here and break for lunch."

Shame slammed back into me like a blow straight to the chest, the air thinning.

"Y-yes." I shifted away from Thera, the back of my neck burning like I'd stayed in the sun too long.

The heir to the Sunkissed Throne did not have the luxury of pretending. Of putting pleasure first.

And even though Rory and I owed each other nothing, even though our roles and stations firmly prevented us from crossing any lines . . .

My gaze cast downward, feeling like I'd betrayed her somehow.

Rory's eyes narrowed, focused like a hawk on the space between Thera and me, but she thankfully said nothing as she clicked her heels and rode away, readying the caravan for a break.

I followed, steering the *Skialogo* to the side of the path, a stone in my gut weighing me down.

"Does Captain Bellatore know about your reading habits?" Thera mused, but there were barbs attached to this probe. "Or your *expert* proficiency in storytelling?"

The compliment fluffed my already-inflated ego, but I tread carefully, the shift in her tone unsettling. "She tells dirty jokes, but we don't really talk about that . . . stuff."

Not that I hadn't wanted to.

Not that it mattered.

"Her loss." Thera slid off the steed, patting his neck appreciatively, and I sank at the loss of her heat and presence. She turned, staring at where Rory had already set down mats to sit on, pulling rations from her pack with impressive speed. "You've never thought about asking her to join?"

"No, that's not—that's inappropriate." I shimmied down, flinging one limb after another over the side. My legs screamed in protest as I hit the ground, a protective panic rattling me. Ignoring the discomfort, I grabbed Thera's good wrist, halting her in her spot. Urgency hastened my speech, but I forced myself to whisper. "Please don't tease me about Rory. She's my best friend, and a wonderful guard. She doesn't deserve the gossip."

Ice and emerald flicked to me, their gemstone hues sparkling in the sunlight. But there was no amusement, no sign of teasing or deception in her expression; just a hunger I had no name for.

"That wasn't a tease. I was serious." King Thera grinned as she stared up at me, dazzling, daunting thoughts turning over in that too-bright gaze. "But I respect your boundaries. Now, let's eat. I'm sure you've worked up quite the appetite."

Thera sauntered off toward the resting soldiers, leaving me with my mouth gaping and my head swimming.

The world was indescribably, irrevocably changed. I was, too, and it was barely noon.

Thera of Erebus had already taken giant bites out of my life, changing its shape. And I wasn't sure I would survive another few days—a *lifetime*—without her devouring me whole.

CHAPTER
FOURTEEN

"We must denounce the downworlders as our kin, for they have tainted their blood black. We may mourn their loss, but we cannot raise what is already dead." —The Commandments of King Alixsander Borealis the 1st, 5 A.G.W.

RORY

King Thera was a dark, manipulative *witch*.

It was the only reasonable explanation for the way she'd enchanted the prince. Enchanted *me*. Her shadows corrupted the mind, a treachery fought in seductive smiles and burning looks.

I couldn't blame Caelum for his attraction to her, a moth to the flame she'd cast. I'd almost fallen prey to her enchantment, our moment in the tent together just as unreasonable, *inexplicable*.

But watching them together on that horse, day after bloody

fucking day, *listening* to them tell dirty stories to each other like no one could hear them ...

By day three, I'd had enough.

Breathe, Rory.

Promise.

It was the only tether to my patience, the inhale-exhale that steadied my raw, grated nerves.

Yet even that faltered, the repetition no longer a comfort, but a dark, perseverating thought that consumed the last few drops of my sanity.

Perhaps it was the thin mountain air, the sun looming closer as we conquered ridge after ridge. Or maybe it was my sore, stiff muscles, my body not conditioned for long, stagnant days on the top of a bouncing horse. My lungs struggled to grasp at deep gulps, my ribs pained and my mind a racing tumult of thoughts.

Before I could well and truly pitch a fit, just before twilight, our caravan headed over another rocky crest; tall, piney trees blissfully guarded us from the blade-sharp winds. Though we were high up, the purple-bruised sky spoke of oncoming night, the sun gratefully dipping below the neighboring peak. A river babbled nearby, drowning out Caelum and Thera's murmurs and giggles, offering me a respite I didn't know I needed.

I exhaled fully—the first in miles. "We camp here."

My men didn't hesitate to dismount and begin the preparations. Though Julius was the only one who could feel the soul-deep itch through our shared tattoo, perhaps my whole garrison had been fighting off the poison of the *Sykagos'* taunting magic.

I walked up to the regents, holding my breath, like that might somehow shield me from her intoxicating fumes. "We'll rest here for the night, Your Majesties."

"Thank goodness." Caelum stretched as he swung his leg over their shared steed and half-fell to the ground, his face a deep red from sun and sin alike.

Thera eased down next to him, that wicked enchantress's grin ever-present on her face. "Ready to be away from me so fast?"

"No!" Caelum waved his hands, a flailing fly caught in the spider's invisible web. "My ass is just sore."

Heat lit *my* cheeks—along with a hot, simmering rage—as King Thera dragged her gaze over his backside, as if inspecting said complaint.

"Goodnight then, *My Prince*. Take care of that ass," she drawled.

Whatever tentative truce we'd made in her tent the night she was injured was gone. She was my enemy—one that fought with shadows and sorcery and other seditious weapons.

For the first time since King Kato had handed down my orders, the idea of killing her *thrilled* me.

She retreated toward her escorts, her commander and ambassador wearing similar masks of distaste.

My expression echoed theirs. Perhaps this . . . spell . . . Thera had over Caelum was a unifying cause between both of our peoples.

Caelum watched Thera go, his eyes shading violet in the twilight dim. A green, envious thing twisted so harshly in my middle that a stitch tugged my side.

I spun on my heel and walked toward the assembling camp before I put my fist through someone's face.

Breathe, Rory.

Promise.

Like my fury had summoned him, Julius fell into step at my side, his heavy footfalls crunching over the beds of pine needles. "What's got you in a bind?"

I fiddled with the *Zo'is* gauntlets on my wrists; the metal chafed, much like the grating scrape of my annoyance at my back. I wished I could unleash my magic on her, see how well she fared under the *Zo'is'* heat. *One day.* "They're insufferable."

Julius turned over his shoulder, but I nudged his side before he could draw attention.

186

"I think it's nice they're getting along." He rubbed the spot I'd hit—perhaps a smidgen too hard—but blessedly kept his voice low. "Though I guess I'd prefer if they were quieter. Do you think the Prince knows we can hear everything?"

I stopped, my fingernails drawing blood from my palms. Of course, Caelum knew all the soldiers in my garrison were *Zo'is*-touched. Our tattoos gave us connections to our *Vinculum*, let us draw on each other's energy and resources, but they also exacerbated our senses—our hearing, our smell, our vision. Made us the apex predators.

Made it *incredibly hard* to drown out Caelum's desire-driven tales and Thera's hypnotizing coos of approval. Like a repeating chant, they both sang their parts; and even half-whispered, the whole squad was caught in the trap, our bodies all attuned to whatever narrative they chose.

Black magic, all of it.

"I don't care," I lied, but my eyes pleaded for help. "Want to spar?"

My *Vinculum* sighed, squeezing my shoulder. The contact gave way to a small trickle of relief.

"After eight hours straight on a horse? No way in hell, Rory." His lips pressed into a frown as my expression clearly mimicked said dismay, my momentary relief gone. He didn't rescue me this time. Couldn't. "Look, I love you, but even I have my limits."

With a groan, I rocked forward, my head falling into his chest. "I need an outlet for this anger."

Yes, that had to be the name for this cramp, this tangled, throbbing thing that yanked through me day after day, that left me breathless atop my horse as I failed to shut it all out.

Jules forced my head back with a single finger against my forehead, one eyebrow raised as he peered down at me, gaze all-knowing. "Oh, *that's* what that is? Interesting."

As if the insinuation wasn't enough, a flare of something hot and sweet shot through our bond—my emotions mirrored back at me. A reminder that I couldn't lie to Julius any more than I could lie to myself.

A shudder ran down my spine. "You're not helping."

Jules bit his bottom lip, holding back the laughter that shook his shoulders. But he jerked his head toward the encampment a few dozen paces away, to where the soldiers finished setting the tents for the night and stoked the fire beneath the cauldron for stew. A few of them had stripped their armor already, dressing down for the evening lull.

"You know, Second Lieutenant Argentis has eyes for you." Jules kept his voice low enough that even their enhanced hearing wouldn't register.

"Syrax? That prat?" My gaze fell onto the egotistical elf as he brought down a silver hammer onto an unsuspecting tent-spoke with vigor. His helmet off, long brown hair dusted across his shoulders in straight curtains, emphasizing the solid build of his muscles. He'd already paired down to just his undertunic, the white stained with sweat, revealing hints of the broad expanse of his amber chest.

He *was* something to look at, that was for sure. But a shame his beauty did little to hide his obnoxious mouth. I'd kicked his teeth in a few times during our training days, but I'd never silenced him fully.

"He's a prat, but he's good-looking." Jules echoed my inner monologue with a snort. But his tone sobered as he leaned closer, rubbing circles across his tattoo. "Listen, I'd never tell you what to do with your body, but that tension isn't good for either of us. Syrax isn't anything special, but at least you know he won't be clingy after."

That, thank the sun and stars, was true enough. Syrax had slept through half the barracks already, men and women alike, without ever signaling anything close to real attachment, much to many of his bedfellows' dismay.

But perhaps Julius had a point. Perhaps the best remedy for the poison that infected my soul was the same as many of the toxic tinctures I'd consumed in my life.

Sweat it out.

Breathe, Rory.

Very few aches a good roll-around couldn't stretch out. Besides, it wasn't like that form of recreation was uncommon in the barracks. Though I was Captain now, no longer a petty foot soldier, the culture was the same. We watched each other's backs. We fought at each other's sides.

And we met each other's needs.

"You're a pain," I shot at Julius and mustered my willpower.

My *Vinculum* laughed, shoving me forward with his shoulder. "Have fun, Cap'n!"

I rolled my eyes but trudged toward the rest of the guards.

"Rory?" Caelum's eyes flicked up at me as I passed where he sat on a stump, gnawing at a dinner roll, but aside from a quick, curt nod, I gave him little attention. I had to rid myself of his voice—of its sweet timbre as it had caressed each sordid word he breathed in Thera's ear—if only for tonight.

I felt his stare following me, and it took all I had not to meet it, guilt simmering beneath everything else that drowned me.

"Fortis, guard the prince!" I hollered instead, knowing my *Vinculum* already had my back, as always.

Having finished his hammering, Syrax stood with his *Vinculum* —Corporal Dama, a short elf that overcompensated for his height with bad breath and a big attitude—admiring their handiwork as beads of sweat rolled down their backs and wet their tunics.

"Do you think she gets naughty with those shadows of hers?" Dama sneered under his breath as he gazed toward the Erebushi faction, not seeing me approach.

"I dunno, but I know if it were me, I'd have her whipped into submission real fast, instead of letting her trounce around like she's in charge." Syrax scoffed, and I almost turned on my heel and fled, the sound scraping beneath my fingernails. That *stupid mouth* of his kept flapping. "Some of us are just alpha-elves. Meant to lead."

My eyes rolled so hard that I was concerned about their permanent residence in my face, but I cleared my throat. I didn't need to like him to fuck him.

"Second Lieutenant," I ordered, and both elves spun about-face so fast, they almost toppled into each other. I subdued a smile, my hands stuck behind my back. "Come with me. We have things to discuss."

"Yeah, of course, I mean—" Syrax shot to attention, wiping his sweaty face with his unclean shirt. He cleared his throat. "Yes, Captain."

I walked away, knowing he'd follow.

"Go ahead, Syrax, you're quite the alpha," Dama called after him.

I covered my laughter with a cough.

The sunset dipped into darker territory now, shadows dappling the sky's uppermost crust in deep indigo, which suited my needs just fine. I had Syrax follow me all the way to the river—far enough away from the path to not be seen, and loud enough to cover any *conversations* we might have.

When I was finally satisfied with the quiet, the background noise of the river soothing my senses, I turned to face him.

Breathe, Rory.

Syrax scratched his head, stance both casual and cautious. "What's this about?"

I faltered, heat filling my cheeks. Sun and stars, was I really doing this? I shifted my weight between my feet, desperate for even ground to stand on. "I don't really want to *talk*."

Eyes narrowed as his hand dropped to his side. "Oh?"

I clenched my fists. No going back now, and I'd be damned if I didn't commit to finishing what I'd started. I lifted my chin, letting authority drip from my words as I took a set closer. "Julius says you've been eyeing me?"

A pretty blush reddened his cheeks, one corner of his mouth twitching as he fought a smirk. "I'm sorry if I've offended you. I'm just paying attention."

I dragged my gaze over him—paying just as much *attention* to detail, from his boots to the crown of his head. His leathers hugged the solid muscles of his thighs, tapering into the thin 'v' of his waist. But the shape flared out as his broad chest rose and fell, his breath hitching as my gaze lingered on the sweaty expanse of his shoulders.

Finally, I met his gaze—a lovely shade of hazel that mimicked the pine around us. "Are you going to do anything about it?"

A sharp inhale, his eyes snapping wide. "What?"

Rallying all the battle-tested, fire-forged courage I had, I stepped forward yet again, breathing in his musk.

"You heard me." I reached out—my hand splaying flat across the divet in his chest. My voice dipped husky. "Are you just a watcher, or do you want to *do* something about it?"

Thank all the fucking stars, Syrax needed no further encouragement. A wide smile split his face. "Sun-fuck-me, yes."

His mouth claimed mine a second later, no hesitation as it sought to devour. No gentle introduction, no testing the waters, but a quick taking of what he wanted. What I needed. I met him stroke for aggressive stroke, my fury and pent-up frustration relishing the battle of tongues and clashing teeth.

His hands gripped at my sides, propping me back against a tree, long fingers pushing up the fabric of my tunic. He palmed my breasts; greedily, insistently, my nipples budding at his command.

My mouth ripped from his, exploring down the side of his stubbled cheek, down his neck, tasting and claiming more of him.

This is what I needed. Carnal, vicious pleasure. To let Syrax swallow down my thoughts and aggravations with each pass of his burning touch.

"Greedy, are we?" He groaned in my ear, angling his hips to

mine, pinning me against the rough tree bark. I rocked against him, the friction a welcome contact, but I shook my head.

My hand wound around his throat, thumb pushing against the artery pulsing beneath it to silence him. "Hush, no talking."

He shivered, eyes rolling back in a wave of pleasure. "All right," he choked out, and I released him.

He attacked again, harsher and more demanding, his mouth and tongue a sloppy frenzy as they surrounded mine. I reached down in the minimal space between us, quickly dismissing the laces of his trousers from their duty, then undoing my own with stumbling, hurried fingers.

There was little ceremony as we shucked off our pants, as he flipped me over and entered me in a quick, decisive thrust.

I braced against the tree with my arms, pleasure and pain a furious mix as he pounded with abandon.

This is what I needed. Agony and absolution. Torment and liberation.

"Oh fuck, you're so tight, oh *yes*—" He grunted as he smacked against my ass, my pleasure fleeing with the intrusion of his unnecessary commentary.

I untangled from him, and surprise lifted his brows. I pushed his chest with both hands, and he stumbled back onto the riverbank. But before he could get back up, I climbed over him, straddling his hips and lowering myself onto him in an unapologetic maneuver. His fingers gripped my thighs, his gaze hooded and hungry.

"I said no talking." I grinned down at him as I lifted and lowered myself again. And again. And again.

Again, until all thoughts of Caelum's *reading list* fled from my mind.

Again, until the image of Thera's dark—and beautiful—visage was barely a faded memory.

Again, until my pleasure rose and my breath shallowed, this time my hammering heart racing as I chased my release.

Breathe, Rory.

My eyes closed, head tilted back, sweetest muscles tightening as Syrax's steady rhythm and circling thumb pushed me close to the precipice . . .

A twig snapped, and my eyes flew open—

Ice and emerald stared at me from opposite sides of her face, that stars-damned *smirk* curling as my toes did—

From ten paces down the river, Thera's gaze did not leave mine as my whole being trembled, falling over the edge, and I came hard enough to see stars.

I'd washed *twice* after my romp with Syrax, scrubbing harder than a scullery maid in need of a raise in the near-freezing river, but it was no use.

Nothing could wash away the burning stain of Thera's eyes on me.

She'd fled so fast, part of me was hesitant to admit it'd happened at all. Like she was just a figment of my imagination, a shadowed phantom I'd conjured in my rage and moment of release.

But the scald of her glare had marked me, an unseen scar on my most vulnerable parts that wouldn't disappear, a festering spot of darkness on my soul.

As was the truth I'd been reeling from, even as Syrax and I dressed and parted ways with little affection:

Whether she was real or imagined, whether she'd seen every-thing or had only gotten a glance—

I'd liked it. I'd *wanted* her there, conjured either in fantasy or reality.

I hated her for it.

Hated me, too.

And even though I'd slipped into my tent that night without

193

seeing her or Caelum, sleep evaded me. The imprint of her stare still there every time I'd tried to close my eyes.

The next morning, as the first rays of the sun peeked through the flaps in my tent, I hurried to pack my bags. Maybe if I focused on a task, I could shut out all thoughts of the witch from Erebus and what her and my best friend would do on today's trip.

Unfortunately, thanks to my incredible training, I had my things tucked away and my tent collapsed in record time, my distraction short-lived.

Well, if I had to suffer, so would everyone else.

I signaled an early start. All the elves in my command—even Syrax and Julius, the ungrateful traitors—groaned, and I barked orders until the entire camp was ready before the sun had even fully found its way above the tree line. I hovered over Dama and his grunts as they prepped the horses and wagons, carefully avoiding the royals from both kingdoms.

I didn't know why Caelum was on my 'to-hide-from' list, as I doubted Thera was bold enough to tell him what she'd seen. And even if she did, why should I hide it? Syrax was not a lover, but a simple means to release. And I was an elf in my prime with needs like any other.

And he was my prince. A *betrothed* prince, one who could never meet those needs for me, no matter how many times I'd fantasized about it in the most private parts of my mind.

It didn't matter. Couldn't.

Still, I avoided him for a solid hour, not even sparing a glance his way while the garrison readied to leave.

"Everyone move out," I grumbled when there was no more putting off the inevitable. I did not look where Caelum and Thera stood by her freakish horse, instead training my glare directly toward some of the grunt soldiers who'd do well to fear me a bit more, a few of them even muttering under their breaths at me.

They'd regret it, if they survived today.

I'd been so focused on my targets, I didn't hear her sneak up on me, *again*, until that sing-song voice was right in my ear. "I'm feeling much better today. I think I'll ride separately."

I spun on her, fighting the heat that rose to my cheeks against my command as I took her in. Dressed again in her casual riding clothes, her normal smirk was abandoned, her arms resting comfortably at her sides instead of rigidly like the last few days.

I tensed, waiting for her to mention anything about the woods last night, but she just tilted her head. "Well, Captain? Where should I ride?"

It was strange, that she asked rather than barking a command. I narrowed my gaze.

Dama groaned next to me. "We'll have to rearrange—"

King Thera gave him a look that could shave the fuzz off a peach, and he shut his mouth. Smart fucker. Her mismatched eyes locked on mine again—just as they had last night—waiting for an answer.

I'd be lying if I said I didn't want to separate her and Caelum, even just for a day, giving us all a break from their narration. But the sudden change of pace was alarming.

Thera of Erebus was utterly unpredictable.

"We're almost out of the mountain. It'll be fine." I clapped the blanch-faced corporal on the shoulder as I reassured both him and myself. No reason to look a gift horse in the mouth. I raised my voice so the others could shift preparations. "I'll ride center next to the Prince. Fortis will take the lead. The Erebushis can watch their king from the back."

Thera winced at my not-so-thinly-veiled dismissal, but I ignored her.

"Yes, Captain." The guards—already aware of my winning mood—shouted in unison, the sound music to my ears.

Perhaps today wouldn't be as terrible as I imagined after all.

Thera nodded, walking away to where the impish ambassador and the scowling commander waited, not looking back—another favor I didn't know I'd earned. Perhaps she was testing me, baiting me—making me think the night before was all in my head, or waiting to use it against me later.

But frankly, I didn't care if it gave me space from that stare of hers.

I sauntered over to my horse, the garrison busy and noisy again as they all finished the last preparations, and took in a deep breath.

It dried up in my chest as Caelum approached, a tentative smile on his face. "This will be nice."

The early light bleached his hair pure white, a halo framed his dark skin. The breezy cut of his tunic would've left anyone else freezing in the morning chill, but Caelum had always run hot—like the sun lived right there in his slightly exposed chest, warming everything it came in contact with. I supposed it was a side effect of his illness—his nervous system never regulated what it needed to, whether it be his pulse or his temperature. But his mother used to say it was because his heart was too large, too full of light and love to be contained.

I was inclined to believe her.

This was the boy I knew; bright, angelic, inviting. But it was that same soft mouth that'd been chanting the Dark King's spell against the shell of her pale ear, those same violet-hued eyes that had barely shifted since they'd first seen her.

It didn't matter. Couldn't.

I guarded myself. Turning back to my horse—a dappled mare named Csaria—like her cropped hair was suddenly the most interesting thing in the world, I asked, "Can I help you, My Prince?"

Caelum brushed Csaria's neck with gentle fingers. "I have barely seen you all week."

His stare heated my cheek, insistent and inviting all at once.

I clipped a polite smile. "You were quite occupied with King Thera, Your Highness."

"We've been getting along well. It's good." He shrugged, but he shifted on his feet, stroking Csaria like it soothed him, not the other way around. "The city will be very different, especially when we reach my father."

My gut knotted, protective instincts kicking in. The city wouldn't take kindly to Thera's presence. While the mountains were brutal, they paled compared to the rocky ranges of high Luxian society, and my stomach flipped at the thought of my best friend having to contend with the sheer amount of vitriol tomorrow would bring.

But Caelum didn't need my protection anymore. He had his betrothed for that now.

At least, that was the lie I told myself as I moved to mount my horse. "It'll be fine, Your Highness."

"Rory, hey, wait—" Caelum's fingers wrapped around my wrist, and my *Zo'is* bracelet flared. I met his gaze . . . and the vat of sadness and longing waiting in their sky-dappled color nearly knocked me right back off my mount. "Can we talk? *Privately?*"

Every muscle in my body clenched.

I was a fighter and survivor, battle-tried and tested. But I'd never found an effective way to steady my strength when Caelum Borealis *begged.*

My protest lacked conviction. "We're wasting daylight."

"Please, just for a moment?" he whined in his somehow endearing way, but he knew he'd already won. The first hint of a smile softened his face as he jerked his head toward the trees. "Just over there. Pretend you're escorting me to relieve myself or something."

The fight fled me, my body responding on its own to his call, as it always did. I grit my teeth together for show, but the battle was already lost. I slid off Csaria and crossed my arms. "Fine. Make it quick."

The others didn't mind the delay as I made our excuses—most of them happy to be rid of me and my foul mood for even a few minutes. But Julius shot me a quick glance, rubbing at his chest; an unspoken reminder that I wasn't alone—not in this, or ever.

I felt a flare of his affection run through me, and it steadied me as I waded after Caelum into a nearby thicket of trees.

Breathe, Rory.

When he finally paused and turned to face me, the tinge of humor that'd graced his expression was gone, replaced instead with an exhaustion I hadn't seen on him in years.

He hadn't been sleeping, and I'd been too in my own envious head to notice.

"What did you want to say?" Guilt scraped beneath my skin, but I held firm.

"We've been . . . off, since Quinton. It feels *wrong.*" He ran his hands through his ivory hair, the silken strands still somehow perfect despite the last few days in the elements. His tone was heavy with a sincerity and somberness I rarely experienced with him, as those too-bright eyes stayed locked on mine. "There are a lot of . . . changes happening, and while most of them are bigger than us, I don't want our friendship to shift because of it."

I bristled, images of a certain dark-haired, strange-eyed *change* reinvigorating my frustration once more. "Seems like you have plenty of new *friends.*"

I expected Caelum's normal sidestepping, his gentle way of disarming even my worst moods, but he scoffed, the sound a scald on my soul.

"I could say the same for you." His fists clenched at his sides, the most violent I'd ever seen him. "I mean, Syrax Argentis? *Really?*"

Thera told him, then.

The mixed sting of the violation of my privacy and the condescension dripping from his tone was gasoline on an already-burning fire. He would not embarrass me, not when he had so little shame for his own recent activity.

I stalked toward him, my chest inches from his, mirroring his contempt. "Why don't we both avoid commenting on each other's taste in bedfellows, shall we?"

His expression went entirely blank, an iciness freezing over it that sent a chill down my spine. "So you have slept with him?"

He'd just assumed, then?

"What does that matter, Caelum?" I hung on to my anger with all my might, avoiding the pit of hurt that burst open beneath my feet. I had given him my life, dedicated it to his service, and this was the thanks I got? Rejection and judgment all wrapped up in one? Cruel parts of me tamed my tongue, using it for their own agenda. "What's your *problem*? Does story-time with the King not cut it for you?"

I was done protecting him—from the world and from me.

It was time I protected myself. My bleeding, wounded heart.

It still didn't stop his words from slicing through it mid-beat. "If I didn't know better, I'd say you sound jealous."

Jealous.

Of course I was fucking jealous. Despite knowing I'd never have him for myself, seeing him flirt and change before my eyes with the one I was supposed to hate more than any other killed me in a way I hadn't projected, not even in my worst nightmares. Sun and stars, yes, I was jealous, and *confused*, despite my better judgment. Because for all that I tried to deny it, for all the ways I wanted to paint her as a witch, I didn't hate Thera. Not the way I wanted to or could before, when she was just an idea.

She'd saved Caelum. Protected him when I couldn't.

But none of that made my mission to kill her any less real. And it didn't quell the yearning, horrible fire in my veins that burned every time Caelum merely looked my way, the stupid, selfish parts of me still holding on to a hope that was never mine to begin with.

Unruly tears streaked down my face. "It doesn't matter if I'm jealous. My feelings don't matter at all, in any of this."

Caelum's mouth fell open, eyes scanning my face as the tears fell onto the leafy ground. As they nearly drowned me in truths I'd fought for too long.

I loved Caelum. And it didn't matter. *I* didn't matter.

199

"My feelings mean nothing, too, Aurora." His voice was quiet, but there was something raw in his expression, something that reflected the ache in my chest. Something that made the sound of my full name on his lips not just bearable, but *lovely*. "I'm making the best out of this situation, and I'll admit it's been far better than I imagined when I first learned I'd been offered to the *Sykagos*. But that doesn't mean I chose this. Or that I didn't wish that *we*—"

He stopped.

He stared.

But he didn't continue. Those words just hanging above us like a guillotine, just like they always did. Always hovering, but out of reach, waiting to slice us in two.

"Say it," I pleaded, my voice thick with all the unsaid words I'd been forced to choke down for too long. "Just once."

A silly wish. Even if he uttered every word I'd ever wanted to hear from him, it wouldn't change anything. *Couldn't.*

"You know I can't," he said instead, and his hand brushed away the evidence of my last tears from my cheek. But he didn't drop his hand, even when there was nothing left to erase, long fingers just waiting there, warm and *wanting*. He swallowed hard. "Neither can you."

"I know." I pressed my cheek into his touch, both of us toeing this red line as close as we could allow ourselves. As close as we could ever be without falling over an edge we couldn't climb back from.

But then, for the first time in his life, Caelum stepped over. Just a single step, a rebellious, riotous push of boundaries that he'd always heeded—

His other hand raised until he cradled my face in his soft palms. That violet stare said so much more than words ever could.

"But I want to. It's not fair to you or your position, but I want to," he said, the words like a prayer, one last foolish plea to stars that did not listen. His mouth moved, only inches from mine, as he held my face like he held the whole world. "I'll always want to—

want *you*. And even if it can never be more than that; a desperate, aching want, even if I'm alone in it, I will never be free of that secret wish."

It didn't matter.

Couldn't.

But my finger traced his waiting lips once anyway—just once—a last gift that I couldn't keep, but would never forget.

And then I stepped back—back into my duty, into my position—despite the deep, soul-shattering pain that stabbed through my middle. Then, I wiped the same thumb across my mouth. The closest I'd ever get to truly tasting him. Shuddering as he tracked the motion carefully, *intentionally*.

"You're not alone," I whispered back, but it didn't matter.

Couldn't.

I said it anyway. "I will always be by your side, Caelum. Step for step. In my duty, and in this."

I stalked back toward my horse without another word before I nose-dived into choices I'd regret.

But even as I entered the clearing with the rest of the garrison, even though Caelum was the only person who followed—a respectful five steps behind . . .

I couldn't shake the feeling that I'd been watched, again.

CHAPTER
FIFTEEN

"Lux is not the enemy; Fear is." *—An excerpt from Queen Glori-anna's letter to the Elysian people, circa 2 A.G.W.*

THERA

It was easy to forget.

Traveling through the mountains, cold and rocky as the journey was . . .

So easy to forget the sting of hatred against my skin. The way eyes could flay the flesh from my bones. The way strangers could hate so purely, so perfectly.

Easy to forget that I was alone.

Easy to forget the killing power that lived inside me.

Easy to forget the lives I'd devoured to earn their hatred.

After I'd saved Prince Caelum and the captain had healed me in my tent, a tentative peace had formed that made forgetting easy as breathing. Though still wary of me, the guards gave me little trouble, aside from a few snickered comments here and there.

I preferred the murmuring to the pure, silent contempt and fear they'd harbored when I'd first arrived. Uninventive as some as their digs were, the fact they spoke of me at all meant they were warming up, ever so slightly. They didn't even flinch anymore when I passed, and I had heard none of them call me the *Sykagos* out loud in days. I could handle the hazing and ribbing if it meant a future of mutual respect.

Especially as Caelum's unexpected charm and adventurousness had eased the ache in my body and my heart, a welcome gift from my betrothed I hadn't expected. His stories surprised and excited me; though he was his father's dutiful son whenever King Kato was present, there was potential in him. Perhaps with some tutelage and a push, he'd be something more. Something *great*.

And even though Rory grumbled and glared for most of the journey, there were moments—brief, shining—where her burning eyes softened and *invited*. Moments where she lingered just a second longer, fighting whatever denial she wrestled with. Like when I'd caught her in the woods with the Second Lieutenant. She hadn't scrambled off him or hurtled an insult at me or any other normal, appropriate response, like Nyxia had the few times I'd accidentally walked in on her between some maid's legs or atop a poor soldier's cock. One time, she'd even thrown something at my head, giving me a bump that lasted a week.

But no, Rory had captured me in her gaze, and didn't let go until she'd found her release.

I'd taken it as a sign that maybe Lux wasn't so bad after all. That maybe, if the captain could find something redeemable—or at the very least, *interesting*—about me, then perhaps the rest of the sun-bleached continent could do the same one day.

I'd forgotten.

I couldn't any longer.

When we finally made it out of the Polus Mountains and into the outer city, there was no pretending. No forgetting.

A small unit—six men—from the King's transport met us on the outskirts, two of those awful, noisy tanks in tow.

These soldiers didn't warm up to me like the others had. They wrinkled their noses at me like I smelled of piss, baring their teeth in grimaces from across the field. Hands clutched weapons with white-knuckled grips, and I didn't need to be a mind reader to know how they fantasized about skewering me for merely existing.

Rory dismounted first, crossing over to discuss formations with their leader, a broad man with a scraggly beard and stringy brown hair that reached halfway down his back. A prominent soldier, given the Luxian custom of only cutting it after defeat.

Even as she spoke to him, he shot dark glances my way, like he'd chop it all off in a heartbeat for just a shot at me.

She returned, a frown on her face. "We're traveling through the city proper instead of through the back channels. Apparently, there have been Shadowborne sightings in that area in the last few days."

Lieutenant Fortis crossed his arms, his brows taught. "Really? This far out of the mountains?"

"Isn't that strange?" I pursed my lips. I wasn't an expert in Luxian geography, but even I knew in my many sieges on the city that the Shadowborne rarely left the dark outskirts of the continent, the population topside far more controlled than it was back in Erebus.

Rory's eyes flicked to me for a second—a fleeting accusation—before she nodded at her *Vinculum*.

I'd forgotten.

In Lux, everything was the *Sykagos'* fault.

So, when the others moved into those buzzing, clanging contraptions, I'd chosen to ride; a desire to truly see Lux and the people singing through me. And it was time they saw me. Time they got a glimpse of the king behind the monster they so desperately clung to in all of their cautionary tales.

Their prejudice was born of ignorance, just as mine had been.

I refused to rule blindly. If Caelum and I were to both truly unite and take care of both of our homelands, at least *one* of us had to get to know them, and the boy currently lacked in that regard.

He chose to ride inside a tank for his protection, much to my disappointment. Not just because I wanted his company, welcome as it was, but because it'd be foolish for us not to present as a united front. Still, I sat atop Asteri, ready to make peace with the continent that'd scorned me and my people.

I should've anticipated what I'd see.

Even here, on the very outskirts of the city proper, the glass and metallic buildings were packed tightly together, homes stacked on top of each other like crates. Citizens poured out of the too-small thresholds like spiders from a den. How the structures stayed standing baffled me, tall and thin and fragile as they all were, especially as the tanks rumbled through the narrow streets shook their very foundations. But the commoners didn't seem to mind—that, or they were so used to the lack of stability by now, they didn't even notice the rumbling beneath their feet.

I met their gazes as I passed—a woman with two crying babies on her hips and a toddler hanging on her legs in dirty, torn clothes. Another woman dressed in flashy fashion, her hat nearly as tall as Asteri, her bassinet carrying a small, yappy dog instead of children. A man with soot from the Zo'is mines permanently staining his hands and face azure, his eyes bloodshot from whatever substances he medicated himself with afterward. Another elf, older, with a perfectly quaffed mustache and recently shaved sideburns, like he'd come back from the barber's and dropped in to see what the fuss was about.

A man handing a woman a small, blue-stained sack—likely illicit Zo'is.

A woman clanging an empty tin cup at the street corner, begging the other townsfolk for extra coin.

A boy in clothes too big for him—hand-me-downs, then—

selling little Sun-crested Luxian flags to men in suits tailored to fit them perfectly.

Yet despite their varied classes, the hundreds of them, the *thousands*, all shared the same expression, their empty stares reminiscent of my homeland—of my people, just as desperate and exhausted.

And when I made eye contact with those lining the path, when I tried to see, to *understand*, anger captured their expressions, distorting their features to spitting, grotesque displays of pure hatred. Extra guards held the barricades, the commoners hurling their rage and fear at me.

Though there were so many, the chorus was unified.

Kill the Sykagos!

Murderer!

Freak! Monster!

None of them blamed Caelum. None of them shouted Kato's name.

I stopped looking, instead directing my gaze forward and my horse straight, even as he whinnied nervously beneath me. But my chin would not dip an inch, even with the weight of my father's crown resting on my head today.

A king bows to no one.

"Fucking Luxian bastards," Kappas muttered behind me, his steed chuffing in confirmation, and then, louder, "What a warm welcome from your chosen people, *Mi Vassilla*."

He said my title with the same poison as the Luxians casting curses on my name.

I'd forgotten.

The *Sykagos* was always, *always* alone.

We kept moving, and though the buildings grew even taller, their crystalline structures blinding in the midday sun, they spread out as we drew closer to the inner city. The wealthier district, where higher-class merchants and nobles dwelled.

I supposed they could afford more space, their looming and

gaudy homes sitting atop little green patches of trimmed grass and orderly flowers. Statues lined these streets, bronze and stone depictions of Luxian's greatest heroes: Kato and the great King Alixsander.

And among the elite, the song of the people did not change. If anything, it became more personal, more vicious—less weighed down by exhaustion and instead bolstered by their obsessed reverence for the Luxian crown.

Erebushi whore!

King Theron's monster child! I bet her mother was a Shadowborne beast.

Diavolos scum! I wonder how long until she swallows up the princeling.

To my surprise, Captain Bellatore trotted up beside me on her dappled mare, shooting dark glares at the gathered masses we passed.

They'd crossed the line, insulting her prince, her *beloved*.

But as shouts dwindled to murmurs under her reproachful stare, my gratitude was real all the same. Whether she was an ally by choice or by force, I'd take the assistance.

I lifted my chin a little higher.

I would not forget again.

I willed my mouth to smile, fiddling with Amma's ring for strength. "How kind of you to join me, Captain."

Rory grimaced, her keen eyes scanned the masses. "Your Majesty, we should retreat into the tanks for the rest of the journey."

It shouldn't have mattered. She was not my friend, no matter how *interesting* we found each other during our voyage. But still, a glimmer of discontent rattled through me, an unsettled ache that would not quiet. I shot her a sarcastic smirk. "Why, so you don't have to face the fact I'm not the only monster in this world?"

I gestured to the masses; to their red, angry faces, their cruel, heartless shouts. They would one day soon be my people. My monstrous hoard, made of the same vitriol and venom I was.

Rory raised a brow at me, biting her lip to stifle her own grin, and I balked at her.

"The tanks are faster." She flattened me with her matter-of-fact tone, but the twist of her mouth fell. She trained her gaze toward the towering, glittering city beyond. "And trust me, these elves are the least of the monsters you'll be dealing with today. King Kato has arrived at Stellaris, and he's already called court."

It took all of my willpower to hand over Asteri to the guards and climb into one of the obnoxious tanks, but Rory was admittedly right.

It took under an hour at full speed, and though the harsh, *Zo'is*-fueled lights stung my eyes, it was a respite from the horrified faces and terrified shouts along the streets. Within the small cabin, the only noise I could hear was the droning, unnatural buzz of the engine.

When I climbed out again, the sun a brief, blinding flash, the looming presence of Stellaris stared down at me, another obstacle to overcome.

I craned my neck as far back as it would go, and still, within the courtyard, there was no seeing the top spires of the crystal-laid palace. It stood almost as tall as the Polus Mountains at its back,, a goliath towering over the rest of the world, shouting its superiority from the hilltop. It jutted up from the expansive, trimmed-hedged gardens and forests surrounding it, the Elven-made brilliance an affront to the natural beauty of the nearby terrain. Gems and metals I had no name for encased the obscenity in glittering light. Glass spires and swirls decorated every inch, making it impossible to appreciate any of the designs, all of them competing for focus beneath the blinding sun's sparkling rays.

The hedges and statues—all carved to match Alixsander and Kato's images—pointed toward the entryway, leafy arms extended in exalt. Gold and silver double doors waited atop a tall, glass staircase, opened like a beast's jaws, ready to devour me.

"It's beautiful, isn't it?" Caelum approached with his hands behind his back, admiring his home with starry eyes.

It appeared we had different tastes in decorating; another challenge to manage before we wed.

When one lived in the dark, the details didn't matter as much as the functionality of the design. The Tygian Palace was built from stone and iron, made to withstand and protect. The furnishings were simple, carved from dead trees or cleaved from rock. Art was drawn in charcoal and ash. Textiles were roughly spun from what little grew. And even though I had a taste for the finer things—half of my wardrobe crafted from spider-silk or velvet—I treated each item with reverence. Craftsmen were honored in Erebus; it was a testament to true creativity to make something beautiful out of nothing.

Lux lacked the same appreciation, losing the plot to abundance.

"It's certainly like nothing I've ever seen before." My shadows itched to break free of my palms. "I see now why everyone in the outer city wanted to protect it from my disgusting clutches."

The Prince's brows furrowed, confusion and upset wrinkling in the space between them.

I would not coddle and coo at him like his father and keeper did. If he wanted to sit in this castle and shut out his people, he could. But I wouldn't shy away from the truth with him.

I respected him too much for that.

Caelum opened his mouth—to offer a placation or a protest, I'd never know—but I brushed past him, finding Nyxia among the bustling guards as we readied to enter the palace.

"Ready for enemy territory?" I looped my arm through hers, tucking my friend close to my side. In her presence, my shadows eased, the defiant itch soothed.

209

A purely wicked smile stretched her features. "The real question is, are they ready for us?"

I let my friend's courage supplement my own and shoved my shoulders back.

Stavros, Nyxia, and I had gone over my plan for this moment for years, noting exactly the tone we'd need to set amongst the courtiers.

With Caelum, I could allow more of my true self to show, a softness necessary to invite him in.

With the laypeople, I'd have to cultivate something even more nuanced if I was to gain their trust and cooperation—an empathy that they hadn't been afforded in ages, and an accountability for my part in their plight.

With the hungry, greedy dogs that ran the Luxian upper crust, I'd need to speak a language they knew; the only one they bothered to translate at all.

Strength. *Fear.*

I started up the stairs; the Luxians scrambled, calling for me to wait for the delegation, but I ignored them.

A king waited for no one.

My steps echoed loudly across the marble-laid mosaic floor, the blues and whites stark against my black boots. It would have been proper for me to change out of my riding clothes—finely made as they were—and into a gown, but I wouldn't waste my time with pleasantries today.

Deeper inside the entry hall, chatter floated from the crack in another set of large, carved-wood-and-inlaid-gold doors. Two guards posted on either side jolted, drawing their swords.

"We will not be drawing our weapons on the King's most honored guest." Rory scrambled in, panting to catch up with me. The guards lowered their weapons, stabbing me instead with dark stares.

I soaked them in, letting my shadows purr with the taste of their animosity. They swirled in delicate bracelets around my wrists; not threats, but reminders. So the Luxians wouldn't forget again, either, what I could do. What I *would* do, if pushed to it.

The guards took two smart steps back as I burst through the doors and into the grand receiving room, ready to greet the entire Luxian court with my grin on my face.

The music screeched to a halt, a few horrified gasps marking the final chorus of a song I knew all too well. Nobles—dressed in that loose, puffy Luxian fashion, most of them in various shades of white, blue, and gold—scurried out of my path, huddling together like it would keep them safe.

Windows stretched from the floor all the way to the vaulted ceiling, the light pouring in and bathing the marbled floors in gold. It was all so bright, *blinding,* but I soaked in the warmth, my shadows growing darker against the sun's intrusion. My father's throne had been simple—unadorned, forged from the same iron ore that wrought the Tyrian Crown atop his head.

For all his failings, Theron Umbrus had not been a vain man; no use worrying about aesthetics when your people could hardly see a damn thing.

But even in the darkness of Erebus, *appearances* mattered.

Theron knew this—knew how imposing his silhouette loomed against the dim orange glow of meager candles. Knew how to gaze at his subjects in such a way that his brow cast a shadow across his face and devoured the glowing whites of his eyes.

Knew that looks could be deceiving. That threats appeared larger, more terrifying amidst the vast unknown of darkness.

As a girl, I'd sit in the throne room, casting my own meager shadow—and I'd watch. Watch my father grow in size and strength, watch as he altered his presence to fit the room he was in.

On this dais, King Kato lounged upon the Sunkissed Throne, his crown crooked on his head. The thousands of gold spires—meant to resemble the rising sun's rays--protruded from behind him like the spikes on a many-horned beast. Blue *Zo'is* pulsed through the metal, a poisonous creature's colorful warning.

In Lux, light shone too brightly, dispelling any chances to trick the mind. But Kato knew how to make his own shadows, it seemed, using the opposite technique my father had. Where Theron cut a fearsome, untouchable image, King Kato made everything casual. *Relaxed.* Like he was used to being a predator no one even thought to contend with, a lion sunbathing in an open field without a worry in the world about what might be lurking in the grass.

Unbothered, the king clapped his hands together—and didn't rise from his cushioned perch.

"King Thera!" He raised his gold goblet before taking a long swig—holding me at his pace, a tactic Stavros and I had both used many times to perturb my father. "So glad to see you've arrived safely. I take it your journey wasn't too unpleasant?"

I smiled while the Luxians I'd traveled with filtered into the room. From the corner of my eye, I caught Nyxia and Kappas lurking along the walls, the courtiers trembling as my companions passed.

Caelum stumbled in beside me, his face a shade of red that brought out the violet of his wide eyes. He bowed and mumbled a hello to his father. The King barely nodded to him, gaze still trained on me, fingers tapping impatiently against the armrest of his seat as he awaited my response.

I held my tongue until the others stopped moving before answering—using his own delay against him. Then, to the horror of the onlookers, I linked my arm through Caelum's, giving it a gentle squeeze. "Your son was quite the entertainer on the way. A true gentleman. We had plenty of exciting chats about the future. And I was so impressed at how many of your citizens could fit along the streets." I scanned the room, letting my voice carry as the other nobles cowered along the corners. Caelum himself looked ready to explode, from embarrassment or excitement or both, I couldn't tell. "It was quite the welcome."

Someone—likely Nyxia, the imp—stifled a laugh with a cough.

King Kato's smile did not fall, but his eyes narrowed to spikes that matched those on the throne.

"Excellent. That must explain your tardiness." He chuckled, raising his glass again to the onlookers—the perfect model of an unafraid, unimpressed monarch. "Court began over an hour ago, but no matter. I'm glad you're here now, so we can make proper introductions."

The dig was shallow but well-placed, a few of the courtiers daring to laugh under their breaths at their king's jest. Kato knew this dance just as well as I did. He straddled the fine line that separated fear and strength with mastery.

I let go of Caelum's arm, my shadows stroking the side of his face once before retreating to me.

Caelum shuddered, and the room quieted to an uncomfortable silence, laughter dying on their wagging tongues.

Kato might pretend he was unafraid, but his dogs could not.

I stretched my arms high above my head, and several people flinched as I let out a fake yawn.

"Actually, I'll retire to my chambers now." I cracked my neck, stretching the tight muscles. "All this sunlight has simply zapped my energy."

Finally, the king balked, his mouth falling open. He recovered quickly, but he scooted further forward onto his silly chair, his knuckles white where they strangled the armrests. Like he was physically restraining himself to not leap from the dais and strangle *me* instead.

There it was, the fear I'd been dying to taste. Not of me—no, the fool saw himself as my equal, a grave mistake—but of losing the room. Of being perceived as less than the almighty, god-like ruler he'd painted himself as.

"Surely you're hungry?" His voice was pleasant, *practiced*, but it wavered ever so slightly as his control slipped. "My courtiers have all waited to dine with you, Your Majesty."

"Yes, I haven't been this excited for a meal in ages," one brave courtier said, a man wearing a pale green chemise, his earthen coloring just a shade off from everyone else.

I trained my smile on him—my teeth bared.

"My regrets to you, then, but please, enjoy all of your food." I shrugged, and a few relieved sighs echoed from the masses. They didn't want to dine with me more than I wanted to stick thorns up my ass. Their relief was short-lived as my shadows coiled around my waist like a cobra. "I've eaten more than my fill on the journey."

King Kato's throat bobbed as he stared at my vicious shadows. With fear, yes, but . . .

My hackles rose. There's something else in his perceptive gaze, something dark in his widened pupils.

Hunger. *Desire.*

"I see." He clicked his tongue, and he sat back, relaxing into the throne again.

I didn't want him relaxed.

Strength, fear.

A king bowed to no one.

I cleared my throat, knowing every ear in the room trained on each and every syllable pouring from my lips. "Speaking of provisions, we brought back a prisoner. He's still out of sorts, but I will need to question him myself tomorrow. Please see to it he's being well-fed until then."

The courtiers murmured at my demands and revelations, and the king blanched, bronze skin paling as light as his hoard of marble and opal.

I continued, firm and sharp, "And we'll also have to discuss the Shadowborne attack in the summer palace, as well as the sightings in the outer city—I have my questions."

It was a risky play—revealing the Shadowborne's involvement. If the plotter was in the room with us, then I'd be putting them on high alert, and could give them the time and foresight needed to evade me.

But the courtiers needed to see their charlatan king for what he was. *Powerless.* And I needed to remind him exactly how he measured up.

This was his court.

It would be my battlefield.

And when he grimaced at me—that easy, aloof facade cracking beneath the weight —I savored the victory.

"Those are sensitive matters we can discuss more at a later time." Kato's voice was a low rumble through the room.

I feigned a small, apologetic nod.

"Yes, of course. Enjoy your little party." I turned my back on him, already on my way, even though I didn't know where I was going.

A king waited for no one.

Though it was a shame that I couldn't see the look on his face. But based on the delighted grin on Nyxia's, it was *priceless.*

"Captain, please see Thera to her rooms," the King called out.

Bellatore's steps clapped across the floor as she rushed to join me, Kato's most loyal dog nipping at my heels. My two advisors did the same as I sauntered back through the doors, the guards bumbling out of my way again. Bellatore paused to bow and say her goodbyes, but Nyxia, Kappas and I didn't wait for her, already half into the long hallway.

"*Mi Vassilla*, I request I go and see the prisoner now," Kappas said once we were out of earshot, his hand tight around his sword. "I do not trust the Luxians to keep him alive."

I narrowed my eyes at Kappas—he'd been quiet since our arrival in Lux, the loud warmonger somehow tamed by the sun. His comment in the street today had been his first real complaint in a long time. Parts of me worried he was plotting something, but whether I liked to admit it, his instincts were sharp—decades on the battlefield making intuitive decisions did that to an elf.

And, admittedly, I shared his concern. I didn't trust the Luxians at all, and I wanted to know my enemies. Wanted to know what the faction in the woods were after, and how they knew we'd be there.

The only truth I currently possessed was that they had almost killed twice the Prince in a matter of as many days.

Which meant someone among the closest, most elite circle of the Luxian upper crust wanted my betrothed dead. And had almost succeeded.

Whoever had called the hit would likely want their only living accomplice too dead to talk.

I nodded to Kappas before slipping a paper with my royal seal on it from my sleeve. It would gain him access to the prisoner . . . and would protect our asset. "See it done, Kappas."

Kappas frowned before stalking off, nearly bumping into Rory as he pointed himself toward one of the idiot guards—likely to bully him into taking him to the dungeons.

Bellatore raised a brow as she neared Nyxia and me.

"Follow me," she said, keeping her mouth shut on the matter.

Nyxia and I did, pointing east.

"Why don't I join you?" Caelum's tenor carried through the hall's arched ceilings, halting us in our tracks. He bounded up to us, adjusting his ivory-embroidered shirt, his cheeks aflush from the movement.

A thrill bubbled in my veins at his arrival, even as Rory went rigid next to me. I'd written the Prince off as spineless today, just a boy desperate for his father's attention, but to walk out of court after I'd made such a spectacle? That was no small rebellion for a doting prince. That was practically a declaration of independence.

Or, of something else just as wild, if his breathless smile indicated anything. "I promised you a tour. What do you say we start now? Unless you meant you were really tired, and it wasn't just a ploy to get out of court."

Nyxia snickered, gaze raking over Caelum like a cat about to pounce on a mouse. "Will we get a *story* as we go, Your Majesty?"

"Play nice, Nyixa." I pinched her side, and she stuck her tongue out at me. My hand found my hip as I looked at Bellatore. "Well, Captain?"

This would be my battlefield, this palace, this kingdom. But if I was to conquer Lux without bloodshed, I'd need to win over its key soldiers.

She blinked, taking a full moment to realize I'd spoken to her. Her head swiveled between the Prince and me as she weighed her choice, as if surprised to be the one making it at all.

"I suppose King Kato didn't say we had to rush." Her hand gripped the hilt of her sword like it was a comfort at her side. Her lips pursed. "But I do have other assignments to take care of."

"Go ahead, Rory. I can take it from here." Caelum squeezed her arm—a simple, quick touch—but it revealed too much, especially as her shoulders relaxed beneath it. Nyxia had told me of their private moment in the woods, the spy stumbling in on their strangled confession, but this still posed both an opportunity and a problem for me to solve.

I expected the captain to protest with her typical icy retort, but she wrung her hands in front of her, gaze darting down the hall.

Curious.

She straightened, clearing her throat. "If you need anything, there are guards at the end of every hall, and they can call other attendants for assistance."

Whether it was a sign of her ignorance toward the attempts against the Prince, or a sign of her trust in my ability to keep him safe, I didn't know. But one thing was clear—she'd stopped marking me as a threat to his life. She trusted him to wander the halls of this massive obscenity with the two of us as his escorts. Of course, there were guards around, but she'd seen what I could do before.

I didn't know whether to be honored or suspicious.

"And if I want to get in touch with *you*, Captain?" I batted my lashes and stepped closer, trying to read beneath her facade, testing the limits of this newfound—whatever it was. "Who do I call?"

Rory's throat bobbed, but then she covered it with an eye roll.

Without a word to me and a quick bow to the prince, she stalked off, leaving me reeling with puzzle pieces that fit, but didn't quite click into place.

My shadows ached to follow her, dark whispers scratching at the back of my mind, but I ignored them, turning to Caelum— whose gaze also followed Rory down the long hall, violet darkened by wide pupils and hooded lashes.

I linked my hand through his, pulling him back to the moment, and earning a flash of heat across his high cheekbones. "Well, Prince Caelum, shall we?"

His starshine smile brightened even my dark heart, shadows clearing from cracks I'd thought permanently unlit.

Tugging my hand, he led me through the vast expanse of the halls, not flinching as the posted guards gaped at our joined fingers, his head high.

For the first time since I'd met him, he looked like he had the makings of a king.

We wound around corner after corner, Caelum pointing out the half-a-dozen busts of King Alixsander and telling stories of each gaudy art piece along the walls. *A commission by the great elf Manto Santorini, a brilliant sculptor. A portrait by his ex-wife, the late Selena Santorini, who had always tried to compete with her former partner after he left her for an opera singer.*

But with each new twist, my heart sank deeper into a pit. His hand went from a soothing touch to a weighted anchor, holding me in place as wave after wave of horror and resentment slammed into me.

This was not a castle. It was a fortress, designed to hoard all the wealth and resources inside, and shut everyone else out to fend for themselves. Erebushi and poorer Luxians alike.

"This is the hall of commerce, where most of the meetings are held to discuss finances," the Prince said.

We'd entered another long, overly decorated hall. Even in the further reaches of this blasted castle, every marble column was inlaid with ornately carved designs, every wall covered with silken tapestries or gem-encrusted picture frames. The skylights dyed it all in endless, sharp gold, the pools of warmth fighting against the cool glow of the dozens of *Zo'is* lamps that burned even in the bright of day.

My head pounded as I struggled to focus on his words amidst such offensive radiance. "On the other side is the Hall of Justice, where smaller trials are held. My father's offices are in the tower just past that."

Nyxia yawned, slumping against one of the columns. I unlatched my hand from his.

"Stellaris is very fortunate to have so many rooms for different meetings," I grit out, my patience wavering.

With the enraged townspeople I'd seen this morning, I'd been the focus of their hatred, the symbol of despair and darkness. Did they understand the true opal-and-gold-crusted cause of their misery?

"There seemed to be a preference for tight spaces in the outer city."

Caelum blinked, that cloudy ignorance dulling the edges of his gaze again. For someone so enraptured by literature and history, he had little understanding of life. Whether it was feigned or forced, he was far too comfortable in it for my liking. "The architecture here is several millennia old, whereas the outer city is mostly newer developments."

I fought back my scathing review of his assessment, instead nodding like his words had any sense or meaning. "I see."

"Where are the kitchens?" Nyxia shoved off the column and cracked her neck, a frown wrinkling her tiny face.

Caelum cocked his head to the side, like it was a strange question to ask. "The floor below, I believe, with all the other servants' halls. There is also the laundry hall and the storage spaces."

She grinned. "I suppose I'll go searching."

Caelum waved his hands. "No need, we can send a servant—"

But Nyxia was already walking off, probably in the wrong direction, flashing her teeth at the guards as she passed, ready to make trouble.

I patted his arm, stifling a laugh, grateful for my friend's interruption. "Never mind her, she has a short attention span. She'll make her way back."

A frown tugged Caelum's mouth, his brows pulling together. "But she doesn't know where anything is."

Some of the disquiet in my chest eased. For someone so oblivious to the plight of his own people, Caelum had a knack for fussing over those he'd deemed his friends. I'd been the object of his consideration more than once now, and while I hoped he'd learn to expand his borders to include more of his subjects, knowing he had the capacity for empathy gave me hope.

A rare, dangerous thing, indeed.

"That has never stopped her." I shrugged, tucking my arm through his again. "Come on, My Prince. Show me this awe-inspiring library of yours."

Elation claimed his features, galaxies sparkling and colliding in that wide stare. "Follow me, King Thera."

And I did, around another two corners and up a flight of stairs, until we stopped in front of a pair of giant wooden doors, waiting for Caelum to catch his breath again.

Giving him a moment of privacy, I studied the doors, carved with the same swirling markings that decorated the rest of the castle. But it was refreshing to see the natural, deep color of the wood, the ancient rings and markings beckoning us in.

"The doors were a part of the original castle, before Alixsander's mining efforts and subsequent renovations," Caelum said, his voice quiet. "They're carved from the Willow Grove outside. Some say they are older than Elvenkind itself, forged from a race that roamed these lands before the elves or the diavolos ever existed."

I traced the wood, the slight grooves catching beneath my fingertips. "Beautiful."

The doors cracked open without warning, sending us both stumbling a step back to avoid being knocked over.

"Your Highness." The aged woman bowed low, and I worried that her crepey skin would fall off her face. But when she straightened and her dark eyes found me, all concern fled from my heart as pure, unadulterated hatred claimed her expression. "Oh, sun and stars, *no*."

Caelum lifted his chin, sliding a hand across my back. "Mistress Grotchkin, this is King Thera—"

The woman hissed. She slunk closer, her teeth bared. "I know what you are, *Sykagos*, and I will not have you defiling my library with your darkness."

Her words punctured my lungs, the air dragging in shallow pulls.

I wanted to smack myself. I'd forgotten, again, *already*. Just because I was in the castle, just because I was away from the courtiers and angry townsfolk—I was not welcome in Lux. Not just unwanted but *despised*.

My shadows writhed around my wrists, ready to shift into claws and snatch her by the throat, but I managed a grin instead.

"Oh, so you *do* know me." I licked my lips.

Caelum's hand stiffened at my back—in my defense or in a warning, I couldn't tell.

I pressed on. A king bowed to no one. "Then I suppose you know what I do to those who dare speak to me like that?"

The old crone took a faltering step back, but she raised a trembling finger at me. "I swear on King Alixsander's will, you will meet your end in the most horrific way possible. You can threaten me and my people all you want, but I have endured here for centuries, and I will not stand—"

"Mistress Grotchkin, pack your things immediately." Caelum's voice rumbled low as it sliced through her warbling tirade. His hand abandoned my back, but as he stepped around me, his shoulder blocking the crone's view, something wicked and delighted spun through my limbs. "Your employment is dismissed as of this instant, and you no longer have clearance to be present here."

The woman gawked at him. "What? You can't do that—"

He held up a hand to silence her, no room for argument in his unbending tone. "I can, and I am."

She paled, her whole form shaking with unbridled rage. "Your father will hear—"

Caelum stepped closer, and for the first time I realized how *tall* he was. His chin bent almost all the way to his chest as he glared over his nose at her.

"Oh, my father will *certainly* hear about how you just threatened an ally to the throne. Your future Queen Consort, and my *betrothed*." His tone blistered, the flicker of starshine I'd seen in him now scalding like a meteor burning through the sky. "I'm sure he'll take it well. Why don't you run along and tell him, so the rest of us can place bets on how long it'll take him to relieve you of your head?"

The woman's jaw snapped shut so hard, I thought she might break her teeth. With a sharp inhale, she stormed past him, spitting at my feet. "*Sykagos.*"

"Nice to meet you too!" I called after her, frowning as I wiped the spit from my boot on one of the silken tapestries hanging outside of the library.

Caelum did not turn away as he watched her retreat, that same blaze still darkening the blue of his eyes to a frightful purple, his fists clenched at his sides.

A king bowed to no one. And from this angle, it looked as though Prince Caelum was learning to keep his head erect under pressure.

I placed a hand on his arm—these casual touches between us normal now, after so many days pressed tightly together.

He melted beneath my fingers, and heat pooled low within me.

"You know, I am not helpless. I can fight my own battles."

He shook his head, and the lingering tension dispelled from his lanky frame. He flashed a tight smile. "Oh no, that was personal. I've been looking for a way to get rid of Crotchkin for years." His hand found mine again, the feeling of his fingers was both familiar and welcome. "Come on, Thera. We've got a library to explore."

In a singular, smooth move, he kicked open the door and spun us both through it, setting me off my center as the world tilted and came back into focus.

When I caught my balance and my eyes adjusted, my heart nearly cracked open my chest to jump out.

In every direction, tall, endless shelves soared toward the domed-glass sky, spines of tomes in every color a kaleidoscope of brilliance. Staircases and ladders wound around the circular space, like pathways to the heavens themselves. The light here filtered with specks of floating dust.

I braced my hands on one of the finely crafted tables, craning my head back to see the very top of the stacks in dizzying wonder. "This place is—"

"Amazing." Caelum's breath whispered across my cheek as he settled at my side, heat caressing my arm where we brushed against each other.

I'd never been one for overwhelm—it was an emotion that didn't serve weapons well, and my father had done his best to eradicate it from my being. But standing among the thousands of books, amidst so much history and knowledge that could all potentially hold the key to saving my people, to bettering this world . . .

It was all too much. Too wonderful.

And to have him here, to have him staring at me like I was just as special and incredible . . .

For the first time since I'd claimed the shadows as my own, I saw the light at the end of a long, hard tunnel.

A single, vulnerable admission flew from my lips before I could stop it. "There is so much . . . I don't know where to start."

With the library, or with this dangerous hope that'd rooted firmly in my gut against my wishes.

Caelum laughed, sincere and playful, but then his gaze dipped to my mouth, and the humor eddied away. "I have a few recommendations. I'll show you the romance section, if you'd like."

My stomach knotted with a welcomed squeeze, my senses already overstimulated and craving something to bring me down to earth. Craving *him*, this starkissed future king, and the soft light he offered amidst a lifetime of dark nights.

"Oh, you'll *show* me, will you?" I teased as I slid my hand up his arm, looking up at him through my lashes. "Is there a stack for that?"

I expected him to blush and balk, our practiced dance, but he reached out, a soft finger trailing against my cheek. He tucked a lock of my hair behind my ear, and his hand settled against my neck—right above my fluttering pulse.

"You are welcome here, Thera. Whenever you want or need." His stare was impossibly soft, yet it still cut through me, sliding beneath all my thought-to-be-impenetrable walls. "My library is your library. My kingdom, your kingdom."

I swallowed the lump that choked me, foreign tears budding against my lashes.

With him, it was so easy to forget. Easy to believe that maybe I didn't have to be alone. That hands could hold and caress, not just wound. That stares could make me soar, not just strip me of my dignity.

I detested and delighted in how vulnerable my voice sounded as I finally formed words. "I like the sound of that."

And when Caelum's lips pressed against mine—one small, innocent kiss, there for a breath of a moment and gone the next—I realized how easy it could be for a king to fall.

Into him. Into forgetting. Into something I didn't have a name for, not yet.

Someone cleared their throat, and I jolted back, knocking my hip into the table with a wince. "Prince Caelum, King Thera."

Lieutenant Fortis stood in the doorway, graciously staring at the floor like it held all the secrets to this library of wonders.

Caelum tucked his hands in front of himself, his cheeks blood-red. "Yes, Julius?"

I bit my tingling lip to hide a laugh, as if my heart wasn't still slamming against my ribs.

Fortis lifted his head. "Prince Caelum, you should get back to the party. Your father will be waiting, and it's best if you explain the situation with Crotchy to him." He bowed with an apologetic smile. "I'll take the King to her chambers."

Caelum sighed and nodded, trudging to the door, ready to face the consequences of his rebellion. And though I mourned the loss of our little peace, parts of me sang at the idea of him handling himself against his father.

His gaze—reverent and gentle in ways I'd never known—trapped me from the doorway before he slipped through it. "Good-night, Thera. Welcome to Lux."

CHAPTER

SIXTEEN

"*Stellaris is the heart of Lux. Its defense is a paramount priority of every member of the core, regardless of rank, station, and assignment.*" *–Rule Sixteen of the Luxian Soldier's Codex, written by King Alixsander the 1st, 3 A.G.W, Updated by Commander General Atlas Tiberius, 1989 A.G.W.*

RORY

I had a small window of opportunity.

If Caelum gave King Thera the tour, it could take them hours, especially if they'd wandered into the library. And as much as I hated the idea of them cozying up between the stacks—Caelum's confession in the forest still an endless, dizzying loop in my mind—I had to take a shot.

Commander Tiberius always said we won wars through initiative, and it was time I seized mine.

If I were to kill Thera, I needed leverage. Her strength was

226

unmatched, and if the King's reaction in court was any indication
...

He sent *me* because he couldn't do it himself. Politically, his hands were tied, but I suspected even *he* couldn't pry Thera's crown from her head without a significant sacrifice.

After traveling with her for the last week, it was clear as daybreak; King Thera was the most powerful elf to walk the earth in the last millennia. Her strength, skill, and determination were unmatched, her every step sure and powerful.

If they hadn't tasked me to kill her, if she hadn't been betrothed to Caelum, it might've impressed me. *Intrigued,* even.

But the cold reality sank through my bones, making every joint stiff with fear; I wasn't strong enough to kill her through force alone.

I'd have to be *clever.*

Her rooms were quiet when I entered. A small greeting room with little adornment opened up into a larger bedroom; a square bed with three beige pillows, a high-backed, uncomfortable wooden chair, and a small dresser the only furniture. Undecorated unlike most of the castle—an insult, for someone of the King's standing.

Though considering Thera's frown when she'd first noted Stellaris, it might suit her tastes just fine. The staff had dumped her two trunks off, the metallic black containers eyesores against the creams-and-beiges, not bothering to unpack for her as they might with other nobles.

No one wanted to get too close to the *Sykagos'* cursed hoard.

I was about to dig through all of it.

Starting with the chest closest to the door, I tore through it as quickly and thoroughly as I could, both goals contradicting each other. This one was mostly clothing—black and red fabrics that blurred together, even despite my effort to note the order in which I pulled them out so I could properly restore it all without being caught. Unless the *Sykagos* hid secrets under her skirts, this trunk bore me no help.

In a separate section at the bottom waited more personal garments—lacy, impractical things that brought heat to my neck and cheeks—but Thera struck me as the kind of elf that would march through the halls of Stellaris in her panties alone just to disarm us all, so there was no leverage in her lingerie, either.

I tossed a folded black negligee to the floor with a huff, frustration's many heads rearing within me.

But when a thump sounded, I whipped around, hope springing up in my veins like a full dose of *Zo'is*.

From within the sheer fabric, a notebook tumbled out onto the floor, the face wrapped in a dark leather that practically absorbed the surrounding light. Carefully, I reached for it. My fingers brushed the front cover, and the cover tore open.

It was unlatched.

And inside, line after line of elegant handwriting sprawled across the pages, the hurried words of an elf possessed saturating the creme paper in inky black.

King Thera's personal journal.

I snagged it from the floor and flipped through quickly, finding nearly every page covered in the same frantic writing, each line of script pressing to the very edge of the margins, like she wouldn't waste a single centimeter of space.

Another thump sounded, heavier this time, and panic set my heart to its top speed. I tucked the notebook under my armor before I whipped around to face the intruder.

A breeze from the bedroom window swooshed the silk curtains, and Nyxia appeared in front of it, against all logic. We were four stories high, yet she was *there*, just beyond the plain bed, a cruel smile curving her lips.

"*You're* the little snake." She chuckled, the tinny sound scraping along my spine. The silver blade of a dagger flashed as she swiped it from her sleeve. She twirled it through her fingers—excellent knife skills for a mere ambassador. "I'm surprised; I didn't think you were clever enough."

I shot to my feet, dropping into a defensive stance. My senses pounded a warning through my skull. It should've been impossible for her to scale the walls, the castle's gemstone surface *terrible* for climbing—a design choice with practical defenses. And I should've *heard* her coming.

There had been no warning. Nyxia was as untraceable as a shadow.

My fists tightened, prepared for an attack. Her *nimbleness* aside, I had the physical advantage, but this couldn't come to blows. King Kato would never forgive me for being so indiscreet, and Caelum—

I didn't want to imagine his disappointment if I killed his betrothed's favorite pet.

"I'm—" I scrambled for an explanation, forcing myself to straighten and unclench my fists. I had the authority here, Nyxia's insults aside. "It's protocol. We have to search all belongings to ensure Stellaris' safety."

The lie tasted shallow, but I'd have King Kato's backing if I begged, and better to have Nyxia and Thera pissed over an intrusive policy than suspicious of me.

"And the Captain of the Prince's Guard sees to that personally? Don't lie to me, girl, I can smell it on your breath." Nyxia cut through the excuse like steel through flesh, her eyes tracking over the disarray I'd made around the room before they slashed to me. She prowled around the bed, her knife steady in her hand. "Did you let the Shadowborne in, too?"

"What?" My jaw dropped at the absurd question, fingers twitching toward my sheathed sword. I didn't want to fight, didn't want to deal with the fallout, but I wouldn't entertain such accusations from the right hand of the devil herself. "Stand down, Ambassador, or I will detain you."

The little demon barely came up to my chin, but she smirked up at me with the venom belonging to an elf three times her size. "You can try your very hardest, Captain."

This time, I heard footsteps approaching, though I dared not turn, dared not give Nyxia my back.

I did not trust she wouldn't stab it at the first opportunity.

"What's going on?" Thera's sharp voice dragged my attention away from her spy to where Jules and Thera were in the receiving room, footsteps drawing to an abrupt halt.

Her face held not an ounce of emotion, cold and lifeless as the shadows she wielded. She surveyed the space, eyes catching only for a second on the underwear I'd carelessly tossed aside.

Confusion pulled my *Vinculum*'s brows together as he nervously clutched the hilt of his sword. "Rory?"

Nyxia stepped closer to her monarch, though her stare didn't shift an inch from my face. "I found Captain Bellatore digging for gold through your things, *Mi Vassilla*." She tossed that tiny knife between her hands again. "Should I kill her now, or should we interrupt court and make a game out of it?"

My stomach fell, though I refused to let it show on my expression, trying to calculate my next steps carefully. This could not descend to violence, but King Kato would have my title stripped if Thera took us to court and I embarrassed him so publicly.

The weight of her journal against my chest pressed heavily as sweat licked the back of my neck. Reeling, I searched for a response, for a plan—

"Explain." Thera's command halted all thought.

Nyxia gaped at her king as she looked at *me*, not her disciple; expectant. *Waiting.* But malice didn't hide in her stare, not a trace of judgment or contempt, and the utter lack of emotion threw me off my center even more severely.

She gave me a chance to explain myself. Like she wanted to hear *my* side. My story.

My shoddy excuse was less mangled this time, the sound something more akin to confidence despite the sheen of discomfort that clung to my back. "It's a safety protocol. We have to make sure we've approved all items in the castle."

Thera took a single step. Jules and Nyxia both flinched at the action, ready for anything. But she just waved her hand in dismissal.

"Then go ahead." She sighed, floating toward the tall chair in front of the still open window. She sat, her legs crossed, King Thera making the unadorned space her throne room in less than a breath, a burning grin finally cracking her icy facade. "Though surely I'm allowed to be present while I watch you tear through my *intimates?*"

Heat burned my cheeks, and my heartbeat slammed against the journal—likely the most intimate part of her collection. If I didn't return it before she noticed, she'd know it was me that took it. But it was also potentially my only lead. The only leverage I had. And I wouldn't let it slip through my fingers. "Your Majesty, I—"

Thera snapped her fingers at Jules, ignoring my response. "Give her a hand, Fortis."

Jules stiffened and looked at me, eyes wide with fear, waiting for an order.

Breathe in, Rory.

Anxiety blurred the edges of all my rational thoughts. I breathed deeply, the air blowing away the misty haze. I was a Luxian soldier, trained and tested under diamond-forging pressure. And as always, the best way around a sticky situation was *through*. I'd started this, and now I finished it.

There was no going back. If Thera and Nyxia wanted to watch me work, so be it. It didn't change my trajectory in the slightest. I would search the other chest, find an excuse to confiscate the journal, and I'd read every manic word until I killed King Thera.

I nodded to Jules, marching toward Thera's second chest and opening it with little ceremony. My *Vinculum*, as always, was at my side in another breath, even as his hands shook at his sides, his unease blaring through our shared bond like a siren. But he had no reason to be afraid. The King's secrets were *mine* now, and I wouldn't let her hurt him or any of my loved ones with them.

The second trunk was similarly boring—her accessories and cosmetics taking up most of the space, as well as some spare shoes and the thick cloak she'd worn over the mountains. My brows drew down at how lightly she packed—and how much of her attention had clearly diverted to bedroom activities.

It sat like spoiled milk in my middle, rotten and ruined.

But it wasn't nearly as uncomfortable as the burn of Thera's stare on my every move, the sheer weight of her unmoving presence in her makeshift throne. As Julius and I sorted and searched every inch of her belongings, the king didn't so much as flinch, unbothered as we tore through her life, like she had nothing to hide and even less to be ashamed of.

Nyxia watched with more apprehension. She growled and grumbled whenever we handled things with too little care—a guard dog trained well by its master—but she didn't stop our pursuit.

An opportunity never presented itself to slip the notebook from my armor, their unwavering attention too close for comfort. And as we hit the very bottom of the second trunk—even pressing for secret compartments and finding none—my window of opportunity closed firmly shut.

I'd have to take the notebook, read it, and slip it back into the room later—perhaps pretending it'd been misplaced as I'd made my mess.

Thera finally stood, stretching her neck like this entire affair had bored her half to death.

If only.

"Anything to confiscate? My underwear, perhaps?" She smirked, but it didn't quite captivate her face like it normally did, an exhaustion weighing the quirked side down ever so slightly.

I blinked as I noted the shift, unsure I'd seen it at all. But whatever weariness dragged Thera of Erebus down was not my problem

—it was my *ally*. Perhaps the very chip in her impenetrable armor I'd need to end her once and for all.

Which is why the guilt that roared through my chest surprised me. I cleared my throat, my voice laden with a rare contrition. "We're all clear. Thank you for your cooperation, Your Majesty."

Thera waved a hand and turned to the open window, dismissing Julius and me with both of our heads intact.

Nyxia glared from her corner but said nothing—a dutiful pet through and through. I'd have to keep a closer eye on the ambassador.

Before they could change their minds, I nudged Julius toward the door, ready to be free of this room and start strategizing with my *Vinculum* about what in the Inferni hell I was going to do next.

"Was Caelum *aware* that he was being used as a distraction?"

My feet stuttered to a stop only a foot from the threshold. The crack in her voice did something to me I didn't want to acknowledge.

I turned. Caelum's name on her lips had my instinct to protect jolting through me, but my thoughts crashed into each other, none making sense. The sight of her rattled all sensible parts of me.

Thera stood rigid at the window, her hands clasped behind her, *both* her eyes matching with a darkness that had crawled out of Erebus itself. It sucked me in, an unnatural void that devoured all light and turned my stomach over.

A glimpse of the *Sykagos*. The monster of my nightmares, the eater of souls.

"Did you two plan it together during your little romantic rendezvous in the woods the other day?"

I sucked in a breath.

The hitch in her voice spoke of a vulnerable womanhood I knew all too well—an insecure, girlish part I recognized in myself more than I wanted to admit.

We watched each other, both unmoving and silent as she acci-

233

dentally slipped maybe even more of her secrets to me than the book still hidden beneath my breastplate.

Thera of Erebus was jealous. Lonely. *Hurt.*

By Caelum. By *me.*

And that bothered me more than I liked. Shame and regret froze me to my spot.

But before I could respond—and say *what,* I didn't know—fast-moving footsteps broke the moment in two, reality crashing through the door as Commander Kappas' shaved head tumbled through it. Syrax and Damas pursued hot on his heels, both of whom he'd likely taken as his escorts, entering half-a-second behind.

"*Mi Vassilla!*" Kappas bellowed between pants, panic written across his reddened face. But neither Syrax and Damas sported any humor in their expressions, their jaws clenched and sweat glistening on their foreheads as they both exchanged a dark look with me. Instincts prickling the hair at the back of my neck to standing.

Thera crossed the room in five long strides, shadows nipping at her ankles as the king replaced the girl once more. "What's wrong, Commander?"

Kappas straightened and drew in a deep breath, mouth pressing into a firm line as he steadied himself. Syrax and Damas both gripped the hilts of their swords—knuckles white as they stood *with* the commander.

"The prisoner is dead." Commander Kappas' words shook through the room like an earthquake, disaster striking at all of us with indiscriminate brutality. "The coroner is claiming it's natural causes."

Questions darted to the front of my mind. I looked at Syrax, ready to demand answers from my subordinates. How had this happened? Were there any witnesses? We'd been extra cautious to keep the man alive through our journey, and despite his addled state, his vitals had all been perfectly fine when we checked *this morning.*

No, there was nothing natural about this. This was a hit. An attack from *inside* the impenetrable walls of Stellaris.

Fear, true and caustic, turned my gut over itself; my fingers and toes went utterly numb.

"I'm not the enemy, Captain, and I did not bring darkness into Stellaris." Thera voiced my fears aloud, her tone cold enough to send a shiver sprinting down my back. "It already lived here."

CHAPTER
SEVENTEEN

"The doctors claim your heart is weak, but I know otherwise, my love. You have the strongest heart I've ever known, and it beats the song of a great king." –Queen Dellia's recovered letters to her son, Prince Caelum, circa 2096, A.G.W

CAELUM

Stellaris had always been my home. My birthright.

This castle had memories etched into every glittering surface, the multitude of rooms and expansive grounds my playpen in boyhood, and now my domain as a young man. But in the few days following King Thera's arrival and the prisoner's death, I'd never felt more unsettled.

The disquiet that crept through the halls and whispered around corners set every resident on a knife's-edge.

I didn't need proof to know Thera had nothing to do with the man's death, though luckily for her and Commander Kappas,

236

Rory's men had been there with him to vouch for his innocence. But for Thera to have declared the prisoner's presence before the court only hours before his death didn't bode well for her already shaky reputation, whispers lapping her heels like her ever-present shadows whenever she passed.

And that was all she had done since our kiss—pass me by, no more than polite nods and waves whenever we ran into each other in the halls. She'd taken her meals in her rooms, and aside from a few necessary summons from my father to discuss the issue, she'd taken leave from court as well.

Strategically, I understood. While the inability to keep a prisoner alive and the Shadowborne attack should've reflected poorly on the staff and security of Stellaris and the city, the court of public opinion needed a monster to blame. Lying low was her best option until answers were discovered, or until the next big gossip swept their attention.

Withdrawn as she was, it didn't stop my mind from straying to her at every idle moment. Laying in my rooms to read—taskless now that Grotchkin had fled with her tail between her legs, leaving me tutorless for the time being—even my books couldn't distract from the constant thoughts of *her*.

The taste of her mouth, sweet and soft. The light in her two-toned eyes as she'd marveled at the stacks of the library, like a small child stargazing for the first time. The purr of her teasing voice, the smell of her hair . . .

Her cruel smirk she wore in court, powerful and predatory. Her shadows that prowled before her and caressed me in front of my father, marking their territory.

Stellaris was home, but Thera had moved into my heart in the little time we'd had, rearranging the furniture and making it hers.

At least, parts of it. Other parts were untouched by her shadows, parts I hid and tried desperately to forget; parts that still drifted to memories of the sun peeking through leaves, splattering *her* tanned face in freckles of light, dark gold eyes looking at me in the way I'd secretly prayed for over *years*.

Before those parts invaded the rest of me like weeds in a fertile garden, I needed to see my fiancé.

I tossed the book I was reading onto my pillows—before realizing it was the perfect escape. I snatched it up, toppling off my bed and slipping my boots on as fast as I could without falling over. Checking myself once in the floor-length mirror—making sure my sky-blue tunic was wrinkle-free, smoothing my hair back—I headed out the door, ready to move.

Julius stood sentry outside, as he had since the attack.

Rory had barely spoken to me since we'd arrived home, busy with her duties in the wake of yet another death—and likely ignoring the parts of her that'd slipped out in the woods, too.

I tried not to take it personally that both women I'd expressed affection toward in the last week now avoided me like I was an infected Shadowborne.

Instead, I clutched the book tighter—a romantic comedy about a prince that kidnaps his sister's groom—and set my feet toward my betrothed.

Fortis stepped beside me, becoming my extra shadow, even though I often stood in his impressive one. "Where are we headed, My Prince?"

"Library." I held the book up for him, trying desperately not to roll my eyes. Julius might've been confident and assured in his rank, an excellent fighter, and a good elf all around, but if I had anything on him, it was that he'd likely stopped reading when the books stopped containing pictures.

I hated that it made me feel ever so slightly superior, a pride puffing out my narrow chest.

On cue, Jules' eyes glazed over as he read the spine, already bored by the mere prospect of exercising his brain. "Oh? Do you have a new tutor?"

"Something like that." The corner of my mouth twitched. I'd

learned quite a few things from Thera already, and I was intent on continuing my instruction.

My steps hastened, even as my heart sped in warning.

The sunset baked the library in decadent heat, the magic barrier that protected the spines from fading into a semi-transparent shimmer in the golden light that made me squint. The new head librarian bowed as I entered before shuffling off into the stacks—avoiding any direct contact with me, or with the elf sitting at the center table, her dark form silhouetted in amber.

One foot tucked up on her chair despite the way it bunched her black dress, Thera slouched over the table piled high with books and parchments, her hair wrapped up in a haphazard bun that sat like a makeshift crown atop her head. Shadows danced through her fidgety fingers, and she squinted at the text of the giant tome in front of her, her tongue poking out the side of her mouth as she focused.

My heart swelled and dipped, the sight so unexpectedly unrefined and wholesome at the same time.

Fortis, gratefully, stayed stationed at the door.

I walked forward, my strides just a tinge too long as excitement carried me on a swift wind. Yet she didn't even raise her head as I slid into the chair opposite her, so entirely absorbed in her reading. "How did I know you'd be here?"

She startled and offered a tight-lipped smile that wrinkled the dark bags decorating her under-eyes. "You're more clever than you let on."

My chest squeezed, and I shifted in my seat, suddenly unwelcome in my library. Thoughts spiraled through me as I scrambled for an explanation. Had our kiss offended her? Did she blame me for not being there when the prisoner had died, or for the arrow she took in my place? Did she simply not like me anymore, now that she'd seen more of how boring and incompetent I was?

I shoved the irrational musings back, fingers clenched tightly around the spine of my book. The characters in this one had fought their fears, had stood brave in the face of rejection, and so could I.

Aching as I severed myself from my lifeline, I pushed the novel across the table, the corner of it nudging some of her strewn parchments to the side. "Have you read this one? I was just coming to return it."

Eyes flicked back up to me, ice and emerald softening, but they still lacked their normal gemstone shine, a tiredness lining them in bloodshot red. She sighed, flopping against the back of her chair, shadows dissipating. "I haven't. Is it interesting?"

I grinned at the victory of her attention. "Remarkably so. Funny, too."

She reached for the book, slender fingers clasping around it as she examined the spine before gently setting it to the side. "I'll have to add it to the pile."

Her head dipped again as she resumed her reading, a not-so-subtle dismissal.

A new discomfort squirmed through me, sitting low in my middle. Though I hadn't known her long, this was a different king than the self-assured, skillful, *salacious* ruler I'd come to know. This woman wore her weariness like a cape across her shoulders, her desperation and disappointment both apparent through the bruised skin that clung too tightly to her cheeks, like she hadn't been eating.

Whether I was the culprit, something was *wrong*.

"You look tired." I leaned my elbows on the table, keeping my voice low. The other librarians had clearly given Thera a wide berth, but I didn't want anyone thinking her weak or compromised. I knew too well how that could damage a reputation. "What are you reading?"

Her gaze met mine again, but a darkness lingered in them this time, shadows blurring the edges of her colored irises despite the bright light still pouring into the sun-soaked room. She tilted the giant book upward to reveal the title. "Terribly written fiction."

I turned my head to read the spine. "History of the Great—" A laugh bubbled up from me. It was one Grotchkin had made me half-memorize before I'd departed from Stellaris. "I've read that one. It's a textbook, not a novel. No wonder you're not enjoying it."

Her breathy laughter joined mine, but it held no humor, harsh and shallow. "This is no more of a history than your smut." She shoved the book away, disgust curling her lips. "Are all the texts here this unchecked? Is this what your people *believe*?"

My brow furrowed. "Of course all historians have their different interpretations, but this one is the standard—"

Her finger slammed onto the page. "This is sycophantic drivel." Her voice dipped dangerously low. She yanked the book closer again, a sneer captivating her face.

"*Glorianna was hungry for power,*" she read aloud in disjointed Luxian. "*She betrayed the king by breeding with a lesser Elven-lord from the Inferni, a Shadow Demon named Dymitrius.*"

My stomach soured, my early dinner threatening to rise again.

I knew the passage well. Had read it a dozen times, thinking nothing of it, but to hear it in her voice, in the lilt of her Erebushi accent, to hear the rage and hurt that coated her tongue with each word. . .

Shame licked the back of my neck in a sheen of sweat, the warm room suddenly sweltering.

I looked down at the ink blotted page, unable to meet her stare. "Perhaps the author is a bit critical in their account of the events."

She scoffed. "*Already pregnant with the first half-breed,*" she continued reading, letting her rage carry her voice on an echo through the open space, "*her mind was lost to the shadows, and she would not return to the Stellaris Palace without turning to ash. So using a vast amount of Zo'is, Alixsander sealed the portal to the shadowlands, casting her and the other lesser-elves into the darkness where they belong, protecting his chosen people.*"

The book slammed shut again, booming like a gunshot through my middle. A long stretch of silence pulled taut.

"Is that what I am as Glorianna's direct descendant, Caelum? A half-breed demon? A *lesser elf*?" Each syllable Thera spoke, another wound through me.

I hated how my name sounded like a curse in her mouth. If anyone here was lesser, it was me. I wriggled in my seat, as I used to when Grotchkin would lecture me, my inadequacy my ruin yet again. "The language is harsh and outdated, I will give you that."

"It's *incorrect*." Thera's gaze burned against the crown of my head.

I dared a look up at her again to see the shadows had fully shifted her eyes to black. My throat worked, words lost on me. I didn't know what to think, what to say. . .

"Glorianna was one of the sharpest minds in history—a strategist, a warrior, an innovator. She ran from Alixsander's possessive, cruel nature, and when he wouldn't accept no for an answer, he cast his revenge on thousands of *innocent* elves for the simple crime of being her people."

She spoke with such belief, such conviction, that I wanted to nod in agreement. Wanted to rub away the furrow between her brows, to chase the shadows that'd stolen her mismatched stare from me.

But my head snagged on one of the thorny words, unable to see past it.

Innocent.

There were no innocents in war. Not when Glorianna's followers killed thousands of my people for generations. Not when they were the reason Luxian children were afraid of what lurked in the dark.

Not when the Shadowborne existed *because* of them, stealing the souls of good elves like Quintin and Julius' sisters and so many others.

I fought to keep my voice steady. "I'm sure she believed that, but you know what shadow magic can do to elves, otherwise the Shadowborne would not—"

"Do not lecture me about shadow magic, *Prince*." The room tinged darker as the shadows bled from the corners, fighting the dying sunlight. "You haven't the *faintest* idea of what it can do."

My tongue went dry as dread pooled low in my gut, my jaw clenched. From the corner of my eye, I saw Julius grab the hilt of his sword as the air in the room cooled, like Thera had devoured all the heat like she did souls.

I met her ironclad stare, and for the first time since we'd become acquainted . . .

I saw the *Sykagos*.

Saw the weapon, not the king. Saw the monster from every Luxian nightmare.

I swallowed down the lump of fear, forcing myself to sit straighter. "Is that a threat, King Thera?"

At her name, she blinked, shadows clearing slightly. Her mouth flattened into a line, and her shoulders dipped, the room warming again as tension uncoiled from her frame. But her gaze didn't drop from mine. The blue-and-green bled back into it, like storm clouds clearing from a sky-covered meadow. "It's a *truth*, Caelum. One that everyone in this castle has protected you from for far too long."

Shock erased any fear or shame that'd lingered in my veins, a lightning strike of hope spreading instead.

Protected. That was the word for it, the way everyone had sheltered me. My father, Rory, the staff—they all loved me, that was certain. But none of them trusted me. *Believed* in me. So instead, they hid me from the world, locked the doors and stood sentry in front of them so I'd never get hurt—or learn to protect myself.

All but one.

One person who'd taught me to walk through worlds. One person who'd encouraged my mind to explore even when my feet could not.

One person who loved the shade.

"Not everyone," I admitted aloud, my mind drifting to locked doors I'd protected *myself* from for far too long. But if I were to be

243

king one day, if I was ever to be worthy enough to rule at Thera's impressive side. . . perhaps she would journey into that unknown with me. "There are other books that might offer a more. . . balanced perspective."

Thera stilled, scanning my face as her hands fell to her lap, her own defenses lowering as mine did. "Where?"

I sighed, watching the last rays of the sun dip behind the glittering city. It was time for me to face the dark. "My mother's rooms."

Stepping into my mother's drawing room felt like stepping back in time.

In the decade since she'd passed, nothing had been moved or touched—the furniture remained arranged to her liking, a teacup still sitting on the mahogany table next to her favorite emerald-velvet chair, her reading glasses still strewn atop a well-loved book on matching ottoman. Half-melted candlesticks decorated the mantle of the deep fireplace where logs waited to be lit, both evidence of the long hours spent cozied up here, my favorite blanket still hanging over the arm of the plush couch opposite Mama's chair.

I rested a hand on the wall to steady myself against the peeling teal paint, breathing in the musty air to slow my thundering heart as a wave of sorrow slammed into my middle.

This never hurt any less, no matter how much time had dragged on. It's why none of us could bear to be in here to clean the place out; my mother's treasures entombed with the memories of her etched into this room.

Thera stepped in, leaving Julius to stand watch outside the door. She took in the space, a finger swiping across the dust-covered mantle as she stared out the wide, circular window, the dusky sky casting her in a pink and purple glow. "This place is—"

"Dusty?" The joke fell flat, the air in here too thin for it to soar.

Thera turned, eyes brimming with an understanding that knocked me even more off-center.

"*Cozy*. Your mother had good taste." She smiled at me—a real one, this time—before spotting the wall of bookshelves on the far side. She took in the countless romance covers with a pointed look, brows raising. Then, long strides devoured the room as she ran her finger across the titles, picking one—*A Midnight Affair*—from the shelf. "In books too—*oh*."

The book fell out of its protective cover as she caught it, revealing the truth hidden beneath the dust jacket.

A Comprehensive Guide to the Medicinal Purposes of Zo'is.

Thera's head snapped up to me as she processed my mother's clever trick.

I breathed deeply, letting the stale air sink into my lungs. I needed to do this, for Thera, and for myself. If we were to trust each other, to rule together, I had to stop hiding from hard realities. Had to *question* things if I would make this right. "Before she passed, my mother told me this library holds all the knowledge I would need to be an excellent king one day, and not to tell anyone her secret."

Thera gently replaced the dust jacket and restocked the book to its home. "And you haven't?"

"Not a soul."

It was a memory I'd kept tucked away in the most private corners of my heart, not even sharing with my father, selfish as it was. He'd been devastated after her death, but I wanted something that was just mine. Wanted *her*, in whatever capacity I could keep her. Though even in death, I'd let her down, my avoidance a wall between us. "But I haven't read any of it, either. It's been too . . ."

Painful didn't feel like a big enough word, so I didn't say it. I just let the hollow silence that followed speak for itself. Speak for the vacant, abandoned parts of me that had been carved out when I'd lost her.

Thera crossed to me slowly, skirts floating over the hardwood like they too were being careful not to disturb any of the remnants of my mother's spirit. She twisted the ring on her finger; the silver glinting in the twilight.

"My mother was a warrior, but she was kind." Her voice was far away as she slipped the jewelry off. She stared at the silver for a long moment before reaching for my hand, pressing the warm metal into my palm. "This was hers. It brings me strength."

"I can't—" I tried to hand it back, but she closed my fingers around the trinket, her hands soft as they clasped mine.

"You'll need it if we're going to read these." She gestured with her chin to the teeming bookcases, giving my closed hand one last squeeze before letting go. "Consider it an early wedding gift."

And a gift it was, more intimate and special than any I'd ever received. My throat closed around half-formed words, my gratitude choking me as I slipped the ring around my pinky.

I'd never been strong, not of body or will. But if Thera believed I could be, if she would share some of her unending stability with me, then I'd give her everything I had in return.

So I let her comb through my mother's books, her most sacred belongings, watching from my favorite couch as she gingerly removed each dust jacket to reveal the invaluable titles beneath. Titles written in Luxian *and* Erebushi, even a few in Old Elysian.

A Discovery of Shadowborne Behavior.

The Mechanics of Flight.

Ancient Elven Cultures of the Elysian Empire.

This collection had been my mother's life's work, and finally, it was clear why. Information made men into excellent kings, and these texts were all written by the experts and scientists with enough knowledge to better all of Lux. And they weren't just about my home, either. This selection was far more diverse, even though there was less to choose from. Some titles favored our Dark Sister, books that likely would be banned if Alixsandrites like Grotchkin ever got a whiff of them.

The Plight of Erebus.

Survival in Inferni: A Terrifying Guide.

The Gloriannic Principles of the Female Warrior.

I doubted any of these texts tried to paint either side as the 'lesser-elves' or 'half-breeds.' Shame crept along my spine again even as I tried to make it right; embarrassment over how my privilege and inexperience had blinded me to such blatant affronts.

"This one is interesting," Thera spoke after picking up a book from the third shelf and flipping through its contents, this one thinner than some others, its true face bound in a blank, unassuming leather. "My Old Elysian is terrible, but I *think* it's a personal account of the Great War from a Luxian soldier undercover."

Though I'd been hesitant to read any of them myself yet—I sat forward.

"Can I see?" I extended my hand, and she graciously placed the book in it. I scanned the contents, the words in a hurried script hard to make out, but the name signed to each of the entries was unnervingly familiar. "*Arturus*—that's my middle name."

Thera tilted her head, studying me for a moment before turning again to the bookstacks. "It suits you. We should start here, then. But it will take me forever to translate."

I shrugged. "I can do it."

"You read Old Elysian?"

"I can even speak it," I said.

I closed the journal, afraid that its secrets might jump out and bite me. I'd need more strength before I was brave enough to dive in, a disquiet rolling through me that screamed warnings I wasn't ready yet to hear.

Instead, I watched Thera, her effortless grace, her wide, curious look as she courageously sifted through each book, amassing a small to-be-read pile for herself, unafraid of the world or the knowledge she might find.

"What's yours?" I asked, consumed by a need to know *more.* If there was anything in this room that had the power to make kings, it was her.

She turned, brushing a strand of hair that'd fallen from her messy knot out of her face. "Hmm?"

"Your middle name?"

Her head lowered, and she turned the book she had in her hands over, like the answer to my question might be inscribed there.

"Dymitria," she answered after a breath, and when she looked back up, a mist lined her gaze that made my chest squeeze. "My mother picked it. She hated that I was named after my father, so she called me Dymi instead."

I nodded, an understanding resonating in my heartbeat. Here we were, the inheritors of our father's crowns, both holding secret legacies from our forgotten mothers. Both grieving their absence in quiet ways.

Both trying to improve our kingdoms in their honor.

"Dymi," I repeated, caressing the name with the reverence it deserved.

I stood from my perch on the couch. It was time I stopped sitting around, time I stopped hiding and started doing. For my mother's namesake, and for the king who reminded me of all her good parts. The king that deserved a partner who didn't just accept the distorted narrative he was fed, but who wrote his own. "Tell me more of what I should know, *Dymi*."

A purr escaped her. "What would you *like* to know?"

I hedged closer to her, clinging to her like the shadows that swirled around her ankles. Shadows that never left—but never overtook her, either. Shadows that always drew the line between *Sykagos* and King. "Before, you said I didn't know what the shadows could do."

Thera stilled. "Secrets are currency in this world, Caelum." She looked down at the book in her hands, her gaze shuttered. "And some of them are more valuable than others."

Disappointment flickered through me, but I wouldn't give up so easily today. Not when I'd already trekked so far into uncomfortable territory. I stared at the book, too. *Essays from the Warfront* by Petris Velares, a known Erebushi sympathizer. My voice found its footing. "I know. You're holding my greatest, most vulnerable secrets in your hands. I'd feel less vulnerable if you were clutching my balls."

Mismatched eyes flicked up at me—humor returning to their bright hues. A wicked grin cracked her face. "That could be arranged."

"Tempting." I chuckled, heat pooling low, but I fought the urge to succumb to its delicious draw. "But you're deflecting."

"Fine, you make a strong point." She sighed, resting the book back on its shelf. Then, a long pause, as she chose her words carefully. "Do you know how *Zo'is* works?"

"Yes, intimately," I said, but stopped. Maybe I was a hypocrite, but I didn't need Thera knowing all my weaknesses today. I cleared my throat, mimicking Grotckin's flat tone as I recited the same answer I'd given her just a few weeks ago, memorized perfectly from a textbook. "*Zo'is* is a compound that seeks to bond with other compounds, and takes on the nature of said thing. Alone, it is useless. It needs an energy source to work. For example, the powder is nothing, but add fire to it, and it can be a light, it can fuel engines. Mix it with blood and the electrical impulses of the body, and it can speed up cell repair and bind with that body. It adapts to the energy source."

"Very good, *My Prince*." Thera's shoulders eased. "Water alone is stable. Steady. Add heat, energy, it boils. It becomes lively. Cool it down, take away energy, it becomes hard. Strong. *Zo'is* is similar. It amplifies and strengthens, depending on what is applied to it."

I nodded, understanding the mechanics. "Does shadow magic do the same? Does it take on the darkness of a person's mind?"

Thera breathed deeply, like she was trying to store the air she needed, trying to let it quell whatever rose inside her.

"No," she said finally, the mirth and flirtatiousness gone from her voice. Instead, it was empty, passionless, like she'd hollowed herself out to make room for what she had to share. "The shadows *are* energy, already existing. They seek a host and demand the body to adapt to *them*. That's how Shadowborne happen. To control the shadows, a person needs to be completely grounded. *Disciplined.* One must contain the energy, not ignite it. But it is a very difficult task."

My eyes tore to the shadows that dwelled around the room, my blood running cold. Thera's hands shook; like she, too, was uncomfortably aware of every dark spot in the shaded library.

Spots that seemed to *breathe*. Spots that waited, just like Thera had said, for a willing host to devour.

My throat dried, and I allowed myself one last cowardly act. I grabbed Arturus' journal again, the weight of it somehow grounding me back to the room—back to the light. "Well, this won't read itself. I'll let you know if there is any king-worthy information in it."

Thera stepped closer. The tension in her frame melted with each deep breath, her gaze clearing, and the shadows slinking back to their corners. Her hand pressed over my heart.

"It seems your mother had good taste in that, too. She could see king-stuff even where others couldn't."

I covered her hand with mine, her mother's ring on my littlest finger, as I hoped with all my might she wasn't wrong.

Stellaris had always been my home, but it had also been my cage.

And I was ready to break free.

CHAPTER
EIGHTEEN

"I am not cruel. I am protective. One day, you will see. So will she."
—Excerpt from a letter from King Theron Umbrus of Erebus to General Danae, circa 2078 A.G.W.

THERA

My father used to say the art of shadow magic was the art of control. *Discipline.*

A platitude he blared into my head during every lesson, a scar he carved into my skin during every torturous tutoring session.

Shadows were not wicked, but wild. Untamed, and in their chaos, gave way to the mayhem within. To manage the shadows, one had to have total control over their own inherent disarray. Our emotions; pain, fear, sadness. Our desires; hunger, sex, power. Those uncontrolled urges and reactions were the chaos the shadows thrived on, what they *exploited*; and what paved the path to madness.

It was why he'd never relented—never offered mercy. If I was to control the *Skia*, I had to withstand whatever external chaos he— or the world—threw at me. Had to breathe through it and clear my mind, even when my body ached. Even when my thoughts and emotions betrayed me.

By the time I turned fifteen, I'd mastered the craft. Better than my father ever had. I'd learned not just to suppress my internal madness, but to cultivate it. To track it, like a tiger stalking its prey. To *wield* it, not to make it something other than it was, but to know how to manipulate it to my will.

And like all men desperate for control and discipline, my father had both adored me and hated me for it. I was his weapon—his dark sword set to cleave through the portal and reclaim Lux in his name. But I was also his rival, the only elf to surpass his knowledge and talent, mastering myself more than he could ever dominate and command me.

All he had, I had given him. All he wanted, I had access to.

All he was afraid to lose, I could take from him.

Everyone in Erebus knew it. And now Lux did, too.

It made me both powerful and powerless at the same time.

Taming shadow magic was an easier task than earning friends. The shadows were maddening, but they were pure. Singular intent pulsed through their every fiber, as they didn't seek to hide their true nature, but let it run amok. Whenever I bathed in the dark depths of the Pool of Souls, I'd felt clear. *Clean,* at peace with the whirlwind within.

But the farther I strayed from Erebus, the longer I went without the pools' reaffirming guide, the less clarity I had.

Blinded by the Luxian light, it was hard to tell who my friends were. And if I was to hold on to the control of both myself and of my kingdom, I needed allies. Friends. But elves didn't wear their true darkness on their sleeves like the shadows did. Did not speak of desires and fears with no regret or remorse. No, agendas in Lux hid. They were complex, layered in the distracting, disorienting sparkle that cast mirrored illusions on every interaction.

More of the endless, tedious daylight seeped through the window into my shabby drawing room as I lounged in a deep armchair, reading a book Caelum had lent me from his mother's collection, trying to decipher if I'd been saved by the prince or duped by him.

A slight breeze at the nape of my neck alerted me to Nyxia's arrival—one friend I never had to doubt—tugging me from my thoughts. I didn't bother to lift my head from my book and offered her a wave. "You've been busy."

She slid into the empty chair, her dark hair windswept and her cheeks pink from the sun, still unaccustomed to its unrelenting burn. Still, she sported a grin, a sign of better fortune than we'd been having in the last few days. "I've been hunting."

I let my book fall open in my lap, taking a sip of the already cold tea I'd forgotten. "What did you catch?"

Nyxia crossed her legs and stole part of my abandoned break-fast—a half-eaten buttered biscuit likely as stale as an old shoe at this point. She stuck it in her mouth anyway, chewing as she leveled her report. "I've made some friends among the staff. Most of them are like the others. Afraid. But the scullery maids, laun-dresses, some gardeners—they'll talk."

Despite my exhaustion, the corner of my mouth twitched. "And what do they say?"

Nyxia brushed the sprinkling of crumbs from her tunic and licked the buttery remnants from her thumb before responding, looking fully satiated. "The King fades. Bit by bit. And the people in the outer city do not fare well despite all the resources. There is a distribution problem."

Though I'd barely eaten, my belly felt full, too.

We'd suspected as much, our early reconnaissance suggesting King Kato's wavering strength and the crowded lack that suffocated the outer city under itself were both weaknesses to press. But it was something more to know that the public talked about it, too. A voiced need going unheard, a chaos brewing against the light, giving me the opportunity to lend an ear and gain some traction.

We'd still need support among the nobility—an entirely different challenge—but for the first time since arriving, hope bloomed in my chest. We were making headway.

"Good work, Nyxia."

She shrugged off my praise, a predator still on the hunt for more. "Have you found anything?"

Another victory clanged through my chest, clearing out my lingering doubt and dismay. "Yes, actually. Caelum, of all people, has been exceedingly helpful." I stretched one of his mother's books toward her, still open to the page I'd been reading. "Read this."

Nyxia held the text close, her brows knotting at the center. "'*Zo'is* is a remarkable energy source for the body, but too much of it in too high a dose can cause long-term side effects on the psyche and an elf's ability to heal naturally. The substance can be habit-forming, and with dependency comes a list of other comorbidities.'" She dropped the book back onto the table, sighing and slumping back in the chair. "Dumb it down, please. I always skipped science lessons."

I stifled a laugh. I might've mastered the art of taming shadows, but Nyxia *was* one, unbridled in her desire. No point commanding her to deny herself. Though I'd never voiced it, I always had wondered if she might be part *diavolos*.

"The more people use *Zo'is*, the more addicted they may become, and the less effective it is."

Nyxia straightened. "So you think—"

A shadow danced through my fingertips as I voiced the dark theory aloud. "I think the King is looking for other sources of magic. *Zo'is* isn't working anymore. It's not keeping Kato young, and it seems that the Prince's strange tea isn't managing his symptoms as much, either."

And if I had to make an educated guess, based on the hungry look King Kato had given me in the throne room a few days prior, he had a very specific, very taboo source in mind to help secure their line.

My shadows curled tighter around me, a protective layer against my anxiety. I didn't want to think about what his chaos might look like, that man's desire and darkness, a stench that hung around him despite all the gilded, flowery affects he dressed himself in.

And I didn't want to dwell on the truth I'd already parted with. The secrets that I'd given Caelum . . . secrets he might *use*, if he thought like his father did.

Nyxia sucked at her bottom lip, an apprehension steeling her expression. "What of the nobles? Any potential allies?"

She must've pieced it together, too. I grimaced, my shoulders tensing. None of the nobility had even attempted to have a direct conversation with me yet, though their curiosity seemed to win against their fear finally, their looks lingering longer when I passed them. But I hadn't made myself approachable, either, and given what lies their history books contained, I had doubted if such a thing was possible among the indoctrinated.

Controlling my darkness was easier than trying to control a narrative.

Then again, there were those in the palace already willing to change their minds. Willing to hear, to learn, and to teach.

"Caelum is my only ally in the castle as of now, but I hope to use that to my advantage," I reassured both Nyxia and myself. A king was nothing if not resourceful, and I could challenge my mettle soon enough. "I have a meeting with Kato at the end of the week to discuss wedding plans. I'll look for others before then. How are you and Kappas doing in the search for the traitor?"

Her bottom lip jutted out. "Kappas and I have very different strategies, *Mi Vassilla.*"

I pinched the bridge of my nose; the ache there ever-present as of late. Kappas hadn't been acting up as I'd expected him to. So far, he hadn't started any unsanctioned fights, and his surly demeanor had actually been a boon of protection whenever he traveled with us, discouraging naysayers from voicing their complaints aloud with his eviscerating scowl. But while he preferred direct, clear plans and lines of attacks, Nyxia was far more used to her subversive, subtle methods of information gathering, and the two hadn't stopped bickering all week.

And despite how well their talents complemented each other, and how desperately I needed their support, I was at the precipice of my patience, and had considered simply shipping them both back to Erebus for some peace.

"Work with him. We have no room for dissent among our ranks, and I can't have him making a mess." The plea veiled itself as a halfhearted command. Kappas had been my father's favorite war dog, and I didn't want to see what happened if we let him off his leash. His complacency unnerved me. I still hadn't ruled out that he'd plotted against me the whole time.

My authority slipped the longer I was away from the shadows of my homeland—another problem I tried to manage. "Speaking of, do you have a letter for me?"

I hadn't heard from Stavros since arriving at Stellaris, and I had never been more desperate for some of his cool, gentle guidance.

"Two, actually." Nyxia slipped small envelopes from her breast pocket, and relief pooled low in my gut as she handed them my way, the thin sheets of parchment breathing new life into my veins. "Arrived this morning from one of my messengers."

Plain wax sealed the first envelope, but given the stain of what looked to be *blood* on the corner, I assumed it was from Agyros. My eyes rolled on their own command, knowing the Minister of Medicine had probably tucked vital information between his scribblings of annoying affection, and I'd have to read the whole thing to fully grasp the situation at home.

But as I ran my finger over the seal on the second envelope—Stavros' seal—I had to blink away a surprising surge of tears, my frustration and exhaustion melting. I cleared the lump from my throat. "Thank you, Nyxia."

Nyxia said nothing, thank the moon and mist. She just stood, patting me on the shoulder before heading to the door, giving me privacy I hadn't asked for, but desperately needed. "I'll see you for dinner."

I waited until she was out the door before I tore into Stavros' letter first.

The first line brought tears to my eyes.

Erebus without you is like night without darkness.

I blinked to dispel the moisture, my heart just as empty without my dear friend at my side, but his words fed something in me I hadn't realized had been so famished until now.

I hope you're faring well in the land above, Mi Vassilla. I hear from Nyxia that the food is divine, and I hope you'll render me with an account of all that you've been eating. You have been eating, yes? You've always been a slip of a thing, and you can't afford to skip meals if you're going to remain vigilant. Breakfast keeps the brain alert, and I wager you need all your senses.

I looked at the rest of my uneaten food, and begrudgingly took a bite of the now cold, pasty oatmeal that I'd let sit too long. As if Stavros could see me here and would frown like an old bulldog if I didn't oblige him.

I kept swallowing down the mush and read on.

The council continues our work with little interruption. Hasapis

*finally showed the ledgers your father left, and while the coffers
are abysmally managed with so much of the wealth poured out
into your father's obsession with the military, the situation is not
as dire as we'd assumed.*

A breath loosed out of me. *Good.* We'd hoped to not look too desperate too fast, not wanting Lux to see us as the needier party in this arrangement before we could truly find our footing. So, while Erebus did not have time to waste, we could ration longer. My people were survivors, and they would hold out. We would prevail.

*As for the Shadowborne, they've been quiet. Deceptively so. Of
course, rumors have sparked up in their place, nearly as vicious,
but nothing I cannot handle on my own. I will quell them before
your return.*

That line itched beneath my skin like a rash. If Stavros kept the rumors from me, they had to be vicious. Knowing my people—respected as I was—there was probably speculation that the Shadowborne left when I did. No matter how much I'd done to build my people up, they were not immune to fear, and the unknown elicited terror from even the bravest hearts.

And I was an unknown, an *other*, even by Erebushi standards.

*My only concern, as of now, is you. Your health and your mind. I
know you to be both strong and capable, so perhaps I'm just an
old man worrying for no other reason than it suits my wrinkles.
But I do hope you're being careful.
And selfishly, I hope your business above does not linger a
moment longer than it has to.
Erebus needs you. And I, your faithful servant, do too.*

I folded the letter again—carefully, desperate not to forge any unnecessary creases, and tucked it back into the envelope, setting it on the table. I'd come back to it again later. Not because I'd glean any more useful information, the letter purposefully short and vague just in case it had been intercepted, but because I needed a reminder more than ever of what I was doing here. What I hoped to achieve.

The friends that relied on me to see it through.

Sighing, I moved on to Agyros' letter, hoping it would bring me more news I could use to do just that.

I dreamt of you last night. Your mouth on my—

It took all my strength not to tear it up and throw it in the hearth, forcing myself to read through the poorly written smut, to further down the page to where Agyros bothered to include the useful message.

If we could get an advance on Zo'is, that would help our work here. The quicker we can start healing those already malnourished and weak, the faster we can begin the rebuilding project. I wonder if perhaps your fiancé would offer such a generous wedding gift early?

I bit my lip hard enough to draw blood, frustration curling my shadows around my fingers, the blackness surging across the page and blotting out the ink.

Agyros was supposed to be making do with what he had and giving me information about the status of it all, not begging for scraps from the Luxians. And if I asked Caelum or Kato for the supplies now, if I showed my hand . . .

Caelum might be generous, but it would reveal more than I wanted to give his father. And whether Caelum would offer me information and companionship as he had, there was no way he'd approve resources sent across the portal without Kato's signature.

259

I schooled my breathing and my heart rate back to a reasonable pace.

I couldn't ask for what I needed.

But that didn't mean I couldn't get it *offered.*

Throwing Agyros' letter into the dying fire, I stood, setting Caelum's book to the side and readying myself for the next challenge.

Shadowcraft was the art of discipline, but politics were the art of deceit. Deadly games of give and take, of hide and seek.

And unfortunately for the Luxian nobility, I was talented at both.

The way the crowd parted for me whenever I entered the throne room brought me an inkling of satisfaction. Courtiers lingered there all hours of the endless day, and, as they normally did, they scurried out of my way. I didn't show any emotion stalking toward my target, waiting just where he said he'd be.

It was Caelum's day to sit in court, and I had to admit, he looked good doing it.

Long legs crossed as he sat on the throne, his crown ever so slightly askew atop his white hair, styled down so the soft strands brushed his cheek. And to my surprise and delight, he wore a darker hue than normal—the color reminiscent of the deep purple of twilight—that made his violet-blue eyes pop even more against his deep bronze skin.

His smile captivated his face, gaze dragging over my tight pants and cinched off-the-shoulder tunic. He ignored the man talking at his side completely.

A frown overtook the noble's face as he looked between Caelum and I. He was a tall, slim man, his reddish-brown hair pulled into a slick bun at the nape of his neck. But despite his put-together appearance, wild freckles spattered over his nose, like the stars had accidentally dripped all over him when they'd painted his coloring. An abstract, natural contradiction to the sculpted, gilded order of the rest of Stellaris.

I liked him already.

"Good morning, My Prince." I offered my betrothed a genuine smile despite the way dozens of eyes burned at my back.

One scalding gaze was missing, I noted despite myself. Fortis stood watch among the other guards, but Captain Bellatore was suspiciously absent again.

Both my disappointment and relief surprised me in equal parts.

"King Thera." Caelum's voice hitched over my name. He stood, hopping off the dais in a smooth leap and met me, face to face. A hand brushed against mine, the affection clearing away any of my doubt. "You look well."

I fit my fingers between his before jerking my head to the unnamed noble who still watched us with *interest* instead of disgust. "Who is your friend?"

Caelum turned to introduce him, but the noble wasted no time and cleared his throat.

"Minister Florian Pollux, public relations." He bowed, though his jade eyes met mine—unafraid and unwavering. "It's an honor to officially make your acquaintance. I was saddened when you didn't dine with us on your first day in Lux."

Recognition stirred—this had been the odd-noble-out when I'd first arrived, the only elf with the stones to say anything.

Oh, I *definitely* liked him. Even more so, as he was a potential ally in my court-of-public-opinion problem. "The honor is mine."

Undeterred by niceties, Florian clasped his hands behind his back, his smile genial. "Perhaps I could request an audience with you soon? King Kato has been very busy, and I have many concerns about life in the outer city—"

"I'm sure we'll get to it, Pollux." Caelum's mouth pressed into a tight line and shoulders squared; the first time he ever looked like his father.

I squeezed his arm—to soothe, and to apologize for what I was about to do. For the game of politics I had to play.

"Why don't you meet Prince Caelum and I for dinner at some point this week?" I tilted my head at the Minister, purposefully dragging my gaze over him slowly—critically, as if I sought both his merits and his faults. "I would love to assist you as best we can, or at the very least take your concerns to the King if *necessary*."

It was a careful offer. The promise of potential camaraderie, but not without scrutiny. An allyship that favored him on the surface but bought me something priceless.

Friendship. *Numbers.*

The man's wry smile indicated he knew exactly the pitch I delivered, but he did not balk; perhaps just as in need of powerful companions as I was. He bowed again, deeper this time. "Thank you, Your Majesty. I look forward to it."

"No, thank *you*, Minister."

"Call me Florian." He took my hand, pressing a kiss to my knuckles, before dipping his chin. "Good day to you both."

It was a treat to watch him walk away, re-assimilating into the throngs of courtiers, even as my fiancé crossed his arms. "What was that?"

"Progress." I smiled before sauntering back out of the throne room, enjoying the branding looks from the other courtiers, all of them shifting uncomfortably as they had to reconsider their positions.

I could almost smell their churning thoughts.

Is the Sykagos in with the King? Had power already begun shifting to the prince? Should we seek an audience?

One bold courtier—a lady in a tacky pink gown—was brave enough to step in my way, falling into a deep courtesy. "G-good afternoon, Your Maj—"

I didn't break my stride and swept around her, dismissing her entirely.

Letting the nobles know that my favor had to be *earned.*

I enjoyed the flurry of whispers that followed me out of the throne room.

"Hey, clue me in next time," Caelum panted as he caught up with me. His mouth tugged into a frown as he shot Florian a glare over his shoulder. "I looked stupid."

I slowed, giving him an inch of grace. "Get used to setting your own rules, Caelum." I tucked my hand into his again in a truce—I wouldn't coddle him, but I would be by his side as he found his stride. And that was about to start with an Erebushi version of a wedding gift. "Come with me?"

Caelum paused just outside of the doors, brows wrinkling. "Where are we going?"

I reached up and smoothed away the crease with my pointer finger, and Caelum shivered beneath my touch, the divot disappearing.

"You'll see." I winked before tugging him along toward the front doors of the castle.

Our destination was a bit of a hike, around the front of the massive castle and down a slight hill to the servants' houses and soldiers' barracks. We passed guards and house staff alike, gaping at us as if they'd never seen the nobility tread this way before. But luckily for me, Nyxia had scoped the path last night and found exactly what I'd looked for.

The sun had worn down the rock of the small, stadium-like building with its loving embrace, giving the faded white stone a softer sort of beauty that I appreciated. In the center, a flat, round expanse of sand filled the space, red chalked lines delineating different zones for different approaches, mimicking the blood and sweat that poured from the colosseum's victims and victors day in and day out.

Today—thanks to a little manipulation on my part and a letter to Commander Tiberius about a supposedly 'very important structural inspection'—this pitch was delightfully empty.

Caelum stood at the threshold in his fine clothes, kicking the edge of the sand. The furrow in his brows returned, and his face already red from the walk. "This is a fighting pitch."

"Yes. Very astute observation."

"What are *we* doing in a fighting pitch?"

I shrugged, kicking off my shoes and stepping onto the hot sand, letting it filter through my toes. "Well, I thought we'd fight."

Caelum gaped, still stuck at the threshold's shadows. "Together?"

"No more hiding or protecting." I curled a beckoning finger before squaring my shoulders. "If none of the others will train you, I will. Do you have any experience?"

He took a step in—hesitant. *Nervous.* But then he puffed out his chest, feigning confidence. "Rory has taught me basic self-defense over the years."

He titled his chin up, like that was a badge of honor.

With a coy smile, I circled him slowly, my eyes dragging over his every inch like I savored the view—which, admittedly, I did.

He favored his left side, based on the pronation of his right foot, yet his right hand was dominant, given that it grasped his left wrist as he clasped them both behind his back. His circulation was poor as a result of his illness, but his core was stronger than I'd expected, but—

There it was.

I stopped when I faced him again, my smile growing. "Excellent. Let's begin."

"Now? I—ah!" Caelum had no time to react as I struck at his open spot—a quick tap to the back of his right knee that had him toppling to the ground.

I grinned. "Let's try again."

He glowered and brushed the sand off of his fancy trousers, tears pricking in his eyes. "I wasn't ready."

I stepped in again, a breath from his face, and inhaled. His weakness invaded my senses, but also the willpower that burned beneath the frail exterior. "No, you're not ready. And a good opponent will take advantage of that."

It was not a taunt, nor a prod at his ego.

It was a *gift*. A lesson of survival and control that was bred into Erebushi stock the Prince would need. A gift from a land that had no resources, but still lived on will and resolve alone. Where sickness was not rare, but the norm; where most bodies were underfed and malnourished, but still strong in their resilience.

A land he would one day rule with me, along with this shimmering empire.

This time, when I jabbed him in the right ribcage, Caelum didn't deflect—but he *did* brace himself enough not to stumble, even as I knocked the wind from him.

I paced back, dropping into a ready stance.

"Better." I cocked my head. "But not quite."

To my delight, Caelum quickly unbuttoned his shiny tunic, bronze skin peeking from beneath, and threw it to the sand. There was a softness to his torso, a pretty, untouched canvas novel to scars, but a slight sheen of muscle lived beneath. His skin already flushed, his heartbeat fluttering in the vein on his neck, but he mimicked my stance, flexing his abs and raising his arms ready.

I nodded appreciatively—at both his beauty and his grit—and began again.

Caelum was ready, and lasted a good three attacks before I snatched his arm mid-strike, then used his body weight to flip him over my shoulder.

He hit the sand with an unforgiving thud.

But life was unforgiving. The world. His court. None would give him quarter or rest.

"Ow." He groaned and rolled on the ground, squinting at the sun as he coughed.

I offered a hand. "Calling it quits?"

He slapped it away and hopped up, spitting onto the sand as sweat kissed his skin. "No. Never."

"Good boy," I cooed and surged again.

This time, he blocked me, snagging my wrist. He leaned in. "I'm not a boy."

Heat—not entirely from the afternoon's rays—dipped to my lowest regions.

A quick swivel, and I had his arm behind his back. He grunted, and I twisted the limb at a slightly uncomfortable angle—but not sharply enough to damage. I whispered against the shell of his ear, "Good *prince,* then?"

I wasn't expecting the kick to my shin, and it sent me staggering back, dropping his arm.

"You will see me as a man one day, *Dymi.*" His voice was a low, quiet purr between pants. He readied himself again, his soft mouth pressing into a promising grin. "I swear it."

Something about my name—my *true* name—on his lips sent a shiver of desire down my spine.

But flirtations wouldn't distract me. I had mastered my wants ages ago.

His muscles moved, his ribs expanding and shuddering with each drag of air; his left leg shaking as he favored his right, the sweat now running a stream down his chest.

He was hurting.

Weakened, all the King's 'protective measures' keeping him compliant and impotent.

But there, in the glimmer of his blue eyes in the bright sun, I could see it.

Caelum Boreallis had the makings of a king. He just needed someone to see him. To *show* him.

He had given me his mother's knowledge. I would teach him what my father taught me.

"*Very* good." I sucked in a breath, vanishing the pain in my leg with a thought, and winked at my fiancé. "Again."

I was on him in a moment, straddling his torso, relishing the movement of his chest rising and falling beneath me. Breathless, his hands clasped my thighs, and he stared back, eyes blown wide with desire.

But one lesson of my father's, that I'd perhaps forgotten, was to never assume you had the upper hand. To always expect the unexpected.

Maybe, if I'd kept both eyes open and hadn't been so intent on seeing *him*, I would've noticed Captain Bellatore barreling toward me before she slammed into me, pounding me into the sand.

"Don't you fucking touch him."

CHAPTER
NINETEEN

"I've spilled the blood of so many elves, a chicken's life should mean nothing to me. But if I cannot ration my damnation, I can at least inhibit my diet." —From Thera Dymitria's personal journal, circa 2100 A.G.W.

RORY

Erebus is cold tonight. Not in the absence of light, though that
chill never flees.
But in the absence of mirth. Of hope.
Hungry bellies and scattered hearts are much harder to warm.
The guard passed out blankets and coats today—the last of our
stores—but I doubt it will chase the frost from people's expressions.
They wait for something to happen. For someone to do
something.

It will have to be me.
I hate it.
They don't know how cold the shadows can be. How the pool
bites my skin to raw. But I'm numb to it now, impervious to the
everlasting chill.
I don't know what that makes me. Am I a survivor? Or am I built
wrong? Am I—

Thera's journal snapped shut, and my throat closed over misplaced emotion.

The woman I met in these pages couldn't be the same swaggering, salacious elf that prowled the halls of Stellaris. Couldn't be the *Sykagos* that tore through battlefields of men like they were soft clay. There was no way to rationalize one with the other, no way to assume both could even exist in the same *world*, never mind the same body.

The woman in Thera's journal was so *lonely*.

She wrote of many things; the margins of her journal bursting with scribbled, chaotic thoughts like these. Of the cold and dark, and of her favorite recipe for something called *tofu* stew. Of ingenious ideas for irrigation and crop rotations, and of the medicinal properties of herbs that somehow grew with no light.

She wrote of her fears that wrenched her from sleep, the nightmares of a creature she referred to as the *Katka*—the *evil*—that ripped her to shreds. Her daydreams and desires, of her tumblings with nobles and civilians alike—those she'd bedded for information, and those she'd laid with for pleasure alone.

She wrote of loss, a pain for her long-gone mother that hadn't faded after decades.

Of worry, for her people that still suffered; their war one of starvation and sickness.

Of hope, for the future she was trying to build.

Of compassion. *Joy.*

But not a single page held the dark creature I'd seen in battle. Not a trace of the monster I could use to justify her death.

Only the King, the dutiful ruler of her people, lived in the pages of her journal.

And the lonely little girl.

It had to be a trap. A design to lure whoever found it into a false sense of safety. She'd written in Luxian, for Sun-fucking-sake, meant to be read and found by the enemy.

Or kept away from those she dwelled with.

But it didn't change the fact that every line, every *word*, made it harder and harder for me to remember that I was a soldier with a task. A guard with a duty to protect.

The headache between my brows pounded like a blacksmith against an anvil, heavy throbs sharpening me into a weapon. I'd avoided her, and Caelum, for days, not knowing how to look at either of them. Instead, I'd opted to sit in the barracks and read in the lowlight of the mess hall whenever I didn't hunt for the traitor or report back to King Kato. It was outside of my normal duty— which meant coming up with piss-poor excuse after piss-poor excuse to get Julius to cover my normal rotations, but I'd be lying if I said I hadn't appreciated the reprieve from the role.

But there was no hiding from the surge of emotions that tracked down my cheeks in heavy droplets.

I felt Julius before he found me like that, my tattoo itching as he became the first to taste the fury of my aching head and tangled heart.

I wiped away the evidence of my tears from my cheeks with a quick sweep of my sleeve as his footsteps approached, the bond between us loosening as the distance closed.

He appeared through the doorway and levied me with a knowing grin. "You okay? I thought I felt you *crying*."

"I don't cry," I lied, knowing damn well my eyes would be a bloodshot telltale of the truth.

The corner of his mouth twitched up. He nudged the book and

sat on the bench across from me, tearing into a slab of jerky with his teeth. "You read? Since when?"

I rubbed my forehead, hoping to coax the beast into submission. "Shut it, will you?"

Jules waved the jerky at the journal like it was a wand, and I instinctively pulled it back—out of the oily meat's reach. His eyes narrowed. "Is that Thera's? What does it say?"

Of course, I hadn't completely lied to Jules. I'd told my *Vinculum* the truth of my petty theft, simply leaving out the part where I was using it to find a way to kill her. Instead, claiming that Tiberius had suggested I know Thera better, to protect Caelum more effectively.

"Nothing damning." I tucked the journal under my leg. Of course, this wasn't any of *my* personal information—sun and stars, I was the real snoop—and I knew Jules could feel the discomfort climbing down my spine. But it felt wrong to let him read; wrong to let anyone else know about the girl inside. "It's a dead end."

Jules didn't press, Sun bless him, but his shoulders didn't relax either, a tension still in his stance tangling with my own.

I sighed, snagging the jerky from his grip and chomping off a piece for myself. "What's eating *you*?"

"I've been on edge since we got back to the city." His leg bounced beneath the table, that anxiety unraveling as he finally spoke. "Any leads on the attacks or the prisoner?"

My head throbbed again at the mere mention of yet another task I was burdened with—and *failing*.

"No. They're stealthy." The cured treat soured in my mouth, poisoned by the harsh reality that rolled in my gut like bile. "And they know Lux too well."

There hadn't been a trace at the scene of the prisoner's death, none of my men noting anything suspicious during the transfer. Nothing from the coroner that could help. Nothing back in the forest. The team we'd dispatched there finding the other rebel bodies already burned and any evidence discarded.

And nothing, absolutely *nothing*, that linked Thera or her

people to the crime. Even Commander Kappas, who was the most suspicious of the Erebushi faction, always had an ironclad alibi.

Whoever had conspired wasn't just good at it.

They had full access and power. Resources.

It limited who could have pulled it off and left me with several uncomfortable suspicions I didn't dare voice aloud.

"So our fears are confirmed." Jules leaned forward even though we were the only two in the hall. Which was safer—the walls had ears in Lux. While no one ever outright said it, I suspected *Zo'is* listening devices had been shoved in key hiding spots. "Does the King know yet?"

Nausea waved through me, my fists clenching.

I had no updates for King Kato. No answers to any of the questions he'd tasked me to uncover.

And now, I had no leverage against the *Sykagos*. No weaknesses I could exploit, aside from some mommy issues that might sting, but couldn't truly wound.

"No. I have a meeting later that I'm avoiding," I said honestly, my *Vinculum* the only one I *could* be honest with anymore. At least, in part. Lies still lingered between us. Deals and secrets I kept close to my chest.

I needed to change the subject before anxiety could trap me again, my head too heavy and battle-beaten to focus. I picked another question I'd been circumventing. "If you're here, where is Caelum?"

Jules relaxed, his leg ceasing its bounce as we entered safer territory. "I thought you were avoiding him, too."

I flipped him my middle finger. "Just because you can feel my feelings doesn't mean you get to be a smart ass about it."

He beamed, glee beating through his chest and, by extension, mine. "But that's why you love me most."

Despite the effort I put into maintaining my glare, the corner of my mouth tugged toward a smile.

Stupid *Vinculum* magic. It was hard to stay cross when your bonded had the disposition of a puppy.

"Fine." I sighed, Jules' sunshine chasing away the storm clouds lingering in my head. I pushed up from the table—careful to tuck Thera's journal in my knapsack.

My moment with Caelum in the forest had rewired parts of my brain, had shifted the fabric of our dynamic irrevocably. But that didn't change the fact I still was his friend before all else. His guard, with a duty to protect.

"Where is Caelum? Court?"

It was time I stopped running from my charge. Time we had a chat about what happened in the forest, or at the very least, how he'd fared since. If there were traitors in Lux, I needed him *safe*, not surrounded by them all, waiting to strike.

But Jules shook his head. Grimaced. "No, he left with the King."

Dread pulled my brows close again. The King was out in the Inner City today unless something had changed. "Kato is back? But I thought he was out—"

"No, Thera."

I paused. Breathed in. Out.

Then, on a single, rattling breath, I said, *"You let him leave with the Sykagos?"*

Jules frowned. "Are we still calling her that?"

I shoved back from my seat, the last of my control snapping under the pressure. "It's what she is!"

Not the girl from the journal. Not the girl from the journal.

"She's his fiancé." Julius rose from the bench, towering over me. But even as he used his height to his advantage, his gaze softened —something akin to *pity* watering in the gold flecks of his eyes. "And you know damn well he's safe with her."

"You don't get to decide that. You're his guard, Julius. You *guard* him." My fists clenched at my side, but even as the words exited my mouth, I knew they were useless. This was not something I could fight my way through, not something I could project onto Jules.

Caelum *was* safe. Thera had saved him once already, and as far as power went, she was unmatched. With a killer roaming loose through Stellaris, Julius had a point.

Thera was the only truly untouchable elf here, which made her an exceptional bodyguard.

But that role was not hers to take, no matter how lonely she pretended to be. That duty was mine, one I'd sacrificed every dream and future for. One I held closer than anything else.

One that I'd been avoiding, shirking off to Julius.

"No, *you're* his head guard, *Captain*, and you haven't taken a shift in days. You want to make sure he's okay?" His hand gripped my shoulder hard enough to bruise. "Go check yourself."

It wasn't an admonishment, but a challenge.

A dare.

Stop hiding. Breathe, Rory.

If I wanted Thera to stop stepping in, I had to step up.

My frown was forced. "I should write you up for this."

Jules scoffed, but something in his shoulders unknotted. "Save that fire for your meeting with Kato later. You'll need it. But go find the prince first."

"Fine. Where is he?"

"They went to the training pitch."

I had to blink away streaks of pure crimson from my vision. "They went *where*?"

Jules stiffened. "To the pi—"

I didn't wait for him to finish.

The fucking fighting pitch.

Unguarded. *Uncovered.*

In the middle of other bloodthirsty warriors that might want a piece of the *Sykagos*. That might trigger a fight—and get Caelum caught in the crosshairs.

My heart was a demanding drum in my chest, and I marched to its beat all the way to the arenas, my stomach knotting around the few bites of jerky I'd eaten. Panic pushed my pace faster, my lungs dragging more air as I fought to *breathe.*

Caelum's health concerns aside, Stellaris was not safe. Not for anyone, but especially not for Caelum right now. Both attacks were too close to him to be a coincidence.

And Thera had led him to the one place where anyone could easily take him out from the rafters or the stands, weapons galore at their disposal . . .

She would get an earful, and Caelum needed a reality check.

He might be engaged now; he might enjoy flirting with Thera and messing around . . .

But there were actual threats afoot, and Lux needed its heir protected.

I crossed the threshold of the first colosseum. Grunts and moans carried from the sand, and all plans blew away on a dry breeze.

Maybe it was the headache. Or the confusion, brought on by the journal's enchantment. It could've been the weeks of tension and stress, the nights of little sleep and several agendas that demanded my attention, King Kato breathing down my neck on all of them.

Or it was that Caelum—*my* Caelum—laid defenseless beneath her, the Sykagos poised above him, ready to strike again.

The world tinted red.

And I *lost it.*

I was on her in a second, her lithe body hitting the sand with a thrilling thump that sent a jolt of primal victory shooting through my veins. I pressed my hands against her shoulders, my knee rooting her in place, and a growl worked up through me. *"Don't you fucking touch him."*

"Rory!" Caelum bellowed from behind me, but the ringing in my ears drowned it out.

Beneath me, Thera smiled. "If you wanted a turn, you could've just asked."

My distraction cost me.

She bucked up and hooked her leg she somehow got free across my torso, the grappler's move precise and brutal. With the down-swing, my head jerked back, and she used her momentum to swoop on top of me. Sand flew into my eyes, blurring my vision.

Her hands pinned my wrists above my head, and she straddled my torso, heat surged through me like sunlight.

Anger. That had to be anger.

Anger, I knew. Relished.

I shut out the rest of the world, sweat and sand and some kind of unfamiliar perfume. Closed off my senses to the heat of the sun above and the body on top of me.

My opponent, my enemy, had my sole focus. The sting of my knuckles and the fury of my fists.

I kneed up, smacking her spine, and she winced, but didn't move, surprisingly dense for her size.

"Stop it, both of you!" Caelum screamed again, but I didn't let my focus drop.

Thera leaned in, her hair a veil between us and Caelum, and she winked. Her grip loosened. "Let's put on a good show for him, shall we?"

My next punch hit her straight in the jaw with a satisfying boom. Pain jolted through my knuckles, but I didn't care, adrenaline springing up inside of me.

Thera toppled hard but scrambled back to her knees.

Wiping the sweat and sand from my eyes, I went to lunge again, but boots blocked my path.

"*Aurora!*" Caelum's face had gone a deep red. He stared down at me, rage dripping from him like sweat.

My name hit me like a kick to the gut.

Caelum never yelled. Never spoke a notch above gentle. And he certainly never said my name with such disdain and disappointment.

I scurried to my feet like a kid caught with her hand in the sweets jar. Shame coated my limbs like the sweat cloying to my underclothes, but I stamped it down, instead letting the familiar anger talk for me. "She was hurting you!"

"She was *training* me." Ragged breaths shook through his chest. He glared at me with such a force, it nearly knocked me back down to the earth.

I mustered the last of my authority and shook my head at him. "*I* train you."

Caelum blinked, face falling for just a flicker of a moment—

But a scoff from Thera tore my attention. She brushed off her pants, sand cascading from her like glitter in the light. "If that was the result of you training him, then you're a terrible instructor."

The last threads of patience—the last of any empathy I had for the journal girl—snapped, recoiling with a brutal slam.

A dangerous blend of pride and fury burned through my shame, and I stormed to her, stopping mere inches from her face and gave her a withering stare. My voice dipped low. "You are crossing a dangerous line. My duty is to protect him, and I will end you if you think of laying another fucking finger—"

"Your definition of protection and mine are different." All teasing evaporated from her expression, and she leaned closer. Shadows darkened her stare, and even though she was shorter than me, her presence loomed like one of Stellaris' towers. "He is *soft*. But he has potential. He needs to learn to protect himself. Otherwise, whoever is after him will succeed."

I bristled, fear licking up my spine. "He doesn't need to protect himself, I will—"

"I am *right here*." Caelum pushed between us, cutting through the tension like a blade. He positioned himself next to *her*, bright eyes misty with angry, burning tears. "And you are not always there. You haven't been there in days."

It would've been better if he stabbed me. Better if he gave me a scar to match the ugly one across my face than to accuse me of abandoning him.

But I had. I'd been avoiding him since the woods, since we'd come close.

"Caelum—"

"I'm done." He snatched his discarded tunic from the ground, then leveled Thera with a look dirtier than the silk he had clutched tightly in his white-knuckled fist. "And I am not soft. I am *new*. There is a difference."

I expected her to bicker back, to scoff.

But she took a step closer, a hand outstretched.

"I know. I'm sorry," she said.

The word threw me off my center, so unexpected and kind from the *Sykagos*. So reminiscent of the lonely girl.

"We can keep working at it together."

I shook my head, brushing off the enchantment before it could drag me under. "Over my dead body."

I was powerless to stop the *Sykagos* from marrying Caelum or winning his heart. But I would not allow her to put him in danger, even if it hurt his feelings to do so. Even if protecting him physically meant wounding his pride.

"That's *it!*" he shouted, his gaze burning my flesh to an uncomfortable itch. "I have had *enough* of you looking down on me! Of both of you looking down on me!"

Thera winced. "I don't—"

"You do." He pointed between us both. "You all see me as the fool prince. And I know I am. I know now that everything I thought was true was a facade, and that I have no skills as a ruler. I am weak." His voice broke off, cracking in a way that shattered my heart into pieces. His chest heaved as he caught his breath, staring at us both with such contempt.

For a moment, I wondered if looks could truly kill.

"But I am not useless, not anymore," he said, his voice distant. Cold. More rigid and impersonal than all the lifeless gems encrusting the castle. "You two can both either work together and *help me*, or you can both get out of my fucking way."

He didn't wait for a response and stalked off, a limp in his gait. He didn't look back either.

Shock and shame rooted me in place. Like the pitch was made of quicksand, threatening to drag me under.

Until Thera blew out an exasperated breath.

"Don't just stand there gawking. Go after him."

I spun on her so fast, the world tilted. "What?"

Two-toned eyes stared back, a sadness dulling their vibrant hues that revealed the girl from the journal, not the king. "Go. Before you lose him."

Biting back the last of my rage, I nodded, sprinting after my prince.

Leaving the girl lonely and cold again.

CHAPTER
TWENTY

"*Love is a fickle, wicked thing. It can defy gods and topple kings.*"
—From "*The Lover's Plight,*" *by Luxian Poet Obilos Hammon,*
889 A.G.W

CAELUM

I ran as far as my feet would carry me, all the way to my mother's willow grove despite the protesting twinge in my left shin and the sharp sting rattling through each breath. I would need to double up on my *Zo'is* tea later if I wanted to survive, but I didn't care.

I should've stayed. Should've proven my words with action for once, should've stood my ground and shown both Thera and Rory the man I wanted to be. The king my mother believed I *could* be, with the right training and accommodation tools.

But my retreat spoke volumes, my weakness only good for running away.

I was so fucking tired of running. So fucking tired of falling and failing, of not measuring up or standing tall. Of not being a man my father could trust, or one that would make my mother proud.

Thera was right. And so was Rory. I was *soft*. And that made me a target, one that couldn't defend myself even if I tried. One that put other good people in harm's way. Like Quinton.

I'd veiled my cry for help beneath a sharp admonishment, but I couldn't blame them for seeing me for what I was. Couldn't strengthen my muscles or make my reflexes faster with words alone. Couldn't make my lungs cooperate or my heart stay steady with willpower. My condition was hereditary—no remedying a nervous system that didn't fire right.

And no cure for the ignorance of those avoiding the truth.

I collapsed on the bench beneath my mother's favorite tree, the shade hiding my shame from the rest of Stellaris.

Tears bit my eyes, spilling over, and I tucked my knees to my chest. If my mother had lived, would my father have given me more room to learn and grow? Would he have been less concerned and protective? Would she herself have taught me, helped me cultivate myself into someone worthy of her kingdom?

My thoughts consumed me, and my sobs sniffling out of me, droplets becoming a downpour.

I wanted to be stronger. Wanted to learn. Thera had given me a gift today—a chance to try. To understand my own limitations, and to push past them. A chance to learn how to work with my body, instead of against it.

But I couldn't grow in a box. Couldn't change if the rest of Stellaris . . . if Rory . . . wanted to smother and overbear. If every time I stepped out of my cage, someone dragged me back and locked the door again.

A snapping twig tore me from the pity-party-for-one.

Rory crossed beneath the canopy of leaves.

I stood, my head rushing with the action, and I quickly wiped away my tears. Of course she'd know where to find me—her primary duty in this castle was to know my movements better than anyone else. To know my weaknesses.

I shoved them all down, sheathing my pain behind an armored facade. "What do you want?"

She inhaled, the dappled shadows darkening the pity written across her face.

Pity. *Again.* So thick and cloying it chased away the sadness, my projected fury surging to the surface again.

I turned to go.

"Wait, please—"

"Go away, Rory."

"No." A hand caught my wrist, turning me back to face her. This close, the pity took on a different hue, concern laced across her drawn brow, and something else I didn't quite understand glimmering in her eyes. She blew out a sharp breath. "*No.* I'll never stop following you."

I tugged my wrist back. "That was an order, not a request."

I wanted her help, not her constant coverage. Not her ever-present shadow, too wide for me to step out of, the shade too dark for me to drink the sunlight I needed to flourish.

But nothing about Rory's planted stance indicated retreat, her feet sturdier than the roots of the tree concealing us.

"If you want me gone, fire me like Crotchkin." A bitter laugh escaped, and she leaned closer, a mighty oak somehow towering even though she was a few inches shorter. Fists clenched at her side. "But I won't ever stop protecting you. Even if you don't like my methods. I meant what I said. *Step for step.*"

The mention of our moment in the woods skewered soft parts of me. Abandoned, needy parts that wanted nothing more than to pull her closer instead of pushing her away. Parts that had missed her fiercely in the last few days, parts that would betray my duty and fall into her warm gaze instead.

But those parts did not make a good king, or a good friend.

My jaw clenched. "I don't need your protection."

I needed . . .

Fuck, I didn't know what I needed. But I knew I didn't need to feel like a child anymore. Didn't need my best friend and guard to hold my hand and wipe my nose for me. I needed to feel like a man, like an adult, like a king.

"But *I* need to protect you." Rory stepped closer again, reaching for my hand, spearing her fingers between mine. Staring at me so fiercely, it felt as if my skin would catch fire. "Not because you're useless or weak, whatever crap you spewed out there. Suns, you might not be a soldier, but you're smarter than anyone else I know and that's strength, too. I protect you because *I* care. Because you're *special*, Cae."

At that, all thoughts stumbled. Paused. *"What?"*

"I'm *nothing*. Unimportant. My life matters to no one." She squeezed my hand tighter, her desperation a vice around her tight voice. "But you? You are priceless, to Lux and to me. I don't care if you *can* do it yourself. I'm staying here."

Unimportant.

Nothing.

The words reverberated through me like one of the tower bells that sang their twilight call every evening.

Aurora Bellatore was not nothing.

She was everything.

But I'd felt so sorry for myself that I hadn't realized Rory had felt just as unneeded. If I learned to guard myself, if I let Thera teach and train me . . . Where did that leave her?

I wrenched my hand free before I did something I regretted. Before I pushed away again. Or reached too close. "Don't say that. Don't say you're nothing."

"It's true." She winced, something dark flashing across her expression.

The civilized box I'd always lived in shattered.

"Listen to me right now, Aurora Bellatore." I grabbed her face

283

with both of my hands, gentle but stern, her scarred, raised skin warm beneath my fingertips.

My gaze scanned every important, incredible thing about her—her gold eyes that shone like sunlight and warmth. Her sharp cheekbones that cut as fiercely as her tongue could. Her strong jaw that spoke of her grit and determination. Her soft lips that shielded the underlying kindness that she often saved only for me.

"You are the only thing that has ever mattered to me. And I will get stronger so I don't have to watch you fall on your sword every time trouble finds me."

I don't know which of us moved first.

Don't know if I pulled, or if she leaned.

But there was a breath, a pause—

And then we collided.

Her mouth met mine, taste for taste, *step for step*, clashing and comforting as the thousands of unsaid words and *almosts* flowed wordlessly between our joining lips and tongues.

She tasted like summer mornings and sand. Like sweat and hidden sweetness. Like undisclosed desire and dangerous freedom. My hands clutched her waist, gripping her desperately, and she wound her arms around my neck, fingers latching through the hair at my nape.

Teeth grazed against my bottom lip, and a shudder ran up my spine. Years of tension and wanting rising through me as I tugged her closer, aching for *more*.

Bark hit my back, startling me back to reality.

Lips stilled. Breaths caught.

Rory pulled away first, hazy pupils blown wide. "Caelum—"

"We—" I gasped, my chest heaving as my heartbeat slammed against my ribs. "I shouldn't have . . ."

I shouldn't, but sun and stars, did I want to again.

She shook her head, but her gaze snagged on my mouth. "That was me, I'm—"

Footsteps crunched just beyond the border of the willow's curtain. A throat cleared. "Captain?"

Rory flew back, the haze clearing, and cold reality doused us both.

Julius brushed back the branches, a blush creeping across his face that said more than words could. "Um, sorry Captain, but King Kato is back."

"Coming." Rory smoothed the frayed strands of her braid—had I done that, or was that from her fight with Thera?

Thera.

My betrothed.

Fuck.

Rory followed Fortis, casting one last sidelong glance my way. "Your Highness, go to your rooms, please."

I heard the *we'll talk later* beneath it.

But even as I watched her go, even as I savored the lingering taste of her on my lips, I knew not a single word in any language could fix the mess I'd just made.

———

In my rooms, back in proper attire and with the curtains drawn and the door tightly shut, there was no hiding from what I'd done.

I'd kissed Rory. And she . . .

I'd always hoped, deep down, that the pining was mutual. But it had always felt distant. More like the desire for an alternate life, or a wistfulness toward a daydream, not a true passion toward *me*.

To *feel* her want was another beast entirely. To relish her mouth against mine, to taste her on my tongue . . .

I couldn't linger in that. It should've never happened. Not because I didn't want it, but because I couldn't. Rory was my guard. I was engaged.

So instead of wallowing in regret and desire, instead of blud-

285

geoning myself with guilt while replaying the breathy noises Rory made in my head over and over again . . .

I read. Escaped into Arturus' journal. Translating a past that had nothing to do with me.

It was slow at first, the Old Elysian harder to decipher when it was written colloquially instead of academically. But word for word, I let my mind drift.

1775 A.G.W. Inferni, Erebus. Fort Tygia rebel camp.

I am confronted by a ~~difficult~~ (no, not difficult) *challenging reality. It is my fifth week among the Erebushi clans, and I have not found any evidence of the espionage my commander has tasked me to find. But I have found something far more dangerous.*

General Danae is an ~~energetic~~ (no, that wasn't quite it, either) *enigmatic leader. She is one with her subjects, not a lofty ruler above them. She knows each peasant and peddler by name. Knows their lives, their children, their interests. Knows the farmer's wife deals with poor joints, especially in the colder months. Knows the healer has a taste for mint chocolates, and he is more likely to assist others when supplied with the delicacies. She also knows I can't be trusted. I think I was made the first night I arrived—and yet she did not order my execution or torture me for information.*

She invited me for supper.

It's clear that this, too, is a ploy for sympathy. A facade she uses to charm her people and to mask her brutal nature.

It's ~~effective~~ *charming.*

I reread, editing the few words I guessed at based on context. But my limited vocabulary aside, Arturus' self-awareness was a surprising twist. Not that I blamed him for finding the general so alluring.

Thera was like that. Warm, intelligent. Dedicated.

Rory, too.

I rubbed my forehead. This was supposed to help distract me from my mess, not make me think more of it.

Still, I couldn't help myself as I dove back in, finding another entry about the general, dated a few weeks later. This one was even more tricky, and a headache formed beneath my brow, but I didn't mind as the narrative sucked me in.

1775 A.G.W. Inferni, Erebus. Fort Tygia outpost.
Danae invited me to ~~food?~~ ~~rest?~~ dine with her again this
evening.

A first name basis this time? Interesting.

Of course, I played along, understanding my station and
mission. I have not forgotten.
But the general seemed different tonight. Her shoulders sag
under the weight of something heavy, and there is a ~~distracted~~
concerned air to her normally warm presence.
This should trouble me as a soldier. Should give me even greater
cause to investigate and identify what has such a powerful elf
worried.
Instead . . . I offered comfort. Drank tea and sat in silence with
her. Spent an evening as friends.
I will not be sending this letter to command. This reflection is
mine alone . . .
And yet I cannot make sense of the heaviness I saw tonight. It
must mean something is coming. I should warn ~~my people~~ the
upworlders, or find out more.
I know myself well enough to know that I won't. Not when I feel
as though I've made a friend for the first time in—

A knock on the door tore me from the pages before Arturus'

words could devour me, a chill running down my back, but new heat rose to my cheeks.

Go to your rooms, please.

Rory.

I'd hoped to postpone this conversation until I had answers for myself. Until I knew how to set clear boundaries again and atone for crossing them. Or until I had the courage to do something about it.

Yet despite my better judgment, I opened the door, instinct propelling me thoughtlessly forward. "Ro—"

A mismatched stare and a smirk waited on the other side, and I froze. "Your Majesty."

Thera dressed for war in a tight black dress that could kill a man, her sharp angles ready to strike like the scales of a black viper. But her smile softened.

"We have a meeting with your father. Walk with me?"

Shit.

Another thing I forgot about when I was off playing pretend with Rory. I hadn't even prepared for this meeting about the wedding, and I had wanted to use this as my first chance to show my father I was capable.

Another failure to add to my growing list.

I nodded to Thera, grateful to not be alone.

But guilt still churned in my core as I fell into step beside her, our shoes matching tempo as we made our way through the maze of Stellaris to my father's meeting rooms.

Thera eyed me closely. "How is your translation going?"

I cleared my throat, trying to dispel the lump of disquiet that coated my chords in shame. "Interesting, so far. Arturus was a spy sent during the second wave of the war tasked to uncover Erebus' tactics for getting through the portal, but he has a very interesting perspective on the people. Some phrases make it seem like he was truly *one* with them. He details a lot about a female general, Danae, that has captivated his attention."

Thera missed a step, stumbling. Her eyes widened.

"Interesting indeed." Her tone was tight as she caught herself, her typical grace returning to her fluid stride. "We could read together later, if you'd like?"

My chest ached. I could visualize it perfectly, much like Arturus' tea-time night with Danae. The two of us, tucked away in my mother's study, reading in a comfortable silence. Sharing new information with each other in the breaths between paragraphs. Sipping tea, or letting it go cold as we talked and bonded. As we learned to rule together.

"Maybe." My smile didn't meet my eyes. I wondered how she'd feel about that if she knew what I'd done. After she'd tried to help me today. After we'd given each other so much trust, only for me to break hers.

Her mother's ring on my pinky was a scalding brand against my skin.

I didn't deserve it. *Her.*

But as we climbed the stairs to my father's study, a gut-churning exhaustion and anxiety quickly chased away shame and doubt. My legs and lungs burned with every step, a tingling sensation in my fingers. My breath came short, each lungful of air hot and heavy.

My head spun, heart speeding like a runaway stallion.

We passed the last step, and Thera's hand found my back. "Are you all right?"

No, nothing was all right. This was why my father kept me away from training pitches. This is why I didn't push myself.

I opened my mouth to say as much, but shut it quickly.

Silhouetted in glaring sunlight pouring from the giant window at the top of the tower, Rory and Julius both stood outside of my father's rooms, my father, Lord Pall, and a few other delegates between them. Rory's eyes met mine, then flicked to Thera at my side before widening.

My stomach lurched and my heart rate doubled.

289

Of course, she'd be here. Had I waited in my rooms, she probably would've come to fetch me in just a few moments.

If I complained now, she'd never let me leave my rooms again.

I averted my gaze, instead focusing on my father's too-bright smile.

"Ah, you're early! Look at you both, getting along so well." My father's eyes narrowed, and he pushed open the door to his study, his smile trained on Thera alone. "Come get settled, we have a lot to discuss."

Sucking down a gulp of hot air, I obeyed.

Bodies packed into the room, filtering around the oak meeting table. For once, stacks of papers didn't cover it—likely a protective measure. My father took the head, as usual, Lord Pall to his right.

Normally, I sat on his left, but that would put me farthest from the door—and facing Rory.

I didn't know if I could handle several hours of staring directly at her, not without breaking into a sweat or my heart rate giving me away to everyone in the room. Not without her noting the change in my condition and exposing me to my father.

So instead, I took the seat next to Lord Pall, my back to her.

I could feel her gaze burning holes in the back of the stiff metal chair, but we'd have to add it to the list of apologies I owed her the next time I got her alone.

Thera raised an eyebrow, but took my normal seat to my father's left, right across from me, and the rest of the attendees—Lord Pollux, our Minister of Public Relations, and Lady Mirena, our Mistress of Art and Decorum—entered, the first casting a curious, hungry look at Thera that made my stomach flip, the second shooting her a glare that could peel paint. She'd been the one who'd tried to talk to Thera earlier, only to be snubbed.

Ambassador Nyxia and Commander Kappas filled into the open seats next to their king, both Erebushis on edge.

I exhaled.

My father raised his hand. "Let's begin."

This would be a long, long evening.

I wished I was wrong.

I wasn't.

The agenda started simply enough with both kings bickering back and forth about the wedding feast, Thera insisting on some lighter, vegetable-friendly food, my father lecturing her about the Luxian tradition of fresh game cut from the hunt the day before. Then it moved to attire, my father insisting on the stuffy, old-fashioned ceremonial robes while Thera flat out laughed in his face, declaring that she'd rather show up naked. Lady Mirena tried to pipe in at that, only to be silenced yet again by Thera, earning a laugh from Lord Pollux.

But even as they battled, words clashing like swords, I barely listened, my head swimming, and I fought to keep my breathing steady.

I thought not being able to see Rory was a blessing.

But it was worse, my imagination running away with the *what ifs* that I couldn't disprove without locking eyes on her.

What if she was glaring at me? What if Thera noticed? Would she think it resulted from our argument out on the pitch today? Could either of them—their senses enhanced—hear my racing heart? Could Julius? Had he told anyone about what he'd walked in on? He wouldn't rat out Rory, but that didn't mean he wouldn't warn others about what kind of elf I was. Inferni Hell, what did he even think happened?

All the while Thera's gaze—brutal and brilliant and soft—kept flicking my way, waiting for me to interject. To stand up, to be the one-day king I'd promised her I'd be. To be the elf she deserved, as idle chatter about menu and decor shifted toward a sharp-edged debate about security and safety measures.

But my tongue remained a numb, lame thing in my head, unable to muster the strength for even a word.

"It's unsafe to let the general public in. There have been too many threats already." A shadow curled around Thera's ring finger

—the skin there somehow even paler than the rest of her, usually sheathed by the ring I now wore. "For the wedding itself, I understand, but the ball beforehand should be an intimate affair."

"I hear your concerns, but our guard is well-trained." My father's smile hadn't cracked an inch, but he rapped his fingers against the arm of his chair, a sign that his patience wore dangerously thin. "We need to show the common folk that this union is one of peace and prosperity. It has to be public. Our kingdom deserves to celebrate, no?"

Thera offered a placating nod. "Normally I would agree, but unless you have any leads on who has been staging the recent attacks, it is ill-advised."

Lord Pall's head bobbed back and forth between the monarchs as they sparred.

"Either way," Pollux, ever the peace-keeper, said, "we can frame it to the public carefully. If we close the ceremony, we can always have the papers circulate it as a true love match. We can print portraits of the lovely couple to emphasize our point."

Thera offered the Minister a co-conspirator's grin.

I stayed quiet.

Nyxia scoffed—at my silence or at the Lord's smooth mouth, I would never know.

"And what about the Erebushi people?" the tiny woman challenged. "With Thera here, Erebus does not have the magical resources to open the portal, but there is clearly an abundance of *Zo'is* in your coffers, Your Majesty. Does Erebus not get to enjoy the celebration? Do your papers not get *circulated* among our lands?"

"We simply don't have the time to vet anyone from Erebus beforehand." Lord Pall finally found his voice, even as mine remained trapped. "We'll have to celebrate there separately."

"Celebrations require something good to happen. Our people have nothing to *celebrate* while they suffer." Kappas slammed a fist on the table—the first to make an outright show of anger—but Nyxia nudged his side.

Thera ignored Pall and Kappas entirely, her focus unwavering from my father.

"My citizens are not the ones trying to kill your son, Kato." Thera cut through the noise. Like they had in the library, her shadows writhed at her fingertips, agitated and drawing all the heat in the room. Thera cleared her throat, but the shadows didn't quiet. "My people need a show of support if I'm going to enter this union."

My stomach dropped at the softness in her tone.

Thera was alone here, Nyxia and Kappas her only allies, as her newly appointed throne sat empty in her homeland. As her people still starved, waiting with baited, borrowed breaths to hear from their distant king.

All the while, my people wrote books about them being lesser demon-kin elves. While my kingdom thrived in excess, ignorant to their dark sisters' and brothers' plight—just as I had been.

My father glanced at the shadows, his lips pursing. His gaze darkened with some of his own, a shade I didn't understand from him.

He was going to say no.

"Thirty guests," I blurted.

Heads swiveled to me before I even realized that had been *my* voice, my mouth acting upon its own agenda for the second time that day. I tugged at the collar of my tunic, my neck heating as I baked in the attention. "We can make that happen, can't we? Thera deserves to have some of her people represented at her own wedding."

My father's eyes widened, but he covered his shock with a placid grin. "How generous of you, my boy. Your heart is inspiring. But we can't—"

"We *can*, though." For the first time in my life, I cut my father off.

The resounding silence sucked the air from the room. No one moved.

My father stared like I'd called him a bastard.

I swallowed the lump in my throat.

Reaching out to the only lifeline I had, I turned in my seat and met the gaze that'd melted holes in my back all afternoon.

Rory's golden eyes were rounder than the sun at noon, but she did not look away.

I hoped she could read the desperation and overdue apologies in the pitiful look I offered as I fed her to the sharks circling me. "Captain Bellatore and my private guard can spare resources, can't they? It's not their normal assignment, but I'm sure they are up to the task."

But Rory didn't run away. Her back straightened. Protecting me, like she always did. "Yes, Your Highness. We can make it work."

I tried not to read into that line.

"Caelum." A broad hand on my shoulder tore me away from Rory, my father's voice tender instead of the bellow I expected at my disobedience. Soft, like he spoke to someone he saw as a boy, a child. Someone he saw as *weak*. "I hope you know it's not that simple."

I would not be weak, not anymore.

I flinched out of my father's grasp. Tried to mimic Rory's impossibly straight posture and Thera's regal chin-tilt. "With all due respect, Father, this is my wedding, and if I'm going to rule with Thera in Erebus, I need to garner respect there, too. It's essential that we invite them in, or they'll never accept me."

Kappas scoffed, but I tuned him out.

My father blinked, clouds clearing from his gaze. Like for the first time in my life, he saw something different.

Something I wasn't sure he liked.

His hands flattened against the table, tension easing from their clenched fists.

"Fine. Twenty guests, and only for the actual wedding."

"I thought the banquet before was open to the public, Kato." A real smile broke across Thera's face, but she did not direct it at my father, even as she spoke to him.

No, her mismatched stare was trained entirely on me.

Flames licked my cheeks. I'd impressed her. Given her back a fraction of the strength she'd offered me.

Mere hours after betraying her with the woman standing guard behind me.

"A deal, then," my father chimed in—always regaining control, like this was his bargain, not mine.

This time, I was happy to let him take the reins, my chest heavy with a whirlwind of feelings I had no energy to quell.

My father leaned forward. "We open the banquet to anyone that can make their way into the city—Luxians and Erebushi alike —and I can spare the resources to invite twenty of your guests to the wedding personally."

Thera nodded, finally facing my father, relieving me of the weight of her stare. "And to assist with the issue of protection, Commander Kappas will lend his support in the vetting efforts beforehand. He's so excited to collaborate with Captain Bellatore."

"What?" Kappas blurt, broad hands gripping the table.

Thera flashed him a smile. "The Erebushi will need someone they trust, Commander."

The broad elf's jaw worked hard, and he clamped his mouth shut, going silent once more.

Rory's throat cleared behind me. I didn't have the courage to spare a look. "That works for me."

Great. My guard, the woman whom I'd stepped out of line with, and Thera's Commander, who I was pretty sure had been looking for an excuse to punch me since the day we'd met, together on a project to help wed Thera and I.

Such a fucking mess. I ran a hand over my face.

My father sat back, lounging into his chair. "Then we have an agreement. This meeting is adjourned."

"That we do." Thera stood to dismiss herself, and I exhaled for the first time since she'd showed up at my rooms.

Pushing back from the table, I stood too, turning to Rory. A breath passed between us, unspoken words flowing in the silence.

I needed to talk to her. Needed to clear the air—

My father cleared his throat. "Stay behind, Captain. I need to have a few words with you if you're going to take this assignment."

"Yes, Your Majesty," Rory answered, her face blank.

My shoulders fell.

I did my best to hide my disappointment, straightening out my tunic and heading for the door.

Thera fell into step beside me again before Fortis could. "Allow me to escort you back, My Prince."

"Thank you." I nodded, stealing one last look at Rory.

Her throat bobbed, and her eyes met mine for a breath, but then they cast toward the floor, silencing anything between us.

Later, then.

I followed Thera out the door, leaving a part of my heart behind.

"Your Majesty—" A voice halted us in the hall, Pollux worming his way out of the door right on our heels. "When would you like to schedule that dinner?"

Thera fastened on her political smile—one I'm sure a clever elf like Pollux could see through. "Ahh, Minister Pollux. Your excitement is admirable, and I admit, I'm interested in hearing more about your concerns. But right now, I'm escorting my love match to his rooms, and if we are to make your job any easier, it is best that we take the time to get to know each other."

Pollux tensed but offered her a similarly false grin. "Yes, you're right. I was overzealous."

Thera laced her hand through mine, my pulse thrumming beneath her fingers. Then she nodded to Nyxia, who'd just slipped through the threshold. "My ambassador will assist you. She knows my schedule by heart."

Nyxia bowed her head, dutiful as ever, and Thera dragged me after her before anyone else could snag our attention.

We were quiet as we trekked down the tower steps, slow enough that I didn't get dizzy, our shoes against marble the only percussion as they echoed. But no matter how awkwardly the silence clung to the back of my throat, I couldn't break it, my guilt a gag that choked me.

I kissed Rory, and now my future wife escorted me around my castle. Mere weeks before our wedding.

And I had no idea how I felt.

I knew how I *should* feel. I should be remorseful, should apologize to Rory and tell her it was a mistake. Should ignore her outside of her duties as my guard and cut off all further ties. Should beg Thera for forgiveness and commit myself to her fully for the rest of my life.

But as much as I wanted Thera, as much as our brief, blissful kiss in the library had only made me helplessly, hopelessly desperate for more . . .

There was no forgetting Rory. No erasing her from my narrative, our story of forbidden longing etched into uncleavable parts of me.

Thera sighed, finally shirking the veil of silence for us both as we approached my chambers. "Do we want to go to your mother's library and read instead? I could use some mental stimulation after that mind-melting drivel."

I stopped mid-step.

Breathed.

Then, because I couldn't hold it in any longer without bursting, "I kissed Rory."

Thera slowed, blinking at me.

I braced, waiting for the rage and revenge I deserved. Waiting to be flayed and flagellated like the adulterous scum I was.

But she simply tilted her head, a smirk capturing her full lips.

"Does that inhibit you from reading? Captain Bellatore is

competent, and no doubt skillful in *all* pursuits, but I'm quite surprised. I didn't think she had that kind of power—"

"You're not—" I gaped, shock numbing my extremities. "You're not angry?"

Thera's grin fell. "Did you want to kiss her?"

I swallowed, hands shaking at my sides. Lying did neither of us any good. "Yes."

Thera remained expressionless. "And she consented as well?"

My thoughts drifted to the willow grove. I still didn't know who'd started it, but Rory had definitely, *enthusiastically* participated. Had pulled me closer just as much as I had tugged her tighter.

I met Thera's gaze. "Yes. She did."

Again, I waited for her to hurl accusations at me. For her to curse Rory and me both to the pits.

"Then what is there to be angry about?" A smile broke across her face, but it didn't quite meet her eyes. Somehow, that was worse.

"I was unfaithful." I stepped closer, scanning the halfhearted smile, searching for the crack that would reveal her waiting contempt. "I had a moment with another woman—"

Thera held out a hand. Pressed it to my chest, fingertips firm but gentle. Ice and emerald eyes smoldered. "Captain Bellatore is your guard, and you and her will have to discuss what this means for that dynamic and whether that's appropriate for her position." The smile fell as she shrugged, and something else captured her expression. Something simmering and inviting. Her face was only inches from mine, her whisper brushing across my skin. "But I do not care if you kiss or even fuck a thousand other women, Caelum. Life is too painful to forgo pleasure where we can find it, and I certainly won't. As long as at the end of the night, you find your way back to our agreement and *my* bed."

Her words rocked through me, something curling low and tight in my abdomen. Her mouth made a brief, momentary pass against mine, and all thoughts vanished. So subtle and quick, it was barely the shadow of a kiss. A far cry from the overwhelming heat and passion Rory and I shared earlier.

Still, a shudder ran up my spine. The *absence* of Thera's kiss felt almost as intense.

My eyes fluttered open again—when had I closed them?—fingernails biting into my palms, and I fought to ground myself.

"You'll have to tell me more about how this plays out." Thera winked and backed away, leaving me breathless and blinking like a fool. "But if you will not join me in the library tonight, I'll excuse myself with a book and something to eat. Maybe a romance you recommended. I've earned a break."

She was gone before I could manage my tongue into words, before I could form a full, coherent thought.

But as I slipped back into my room and sank against the door-frame, more lost than I'd ever been, two truths came to mind.

One; I was unworthy of Rory or Thera. I deserved neither of their attention, and if I didn't start acting with my head instead of my wounded heart, I'd hurt one or both.

And two; I played a game where I did not know the rules. And no matter what happened next, I would lose.

CHAPTER
TWENTY-ONE

"A populace needs to be fed to be loyal. But there is something to be said about a people that have learned to feed on dreams." –From Thera Dymitria's personal Journal, circa 2086 A.G.W.

RORY

"**S**tay behind, Captain. I need to have a few words with you if you're going to take this assignment."

Ice pooled low in my gut, but I fought to keep it off my face. Fought to tear my eyes away from Caelum, away from the disappointment and plain-as-daylight desperation written across his slumped shoulders, instead focusing on his father.

On King Kato, who'd surely have me stripped of my title if he found out what I'd done in the pitch today, or in the willow grove afterward.

Hands gripping my waist rougher than I thought they could. Soft lips blazing fire as they met mine . . .

No, no more thinking of *that*, or I'd out myself. I stood taller. There was no more avoiding this meeting. "Yes, Your Majesty."

Across the room, Thera raised a brow at me before following Caelum. Whether it was because she could sense my leaping heart rate or could smell the guilt and desire mixing low in my scent, I didn't know.

I would have to speak with her later. To apologize; to thank her; or to finish what I'd started on the pitch.

The others filtered out after them—Nyxia spearing me with a glare that could cut through metal as she took up the rear—leaving me alone with the King.

Another monarch that I owed a 'sorry.' So far, I'd failed every initiative he'd given me, instead chasing after his son like I was owed something more.

"They're getting along well if Pollux believes we can trick the public into thinking them a *love match*." Kato's deep voice rattled through the now empty room.

I didn't need him to clarify.

I turned, fighting for neutrality across my features. "Yes. King Thera has been very kind to Caelum."

Another vicious vision slashed across my mind's eye.

Thera, poised on top of Caelum's shirtless, breathless form. Her long hair, dangling over his chest like wisps of night.

Envy and shame fought for dominance in my chest, a rugged wrestling match much like the one we'd shared. Not that I could judge, after I'd attacked her and then practically mounted him myself.

Kato didn't notice the tick in my jaw. He shoved out of his chair and walked over to his desk, barely looking at me at all.

"Good. Make that your focus for the next few days. Include yourself in their time together as best as you can."

He waved his hand as he sat down, scooping up a stack of papers with the other—a clear dismissal.

It took all my willpower not to clench my fists.

That was it? No discussion of the recent attacks, no updates on the conditions in the city proper?

There were people dying in Stellaris. Dying on our soil to two unrelated, but equally worrisome, *unnatural* cases. A Shadowborne attack in the summer palace, let in by one of Caelum's closest attendants. Rebels that somehow knew our route that had tried to kill Caelum, and then managed to off our only informant without a trace. And yet, the only thing King Kato cared about was Thera's death. One I'd sworn to him.

It now seemed far less necessary than I'd originally imagined. Especially with other, more direct threats right within the palace walls.

"I will do my best." I schooled my voice into a careful calm, planting my feet with the last of my strength. "But there are still no leads with the murder investigation—"

Cold eyes flicked up—I didn't realize how chilling their hue of blue could be when Caelum's warmth didn't shade them. "Captain, you read the coroner's report. The *Sykagos* scared the prisoner to death. His heart gave out." The king returned to his papers; his voice just as chilly as his gaze had been. "There is no need to investigate."

I should've let that be my out. I should've been grateful that he didn't tear me to shreds for not having any leads or results.

But I was a guard before all else. My duty was to protect—and that had not changed, even with everything else that had happened. And if Stellaris wasn't safe, if Caelum wasn't . . .

Nothing else mattered.

"I am worried about the safety of the palace, Your Majesty. Especially with the wedding fast approaching."

He sat back in his chair. Appraised me for a long moment. "Your concern speaks of your diligence. And I will need that same focus with inviting . . . our Erebushi guests." His lip curled in an unveiled grimace. "But do not forget your primary aim, Captain. The budding relationship between Thera and Caelum is likely the easiest way for you to find her weak points. All other threats are small compared to her power. You've seen what she can do."

The chill crept up my spine. I *had* seen.

Men, torn to shreds like they were made of paper. Blood and gore, dripping from long, shadowed claws. Screams, piercing the battlefield for miles, a chorus of pain and fear that throbbed against my eardrums. Darkness, creeping over the spilled red and pink as the Sykagos sought more victims.

But in the last few weeks, I'd also seen what she *didn't* do. The control and restraint she exercised, even when she had a clear advantage. She offered kindness, even when her objectives could be accomplished through violent means. The discretion she moved with, even when she could've spilled secrets as easily as she had blood.

"Go. Before you lose him."

The loneliness.

I shook my head. Smiled at King Kato. "No, Your Majesty. You're right. I will see that I use this opportunity wisely to track her movements."

I had meant what I said to Caelum.

It was my duty to protect him, even if he hated me for it. And until I could fully trust Thera, King Kato's point held true. I had to see more for myself. Had to watch for any weaknesses, or anything that would put Caelum in danger.

Or, perhaps, proof that she wasn't the threat we assumed she was.

"Good." Kato grinned back and then returned to his papers once more. "Dismissed."

This time, I didn't press, instead marching to the door without a look back.

It didn't take me long to find Thera in the library, not with the castle staff fleeing the space like roaches from lantern light. Several librarians clattered past me as I marched toward their hub, the scowls on their faces clearer than any map.

King Kato wanted me to dig deeper. To stick to Thera like one of her shadows until I could figure out what made them tick.

And after the right hook I'd knocked her with this morning, I had some groveling to do.

I didn't think about the other infraction I'd levied against her today, about the soft lips and breathy moans I'd stolen from her betrothed.

I shook my head free of those thorny thoughts and pushed open the giant, carved doors, ignoring the flush that crept along the back of my neck.

Still, I didn't expect the wave of real guilt that slammed into me as I found her bent over a book, a fist knotted in her long hair with her brows pulled tightly together. *Zo'is* and lantern light warred to light the space, competing swaths of blue and gold casting dark shadows that hugged Thera's chair like they belonged to her alone.

Other shadows lingered, too, that seemed to disobey their master—the dark circles beneath her eyes, heavy and weighing her down.

It was likely the same expression she wore whenever she wrote in her journal, the very same one I had stowed safely back in my quarters. One she had to know was gone but hadn't asked for yet—another example of her mercy.

"What brings you here, Captain? Looking for a book?" She didn't look up as she spoke, still frowning at the old, withered text in front of her.

A few long strides swallowed the space between us as I approached, dredging up the best of my courage and swallowing down the last of my pride.

Her head finally tilted up, brows raising to her hairline.

And I *knelt*, my head bent low as I bowed.

"I wanted to apologize for today." My braid fell forward as I hung my head, the closest to total prostration I'd ever get, my tone as sincere as I could manage. "My behavior was unacceptable and unbefitting of my station. And I . . . " I swallowed, that tiny kernel of genuine shame sticking in my throat. "I'm grateful that you did not seek to punish me for my poor choice."

I kept my gaze on the marble floor, watching the shadows draw closer to Thera's crossed legs.

An airy chuckle. "Which poor choice? The one to attack me on the pitch, or to kiss my betrothed after?"

My head snapped up.

She *knew*? Had Caelum told her? Or had someone else seen— no, Jules said he was alone, and he would never . . .

But she knew. And she still hadn't asked Kato to relieve me of my head. Hadn't embarrassed Caelum and I in front of the King, hadn't called off the engagement and demanded my death as repayment.

Meaning she either didn't care, or she had an even more nefarious revenge plot up her tailored sleeve.

My heart pounded against my ribs, an incessant, furious rhythm as I scrambled for words. For any explanation that would spare Caelum from the weight of my mistake. "Your Majesty, I—"

"Relax, Bellatore." Thera bit the inside of her cheek to stifle her laugh. She leaned back in her chair, silken locks falling over her shoulder as she eased into it. But there was still a tightness around her eyes, something simmering in her expression I couldn't name. She held up a single finger. "You're forgiven for both, on one condition."

I gulped as a shiver ran down my spine and settled in my toes.

Conditional forgiveness could be a dangerous game when the *Sykagos* held the strings. But I didn't have any other choices, not if I wanted her to keep her discretion and keep Caelum safe. So her puppet, I'd be. "Anything, Your Majesty."

The tightness vanished from her face. Gemstone eyes sparkled in the evening glow.

"Spar with us. Help me train him properly." She smiled. Not smirking or grinning or sneering, but *smiling*.

"*What?*"

"Bring the Lieutenant, too, or any other of your men if that makes you feel more at ease."

I exhaled. Studied her face for a long moment, waiting for the punchline.

It didn't come.

She meant it. There wasn't a hint of anger or scalding scrutiny, not a single glimmer of jealousy or even well-earned annoyance.

No, Thera's only concern was still Caelum's training. Caelum's well-being.

Which meant that at least for now, despite all my instincts demanding otherwise, our goals aligned.

"Of course." I stood, my legs still numb and shaky beneath me. Like for the first time in my life, I wasn't sure where I was treading. "Please . . . please don't be angry at Caelum. It wasn't his—"

"What you and the prince do together is your business alone, not mine." Thera pushed back from her chair. Standing straight, she wasn't much shorter than me. She stepped closer, and her smile found its sharp edge. "But know that even though I'm willing to share, I am not willing to concede. You will have to learn to live with me, Captain Bellatore."

My stomach knotted. Her words darkened by two contrasting themes. Equal parts threat . . . and *invitation*, somehow woven together in the husky dip of her voice.

She reached out, and I flinched, bracing for the sting of a slap—

Featherlight fingers tucked a strand of hair behind my ear. I stilled.

"I'll see you and the Prince first thing in the morning, Captain." Thera withdrew her hand, snagging her open book from the desk before sauntering past me, stealing the heat from the room. She paused at the door. "Rest well."

Maybe it was the adrenaline high from surviving not one, but *two* meetings with separate kings, or maybe it was the fear still lingering at the back of my mind, knowing that it couldn't have been *that* easy. Knowing that the sword would swing at my neck as soon as I least expected it.

Or maybe it was the tantalizing memory of willow branches and warm lips that had haunted me all day, the delicious heat that never fled from my basest parts. Or maybe it was the chill of breezy fingertips that elicited goosebumps down my back, that'd driven me mad with barely a touch.

But whatever it was, it made me bold as I burst through Caelum's doors. Bold and *stupid.*

Caelum, who'd been slumped across his favorite reading chair in the corner, spurred to standing, his tunic crumpled and his eyes wide. "Ro—"

His sentence broke off as my mouth crashed into his.

He froze for a moment, but in the next breath, in the next pass of my lips across his, his hands knotted into my already failing braid, tugging me closer. A small moan built at the back of his throat, and I shuddered at the tension pooled in my lowest parts.

My hands fisted in his shirt, wishing I could tear the fabric off. Wishing I could have him, right here and now, in all the ways I'd imagined since maturity. In all the daydreams I'd planned and replayed in my head, over and over and over again.

He staggered back from me, catching his breath as he gained control before I did. Pupils blew wide, desire etched into the violet-blue, but the corners of his mouth tugged into a frown.

"I don't *care,*" I spoke before he could, my voice low and hoarse with want.

He opened his mouth to retort, but I held up my hand.

"Whatever noble apology you're about to say, whatever well-intended excuse about my honor or the long-term outcome of this you're thinking up, save it."

He swallowed. Breathed in, taking deep dregs of air that puffed and collapsed his chest. "We can't, Rory."

Rejection stung through me, more fiercely than a blade through the gut.

But I had survived deep wounds before. And I was tenacious.

"Why *not?*" I pressed, my voice barely a whisper. "Because you have to marry Thera? Because people might find out and talk? Because I'll be disgraced?"

Caelum winced. "Yes."

Something still lived in the violet of his eyes. Something reckless and wanting, just like this foreign, rule-breaking thing that captained my tongue.

My hand found his chest—a daring step across the line. "Tell me it's because you don't want me."

A groan. "I *shouldn't* want you."

"But you do," I challenged.

He nodded.

My heart soared.

I'd never let myself want anything, not really. But I wanted Caelum more fiercely than lungs wanted air. I wanted him more than I cared for anything else, more than I valued my life.

I'd been holding back for too long, waiting for a maybe. *Maybe,* I'd be able to kill Thera, and King Kato would reward me, and I could want, then. *Maybe,* Caelum would never find out, and forgive me for my part in it all.

A very tentative maybe. Unstable at best. One I had no guarantee I'd survive.

And I was so tired of waiting for a maybe that might never come.

The admission flew from my lips, freeing itself from the ironclad cage I'd kept it in. "I shouldn't want the man I'm supposed to protect, especially knowing I can never fully have you. But I do. I want you, Caelum."

His head fell forward, forehead resting against mine. His voice scraped against his throat, sending a sharp chill through me. "And yet—"

"And yet nothing. We have two choices." My palm cradled his face—his skin so smooth, even with the sheen of fair evening stubble dusting his chin. Still, I made myself keep my voice steady as I offered him an out. "We can pretend this never happened, we can go back to being *us*, and secretly wonder and pine for the rest of forever."

Caelum paused for a long moment. A hand trailed against my neck, fingertips brushing lightning over my tattoo. "And the other option?"

I dragged my thumb across his full lip. "We could enjoy this while it lasts. And when it blows up in our faces, we can burn together."

His mouth parted on a shudder, like he would cross the distance between us. Like he would kiss me again, and let the fire consume us both.

He stepped back, his forehead wrinkling. "I spoke with Thera."

I sighed and tried to keep the disappointment from showing across my face. Of course, he'd already told her. It was a relief to know she hadn't had me followed. And it spoke to Caelum's virtue. Even if I would risk everything, he was not about to throw away his crown and his kingdom over a *kiss*, not without a conversation with his betrothed first.

But I'd had my chat with Thera, and her words lingered unexpectedly.

Though I'm willing to share, I am not willing to concede.

I wouldn't either. "I spoke with her too. *Apologized.*"

Caelum's jaw dropped. "You . . . *what?*"

"We're going to teach you to defend yourself together." I

smiled, shoving down the hurt that boiled in my blood. If this was the most I could have of him—stolen moments shadowed by the *Sykagos*—it would have to be enough. "We're learning to *share*."

Caelum gripped my hand and squeezed. A muddy canvas of mixed, complicated feelings splaying across his face. But among them, there was still that want. Want, and something that resembled hope.

Cae cleared his throat but didn't drop my hand. "I need some time to think."

"That's . . . fair." I tugged away, turning for the door. He needed time, and that was understandable, but I needed space before I did something that he'd resent me for. Something that would consume all of Stellaris if I wasn't careful. "I'll see you at dawn."

"Dawn?" Caelum whined, the sound so familiar that some of the tension in my middle unknotted. "What could possibly be important enough to start at *dawn?*"

A laugh bubbled out of me.

"You want to train?" I shot a look at him over my shoulder, a smirk curling my lips. "Welcome to bootcamp, My Prince."

CHAPTER
TWENTY-TWO

"*In the Lunarium clans, elves are not born, but made. On the first full moon of their 25th year, they chose a new name for themselves, signaling their rise to maturity.*" —*Excerpt from "Elven Cultures of the Elysian Empire" written by Historian Philida Xenos, Circa 317 B.G.S.*

THERA

Words blurred together on the pages of my book —*Elven Cultures of the Elysian Empire*—the ancient language thick and cumbersome to my already aching head. If my betrothed and his guard hadn't distracted me, I might've enjoyed this read. This much firsthand information on prewar Elysia was practically unheard of since the schism, and it was worth reading even if the translations would take me twice as long.

Night yawned wider through the giant windows and my eyes drooped further, and with the captain's interruption, I conceded the battle and headed back to my rooms, taking the book with me.

The ancient Lunarium and Solaris Clans of the Elysian empire could wait until morning.

I needed my beauty sleep before tomorrow's adventure.

"You're later than I expected." Nyxia waited in my sitting room, helping herself to the passive-aggressive dinner tray that'd been left for me. Half of a roasted chicken that, of course, I wouldn't eat, and what thankfully looked like a bowl of vegetable soup, likely cold by now. Nyxia sucked the last bit of flavor from a clean picked leg bone.

I tossed the book onto my table before throwing myself at the plushiest chair, sinking into it. "Library. I was having a chat with Captain Bellatore."

I lifted the bowl to my lips, taking a deep—*chilly*—sip.

Nyxia's eyes darkened. She stabbed her chicken bone at me like a rapier. "About what I'll do to her if she dares to lay a finger on you again?"

I snorted. Nyxia hadn't been pleased when I told her of the brief encounter with rage-fueled impulses. But luckily for Aurora, I had enjoyed our little tiff just as much as she had, the break in tension the only respite I'd had for my stress in days. Typically, when the world got overwhelming, and I didn't have the Pool of Souls to cool me down, I much preferred *fucking* it out of my system, but the fighting would do . . . for now.

I shook my head. "About her and the Prince sharing an intimate moment."

Nyxia's head tilted, mischief winning over malice in her expression. "That's unexpected. I didn't think either of them had the stones."

"Me either, but I'm rather pleasantly surprised." I grinned, curling deeper into the chair. I thought it would take far more prompting for the rule-loving captain and the timid prince to break their celibacy, but the turn of events was not a bad one.

Information was power, and now I had them both in a delicate position where they relied on my mercy. Not that I wanted to ever have to use that advantage, but it was the perfect way to build trust with little effort. Trust the three of us desperately needed if I were to keep my kingdom and my future consort safe.

My only qualm was that they hadn't asked me to *join* them.

Yet.

I rubbed my eyes with the heels of my palms, banishing that particularly delicious vision from my skull. The events of the day throbbed against my temples, my head pounding no matter which pressure point I pressed. "We have more important things to focus on."

Nyxia wiped her hands on her shirt before reaching into her pocket and brandishing a letter.

"Like this?" She dangled it in front of me, close enough so I could make out the black ink swirling on the outside. It was addressed to King Kato.

I shot forward in my seat, snatching it from the little devil.

"It was on his desk earlier, and I thought it might find a happier home here." Nyxia didn't hide the pride in her voice.

I smiled so broadly, it hurt my cheeks. "You're a menace."

Nyxia shrugged.

I unfurled the letter, careful not to crumple the edges in case we had to sneak this back to its home.

A quick scan banished the smile from my face.

The report was brief, written in shorthand in the margins of a map, but the message was clear.

Ninety-eight Shadowborne attacks in the last three days, mostly in the outer city, but nearly a dozen closer to Stellaris.

Ninety-eight attacks.

Triple the amount from a month ago, if Nyxia's informants were to be trusted. The Shadowborne in Lux were still a problem, but typically they'd made their home along the coastal outposts, occasionally daring to hunt in the outlying mountain villages, with the rare outer-city sighting when they got too hungry.

But ninety-eight events, all within the city limits?

A shadow crossed Nyxia's face, mirth disappearing from the room. "Shadowborne activity increases everywhere. But it is all too easy. Look at the geographical pattern." She pointed to the markers at the bottom of the page—at the near perfect crescent that indicated where the Shadowborne had been. "It all seems . . ."

"Planned," I finished for her.

Shadowborne were lawless. Succumbed to madness, transformed by their own inner monstrosity. The shadows did not plot and patiently plan.

And in all my years defending my people from them, I'd never seen them hunt in such an *orderly* fashion.

Which meant we had a strategist on our hands. Likely the same one that'd conveniently let the Shadowborne into the Summer Palace.

I crumbled the report in my fist, tossing it toward the fire. Flames devoured it hungrily, even as my appetite vanished.

"How involved is the King?"

"There is still no evidence that he gets his hands dirty, but my guess is he isn't doing anything to stop it, either. This proves he knows."

My shadows crept closer. Rage licked the back of my neck, oppressive and demanding. My nails dug deep graves in my palms, murderous and hungry to lodge themselves in the King's neck instead.

King Kato was either far more nefarious than I'd been giving him credit for, or he, too, had given in madness. Into apathy and lawlessness.

Either way, he was *dangerous,* and if he didn't start protecting our kingdoms from ruin, he would have to be dealt with.

I didn't want to think what that would mean for my budding trust with Caelum, but I'd always choose my people first.

I inhaled sharply through my nose, focusing on the plain, white fabric of the chair's upholstered arm. Breathed in, out, as I counted the thin, tattered threats. Coaxed my anger back into its cage.

If things went according to plan, I wouldn't have to choose at all. When my voice felt like my own again, I turned to Nyxia. "Captain Bellatore and I struck an agreement. We train the Prince at dawn."

Nyxia pursed her lips. "While that sounds . . . helpful, we have enough on our plates as is, especially now that we can send for more of us."

At that, my heart leapt. Though my meeting with Kato had been mind-melting, a single, beautiful boon had come from it.

My people would get to visit Lux. Would get to feast and dance and bask in the sunlight, a taste of what was to come when my marriage settled. A reminder of what I fought for.

And I wouldn't have to fight alone, not if Stavros would come. My advisor would know how to navigate these treacherous waters.

Waters Caelum still trod in, unaware of the sharks nipping at his ankles, with no rescue boat in sight unless we taught him to swim.

"Our people are counting on the Prince's survival just as much as they are mine. Training him makes us all safer."

For the first time in years, I wasn't as confident as I pretended to be.

For all its finery, I didn't know if *safe* existed in Lux. It certainly didn't exist in Erebus.

And maybe we'd fought amongst ourselves for too long to notice that there was no Elysian peace left in this world.

Nyxia nodded, dutiful as ever. "Then, if that's the case, I have an idea you will not like."

I was wide awake by the time dawn purpled the sky—nightmares chasing away any chance of deep sleep. I dressed quickly, opting for a soft pair of slim fitting trousers and wrapped linen band around my breasts. The sun would likely roast me in my leathers if I dared wear more, my body still not accustomed to the direct heat.

Maybe I'd even get a tan. Or a burn.

Either way, I'd likely get a few looks.

I hadn't lied to Nyxia—the Prince's safety was my priority, and my betrothed needed more assistance if he would survive. But I needed this just as much as he did. Needed to *play*, holing up in the library no good for my mental state. Needed to move, to hone my body into something that could contain the shadows. To remind myself of the discipline that'd been etched into my skin with every scar.

To reunite with the art of control—something that'd been slipping in my time in the light.

I padded into the hall, smiling at the guards posted outside my chambers—both of whom gripped their sword hilts tighter, sweat on their brows—in a decidedly excited mood, and made my way toward the pitch.

Another form blocked my path, stepping out of his room just down the hall.

Dread pooled low in my gut, my mood short lived.

Kappas dipped his head—a poor excuse for a bow. "Mi Vassilla,"

I forced a smile, shadows itching beneath my skin, unhappy with any delay in their carnal feast. "Ah, Kappas. Good to see you out and about so early."

A hand twitched at his side.

"Might we talk?" His lips pursed in apparent distaste, his gaze trailing my mostly bare skin. To his credit, Kappas was one of my father's men that'd never made a pass at me, though I suspected that had more to do with his thinly veiled infatuation with my father.

But if he was here to lecture me about my outfit, I didn't have the time, not with that need still wriggling in my gut.

I moved to step around him. "I'm actually busy—"

He caught my arm.

I raised a brow, glaring at his fingers clasped around my elbow, and he had the sense to drop his hold.

He cleared his throat. "This is urgent."

I crossed my arms, my patience thin. "At dawn?"

Kappas glanced at the guards down the hall. "I have a lead on the prisoner's death."

At that, my shadows honed their focus, a chill running down my spine. "Talk quickly."

Kappas nodded, tugging me toward a shaded alcove adorned with yet another bust of King Alixsander—likely so no one nearby could read our lips. I had my spies, but whoever was behind the attack clearly had ways of obtaining sensitive information as well.

"After our meeting with King Kato yesterday." Kappas kept his voice low—just as aware of the potential listeners as I was, but willing to take the risk. A frown emphasized the wrinkles around his lips. "I realized that Lord Pollux had been on his way down to the dungeons after the attack. The Luxian guards and I had run past him on our way to you."

I stilled, but the shadows writhed.

Pollux, the over-eager Public Representative that breathed down my neck for a chance at dinner. Who had both access to King Kato—and to the inner city.

I directed the flare of contempt that ran through my veins at Kappas. "And you conveniently forgot this until now?"

His brow furrowed. "The visitor log books don't register that he attended, and in the flurry, I didn't—"

"Someone in your position should know not to be swept up in a *flurry*." My sharp tone ricocheted off the marble walls.

Kappas's jaw tightened, but he withheld his response.

Sucking in a breath—steadying my control—I wrangled my voice back into submission. "And if he wasn't included in the logbook, we have little evidence."

Or motive, other than the ambition that every courtier in this sun-bleached snake den possessed.

But if Pollux wanted to share a meal, I would oblige. And if he was involved in the deaths . . .

I might just make him the main course.

I took a step back—into the full brightness of the hallway.

"Thank you, Kappas. I'll take it from here."

Kappas nodded and swept one last disapproving glance over me. "Be careful, *Mi Vassilla*. You are bold to be unarmed in such a place."

A shadow curled around my fingernail, sharpening into a claw. I grinned and watched Kappas' throat bob. "I'm never unarmed."

And if I didn't go hit something soon, all of Lux would soon be reminded of the *Sykagos'* weapons.

Nyxia was already at the pitch by the time I arrived, dressed in black from head to toe, a frown on her face. The rest of our meeting the night before had gone just as poorly as the first half, our plans all balancing on a razor's edge. And we would need to factor in what Kappas told me about Pollux before we moved.

But she wasn't alone, so we'd have no opportunity to chat more this morning.

Captain Bellatore stood in a tight fit, cropped shirt that exposed the impressive tone of her sculpted arms and abdomen, thin, skin-hugging riding pants emphasizing *other* shapely parts of her. Honey-blonde hair wove into two compressed braids, her raised scars and blue tattoos a macabre—and beautiful—pattern across her face and down her torso.

Caelum waited to her right, a bright smile greeting me. His white hair was pushed back by a strip of blue fabric that matched his loose-fitting tunic—likely a pajama shirt. He shifted his weight between both feet, his excitement palpable. A pretty flush tinted his cheeks today, like his body, too, had decided it would play along. I didn't know the specifics of his condition—and it felt impolite to ask—but it seemed to wax and wane.

Something wriggled in my gut.

They were *handsome* together. Soft and harsh, delicate and sturdy, in perfect balance.

Something dark and wicked like me didn't quite fit.

Behind them, Lieutenant Fortis and the two guards that'd burst into my rooms with Kappas the day I'd arrived—Syrax and Duni, I believed—all wore similar uniforms, which consisted of loose cotton britches and *nothing else*, shirts discarded to reveal well-muscled chests. Even the short one was carved from bronze, the three of them statuesque.

Moon and mist, it'd been way too long since I'd had a good fuck. I almost missed Minister Aygros and his half-pathetic, whimpering thrusts.

Control. Art of control.

I waved and kicked my boots off, the sand cool against my toes. I preferred the texture—the slight nips of pain grounding me back into my body. "You brought an audience?"

"We enthusiastically volunteered." The shorter of the soldiers —Dora, or Dugan?—grinned wickedly.

The taller, handsome one tugged his long hair away from his face with a leather band, and his gaze raked over me, lingering on my wrapped breasts. "No way we'd miss this."

The captain leveled them both with a scalding glare.

I couldn't help the chuckle that worked its way up my throat, or the way my eyes dragged to the spectacular 'v' that dipped beneath his britches. "Well, the pitch is yours. Where do we start?"

Syrax opened his mouth to make a suggestion, but the captain beat him to it, her glare melting into something far more sinister. She *grinned*. "Conditioning first. Fifty push-ups, now. Caelum, you do yours against the wall."

The prince frowned. "You aren't supposed to baby me."

Rory crossed her arms. "Injury does not beget growth. You start with modifications and work up to the harder variations. Now stop whining and get moving."

Caelum's frown didn't move, but he stalked over to the nearest column and pushed against it dutifully.

Rory led us through a series of exercises to warm us all up, but by the time we were finished, breathless and sweaty messes, I was hot enough to fry breakfast on. The sun had just begun its ascent over the columns of the pitch, baking Nyxia and I to a crisp.

The seasoned soldiers looked perfectly content, bronze and gold skin glittering with sweat as the sun sparkled off it.

Caelum was a shade of red that rivaled rubies for its depth.

And that was when the real torture began.

The captain called us all through a series of punches and kicks meant to prepare us to spar. And while repetitive, it had been ages since I'd had someone work me this hard.

Without my father's whip keeping me alert and the cool caress of the shadows numbing the sting, I found it much harder to focus on the task.

Instead, my mind—and my eyes—kept drifting to Captain Bellatore, her muscles rippling with each jab and swing. Admiring her genuine smile and the way her sweat-damp hair clung to the places along her neck and face that I wanted to touch . . .

It was even harder when she started correcting the Prince's form, her hands sliding along his arms and core as she taught him how to brace and swing.

I didn't know if I wanted to be him, her, or simply wedged in the middle.

But my fantasies faded as Caelum's frustration mounted.

"All right, My Prince. Hands up." Rory demonstrated the same set of rapid-fire punches for the third time.

Caelum's brow knit, and he tried to repeat the action—but his elbows were too wide, his stance wobbly. "I'm trying."

"Tuck your elbow!"

He threw his next punch, a shaky, indirect swing that wouldn't do much to ward off a seasoned fighter.

And that would be useless against monsters like the Shadow-borne, who didn't wait for their prey to get into an appropriate stance.

I cleared my throat. "May I interject?"

Caelum's eyes flicked to me—a plea for mercy in their pretty blue hue.

This wasn't working, and he wanted it even more than I did.

"Oh, this will be good." Syrax scoffed, earning snickers from the other guards—Lieutenant Fortis included.

Something prickled beneath my skin. Whether they doubted my ability or Caelum's, I didn't care.

None of them would laugh when the Shadowborne breathed down Stellaris' front gates. Or when the traitors *inside* the palace finally played their hands.

Captain Bellatore sensed my shift in tone, dropping her stance. "What is it?"

"This fighting style is effective for you and these meatheads." I jerked a thumb toward Julius, Syrax, and Domo, all of which promptly stopped their snickering. "With arms like those, you can do some major damage."

I patted her impressive bicep, earning the deep blush that painted her cheeks and the tips of her long ears.

I turned to Caelum, speaking *to* him rather than above him. Inviting him in. "But until you put on a little more muscle, even with that long range of yours, you're going to take a lot more hits than you effectively land."

321

In a sparring ring, that meant bruises, maybe a busted lip or black eye.

In battle, or against a Shadowborne, that meant death.

The Luxians were built like houses and trained to fight from birth, but Erebushi were taught how to *survive*.

Rory gnawed her bottom lip, gaze sweeping over Caelum. "What would you suggest?"

I pitched my voice higher—a lesson for everyone listening, not just Caelum. "For those of us used to dealing with less muscular builds, we must use leverage and holds more. Moves that bring an opponent to ground, and that keep us moving with the attacks instead of bracing against them."

Nyxia marched to the middle of the pitch and cracked her knuckles. Her sights set on Rory, her itch for a fight thinly veiled. "Care if I demonstrate, *Mi Vassilla?*"

Part of me itched for that stand-off too, but I stalked toward the other guards instead. Toward the snickering men that relied too heavily on their statures. To the *boys* underestimating my future consort and me. I stared up at each of them as I passed with utter malice in my smile; Julius first, and even Dingle, who was still an inch or two taller than me. "Any enthusiastic volunteers?"

I stopped in front of Syrax—the tallest and broadest of them.

"Why not?" He took the bait with a shrug and a scoff.

"Oh, sun above, this is going to be good." The short one nudged his friend toward Nyxia.

"Shove it up yours, Dama," Syrax said.

He turned his smile on the little devil and dipped into a ready stance, his hands next to his face and his elbows tucked close, just like the Captain had taught. "I'll promise to take it easy on you, milady."

Nyxia blinked at him. "Give me your best shot, tiger."

He swung first.

And missed; Nyxia rolled beneath his punch to snag his ankle.

The man fell harder than a downed tree, and my spy master went to *work*.

I practically skipped toward Caelum, whispering over his shoulder. "See what she's doing?"

Violet eyes watched closely as Nyxia dodged each blow, instead using Syrax's momentum to snare and subdue, over and over again. The few hits Syrax *did* land inflicted minimal damage as Nyxia spun with them, like a feather flying away the harder he tried to catch her.

The corner of Caelum's mouth titled up. "She's using his size and strength against him."

I grinned. "A single pebble can find its way into your sandals better than a mountain can."

"But it only works *because* she's so much smaller and faster." Rory frowned as Nyxia took out Syrax by the knees, folding herself around him to tug his leg at a brutal angle, earning a curse from the large man. "It's less effective when you're similarly sized, and Caelum isn't tiny."

Caelum's chest puffed up slightly, but it didn't matter. Tall as he was, even if he *did* put muscle on, that didn't change the damage years of being ill had racked across his body. Bones more brittle than most. Lungs lacking the same capacity.

No, Caelum needed to learn how to defend himself even if he was at a physical disadvantage. Needed to learn how to reduce the damage he took, and to endure pain. Because even though Shadowborne weren't much larger than most elves, they would show no mercy.

"You and I are about the same size." I tilted my head at Rory. "Why don't we test that theory out?"

She snorted. "I've got thirty pounds of muscle on you."

"Caelum's opponent will likely have that on him, even if they're the same height."

Rory stared at me for a long moment, her warm eyes devouring me from head to toe. "Fine. But this won't be like last time."

323

Last time when she'd been all blind rage and brutal, murderous intent. When I'd been half-serious and out of practice.

No, this would be different. This was her element; the sand her home and the sun her friend. This was precise training and decades of practice, honed for moments like these.

A moment in the ring with the *Sykagos.*

And I was all in, ready to oblige her and show Caelum what real instinct and instruction could make a person. What discipline and control could offer even the weakest of us.

I lifted my chin. "Sounds like my idea of a good time."

Something that fell between a scream and a whimper echoed from the pitch, drawing our attention to where Nyxia had her thigh wrapped around Syrax's neck, blocking his airflow, and he clawed at her leg. She smiled down at the now-purple-male. "Do you yield?"

Three taps to her leg signaled his defeat.

Nyxia released him, and he sputtered for air as he laid flat on his back, staring up at Nyxia like she was the new sun in his universe.

"Fuck, woman," he wheezed. "Will you marry me?"

"Clear the pitch, you moron." Rory rolled her eyes and strutted onto the pitch, stretching out her neck.

I followed her out, patting Nyxia on the head. "Well done."

She tossed me a wink before sauntering to the sidelines, Syrax crawling after her on all fours like a dog after its new master.

Well, that would be a tough act to follow, but I'd have to make do.

Rory tossed the ends of her braids over her shoulder, focus narrowing onto me. "Jules, you're the referee."

"I want a clean, fair fight." Julius crossed his impressive arms across his chest in a stance meant to be menacing. But I didn't miss the bob of his throat. "No magic."

I smirked, my voice dropping purposefully low. "I don't need my magic, but I certainly wouldn't mind getting a little dirty, Captain."

I expected her to blink or stammer, expected that pretty, rose-soft blush to brighten her cheeks.

Instead, her tongue darted across her lips once, a predator licking its chops before setting onto its prey.

"Keep talking, Your Majesty." Rory's expression was trapped between a snarl and a smile. "And I'll make you eat your words."

"This is a bad idea." My betrothed—moon and mist bless him—muttered on the sidelines. His weight shifted between his feet as he chewed on his fingernails.

"The worst," Julius said, his panic masked by that same false-stern bravado.

Pure excitement shot like lightning through my veins, my shadows a controlled coil in my chest for the first time in weeks.

I hadn't had a proper match since I'd left Erebus . . . maybe not since my father died. And if I was to keep the monster in my mind at bay, it needed to be regularly fed.

Captain Bellatore didn't hesitate to deliver my first meal.

Rory struck first, no warning bell or call. Her lightning-fast punch blew past my ear, and I dodged just in time.

Three more jabs—wide right, high, short an inch—none of them finding their mark.

I smiled and darted back. "Missed me."

She opened her mouth, a snarky remark cocked and ready. I lunged before she could speak. My thighs wrapped around her middle, knocking the wind out of her. She caught my shoulders, but it didn't matter as I threw my weight backward.

My hands caught the sand, and I flipped the captain over myself with my legs, tossing her onto the pitch. I landed straddled on top of her, ready to put her into submission—

A punch landed this time, straight across my jaw, hard enough to bruise.

My ears rang, and the world spun. Fuck, she hit like an anvil. Another hit like that, and I'd be dizzy for a week.

I licked my lips, squeezing my knees tighter so she couldn't throw me. "Oof, that almost stung."

As predicted, she reacted and swung again. I caught her wrist and pinned it beneath me, rearranging my weight. If I could strap my leg across her chest, I could pull her into an arm hold, threatening the security of her shoulder joint.

She leaned in instead of tugging back like I expected. Rory surged upward, so I was planted across her lap. Her free hand skimmed against my ribs, her face only a breath from mine, and her gaze darted to my mouth. "Want me to kiss it all better?"

I stilled, brows raising and heat pooling low in my core, sweet surprise skittering down my back. I gripped her wrist tighter. "Don't threaten me with a good—"

Lifting her arm—and mine with it—she spun me off her, throwing me onto the hot sand. Wind crushed from my lungs, and in another second, she was on me, her knee pressed into my chest, all thirty-extra-pounds of her driving me further into the ground.

Her smile was all teeth. "Yield."

I struggled beneath her, legs kicking up to dislodge her, but it was no use, her stance secure. Without my shadows, I had no leverage, the sand sucking me deeper every time I tried to wriggle free.

I couldn't stop the breathless laugh that careened out of me. "Did you just *flirt* your way to a victory?"

Rory fucking *winked* as she hopped off me, leaving me in the sand like a discarded sandal. She turned to Caelum, who watched with a beautiful blend of awe, fear, and something more *improper* tinting his blushed cheeks.

"And that is how you can use information and other tools against your opponent. Fighting style aside, your fists are not your only weapons in a match." Her voice carried on the back of the warm breeze that dusted up sand around me.

She wasn't wrong.

But maybe had she taken her own advice, she'd have paid attention to me moving through the cloud of dusty sand like one of my shadows.

I swiped at her legs, toppling her unprepared stance with an easy blow, before catching her in a chokehold.

Strong hands fought my grip—confident, even under pressure —but I didn't release.

"Another tip." I winked at Caelum from over her shoulder, my body flush against her back to strengthen my hold. "The battle is never over if your opponent is still breathing. Don't lower your guard."

An elbow jerked back into my ribs—earning the captain a momentary breath. "Cheap fucking move."

But I re-centered my grip, holding my wrist tighter, using my bony arm to my advantage, and pressed deeper into the captain's neck.

"The people that want the Prince dead will *always* make a cheap move," I growled against her ear, my lips skimming across the sensitive flesh. "Besides, I'm put out that you led me on."

She stilled in my arms.

And I swear she shivered.

"All right, enough. It's a draw!" Julius called out in the same moment I let go, sending Rory sputtering forward.

She leapt to her feet, stomping toward me until she was just an inch from my face, eyes hooded and mouth parted, ready to punch me or *kiss* me, I couldn't tell.

I wanted both in surprisingly equal measures.

A hand on her shoulder stayed her either way.

"Captain, why don't the Prince and I give it a go?" Julius tried to keep his voice level, but he scratched at his tattooed chest like it was painful.

Her jaw clenched, and she sucked in a sharp breath.

"Fine."

She stormed off to the sidelines, bare feet kicking up clouds of sand with how aggressively she stomped.

But the Lieutenant's shoulders visibly relaxed, his forehead forgoing its wrinkles. He waved Caelum over. "All right, Your Highness. Let's see how you handle someone bigger than you for a bit."

"Way to rub it in." Caelum snorted, but lifted his head high. If he'd lose, he'd do it with dignity.

A survivor in the making, no doubt.

But even as they walked past, replacing us in the center of the ring, Rory paid them no attention, her chest still heaving as she stared at me, gnawing at her lip.

Her eyes danced with something that devoured worlds. Something that could burn the sun itself to ash, or could even make the shadows scurry away in fear.

Desire.

Murderous desire.

CHAPTER
TWENTY-THREE

"Zo'is is highly versatile. When blended with Turmeric and White Willow bark, Zo'is can evolve as an anti-inflammatory and block the pain receptors in the brain. However, like most pain reducers, an elf can build a tolerance to its effects." –A Comprehensive Guide to the Medicinal Purposes of Zo'is, written by Luxian Physician Euclio Naveas, 359 A.G.W.

CAELUM

Pain was a constant in my life, taking up permanent residence in my body. It made a living room in my lungs, never full enough. A kitchen in my always-spinning head, in my too-flushed cheeks. A bedroom, in the ever-present throb that pulsed through my joints, vacationing only to the tingle at the tips of my fingers and toes.

I'd gotten used to it, learned to live around it like an unwelcome guest, the pain just a fuzzy, distant background noise I could shut out. Even on the worst days—when no matter how hard I tried, I couldn't catch my breath, when my head felt like it was going to explode, when every nerve-ending was coated in fire—I'd learned the practiced art of existing through it. Of curling up into a ball on my bed and counting my heartbeats, or of slipping into the tub and focusing on where the water cooled and kissed my skin. Of sleeping through the noise, escaping from my body into the dreamworld.

My mother had taught me—had coached me through my flares just as she had managed through her own. And pain, though unwelcome, had never been lonely.

But the first morning after training, pain found a new shade.

I woke alone to darkness, my body jolting into consciousness. The flickering *Zo'is* provided the only source of light in the room, like the Sun was still deep at rest, not a single hazy ray peeking from behind the curtains.

And in that darkness, I was on fire.

Instead of the deep, throbbing ache, the pain bloomed in swollen, invisible burns, like every inch of me was inflamed.

It took all my strength to get out of bed and pull clothes over my head, the sting of the silk across my flesh enough to make me wince.

I was grateful the servants had the foresight the night before to leave a kettle of my medicinal tea in my sitting room. I stumbled to it like a man crawling to an oasis in a desert, desperate for relief. With shaking hands, I poured a full cup. I downed it in two gulps, barely registering the bitter afterbite of *Zo'is*.

It was all I could do to breathe and *wait*. A few endless moments passed, and the pain finally abated, the vicious, blazing heat dying to a general sizzle.

But it wasn't gone, and even with my high tolerance, it would be noticed. More than a background sound, but a symphony of discomfort that sang with every movement. Not an unwelcome guest, but an intruder, ravaging every system of my body.

This was not good. There was no way I'd survive another day of training like this; no way my body would keep up beneath the Sun's too-hot stare.

Shame rattled through me as I sucked in my next breath.

I'd have to tell Rory. I'd have to admit to her—to everyone—that I wasn't strong enough for this. That I couldn't keep pace.

A knock interrupted my self-flagellation.

My fists clenched at my sides. That had to be Rory, collecting me like she had yesterday morning, earlier than I'd expected.

Better to get it over with, I supposed.

I flung open the door. Thera's pale cheeks touched pink from yesterday's sun greeted me with a wide grin. "Surprise!"

I blinked, confusion blurring the ache for a breath.

"*Thera?* You're early."

Today, she didn't wear the revealing, wonderfully distracting training outfit she'd sported yesterday, but the plainest outfit I'd ever seen her in, a rough-spun beige tunic and oversized brown trousers that cinched her waist. Her long, dark hair tucked up in a loose bun, wayward strands falling to float in front of her face.

A small leather pack strapped to her back.

"We should skip training today." That grin turned feral. "I want to see the city."

My headache and the early hour slowed my response.

"*What?*"

Thera sauntered past me, inviting herself into my greeting room. "I need a better understanding of the Luxian people if I'm going to rule beside you." She threw her pack onto a chair and sat next to it. Her knowing gaze swept over me once, and her lips pursed. "And frankly, everyone needs a cool down after yesterday."

Embarrassment trickled down my spine. Did I look that out of sorts?

Not that it mattered. My body demanded respite today, regardless of Thera's thoughts or feelings on the matter.

I was about to tell her as much when she clasped her hands

together, jutting out her bottom lip like a little kid pleading for an extra serving of dessert.

"My eyes hurt." She offered the pouted explanation, though I hadn't asked for one. "From the sunlight, and all the reading I've been doing. I think I need a happy view to recover. An easy, quiet day strolling around."

I shut my mouth. Thera had spent most of her time in Stellaris, hunched over a book, kneading her head like it was a constant ache. Mother used to insist that even when I was sickly, I take a stroll through the willows, asserting the fresh air and the shade was better than any medicine.

She was usually right.

A slow walk through the city . . . with frequent stops in the shade . . . I could handle. Counterintuitive as it seemed, light exercise often helped my blood flow normally again and prevented my muscles from stiffening. Plus, it would save me the discomfort of having to admit to Rory I needed a break for other reasons.

And Thera was right. She needed a better understanding of my people, and so did I. The closest I'd ever been to a commoner was Quinton, and even he'd come from wealth. If our journey back from the Summer Palace had been any indication, there were problems I'd overlooked right on my doorstep.

It was time I got stronger. But I didn't need to just improve my body's condition, but my mind's too. My *heart's*.

A good king led with all three.

Maybe a day with my future wife—a true king—would help me sort out my tangled heartstrings, too.

"Okay, I'll get my things." I nodded. Then, sheepishly, "But fair warning, I might be slow today."

Thera smiled so broadly; it lit the pre-dawn room. "I don't mind taking it slow with you, Prince Caelum."

With a gulp, in contradiction to what I'd just said, I rushed as much as my body would allow. I grabbed the plainest cloak I owned, a dull, gray-blue that'd faded with time, but with a light hood that would protect me from the sun if I needed it, and a canteen for my tea, in case this dose wore off and I needed another cup.

But then I followed Thera out the door, my heartbeat a jaunt that for once beat with excitement instead of dread.

I'd wanted to go into the city for ages, and I'd never been allowed. Never allowed *myself*, using my condition as a convenient excuse.

But I'd heard stories of the markets—from Rory, mostly—about the main plaza and the wonders that were commonplace there. Stories of life and love and laughter. Stories of action and adventure and artistry—all right here in Lux. All right under my nose, waiting for me to take a whiff.

An imposing silhouette halted us before we could take off down the hall to write our own story. "Sneaking off?"

Julius stood like a sentry, already dressed in his uniform, a brow raised.

"No, we, um—"

"We're going into the city." She sank into her hip, lashes fluttering, as she looked up at Julius. "Care to join?"

The hair on the back of my neck prickled. Another unwelcome guest.

Julius's broad arms crossed, flexing his corded muscles. But his smile stretched across his face, tension-free. "Do you want my *Vinculum* to kill me?"

"Of course not." Thera reached out, squeezing his impressive arm. "You're far too handsome to get rid of."

Something rolled in my gut, a jealous, seething thing that blotted out the pain. She might have been simply playing to his favor, but of course, there was honesty in the tease. Thera found Julius handsome. *Everyone* did, his physique unmatched, his smile bright. Rory wanted me—her declarations still beating in my best with every passing day that she awaited my answer—but she'd always relied on him. *Needed* him, like she needed air in her lungs and food in her belly.

Would I have to share Thera with him, too? Would she see him as a pillar of support, where I was barely more than decoration, an accessory to take on shopping trips? A side character in a story that was not my own?

My envious tongue could not be tamed. "Rory will be angry."

At that, Julius paused. Frowned. Guilt wriggled under my skin, an itch too deep to scratch. It was unfair to use Rory against him, especially since I was about to sneak out myself, which would surely earn her fury.

Thera was undeterred.

"That seems to be the norm." She rolled her eyes before fixing Julius with a challenging stare that could set the sun on fire. "We're going whether you come or not. Either join us now, or catch up later when the captain insists on escorting us back."

Julius sucked in a deep breath.

Then he loosed a burdened sigh. "She'd probably be angrier if I let you go alone. Things haven't been as secure lately." He looked over his shoulder, like he hoped Rory wouldn't materialize from the early morning mist. "And I needed to visit someone in the city anyway."

Disappointment plummeted through me, sinking all the way to my toes. So much for a stroll alone with my future wife.

"That's the spirit." Thera grinned, skipping ahead down the hallway. "Let's go!"

I should've stayed in bed. Should've turned around and drawn myself a soothing bath.

I pushed through the pain in my legs, following after her instead.

While the disappointment lingered on the journey into the city—a bumbling, jostling ride that did my body no favors thanks to the small, single horse-carriage Julius secured for us—it evaporated completely as Thera and I strolled through the market of Solis' outer city.

The smells, the tastes, the colors were a welcomed assault to the senses. No time to process my pain, not with the myriad of sensations drawing my focus. Without the glitter of Stellaris to blot everything out, the tall, glass-faced buildings that lined streets shone in the rising sun, the hum and buzz of life drowning out all else. In the center of the Plaza, a faded green-and-copper statue of King Alixsander raising his arms to the sunlight, streams of crystal-clear water billowed from his fingertips, feeding into the marble basin of the fountain below.

And like it was the middle of the universe, energy surrounded it like bees to flowers. Elves from every walk of life, in every shape and size, bustled in and out of the storefronts that lined the promenade, while others lounged on nearby benches, basking in the morning sun. Where the paved street narrowed into small, stone-laid alleyways, sprigs of defiant green shrubbery grew between the cracks. An ease filled the air with the song of joy, children laughing as their parents chided after them, lovers giggling as they whispered secrets into each other's ears.

A young man playing a happy morning waltz on a violin, his music amplified by a small *Zo'is* device, as others tossed him copper crowns.

An older man teaching a little boy to play chess on a chalk-drawn board, the little boy's face wrinkled in confusion as the elderly man smiled.

A woman, aimlessly rocking her baby in a wheeled carriage as she sampled a vendor's fresh fruit, humming along with the music to herself and her child.

An old crone, sitting on the edge of the fountain, drawing

portraits of passerbys, her gnarled fingers stained with charcoal and bent with years of mastery.

Joy.

In excess. In abundance.

I could barely catch my breath, but this time, not from fatigue, but *wonder.*

I'd never wanted for anything in the palace, all my meals top class and catered to my door, all my clothes finely made by the in-house tailor himself.

But Solis teemed with more vibrancy and choice than I knew what to do with.

Store after store of garments, in every imaginable color and style; some in the standard, puffy Luxian fashion, others in the more muted, earth-toned daily wear that the servants and soldiers preferred. Shop after shop of food and drink; some wafting with savory, mouthwatering smoke, others spilling over with sugary-sweet scents that made my stomach growl.

The market of Solis *breathed*, like it was the great pair of lungs that the city itself used to draw in air and exhale pure, unfiltered *joy.*

A sadness sank through me, dark and envious, for all the days in this sun-warmed plaza I'd missed. For all the people I ruled over but did not know. For the lives they'd live without me, my role to be a distant character, more of an *idea* than a real person.

Julius, who got to enjoy this part of Lux frequently, broke off from us early to meet his friend at the tavern down the road—a soldier's haunt called *Potio*—leaving Thera and I to our own devices. With his absence, another knot in my chest unfastened.

Free of his imposing presence, we stopped at a patisserie first, a little café called *Saccharo* that sold pastries with every filling imaginable. Rows of choices lined the small glass casing at the storefront, each golden-flaked, decadence-filled dessert beckoning me closer.

I wanted to taste them all. Wanted to come back each morning until I could rank their flavors in order. Wanted to savor every morsel this life had to offer.

Drool formed at the corners of my mouth, and we entered, heat closing in like a warm blanket in the dead of winter, cozy and consuming. Soft lamplight baked the room in the same gold as the pastries. A short, round woman smiled from behind the counter. "Welcome! Can I help you two?"

"I'll take one of those..." Thera said pointing at the display case decisively to a blackberry-stuffed bun for her, and a brown-sugar-and-creme-filled donut for me. "And this onee."

The woman nodded, scurrying to collect each treat and place them in a paper bag. She then rung it up on the register, her smile never falling. "That will be five coppers."

Thera, Sun bless her, had thought far enough ahead to bring coin, fishing two silvers from her pack. The woman behind the counter handed us our reward and thanked Thera profusely for the generous tip.

My eyes snagged on another pastry—a cinnamon muffin that had Rory's name practically written all over it—and my heart sank.

I wanted her here. With me. And Thera.

I didn't know how to handle that.

Walking out of the shop, Thera handed me my pastry from the brown paper bag, a brow raised like she could smell my conflicted thoughts.

I shoved my regret aside and shoved the donut in my mouth.

"This is delicious," I groaned after the first bite, not caring how the sticky creme dripped down the side of my mouth. Sun and stars, the sweet, gooey dough chased away my pain, more potent than my *Zo'is* tea. "I've never tasted anything like this in my life."

"Me either." Thera smiled while she chewed, mouth stained purple. Her thumb swiped the excess filling from my lips before she licked it off with a wink. "I could eat a hundred."

Whether she meant the pastry or me, I didn't know, but heat flared through me all the same, happiness sparking in my chest.

337

"Yeah, sure you could. You have the appetite of a baby bird."

"And you should mind your business." She shoved my arm playfully before darting out the door, knowing I'd follow.

"Have a nice day, folks!" The shop attendant called after us with a wave through the wide window.

The air in my lungs thinned, claimed by a sadness I had no name for.

I was just another customer to her, one that could never be a regular. We lived in the same city, but our lives were inherently distanced by the roles we had to play.

Her, the baker that fed and nourished a city.

Me, the prince that could barely nourish himself. Who sat in his gemstone-encrusted towers, lonely and unaware of the thousands who resided near him.

Thera slowed and waited for me to catch up to her. "A copper for your thoughts?"

I pursed my lips, looking back over my shoulder at the store. "They don't recognize us."

Thera sucked in a breath and stared back at the window.

"There is no joy in Erebus, not like this." Thera fit her arm through mine, steadying me—and herself. "But my people do not suffer alone, because I am with them. But here, there is great division. To your people, it's so absurd to assume the royals would visit, that even staring us in the face, they refuse to believe it."

My chest tightened. Lux had always been my home. Solis my birth city.

And it was as foreign to me as Erebus was.

I clutched Thera's arm tighter. "We'll change that. My people will know me, and your people will know joy again."

No more hiding in Stellaris, behind walls of my making. Behind my guard, or my father. With Thera next to me, it was time to step into the light.

My betrothed smiled. Her face softened. Like that had been the purpose of this outing all along.

A paper fluttered in front of us, swept by an errant wind, and Thera plucked it from the air with deft fingers. Her eyes scanned it quickly, a divot formed between her brows.

My throat clogged. "What's wrong?"

Thera clutched the paper to her chest. Her gaze narrowed. "Do you want to know? You won't like it."

I swallowed the lump and held out a hand. "Please."

Thera, to her credit, didn't hold back. She placed the flier in my hand, saying nothing as I read it quickly.

Only three lines of black text, printed haphazardly—like whoever had made these was rushing. But still, my heart slammed against my chest with every word.

KING KATO BEGINS THE FADE!

DO WE WANT TO LEAVE OUR CITY TO THE PUPPET PRINCE & HIS DARK BRIDE?

FREE SOLIS!

The Puppet Prince.

Weak. *Useless.*

"What is this?" My voice quivered out of me, and I crumpled the flier, looking to Thera for answers.

Her throat bobbed. She glanced toward the crowd again— where more of the fliers floated through the air, some already littering the cobblestone as passersby crunched over them. But a few elves scattered around the outskirts of the clearing read the sheets, whispering to each other.

Thera clasped my hand. "Likely rebel propaganda. It seems not everyone is so overjoyed here. But we can change that, too."

I squeezed the flier in my fist as tightly as I could. I would not be a puppet. And I would not be blind, not anymore.

Thera knocked her shoulder into mine. My rage and self-pity floating away at her touch.

"Ooh, let's go there next!" She pointed to another storefront down the road, a deep red light pouring from its windows. The sign atop said *Intimates* in swirling script.

My heart skipped a beat, cheeks firing red. My dark bride did not let opinions ruin her fun, and neither would I. "Um, sure."

Thera leaned closer, her breath brushing against my neck in a caress that sent goosebumps down my back and all the blood in my body to a singular, rigid point. "Care to join me? Help me pick something out for our wedding night?"

My tongue went lame in my mouth, every story shared on Thera's horse together flashing through my mind in an instant. Soon, they wouldn't have to be fantasies, our wedding night fast approaching.

Another thing Rory would miss.

"There you both are," a voice boomed, hands clapping both of our shoulders. I startled, almost dropping the last bite of my donut. "My buddy was a no-show. Ready to head back?"

I glared at him, then stared wistfully at the shoppe. "You ruin everything."

Thera snorted, and Julius' face fell. "What did I say?"

Thera spun from beneath the Lieutenant's heavy arm, grabbing both of my hands and planting a quick kiss on my cheek.

"Come on, My Prince, don't be cruel to the Lieutenant," she whispered, eyes sparkling with mischief. "Besides, I have plenty of lacy things back at the castle that will do the trick."

Fire speared through me, not pain, this time, but pure desire.

But before my imagination could run wild, before I could fish for a witty, flirty retort....

A scream blared over the bustle of the street, a shrill, stabbing cry that rattled my bones. The crowd stilled, shock freezing every-one. Thera and Julius too, predatory calm running rigid in their stances.

Two, three, *ten* voices joined in unison to echo the haunting shrieks. The glass buildings shook, the sound reverberated off them, the stone street tremoring beneath my feet.

The crowd pulsed, people stumbling back. Horror blanched their faces as they turned to run.

"Help!"

My blood cooled.

A snarl tore through the world.

Gray skin clung to lean muscle and bone, a ribbed spine protruding from the creature's hunched back like a grotesque mountain range. It crawled on all fours, the sharp joints in its legs and arms pointing the wrong way, taloned feet scraping against the stone. Wide ears flicked, listening for its prey. Its snout hanging open as saliva—and *blood*—dripped from finger-length fangs.

I'd never seen one before, not like this. Not *alive.*

Was this what Quinton felt in his last moments? This fear? This limb-numbing, heart pounding, overwhelming wave of pure terror?

I'd never know the answer.

The Shadowborne's ruby stare locked on me.

And all pain was evicted; fear invaded my every inch, blaring a singular command:

Run.

CHAPTER
TWENTY-FOUR

"The Shadowborne disease is transmitted by saliva but must enter the bloodstream of an elf to take hold. However, once bitten, the Skia magic infiltrates the body in mere minutes, and there is no stopping—or curing—the transformation." –A Study of the Effects of Shadow Magic, Minister Kristos Agyros, 2079 A.G.W.

THERA

R ed eyes narrowed into slits. The Shadowborne's deep growl reverberated through the creature's throat as it focused on Caelum, ignoring the dozens of others on the street...

Caelum froze as the Shadowborne lunged at him, his skin waning pale.

Fear sliced through me, sharper than I'd thought it could.

A sword slashed before even my shadows could respond, relieving the beast of its head in one fell, practiced swoop.

Black blood coated Julius' blade, spattered across his uniform. *Zo'is* gauntlets flared to life, blue casting a glow over the man's dark skin. "All right, Your Highness?"

Caelum nodded, coming back to reality. Back to his body. "Yes."

Relief pulsed through me. One Shadowborne was no match for the Luxian guard.

But I'd never hated Nyxia more for being *right*.

When she'd offered to distract Rory while I took Caelum out of the castle, when she'd suggested I use him as bait to see if the Shadowborne would follow . . . I'd hoped, secretly, *desperately*, that we'd been wrong. That the Shadowborne were truly just increasing in numbers because my soldiers had made less patrols. That without the war to quell their ranks, they had made more of a home in Lux.

It was a risky play, to gamble the Prince's safety. But I wouldn't leave his side, my shadows more than enough to protect him, and the risk was worth the reward if it brought us closer to the culprit behind it all.

But I'd made a terrible, *terrible* mistake by putting Caelum's life on the line.

Someone was controlling Shadowborne. They were here, *following* us.

Ninety-eight attacks.

And they targeted Caelum.

My stomach rolled as it all came into focus, the danger not yet gone. Blood dripped from the lifeless Shadowborne's fangs; red, fresh blood. *Elven* blood. And given its preoccupation with Caelum, I doubted it'd stopped long enough to feed fully, which meant . . .

There'd be Turned coming.

The realization threatened to reappear the pastry I'd eaten.

Finally, I moved. I did not have much time, but I had to fix my mistake. I grabbed Caelum's hand and tugged him into a mosaic-laid alcove behind the nearest shop, its awning hiding us from view. "We need to get out of here before—"

Growls—higher-pitched, a hissing rattle more than a deep rumble, strident against my eardrums—confirmed my suspicion like a self-fulfilling prophecy.

My stomach in my throat, I peered around the alcove's archway.

Next to us, Fortis readied his blade again, dropping into a deep defensive stance.

Caelum huddled to my side, his clammy hand fitting through mine.

My shadows coiled tighter.

Perched on Alixsander's obnoxious statue were three more Shadowborne, all recently turned; their skin a shade of pale silver, not fully dark gray, their snouts less pronounced, their ears still short and pointed. But they crawled toward us on all fours, lips pulled back to expose their sprouted fangs.

All of them hungry for first blood.

My shadows eddied from my fingertips, sharpening to dagger points.

"Do not use your shadows here." Julius held a hand to stop me, gnawing at his lower lip.

His gaze darted to the people nearby; some, in stores, faces pressed against the glass to watch the chaos unfolding. Others, still unguarded in the street, scrambling for cover.

Fortis clutched his sword with both hands again, stepping back. "We retreat. The First Legion will be here soon, and they'll take care of it."

Splashing through the fountain, the Shadowborne jumped into the crowd.

The nearby commoners screamed again, huddling to the sides of the narrow road, sprinting for storefronts. Elves fell, stumbling over themselves and each other, cries screeching out—and cutting short—as the unlucky were trampled.

All three Shadowborne careened toward them, two cleaving a path through the running crown. One bit right into the neck of a small woman with charcoal-stained fingertips that wasn't fast enough.

But the third Shadowborne remained still as it sniffed the air—like it hunted someone specific.

Julius grabbed Caelum's shoulder, ready to run.

"We can't leave these people undefended." I rooted myself to the stone. I didn't care if I was discovered, if they all hurled fruit at me later. The innocents needed protection.

My shadows lashed out, tearing the Shadowborne away from the woman. It shrieked as it flew, claws scratching at nothing.

With less than a thought, I snapped its neck, and the screaming stopped.

My shadows dropped the beast back in the fountain, right at Alixsander's feet.

"Please, please, help!" croaked the woman as she crawled to sitting, a shaking hand staunching the blood streaming from her neck, the crimson ruining her canvas.

I took a step toward her, reaching out—

She flinched. "*Sykagos.*"

Her eyes rolled back in her head, and she collapsed.

Not dead, no. She'd turn, too.

A hand bracketed my wrist. Julius, his frown dipped in pity. "Please, Your Majesty, we need to get the Prince out. It is a terrible coincidence he is here for this."

"You think this is a coincidence?" I jerked my hand away, tearing my eyes from the woman. "Caelum is out of the palace, and a Shadowborne attacks here of all places—"

And I'd played right into their hands by using my shadows, conveniently giving every witness here someone to blame. Someone to make the monster.

Sykagos.

That would be the story these people told today—that the *Sykagos* came again, right into the heart of Solis, bringing her hordes of bloodthirsty monsters with her. That would be my legacy, as it always had been, though Shadowborne had existed long before I did.

Part of me—a part born to the darkness of Erebus—wanted to show them all what I was capable of. Wanted to tear down Alixsander's statue, wanted to ruin their pretty little street and teach them what fear and pain looked like.

"Stand back!" A voice boomed over the madness from the other end of the road, the accent gruff as he screamed in disjointed Luxian, "Clear away!"

I whipped to the familiar sound. My jaw dropped. "Commander?"

Commander Kappas pushed through the crowd, elbowing erratic commoners out of his way. But even in the chaos, his night-black Erebushi uniform stuck out against the colors and brightness like a sore thumb, his sword drawn.

He stopped. Gaped.

"*Mi Vassilla*—" His brow furrowed. His sword lowered. "What are you—"

One of the Shadowborne—the one that'd been focused, its body larger than the others—crashed into him before he could finish his question, shoving him into a broken bench. It snapped to bite him, and his broad hands caught the creature's snout, wrestling against its superior strength.

Julius shoved Caelum closer to me, the Prince stumbling beneath the force.

"Take the prince now. If you stay, it'll only be a distraction," he grit out, his usually sunny disposition blotted out by dark clouds. "Your Commander and I will handle this."

A distraction.

A target. A villain.

"The *Sykagos* has brought hell to Lux!" Another cry raised from the crowd.

"Go back to where you came from, Soul Eater!"

"Someone save us, please!"

Julius flattened me with one last look before leaping back into the fray, planting a solid kick to the Shadowborne's ribs, knocking it off Kappas. My commander quickly pushed to standing, a mighty war-cry bellowing from his gut as he swung at the Shadowborne.

The woman on the ground—the one who'd been bitten—twitched. Her fingertips lengthened to claws, the charcoal still clinging to them.

I grabbed Caelum's wrist. "Let's go."

He nodded.

And we ran, through the streets of the city we'd someday rule, leaving our people behind to suffer the consequences of our mess.

―――――

After stealing the horse and leaving the carriage, riding together just as we had through the mountains, we arrived back at Stellaris a half an hour later. Noonday sun baked the monstrosity in a glittering, oppressive light. But my mind was all shade, all darkness, obsidian as the Pool of Souls.

Guards and servants swarmed us the minute we pulled up to the front gates, escorting the weary, shock-worn Prince back to safety. He cast a long, wistful look at me, violet eyes bloodshot from tears, before he dutifully disappeared back into his cage.

Despite the tug in my center that wanted to follow, that wanted to make sure he was all right, I marched instead to my quarters, my shadows hissing through me with every step.

Only three people had known about my venture today: Nyxia, myself, and Julius. But the Shadowborne had found us not even an hour into our trip, meaning they'd have been mobilized soon after we left the palace.

There were eyes on us. Someone had to have tipped off the guards and stablehands for information, and they had to have done it quickly.

Someone with access, who could get to the servants and others in time. Perhaps someone like Lord Pollux, as Kappas might want me to believe, but he'd been trying to get my attention. Trying to get closer, not hide.

No, I needed to look for someone with a clear motive, with a vengeance toward the prince.

Someone who had a convenient excuse or misdirection for every bad thing that'd happened since our arrival, always missing from the equation or otherwise occupied. Someone who conveniently forgot about leads to other suspects, until they needed someone to frame.

Someone like Commander Kappas.

Kappas, who had shown up, sword swinging only *after* the first Shadowborne had died—to clean up his mess, perhaps. Kappas, who'd been unusually quiet for most of this trip, his hot temper under control in a way I hadn't seen from the man in decades. Kappas, who hated Lux more than anything else, who was hungry for a chance to water Luxian soil with blood once more.

My father's favorite war dog.

Nyxia and I waited for him in his rooms—the drab, dusty accommodations down the hall from mine—and I commandeered the rigid, un-upholstered chair by the fireplace for myself. Heat licked my face, and the flames devoured the dry wood, turning it into dust and ash.

My shadows writhed at my fingertips, ready to do the same to whoever threatened the safety of this peace agreement. This deal I'd sacrificed everything for. This future that I'd bled and cried for.

If Kappas had anything to do with it, I'd mount his severed head on my mantle.

"You're brooding," Nyxia warned from her perch on the windowsill. "I don't know that this—"

The door creaked open, and Nyxia fell silent. She bit her lip, swallowing down whatever admonishment she'd been concocting.

Kappas walked in, bloodstained and battle-tired, his back to us, and he shut the door with a heavy sigh.

I kept my eyes on the hearth; on the vengeful, hungry flames. My voice was chilly as it skittered through the room, a direct juxtaposition to the crackling fire. "What were you doing in the city?"

He startled, but quickly composed himself, his centuries on the killing-fields steeling his nerves. His hand clasped the hilt of his sword. "I saved those fools."

I ran my tongue across my teeth, biting back harsher accusations.

Nyxia stilled, muscles clenched at the idea of the War Hammer himself intent on *saving* anything.

She knew too well the destruction his fury wrought.

I'd forgotten.

"*You* saved Luxians?" I scoffed, the sound humorless. I tore my eyes from the fire, fixing Kappas with a cruel, mirthless smirk. "How did you know they'd need saving?"

Kappas stormed closer, hovering over me with teeth bared, flashing us a glimpse of that legacy of power and predatory passion.

"I was following *you*," he snarled, the orange fire casting dark shadows over his stern brow. "In case one of those Luxians put a dagger through your back. And then when the Shadowborne attacked, yes, I protected the fuckers. Because you and I both know what happens when there is an outbreak."

My jaw clenched, thinking back to the woman who'd been bitten. Who'd scrambled away from me, fear in her eyes, like I was the monster . . .

She would have Turned soon after if someone hadn't put her out of her misery. Would have sprouted fangs of her own, would have gone mad with the thirst for blood and darkness.

I sighed, rolling my shoulders back. Whoever had planned the attack now had that nameless woman's blood on their hands, too.

Even if she'd cursed my name.

I went to fiddle with Amma's ring—but it was gone, with the betrothed that almost died today. With the elf who had a target on his back. My eyes narrowed at Kappas. "You expect me to believe that?"

He didn't balk under my gaze. His face reddened, not with anger, but with a conviction that burned brighter than the roaring blaze in the hearth.

Then, he *knelt*, his first sign of fealty to me since I'd taken the throne. "It's the truth, *Mi Vassilla*. I respect the Erebushi crown more than my life. And frankly, some of us"—he peered up, withering Nyxia was a caustic stare—"have gotten too comfortable with your security lately."

I stared at the top of his head, at the bald spot forming there. I'd seen it dozens of times over the years, Kappas always bowing to my father whenever he was in his presence, his reverence for the man unmatched.

Kappas was a warrior. A strategist. A commander that the sadistic likes of Theron Umbrus had trusted with his life and his armies. A man that, despite his untampered emotions and fiery disposition, did not pick fights he could not win.

An elf that preferred to wage his war out in the open, not behind closed doors and beneath false smiles.

I did not trust him.

But I could not prove he'd been involved with this attempt at sabotage, and until I had evidence, I wouldn't cut down any of my people. Especially a man like Kappas, who had legions of his own supporters back home. Who might threaten the stability of the throne I left behind to secure my place in Lux.

Instead, I leaned forward, shadows seeping from my form in hissing droves that blotted out the fire's warmth and light.

"If you have done anything," I whispered in Kappas' ear, "*anything* to jeopardize peace, I *will* find out. And I will end you myself. Just like I did my father."

At that, his head snapped up. Eyes burned with pure, unadulterated hatred. "You *bit*—"

My shadows gagged him before he could finish his insult, snagging around his waist and rooting him to the floor. Harsh words were leashed to muffled groans. He thrashed against the holds.

"*Mi Vassilla*," I corrected, pushing up from the chair, darkness coiling tight around my form once more. I made for the door, calling one last command over my shoulder. "Nyxia, make sure the commander is attended at all times from now on."

My spy master nodded, crossing her arms. "Of course, *Mi Vassilla.*"

I dropped the shadows holding Kappas, and he collapsed to the floor.

"Mark my words." He glared at me, voice a low, trembling earthquake. "You will regret what you have done, and Erebus will suffer for it."

I slammed the door behind me, shadows trailing after me.

Kappas was wrong. The only person who would suffer would be whoever tried to undermine my goals and kill my betrothed. The fucker that sullied my already tainted reputation all while hiding their true nature.

And when I found them, when I caught them . . .

They would learn the full definition of what it meant to suffer at the *Sykagos'* hands.

CHAPTER
TWENTY-FIVE

"A Vinculum Bond is a Soldier's Greatest Honor—and Sacrifice. To share your life force with another brings great potential for both power and pain." –Rule Nineteen of the Luxian Soldier's Codex, written by King Alixsander the 1st, 3 A.G.W, Updated by Commander General Atlas Tiberius, 1989 A.G.W.

RORY

The moment Caelum walked through his doors, I launched myself on him, breathing in his sweat-and-sugared scent, my arms tight around his neck. "Are you all right?"

I'd been furious when he, Julius, and Thera hadn't shown up for training. Seething, much to the chagrin of Syrax, Dama, and Nyxia, the only bastards that bothered to make their way to the pitch.

The little spy had tried to goad me—a ploy, I later realized—into sparring away the annoyance. But after the initial sting of betrayal and immediate anger wore off, burned away by the rising sun, a dread had captivated my every limb, propelled further by the stings of panic and distant fear that trembled through my bond with Julius.

Something was wrong.

And when the reports came in, when the First Legion was alerted to a fucking Shadowborne attack in the Seller's Market of the inner-city...

It was a boon that I hadn't eaten yet, otherwise I would've vomited. My stomach was a mess of knots and worry, churning as I'd paced in front of my post, waiting for any sign, any word that they were all right. That Caelum wasn't...

No, I wouldn't go there.

Caelum was okay. Finally, he was here, in my arms, breathing. Everything else was forgiven as long as he was all right.

"I'm fine." He exhaled into my hair, arms winding around my waist. His body shook, trembling like a leaf in the wind. "I'm fine."

His voice quivered, like he was trying to convince himself, too.

I released him, my hands cupping his face as I scanned him for injuries. "I was so worried."

That was an understatement. When the first hour ticked by and we'd heard nothing further, Syrax had to pin me down while Dama hid my armor to stop me from sprinting all the way to the city to search for them myself.

Though I'd never share that aloud, my face must have told the story.

"I know." Caelum's lower lip wobbled, tears budding in his eyes. He leaned further into my touch, nuzzling against my palm. "I'm so sorry. I shouldn't have—"

I shifted my thumb over his lips, halting the string of apologies he didn't owe me.

I had been angry. *Livid*, that he'd left without me. That he'd risked himself without a word. That he hadn't trusted me with the truth.

But while I'd stewed in my fear, while Dama and Syrax had left me here to cool off, I realized my fault in it all. My protectiveness had been pushing him away, bit by bit. If he'd told me he wanted to go to the city, I wouldn't have allowed it. Would've locked him up, like his father always did.

He was a prince. A young man, in his prime, to be King someday.

He should have been able to go to the market when he fucking wanted to. And I should have been there *with* him . . . or should have given him the tools to protect himself.

I'd need to do both going forward if I would keep him safe.

"Do not miss training tomorrow." I lowered my finger, and Caelum's jaw dropped open. "You need to learn how to defend yourself."

Violet eyes sparkled in the warm sunlight pouring through the open window, tears glittering as they threatened to fall. "I—I don't know if I can keep up. This morning, I was in so much *pain*—"

The mere mention of his suffering was a lance through my side, skewering me with sadness and that same protective instinct. But I shoved it down, focusing instead on what I could control. What I could *help*.

"Even if you're not feeling well, I still want you there. You can learn by watching on the days you're too sore to take part." I stepped back, straightening my shoulders. "But Lux isn't safe, even *with* Jules and I protecting you. It's time we make this work."

Caelum's mouth flattened. His gaze flicked back to the door. "Thera, too."

Her name pierced something between my ribs, my heartbeat kicking and dusting up a cloud of emotion I couldn't name. Something like the itch of jealousy and the sting of worry and the fiery burn of passion all in one. Something conflicted and *curious*. "What about Thera?"

Had she known about the attacks? Or was it a coincidence that she'd been there, too?

Was she all right?

Caelum grabbed my hand, and his warm palm soothed the ache that beat in my chest. "She protected me, too. She used her shadows in front of people, even though they blamed her for it. Sun above, they were so *cruel*, and she was the only one trying to save them."

Oh.

I pictured it, the *Sykagos* unleashed on the street. Cityfolk running for cover, not just from the Shadowborne, but from her.

From the elf *protecting* them, and their future king, from harm, risking her reputation to do it.

Whether Thera had known about the possibility of an attack, whether she'd had a hunch or had no part of it, she'd sacrificed something today, too. Something that would take a long, *long* time to get back.

I chewed my next words, like that'd make any of this easier to digest. "Then I owe her a life debt."

Caelum raised an eyebrow—the first glimpse of his humor showing from behind the clouds of his shock and worry. "I can't tell if that's a truce or a threat."

I snorted. "Both, maybe."

And I didn't know where that left me.

———

It took Julius an extra hour to return to the palace.

An extra hour that, even with Caelum safe in my arms, in his rooms, had my skin prickling with unease and my stomach flip-flopping between relief and dread.

An hour of feeling the gentle pulses of reassurance through our bond, mixed with stabbing moments of itchy sadness and fear that tangled with mine.

I knew the moment he crossed back into Stellaris—the surge of sweet relief and exhaustion that flared through me enough to have me running down the stairs, across the lawns, and into the barracks at full pace, ignoring the strange, judgmental looks I got from other staff and guards as I blew past them.

My *Vinculum* was safe. *Home.*

I found him in his bunk, hunched on the edge of his bed with his head in his hands. His armor and under tunic had already been discarded—likely thrown directly in the laundry—so his bare chest and tattoo glimmered in the *Zo'is* light.

"You're back."

His head snapped up—exhaustion clinging to the bags under his eyes—but he managed a smile anyway, one I knew was just to ease my worry. "Miss me that much, Sunshine?"

Marching into the room, I stopped in front of him.

And punched him hard in the shoulder.

"Ow." He whined, rubbing the sore spot.

I cocked my fist again, threatening to give him a matching bruise on the other side.

"Don't play around." Tears stung at the back of my throat, like everything I'd spent the last hour shoving down bubbled back up like spoiled lunch. "I felt *everything*, and I had no idea what was happening."

With a sigh, Julius pushed off his bed, towering over me again.

"Hey, *breathe.*" He chuckled, massive hand grabbing my head and pulling me into his chest.

Giving into it, I let my forehead rest against him, my arms twining around his waist as he caged me in a bear hug.

"I'm not going anywhere."

"Good." I squeezed him tighter, hiding the tears sliding down my cheeks, and I buried myself further into him. "If you died, I'd kill you."

We stayed that way until our heartbeats both settled, matching tempo to each other once more. Until the flaring tattoos quieted, our emotions reined in and detangled once more.

This was the truth of our bond—a unity that could not be replicated. While my feelings for Caelum were pure, and my own, Julius felt like an extension of myself.

When it didn't feel like my stomach would punch through my throat or my head would burst, we both sat, slumping together like the life had drained straight from us.

This was a fucking mess.

"Something is going on." I voiced the obvious, insidious truth aloud. "There is a fucking traitor in the palace."

Julius groaned, head falling on top of mine. "And they know more about us than we do them."

That was glaringly apparent.

Nothing had gone right since Thera crossed into Lux. Quinton's murder, the rebel attack on our party, the prisoner's death, and now a Shadowborne in the city?

It was all too close to be a coincidence, and Caelum and Thera's union was at the heart of it all.

Someone didn't want the prince to live to see his wedding day. A wedding day that would now have guests from Lux and Erebus mingling together, giving our orchestrator plenty of people to hide behind.

Such a fucking mess.

I pinched the bridge of my nose. Breathed in my *Vinculum's* scent, letting it steady me. "Have Tiberius and the King been notified?"

Julius flopped back onto his bed, covering his face with his hands, and he let loose another deep groan. His hair splayed out behind him, dirty and caked in blood. "Yes. I've already been written up with a warning."

I flicked his side, earning a hiss. A warning was the least he deserved for going along with the Prince, but if he hadn't been there to protect him, things could have been much, *much* worse.

Caelum needed more support, and more of his own training. I'd put it off far too long, and if Kato wouldn't take matters seriously, then I would start.

"Then that's all we can do for now. Tomorrow morning, we train again. We prepare ourselves."

Julius gave a thumbs-up, shutting his eyes, a tired smile on his face. "Whatever you say, Captain."

He was exhausted, and we'd both need our rest for what was to come. But I lingered a moment longer, watching the rise and fall of his chest. Counting each breath in and out.

The thought of losing Caelum was a knife to the chest, not just for me, but for all of Lux. If anything happened to him, it would devastate me beyond reasoning. Beyond understanding.

But losing Julius?

That would be unimaginable. There was no surviving if he was gone, his voice, his *presence*, the very thing that tethered my soul to my body. Like the tattoo that symbolized our bond, he was a part of me, inked deep beneath my skin.

Breathe in, Rory. Promise me.

My voice cracked with the emotion that clogged it. "Don't scare me like that ever again, okay?"

One gold eye opened, peering at me with the warmth of an afternoon sun. "Promise."

CHAPTER
TWENTY-SIX

"When you wed, I hope it is for love. But love is not something that stays on its own. It is a choice made daily, and I encourage you to never forget to make it." –Queen Dellia's recovered letters to her son, Prince Caelum, circa 2096, A.G.W

CAELUM

Warm water lapped against my sore muscles, crisp apple and sweet vanilla wafting on each steamy tendril that rose from the bathwater. But as I sank deeper, letting the water unknot my too-sore joints, even with the soothing aromas clearing my lungs, nothing could wash away the worry that polluted my mind.

It had only been a few weeks of training since the Shadowborne attack, but my body had already gotten stronger. My muscles still ached with such ferocity, I thought I was on the verge of losing a limb every day, and bruises in every shade of yellow and purple decorated my skin like a painter's palette. That was nothing new— I'd always bruised like too-ripe fruit. But this morning, I had lasted longer in the ring against Rory and Julius, demonstrating major improvement.

Yet even as my frame adapted and toned, I had never felt more uneasy. Unsteady.

My wedding was a few days away. My marriage to Thera.

I'd been excited at first. Hopeful.

But now, I was unsure.

She'd saved me that day, and again in the woods, her darkness a welcomed shade. But ever since, she'd still been guarded, keeping her secrets as close as her shadows. Brooding and hiding after training, only speaking to me in short clips.

I appreciated all she'd done for me in such a short time. She'd protected me, but also believed in me like no one else had, and encouraged me to do better despite my illness. To *be* better, in ways I hadn't even considered before. She read me as clearly as a book, uncovering answers in my pages that other people hadn't bothered to seek—seeing me for more than just my sickly cover.

But what did I know about *her*? Aside from the woman who loved her people and her mother, and the flirtatious, dangerous exterior she wore like armor.

Who was she, underneath her crown and shadows?

I blew bubbles into the cooling water and leaned my head back. Maybe I'd have gotten to know her more if I hadn't spent the last several weeks focused on myself.

Myself and . . .

Rory.

Rory, who'd been bold and brave, crossing the lines I'd never could alone. Rory, who'd been so patient for all these years, content to support me in whatever way I let her. Rory, who tasted like sunlight and *home*. Who would adapt and grow with me . . .

Who I couldn't ever leave behind.

Of course, Thera had all but given us her blessing, Erebushi customs far more open to unique relationships that didn't require exclusivity.

But was that what I wanted? What *Rory* wanted? Was that even fair to ask of her?

The Erebushi people might have progressive relational dynamics, ones I respected, but Rory and I were still Luxian. We'd been raised to believe in a single mate for each elf, and even though many of the soldiers and servants were casual about sex, marriage was a sacred act. Many elves didn't even entertain new lovers after their spouses passed on or faded, even if they were alone for decades.

My father hadn't.

But I wasn't my father. I would one day rule differently, and if Erebus and Lux were to unite again, perhaps it was time we started blending traditions.

It wasn't my choice to make alone.

I had to talk to Rory, eventually. I'd asked for time, and she'd been patient, like always, but I would not string her along. And I needed to hear her answers, even if I didn't like what she had to say.

Frustration and fear still knotted in my gut. I stepped out of the bath, wrapping my soft towel around me. My feet clapped against the stone floor, and I shuffled into my closet, drying as I went, quickly shucking on loose-fitting linen pants.

I took a quick moment to admire myself in the mirror. There was a new definition to my middle—shadows that outlined the start of muscles I hadn't known I had. I wasn't cut from stone like Julius or Syrax, but everything looked tighter, like my skin had shrunk when drying out in the sun.

I wondered if Rory and Thera preferred more muscular men. If they'd like the changes...

I shook my head, wet hair spraying droplets of water all over.

I needed a distraction.

Throwing a shirt on, I padded back to my bedroom. I had a few hours before I was scheduled to meet with my father and the tailor to finalize my wedding attire, so I had to keep my brain occupied somehow. Otherwise, it would stray back to the two elves tearing my sanity—and my heart—in half.

Falling onto my bed, I pushed aside the romance I'd been reading—a tale of lovers who were meant for each other, but always met at the wrong time—my head already too full of what-ifs. Instead, I opted for Arturus' accounts again. Hopefully, translating his discoveries would prove to be easier to digest, and would give my brain the challenge it needed.

1775 A.G.W. Frontlines of The Great Bridge of Sidus.

I ~~need~~—No, that's not quite strong enough—*love her.*

Well, shit.

> *Danae has transformed my very soul, and I love her. Her strength, her courage, her wit. But that is not why I write this account. My love is secondary to my fear . . . and my guilt.*
> *~~My people~~ The Luxians are marching on the border in two days. Unprovoked. With evidence that they claim came from me, but I haven't sent any correspondence in months.*
> *They are lying. Like they have for decades.*

My stomach dropped. Frantically, I continued, hands shaking as I grasped the book, rereading each line to make sure I had the conjugation right.

> *I will fight for Danae. I will stand with my ~~peers~~ brothers and sisters on the front lines—not the Luxians, but the Erebushi. I will bleed for them. Die for them if I must.*
> *This may be my last entry into this journal.*

If it is, know that the kingdom is corrupt. The King is not who he claims to be. I do not have the evidence I need to expose him, but even if I found it, I reckon they would silence me. Like they are trying to silence Erebus. Silence Danae.

I checked my work again and again, but there was no mistake.

This couldn't be real. If this was true, that meant the King . . . my *grandfather* . . . had attacked during the second wave unprovoked. That this war had carried on for centuries because of my family's direct corruption.

Not that Arturus had any evidence, but he also had no reason to lie in his personal journal. He'd been a Luxian soldier. A trusted spy. The likelihood that he'd betray his kingdom without due cause made little sense.

Unless he was bewitched. Fooled, somehow, by this Danae character.

I read on through blurry eyes, one last sentence still hovering in black ink at the bottom of the page.

Even if I die, the truth will make itself known. It won't just be Erebus that bleeds for this . . . but Lux, too, will fall into chaos.

It'd taken me an hour to steady my breathing and hide the journal in my closet. Another after that to bathe again, hoping to drown the memory of what I'd read; like if I scrubbed my skin hard enough, it would erase the horror from my mind.

It didn't.

And it took all my newfound strength to dress and march to the tailor's rooms in the palace, Fortis' bulky presence at my side not enough to stop me from glancing over my shoulder after every step, like somehow what I'd read would follow me through Stellaris.

But it was nothing compared to the dread I felt when I noted my father's form at the end of the last hall, his hands tucked behind his back the only sign of his impatience.

Did . . . did he know about his father's supposed treachery? If he didn't, would he believe me if I told him?

Should I tell him?

His lips pursed. "You're late."

I faked a grin that likely looked as feeble and shaky as I felt. "I fell asleep in the bath."

My father's expression softened. Stance relaxed as he unclasped his hands.

"Thank you, Fortis." He nodded to Julius, dismissing him to his post at the door, and he drooped a hand over my shoulder, ushering us into the tailor's quarters. "Come with me, son."

I followed easily. Even if I would tell him, now wasn't the time. Not in the tailor's fabric-crowded rooms, with seamstresses possibly listening in and whispering between the racks.

But the room did little to soothe, dozens of clothing racks bursting with dresses and suits of every color and texture. Claustrophobia instantly clung to my freshly cleaned back, summoning new sweat. The walls were covered with shelf after shelf of accessories, hats and belts and cravats all lining the walls, sparkles and metallics blinding under the light of the many chandeliers.

My father led me to the small waiting area of the frill-infested, lace-laden space, sitting us both on a velvet upholstered bench wide enough to fit several courtier ladies in their broad skirts.

I picked at a snag in the soft fabric, trying not to unravel myself.

My father sighed. "You look troubled."

Of course he'd noticed. Next to Rory, my father knew me better than anyone. He was a king first, but that had never stopped him from being an involved father. From always checking in and hearing me out.

But this wasn't a mess even he could fix, not without me getting both Rory and Thera in trouble for their involvement.

I sat on my hand to hide the fidgeting, clearing my throat. "Not troubled, just tired. I've been doing extra exercises to get in better shape for the wedding."

At that, he nudged my side.

"Looking to impress your bride?" He raised a brow, the corner of his mouth ticking up. "That's unexpected."

My *bride.*

Thera.

The reminder cracked open another pit of worry within me, but something eased with his casual approval.

Whether there had been corruption in my family hundreds of years ago didn't matter now. We were about to celebrate a wedding. The most impressive union and attempt at peace in two millennia. And my father encouraged me, as always, here for me to lean on through the anxiety.

This should be a moment of joy, not fear. Of possibility, not distant pasts.

"We get along far better than I expected," I finally responded, my grin less forced this time. "*She's* unexpected."

That was certainly a word for the King of Erebus, the myriad of secrets and contradictions I had yet to fully unveil, peeling away layer by layer. I didn't really know her, not yet. But there was potential there. Excitement and surprise with every new facet.

"Your mother was like that, too." My father's voice dipped low, whispering so the servants wouldn't hear the crack in it. "I wasn't prepared for how much I loved her. It took time, but she grew on me."

At that, longing speared through my already tattered heart.

I gulped down the ball of thick emotion that rose to my throat. "I miss her."

I *always* missed her.

But now, I wished she were here for a different reason. Had she read Arturus' journal, or had it just been another title in her collection, a dust-magnet that had never made it off the shelf?

And if she had read it, did she know what it meant? Did she

have information to prove, or disprove, the spy's outlandish claims?

Thera and I would have to find time to sift through the rest of her library again for answers. Answers I wished my mother was here to give me directly, with a soothing hug and a reminder that it would all be all right. With a kiss on the forehead and a plan for how I should move forward as a good king.

And an even more wounded part wished she was here to celebrate, too. To pick out my wedding suit and tell me what she thought of my future bride. To tell me to get my head straight and smile for my people.

"Me too." My father clapped his hand on my knee, startling me back to the moment, his voice edging with the same brittle quality it always took when we spoke of her. "She would've wanted to be here for this part."

Tears blurred my vision. I looked up at him again. His eyes had the same misty quality, a rare splay of vulnerability from the man who wore his competence just as comfortably as his crown.

"Your Highness, we're ready for you." The tailor appeared, materializing out of one of the over-fluffed racks. He bowed, his hair flopping forward.

The short man wore a bright, luminescent green suit that rivaled the color of freshly juiced olive-oil, the hue somehow standing out even amidst the rainbow of the room.

I stood, fists clenched at my sides, and followed him through the maze of material into one of the fitting rooms.

This would be a nightmare.

I pulled on the attire he'd laid out for me, and a jolt of bright energy clanged through me instead.

I'd expected more of the overcomplicated, overstuffed formal-wear I'd been forced to don my whole life. But the suit he'd made for me was the perfect blend between traditional Luxian reverence and modern simplicity. A pure, blinding white, the neck high and the sleeves long, their edges billowing at my wrists—a callback to the old wedding robes of Elysia. The torso itself tapered to my waist, emphasizing the length of my legs and making my shoulders look broader. The ivory pants hugged my thighs, the silver and gold buttons adding just enough adornment to make it less plain without overwhelming me. And I didn't even need an attendant to help me dress with this, the pearl buttons lining up the front instead of the back for once.

I thought of Quinton, my chest tightening. He would've stayed with me anyway on my wedding day even if I didn't require his help, chatting about town gossip as I dressed to quell my nerves.

But he was gone.

And I hadn't been much of a friend to him the night he died, nor had I done anything to honor his life since returning home. Stars, I hadn't even bothered to attend his funeral, allowing myself to get swept away in wedding planning and secret journals and stolen kisses instead, without so much as a thought back to him. Not until I had a Shadowborne breathing down my front. Not until I faced the same potential death he had.

What a prick I was.

I might have looked regal—*stronger*, even—but I was still the same listless, foolish prince. The same sickly kid that could barely take care of himself, never mind his people.

Raw, unnamed emotion clogged my throat.

I stepped out of the dressing room, and my father's gaze flicked to me.

"Well?" I asked, hesitant and strangely self-conscious, feeling like a small boy again.

Small and stupid and useless.

But my father stood, light eyes sparkling. His throat bobbed.

And he lifted his sun-ray crown from his head to place it atop mine.

I stilled beneath its weight

My father smiled. "You look like a *king*. Your bride won't know what hit her."

Tears fell before I could stop them. Everything that'd been pent up for weeks spilling across my lashes, staining the silk of my suit.

"I—" I sniffled, wiping my tears, careful not to wet the dangling sleeves. "I'm sorry. You have always looked out for me, and I'm . . . well, I'm sorry I've been so distracted lately."

A moment passed. A breath.

Then my father tugged me close, pulling me into a hug. I was taller than him now—stars, when had that happened?—but still, my forehead crashed into his shoulder, the tidal wave pouring out.

"It's not you, boy." His deep voice rocked through me, and he patted my back before pulling away, steadying me with hands braced on my arms. "This union has kept me busy, too. I'm glad you've been spending time with your betrothed and getting to understand her better. You make a pretty match."

I swallowed the last of my sobs.

We *were* pretty together. But hopefully, we'd be more than that, too.

With Thera at my side, no matter what pasts haunted our people, no matter the failures I'd already amassed as a prince . . .

I could become the king Lux deserved. Could unite the empire again, bringing back the Elysia that didn't stab itself in the back. That didn't let subjects—*friends*—die to the Shadowborne, or let a whole kingdom starve in the darkness.

That didn't lead guards on or revel in their own self-importance when they could be out doing good work.

I lifted my chin, lighter despite the weight of my father's crown. "Thank you."

But gently, I relieved the diadem from my head and returned it to its rightful owner. His reign was not done yet, despite how age weathered his face.

The wrinkles around his eyes deepened, and he narrowed them at me.

"But please know . . . if there is anything troubling you, you can still come to me," he hedged, like somehow, he could see all the secrets eating me alive, all the dangerous games I played and *lost.* He squeezed my arm. "I'm a father first. Always."

I nodded. I wanted to tell him, badly. Wanted him to fix it all for me, like he always did.

But even though I trusted him above anyone else, I knew I had to figure this out for myself for once. Had to let my intuition lead. So instead, I said, "I love you."

My father's face relaxed, a silent agreement that he'd drop it . . . for now. "I love you too, son."

A throat cleared behind us. The tailor fiddled with his puke-green waistcoat. "We have the attire for the feast before, if you'd like to try that, too."

I groaned playfully but stood straighter. "Duty calls."

It was about time I heeded it.

369

CHAPTER
TWENTY-SEVEN

"To love is to submit; to give the beast your throat and ask it kindly not to bite." –Quote from "A Tale of Forgotten Love," A Luxian Epic Romance written by Madea Thisbe, circa 1867 A.G.W.

RORY

O ur mornings continued in the same routine for the next two weeks before the wedding:

At dawn, we gathered in the pitch; Caelum usually half-asleep, Thera looking like she hadn't slept at all, with the idiot duo Syrax and Dama there to 'supervise.' Julius joined us on the days he wasn't busy with his own assignments—and his absence sent pangs of discomfort through my tattoo—but when he made it to training, he was a grounding force for us all, his easy countenance bridging the different personalities together.

And day after day, we'd spar until the sun reached maturity. Until we were sore and sand-crusted and sweat-caked and all smelled like the rear end of a horse. Until I fought and watched Thera so many times, I could retrace her tactics and go-to attacks in my sleep. Until one of us pissed each other off so severely, there would be blood spilled if we didn't call it a draw.

Until we all marched off the pitch, exhausted—but *smiling*—before tracking our separate ways; Thera, usually to the library to do whatever it is she did with all those books. Caelum, to his chambers to nap and soak in the warm tub before court called him.

And me, to my post at his door, or to the barracks to reread the only book I'd had any interest in. To find the girl in the journal again, the same one that met me step for step on the pitch each morning with a smirk and something I dared not dwell on.

I hated every second in her presence. Every moment that softened the blade I kept close to my chest, ready to spear through hers. Every moment that made me feel *alive*, her ruthless warfare the only thing close to a challenge I'd had in ages.

I hated it.

Yet I woke up earlier and earlier each morning, night still a soft blueberry blanket across the sky, my excitement propelling me from sleep. My skin itched to get on the pitch, to challenge Thera again or watch Caelum improve.

Even though I'd been staying awake later, either to read more of Thera's journal or to sneak into Cae's room with him, the two of us laying together and reminiscing as he held me close. It never progressed further than that—sleepy, lazy cuddles and conversations that nuzzled up to the boundary he'd set—but it didn't need to. My heart was already so full, I thought I'd burst.

He could take all the time in the world to figure out what he wanted.

I'd wait.

But sometimes the waiting looked lonely, his room empty on nights when King Kato had other plans for the soon-to-be-wed.

A loneliness echoed in the journal I still hadn't parted with.

Thera had to know it was gone, which should have frightened me, but it didn't.

I cracked it again—habit, at this point—turning to the marked page.

Entry 453.

My favorite, Sun-fuck-me.

I dreamt of Amma tonight. Dreamt she was still here, to sing me through the hurt after a difficult session with Appa.
I dreamt she wrapped my bandages instead of Agyros . . . that instead of his pretty eyes ogling me, I had her warm gaze to soothe and strengthen.
I don't remember what she looked like, not really, but I know Appa says I resemble her too much. It's strange that she brings him pain. He did not love her, nor she him. Their match was one of survival—the only thing that ever matters in Erebus. She was a battle-tested general, and he is the Dark King. Her support meant he could rule with more than fear, her soldiers loyal to no end. But that didn't mean they were loyal to each other, or that there was any love. Amma always said she only loved Erebus . . . and me.
I am no longer loved with her gone. I am needed *and feared, like my father.*
It will have to be enough. After all, love leaves. Fear lingers.
But it doesn't stop me from trying to remember what love felt like. From trying to find it again—to no avail.

Caelum was busy—called away with the tailor and his father to finalize his wedding attire—the night I found my way to Thera's quarters, journal in hand.

I didn't have a plan, not really.

This was even more stupid than stealing the journal.

372

But there was something to be said about the fact that King Thera kept her word—not revealing mine and Caelum's indiscretions to Kato, nor using her leverage against us. Instead, she had been exceedingly helpful, not just when she'd protected Caelum in the city, but since then, too, spending her mornings out in the hot pitch despite the sunburn she walked away with every day.

And she was a good teacher, as much as I hated to admit it— good at accommodating Caelum's health and wellness without slowing him down. Good at lifting his mood whenever he got cross with himself, good at teasing him and pushing him further without being too harsh.

I envied her for that.

And I owed her.

I kept that thought at the forefront as I knocked on her door, pretending that my other debt—the one to King Kato—didn't exist tonight. After all, this might have been my last chance to speak with her privately with the rest of the Erebushi delegation arriving in the morning.

But the door swung open of its own accord after the first knock —a shadow scampering away from the handle as I peered inside.

Thera lounged across her chair, her signature wine-red robe draped lazily across her. A glass that held the same color liquid inside dangled from her fingers. She sat up when she saw me, her robe slipping down her shoulder, splaying the swath of milky flesh that stretched across her collarbone and the top of her breast. "Ah, Captain! What a surprise. I was just settling in for a nightcap."

My gaze diverted to the floor. I gulped.

I thought I'd gotten used to her like that, her slender form on display every morning in the tight-fit scraps of sparring clothes we normally wore.

Something about her unraveled state sent heat to my cheeks.

I should've turned around and ran.

Instead, my feet stayed planted, no matter how desperately I bid them to flee.

Thera stared, as if waiting for me to speak. I cleared my throat. "I'm sorry to interrupt."

A dangerous shrug sent the robe lower. "I don't mind."

Sun-fuck-me-*sideways*. I had to get out—had to do what I came here to do and leave fast,before I drowned in this absurdity. Before I was bewitched entirely. Finding my legs, I crossed to her, taking a deep breath, and unsheathed the journal from its hiding space.

I hoped she wouldn't notice the worn, dog-earned edges on the pages I'd reread the most. "This is yours."

I waited for her surprise or her rage. Waited for her to question or blame.

Her face was impassive as she took it from me, gaze quickly scanning the cover before she tossed it on the table.

"I've been looking for that." She smiled, stare spearing me. A flash of white thigh as she uncrossed her legs and stood. "Clever little thief. Nyxia would be impressed."

A different heat bit my cheeks to red, shame crawling its way up my gut.

Thief.

An accurate account, yet one unbefitting for someone of my title and rank. A station I'd dishonored. I lowered my head, guilt weighing heavy. "I am sorry I didn't return it sooner."

Again, I waited for the accusations and threats. For the ranting disappointment and betrayal I aptly deserved.

For anything, *anything* that would let me fear her, again. *Hate* her.

She brushed past me, swaying to the bar cart against the wall. "Better late than never." She poured more of the bloodstained liquid from the decanter into her own cup before turning over another glass—raising it to me. "Drink?"

I blinked, finding my bearings. Desperately seeking a shadow, a hint of anger or malice . . . any trace of the *Sykagos* in her face.

She tilted her head. "Captain?"

Oh, right, she'd asked a question.

I shook my head. "I shouldn't. I'm on duty."

She pursed her lips—more disappointed I wouldn't drink with her than she had been when I'd admitted to stealing her personal effects. Than she'd been when I'd disclosed I'd kissed her *betrothed.* She lifted a silver tray from the bar—several ripe berries stacked on its face—like none of that mattered. "Strawberry then?"

But it doesn't stop me from trying to remember what love felt like.

I wondered if she was so lonely, so desperate, that it no longer mattered to her how people wronged her as long as they stayed. As long as they gave her a chance to remember.

"I should go."

I didn't move.

She sighed, red-stained lips forming around the fruit, and she took a bite of one. "If you want to go, you're welcome to. I'm not stopping you."

Love leaves. Fear lingers.

And curiosity captured.

Mine got the better of me, and I willed my feet to move—not to the door, but deeper into the lion's den. "Fine. One strawberry."

I reached for one—much like I reached for any excuse to stay— but she beat me to it, snatching it off the top with elegant fingers. They brushed against mine. My hand retreated quickly; not with disgust, but with a flash of something hot and heady. With something that surprised me less than it should have.

The air in the room changed, charged like the sky right before a storm.

She held the berry to my lips—eyes hooded—waiting for me to take a bite.

And for reasons I had no excuse for, I obliged, opening my mouth for her, and she guided the fruit inside. Sweet, tart juice coated my lips and tongue, but I enjoyed it less than Thera did *watching* me, a satisfied hum buzzing in her chest.

"Good girl." She smirked, her thumb swiping the dribble that ran down the corner of my mouth.

A shiver licked down my spine. "I—"

"Sorry, I won't tease." Thera sucked the juice off her thumb but turned away, sauntering instead toward her chaise again. Her hand drifted across the back, shadows dancing between her fingers. "Did you read anything interesting in my journal? Perhaps some reflections on my past lovers? I think I have quite a way of capturing their prowess—"

"I skipped those parts." My ears burned.

A lie.

I'd read every stupid fucking page. Several times. And while I returned to some of her more . . . thoughtful reflections . . .

There had been a handful of lonely, shameful nights in the barracks that had me lingering on some of her other *descriptive* entries. My eyes closing after. Imagining. My hands drifting between my legs. Panting in short, gasping breaths as I pictured each moment.

Pictured myself included.

Thera laughed and leaned forward over the chaise—her robe spreading low enough to fully expose the tops of her breasts, barely sheathing peaked nipples. "Too private? Or too ashamed of how they made you feel?"

I stiffened. Forced myself to look away. "What are you doing?"

Slow, deliberate footsteps shuffled the creme-colored rug. She stopped directly in front of me, her presence demanding attention. Fingers reached out, stroking the end of my braid. "In Erebus, this is what we call *flirting*, Captain."

I balked, taking a step back. "You're *engaged* to Caelum."

"And?" Thera frowned, her head tilting. "You're bedding him, aren't you?"

Rage and embarrassment battled in my blushed cheeks. I crossed my arms, feeling suddenly exposed even though I was the one in the full-coverage uniform and she was the one-half-naked. "Caelum and I—nothing else has happened since we last—"

"And yet I see the way you are together. It's a matter of time."

She shrugged, like it was a simple, unquestionable fact. Like she wasn't talking about her fiancé, the future King of Lux. She stole another graceful step closer, and her eyes narrowed.

I waited for my tattoo to pulse, for my bracelets to burn against my skin at the threat . . . but there was no malice in her stance. Only something far more dangerous.

She grinned. "And I also felt what happened on the sparring pitch between us that first day."

I bared my teeth. "You mean when you took a low blow and pissed me off?"

Her gaze dipped to my mouth again. "You watch me like a woman *starved*."

"I don't—"

"Don't deny it," she snapped—the first crack in her nonchalant façade. Sucking in a deep breath to regain her composure, she leaned forward, her face only a breath from mine.

"You're not the only elf in the palace with enhanced senses. I smell it on you, *Aurora*." Her voice sank, each word barely a whisper, but they rattled low through me all the same.

She did not say my name like it was a curse. Nor a threat.

No, Thera bit into my name like it was something delicious, something to be savored, something ripe and indulgent—and she wanted another taste.

I did, too.

"Don't call me that," I warned her. Warned myself.

"Do you prefer Rory?" A shadow curled around her, and I swear I felt one caress the back of my neck. "Or *Captain*?"

I grit my teeth. "I'd prefer if you stopped talking."

"Make me."

The last hold on my sensibilities snapped.

Clasping a hand against her wicked mouth, I surged forward, like I had every morning on the pitch—

My mouth crashed against her neck.

Not her lips—no, that was somehow too taboo, too intimate.

377

But somewhere between a bite and a kiss, my teeth nipped at the soft, unblemished skin of her throat.

And the world melted.

She moaned, tilting her head, exposing more of the pale flesh for me to taste. Desire crashed through me at the sound, demanding and violent in its fantasies. I licked and kissed and bit my way down the column of her neck, my hand fisting in her long hair, pulling just hard enough to hurt. Thera hissed, but a hand found its way between my legs, a knuckle brushing against the sensitive, desperate apex hidden beneath the too-thick fabric of my pants.

This was wrong. So unbelievably stupid and selfish and wrong.

I hated her.

I was going to kill her.

But fuck, I wanted more. I wanted her to strip me bare and taste me until I shattered. Wanted to shred her stupid fucking robe, bend her over and spank her until she cried for mercy. Wanted to fight and fuck until I figured out how to end her, or until she devoured my soul.

Wanted to see how many layers of her I had to peel back until I could find the girl from the journal.

Pain and pleasure.

Restraint and liberation.

Thera supplied *both*. She shoved me against the wall, steering me as the heel of her hand pressed against my bud in a demanding, possessive grasp.

Blue-and-green eyes caught mine for a minute, shadows darkening them. The same eyes that trapped me and Syrax by the river, their brand still marked against my mind. The same eyes that challenged me on the pitch every morning as we straddled the line between violence and passion.

Then her mouth captured mine in a hasty, insistent swoop.

The taste of wine overwhelmed, and somehow sobered me immediately.

I blinked away the haze of whatever madness had consumed me. I pushed her back. "You're drunk."

Thera swiped her tongue over her lips. "Yes. Delightfully so."

My body shook beneath the weight of my regret and disappointment as it slammed into me so forcefully it knocked the wind from my lungs.

Of course, this is all this had been. A drunken *game*. I'd been the one to tell Caelum that swords and fists weren't the only tools an elf had at their disposal, yet I'd fallen a fool for hers. Had let her play me like I was one of her shadows to manipulate.

And I'd *liked* it.

My fists clenched. "I'm leaving."

Thera blinked back her surprise, but I ignored the fracture in her expression, turning on my heel and marching toward the door.

"Of course, you'll leave." Her voice was so quiet, I barely heard it. "Everyone does."

I froze, just a step from the threshold.

There—just for a second—in the vulnerable ache in her voice, *she* was there.

I dreamt of Amma tonight.

I must have imagined it. Must have conjured it at the moment, because when I turned to face her, Thera's flirtatious, smug-as-sin fucking mask was back in place.

And the girl from the journal was gone again.

"I—" Sun above, why was I still speaking? Why did I still subject myself to this insanity?

But the words toppled out of me senselessly, something vulnerable and desperate in me calling out to the girl one last time, hoping she'd reappear. "I don't remember my mother much, but I remember she always told me my bad attitude would be my downfall. Told me it was easier to invite bees with flowers than with their thorns."

Thera winced. She turned; her face hidden behind her wall of passion-knotted hair.

379

"Inviting bees only gets you stung, Captain." She drew her robe closed as she crossed her arms over her chest. "Thorns protect."

"And fear lingers," I said before I realized what it meant—the truths I revealed to her.

Her head snapped to me, eyes wide, and her mouth fell open.

I didn't give her a chance to speak. I jabbed my finger toward the journal on the table. "But if *that* version of you is real, she will not find what she's looking for trapped away in that silly book, hidden behind all your fucking thorns."

This time, I didn't give her a chance to snag me again, brushing through the door and into the hallway as fast as my legs would carry me.

But with the taste of strawberry secrets lingering on my lips, I'd dream tonight of what might have happened if I stayed.

The next morning, I skipped training.

I didn't know if the others would be there anyway, with the wedding banquet later in the evening and the Erebushi invitees set to arrive in a few hours.

I didn't ask, either.

Instead, I stayed in the barracks, using a sandbag in the storeroom as a target for my frustration and confusion. The musty, claustrophobic closet was hardly a substitute for the rolling sands and well-stocked armory of the coliseums, but it was private, which made it worth breathing in decades' worth of dust as I moved through my exercises.

Punch. Kick. Jab.

Breathe.

Breathe.

Breathe.

Thoughts barraged me with each hit. Each breath.

I'd kissed the *Sykagos*. Kissed Thera. And she'd—

No, no more of that. I would pretend it never happened. Would shove it as far away as possible.

Kick. Kick. Punch.

Soon, the *Sykagos* would be dead by my hand, and this would all be a bad dream. Would disappear like lines in the sand after a rainstorm. And I would mourn the girl from the journal all on my own, with no one else wiser for it.

Breathe.

Breathe.

Brea—

"Oh good, you're here." Julius caught my next punch in his palm. Brows knotted as he stared down at me. "You okay?"

I panted as I looked up at him, tears pricking the back of my eyes. He was shirtless and sweaty, sandy hair hanging in awkward clumps around his long ears, meaning he had been training this morning. But somehow, he'd known to wait until after to come looking for me. Had understood that I'd needed space.

I had no words to describe how *not okay* I was, but I knew he didn't need me to. He could feel it, our tattoo bonding us together. My feelings overwhelming us both.

I shook my head and fell into his shoulder.

Strong arms wrapped around me, a soothing hand stroking my sweaty, messy braid. "You're feeling . . . a lot, lately."

I snorted. That was an understatement.

My arms coiled around his tree-trunk waist, breathing in his sturdiness. There was no use lying to him, not today. Not when I barely had the strength of mind to keep myself standing. To keep myself from running straight to Caelum and telling him everything, or . . .

Or sprinting back to *her* and begging forgiveness for sins I had yet to commit.

"The Sy—" I stopped myself, the name somehow wrong on my tongue. The same tongue that had tasted the truth, that had savored the smoky-sweet contradiction of her smooth skin.

I cleared my throat and my head. Focused on my breathing and on the warmth of Jules against me. "Thera knows how to get a rise out of me."

"Yeah, I can tell," Julius sighed and pulled back, scratching at his chest.

Sun above, I must have been torturing him the last few days. I'd barely felt anything from him in return, my emotions too much for even two bodies to process.

Julius winced as another wave hit us both. "But there is more. Fear . . . and guilt?"

Hearing them named aloud made me flinch.

I had been afraid, but not of Thera, not anymore; of what I'd do if I kept on this path. Of how I'd navigate my way back toward the role I had to play if I let myself wander deeper.

And I'd been guilty since the day I accepted Kato's offer. Every other word out of my mouth had been lie after lie, to Caelum, to Julius, to Thera.

To myself. To my oaths as a guard.

I did my best to quell the surge of shame that tightened through my chest and smiled at Julius. He didn't deserve to bear the weight of my lies, not anymore. "I promise I'll be okay."

I would be, somehow.

Breathe, Rory.

After the wedding, I would go see Kato. Would tell him about Thera's journal, and about how she's been treating Caelum. Would do my best to convince him I could guard the prince without eliminating the *Sykagos*.

Maybe then it would be easier to breathe.

Julius still frowned, patting my head. "We haven't been checking in. You're always disappearing."

"I'm sorry. The sparring has helped." I ran a hand over my face, hoping it would wipe away any lingering traces of the exhaustion and worry that plagued me. "It's been nice to spend time together again."

But the placation didn't deter my *Vinculum*, a bloodhound on the scent. Julius rocked on his heels. Gnawed at his lip. "If something is going on . . . if something was really wrong, you'd tell me, right?"

The list of 'really wrong' things in my life right now was a mile long, but as desperately as I wanted to blurt it all out, I couldn't. Not without getting him stuck in the middle of it, too. Not without potentially making him complicit in several of my recent transgressions.

I would tell him everything after I made it right.

"Of course," I lied, one last time. Hoping that one day, he'd forgive me for it. That he'd understand.

Hoping that it wouldn't haunt me.

With that, he eased, the knot in my chest unraveling as his did, our relief just as contagious as our anxiety.

"All right then, Captain. Let's go get ready for a banquet." He poked a thumb at the pummeled sand bag. "Looks like you've worked up an appetite."

I followed him out of the barracks, Julius always could find the sunny side of every situation.

But I couldn't help but feel like I'd made a mistake. Like I'd missed my only window to tell him the truth and make it all okay.

I'd never wanted to be more wrong.

CHAPTER
TWENTY-EIGHT

"I would burn the world for her, but then, she would be the King of Ash." —Excerpt from a letter from King Theron Umbrus of Erebus to General Danae, circa 2072 A.G.W.

THERA

My father used to say all wars were waged on two fronts; what a kingdom fought to protect, and what a king would sacrifice for it.

I'd sacrificed my reputation over and over again to protect my people. Had become the monster in every Luxian bedtime story, all so my subjects could sing their children lullabies.

But it'd been a long, long time since I'd felt so exposed. Since someone had dared to look into the shadows instead of scurrying away from them.

She will not find what she's looking for, trapped away in that silly book, hidden behind all your fucking thorns.

Somehow, being told I was hiding was worse than being called a monster. Rory's blow had struck true, and for the first time since meeting her, I wasn't even sure she had intended to wound me.

Perhaps she'd even been trying to *help*.

But I didn't have time to dwell on it. Not with the people I'd vowed to protect before myself on their way into unsafe territory.

My delegation was scheduled to arrive the morning of the wedding banquet. I glanced out my window, the cloudless sky staring back at me in mockery. The Luxians were convinced it would rain today, said they could feel the oncoming storm in the air.

Even if a hurricane raged, it paled in comparison to the storm raging in my middle, thunderous nerves clashing together.

Twenty Erebushi people, *sanctioned* to come over the Great Bridge for the first time in centuries. Not warriors sacrificing their lives to open the portal, but civilians invited to broker peace through celebration. My trusted advisors and a few common folk who'd starved in the dark for longer than they could remember. Who'd I'd promised peace to when I'd taken my father's crown.

The sun would soon shine in Erebus.

Captain Bellatore and Commander Kappas—with Nyxia shadowing him—had made good on their agreement, providing an approved list a little over a week ago and sending out messengers with the *Zo'is* needed to help them cross. It'd slightly eased my suspicion of my commander as well, Nyxia giving him gold marks for participation and enthusiasm.

But as I stood on the palace steps waiting, unease crept up my spine.

An hour passed, my foot tapping impatiently.

Then two.

A third.

And when the fourth hour ticked by, when the sun was high and burning down my back, when I realized it was well past noon and I'd have to get ready for the banquet soon, something dark and ferocious growled low in my gut. Shadows writhed at my finger-tips, untamable as my control slipped beneath worry's incessant nagging.

Nyxia approached, her face warped in a scowl that could melt steel.

"Where are they?" I hissed.

"I don't know." Her tongue poked the inside of her cheek, her frustration barely contained. "I'm sure they were just delayed. There *is* a storm coming."

On cue, summer thunder cried in the distance, a vengeful god promising sweet respite from the oppressive heat. But a low-hanging cloud rolled closer over the glittering horizon, a threat of the storm to come.

Storm or no storm, Luxian airships should have no problems traveling in all sorts of weather.

Something was wrong. No, something had *been* wrong since the very moment I'd crossed the portal. From the moment King Kato accepted my bargain.

And if anything had happened to my subjects, if any of them were so much as *nauseous* from the air ride . . .

The responsible party would quickly find out just how much I would sacrifice for those I'd been tasked to protect.

"Find out," I ordered Nyxia as I spun on my heel, stalking back into the palace like a Shadowborne was nipping at my ankles.

If my people didn't show up soon, the banquet might not be the only feast held tonight.

The shadows were hungry for betrayer's blood.

———

I gripped the edge of the washbasin in my chambers, knuckles ghostly pale, and stared at myself in the mirror.

Today's disguise was beautiful. Easily one of my best, my kohled and painted lashes emphasizing the disjointed color of my eyes, my skin warmer than normal thanks to my hours in the sun. My hair hung long, as it usually did, but I'd attempted to weave strands of gold through it, ones that complimented the accents in the long, flowing dress that swished around my legs, the blue silk so fair it was almost white—a Luxian color and design, meant to symbolize our unity.

But the shadows waited beneath this pretty mask, churning in my chest like a storm trapped in a bottle. They mimicked the thunder that crashed outside as the heavy rain pelted the castle's exterior, pattering like a furious war-drum.

My people weren't here.

Stavros wasn't here.

And I was more alone than I'd ever been, wearing my enemies' colors and hoping they'd be mine.

Stealing one last breath—one last grounding look at myself—I marched from the room, ready to waltz into the den of wolves waiting for me. I was already late, but I didn't care.

Head high, Thera. A king bows to no one.

Especially not King Kato and his corrupt court.

I just hoped my fiancé would understand. Kato was too far gone, but my betrothed still had potential. Could still help me bring peace to my people.

If they ever showed up.

Nyxia materialized from a shadowed corner, just a few paces from the main entryway leading to the ballroom. She fell into step with me, her night-black dress a defiant testimony to our homeland. To the people we'd left behind, unprotected and unequipped.

She squeezed my hand in gentle reassurance, and I stilled, halting us both.

Something was wrong. In all my life, Nyxia Drakos had never reassured anyone of anything. "You have a report?"

Nyxia looked up. Gone were all traces of mischief and humor, her expression instead as dark as her dress. "We have a problem."

From here, we could hear the banquet in full swing, the music

387

and laughter floating from within a violent juxtaposition to the fear and rage captivating my mind. It was loud enough to drown out our conversation, even with the retinue of Luxian guards—and their enhanced senses—standing just beyond. "Talk. *Fast*."

Tears—unfamiliar, watery droplets—gathered in Nyxia's eyes, and everything around us came to a halt. "I intercepted another missive. There was a rebel attack as they came through. Apparently, soldiers with the same camouflage as the ones we encountered in the forest pass."

My pulse shuddered to a stop for a breath.

Two.

I swallowed, my voice a rumble through me. "How many survivors?"

The unspoken question clanged louder. *How many dead?*

My hands shook.

"No survivors accounted for," Nyxia answered, her voice a meek imitation of its normal bravado. "But a few bodies haven't been recovered."

I swayed, dizziness racking through me.

My people were dead.

"Stavros?" I clipped his name out despite the way it stung, my voice quivering. My body fighting to stay upright.

Head high, Thera.

Control and discipline.

Nyxia shook her head, and relief nearly knocked me breathless. "We don't know."

My surrogate father was unaccounted for. But that didn't mean he was alive. We could only hope that the rebels had him somewhere and kept him alive for ransom.

Or to torture sensitive information out of him.

Bile melted my throat to ash as it surged up. I shoved down the instinct to run straight from Stellaris, to find Asteri in the stables and ride immediately to find him and the other potential survivors myself.

I couldn't lose Stavros. But I wouldn't sacrifice my only chance at unifying our kingdoms, either. It'd be exactly what the culprit wanted. For me to come running, and to call the wedding off. For the *Sykagos* to slight King Kato and attack Luxians without due cause. Or worse, for me to seek revenge on the prince, their target from the start.

No, I had to stay calm. Had to see tonight and tomorrow through.

And then, I would find Stavros. Would see the rest of my people accounted for and properly buried.

Could deliver these rebels the slow, painful end they deserved.

My nails bit my palms so hard; droplets of crimson marred the pale skin. The rebels couldn't have done this alone. Not without information. Who would've told them the portal would open? How did they cut through the Lucian escort so efficiently?

"How did this happen? *Kappas?*"

It would be one thing if the old goat had hurt more Luxians. But if he'd spilled a single drop of Erebushi blood—

"No, not Kappas." Nyxia's gaze was all daggers and darkness. She stood straighter. "According to the report, King Kato's soldiers never arrived as an escort. The only Luxians present were the two messengers sent by the captain and Kappas, and only one made it back to deliver the missive. And it was addressed to Tiberius, not Bellatore."

Something cold and cutting scraped down my spine, a bone-chilling realization settling deep.

The rebels had beaten us to the punch because they knew when it was coming. Someone in Stellaris, likely in the king's most trusted circle, had fed them information and gave them access.

The King wanted this deal to fall through, too.

"Fucking bastard."

There was no more pretending.

The King of Lux didn't want peace. He wanted to end this war and declare himself a victor. He wanted everyone in his empire to see what a monster the *Sykagos* was, while he positioned himself as the magnanimous, patient counterpoint.

And it seemed he would sacrifice more than he protected to see it through.

A breath rattled out of Nyxia like she, too, came to the same conclusions. "We need to figure out who is truly for peace, and who is with him."

At that, the shaking stopped, my limbs fully numb.

Did the captain know? Had she been involved?

Was last night a ruse to keep me distracted? To get me to lower my guard, just so she could strike?

She will not find what she's looking for, trapped away in that silly book, hidden behind all your fucking thorns.

No, I had to believe she was genuine. *Wanted* to believe. She'd had every chance to harm me, had seen me vulnerable on more than one occasion, on the pitch or drunk in my quarters, and she hadn't taken her shot. And if she didn't know what was going on, Caelum likely didn't either.

But that didn't mean they would believe me if I told them. Didn't mean they trusted me enough to aid my cause.

To help me find and save Stavros.

Another squeeze of my hand tore me from the shadowed clutches of my thoughts.

"Smile, *Mi Vassilla*. We are being watched." Nyxia spoke through the grit teeth of a strained smile.

I glanced over my shoulder. The guards had shifted closer—a subtle change, but enough to notice.

We were expected at the party.

And they'd likely been ordered to watch my every move.

I shut my eyes, relishing the lightless reprieve for one moment. It was no Pool of Souls, but the shadows quieted, and I sucked down a breath. I went to the dark, lonely place in the corner of my mind—as I had every time my father's lash had struck. The same cold, heartless world I ran to whenever I let the shadows run amok on the battlefield.

Head High, Thera. A king bows to no one.

I opened my eyes. Tearing away from Nyxia, I marched to the entrance of the ballroom, passing the guards without a glance or greeting. They shifted nervously.

I shoved the doors open with the shadows erupting from my fingertips, darkness devouring the first glimmers of light as the party unveiled before me.

Nyxia vanished into the mist; likely to blend into the crowd, another shadow intent on doing my bidding.

Gasps and screams echoed from the room, the music screeching to a halt.

With my head high and a smirk plastered across my face, I called my shadows back and strode in.

Fear lingered. My nostrils tickled with the rose-sweet plumes that wafted from their trembling frames.

I would not rise to Kato's bait. Wouldn't go chasing after the rebels or levy any threats tonight.

But I would remind him—and all the quivering, sniveling courtiers—*who* they baited.

As the darkness dissipated, the room came into razor sharp focus. Several long, white-clothed and candle decorated tables lined the edges of the space. Impressive candelabras decorated with strings of crystals lit the space, fighting against the *Zo'is* chandeliers hanging from nearly every rafter.

It might have been pretty an hour ago, the gauzy blue and gold curtains swaying with the breeze that poured through the floor-to-ceiling windows. But now, most of the food was already half-eaten and discarded, the wine cups drained and spills marring the cloths, as the partygoers gathered in the center of the marble ballroom. They'd been dancing and mingling amongst themselves before I'd interrupted, content to celebrate without me. But now, they all stared in complete silence, breaths held.

391

I waltzed deeper into the pit, my intent trained on one spot alone.

Sitting in the middle of the center table—the one closest to the dais and the sun-burst throne—was Kato, a smug grin on his face as he raised a glass to me.

"Ahh, our guest of honor has *finally* arrived!" He clanged a fork against his glass, the strident sound shattering the quiet with its mocking tone. "All rise for King Thera of Erebus, future consort of Lux!"

Courtiers echoed the call, joining in on the barely veiled joke.

"Oh, Your Majesty, that dress is lovely!" A woman next to the king—Lady Mirena, the same one that'd simpered during the planning meeting, the Mistress of Hospitality—sneered, sarcasm dripping from her tone as sticky as the wine spilling onto the floor. "I think my mother had the same one when she was younger."

Lord Pall snickered with her, the beady-eyed man puffing his chest. "How generous of you to pay such homage to Luxian *history*."

I didn't spare them a greeting, instead looking to the king's left with a dismissive tilt of my head. "Sorry I'm late, My Prince."

Next to him, Caelum wore a dark navy tunic, one that rivaled the night for its depth, his violet eyes and white hair in stunning contrast. Silver buttons gleamed and blinded beneath the many lights. And had the timing been better, I might've told him he looked like starlight.

The captain was nowhere to be found.

Suspicion stabbed my ribs again.

But my betrothed pushed back his chair, his mouth parting. Blush touched his cheeks, his gaze darkening as it raked over me. Boldly, *shamelessly*. "You, My King, are a vision."

My King.

The words tore through the room, more shocked gasps rising from the courtiers. Mirena and Pall's mouths both dropped open, and Kato's smile verged toward a grimace.

Any other day, any other minute, the compliment might have

thrilled me. Might have given my heart wings and reassured me of my decisions.

But there was no joy, not while my people's souls wandered Luxian soil, alone and afraid and unable to return to the Aether where they belonged. No excitement when anxiety captained my heartbeat as I thought of Stavros, captured and potentially tortured.

No thrill when someone in this very palace was responsible.

But I shoved all of that away as I approached, smiling like the bride I was supposed to be.

King Kato waved a hand, and the musicians resumed their tune, the courtiers all still half-focusing on us and resuming their chatter and dancing again.

Kato relaxed into his seat, taking the last bite of meat from a roasted boar's leg.

"Caelum, care to offer your betrothed a plate?" He chewed as he spoke, waving the bone toward the scraps of other greasy, slaughtered animals littering the table.

But Caelum ignored his father, a few long strides devouring the space between us, his sights set on me. Fingers filtered through mine—unapologetic in their gentleness.

"Is everything all right?" His voice crashed low, caressing the shell of my ear.

The question disarmed even my most protective parts.

No, nothing was all right. Stellaris's glittering, shimmering exterior had blinded me from seeing how wrong it all was, my hope and ambition blocking my view of the rotted, festering corruption that laid the foundation of this palace.

But Caelum Borreallis was not a blinding mirage. Not made of the same gilded and glittering shit as the rest of this castle.

Caelum was kind and smart and made of king-stuff, just like his mother had said.

And if I let him, he might just be the key to saving both of our peoples.

Shoving down my fear, leaning instead into the parts of me that still hoped, still believed, I tugged him to the dance floor. "Dance with me?"

My betrothed nodded, following me further. Forgetting about his shit father and his schemes to get under my skin.

The courtiers gave us a wide berth as the music flowed, but it didn't matter. Caelum's gaze was locked on mine, soft and scalding all at once, like sunlight that both warmed and burned the longer it lingered. But I let it settle me—let it chase away the shadows and feed the seed of belief that still lived inside.

His hands found my back as mine slid to his shoulders. A breath passed between us as we both synchronized to the tune.

Caelum swept me into the song.

Dancing in Erebus was a rare thing, our people too tired to muster the energy for it. But when we did dance, it was a reckless, feral thing to behold. Our music was percussive—string and brass instruments hard to come by—but anything could be a drum if one hit it hard enough. Bodies pulsed and limbs flailed to the rhythmic thumping, wild cries echoing through the deserted, open plains.

But Luxian dances were all art and practiced grace. All sweeping lines and soaring melodies.

And Prince Caelum Arturus Borealis had a gift for it.

Fluid and floating, he led us around the floor, lights whirling around our heads in dizzying blurs. My stomach lurched, tumbling with us as we spun, but his hands stayed firm at my waist, guarding me from falling over the precipice.

And he was so *close*, the scent of him warm and sweet, his soft heat like starlight.

I gripped his shoulders to steady myself, but it did nothing to halt the spinning in my head.

"By dawn tomorrow, you'll be my wife." He twirled me around, his voice a hesitant contradiction to his sure-footed, confident dance.

My steps faltered.

His words were meant to soothe. To woo, perhaps.

Instead, they unsettled, kicking up dust in my lungs that choked me.

My first and only vow was to my kingdom. To my people.

But tomorrow, I'd make one to Caelum, too. A vow as a wife, as a consort and partner. A vow to give him as much as I intended to take.

I needed him by my side if I would uphold my promises to Erebus. But needing someone was dangerous. It was a sacrifice of autonomy. Breaking off another piece of me and giving it to a man I liked, a man I believed in.

But a man all the same. One who would now have the power to hurt me just as much as he could help me.

"Mhmm." It pained me to smile, so I turned away, trying to find a focal point against the spinning, light-saturated room. "Bright and early."

"I hated mornings as a child," he said, his voice a low hum. "I used to steal more time at night, staying up far too late to read or think, and Rory and my mother would both scold me for being a lazy lump until almost noon." He laughed, the sound just as bright and dazzling as the wheeling ballroom. "But since you've been here . . . I've looked forward to each dawn. To the day ahead each one promises."

My feet planted on their own accord, crashing our movements to an abrupt halt. My gut lurched again, this time for different reasons. "Dawns don't exist where I'm from."

And neither did futures. Neither did hope.

My hands trembled, and I tried—and failed—to keep them steady on his shoulders. My feet stuttered, too, too numb to move no matter how fiercely I willed them to.

A frown tugged Caelum's mouth, and a hand rubbed circles across my back. "Will you tell me what's wrong?"

"I'm sorry." I cleared my throat, shaking off the first clawing grasps of panic. I didn't say the other words that begged at the edge of my tongue, ready to fly from it if I let them. Didn't tell him the truth of what was happening . . . not with so many watching us. Not with perpetrators in this very room, waiting for my guard to slip so they could finish us both off. I leaned in closer—like it was just a part of the intimate dance—my voice quiet. "I promise to talk about it with you later. We have a lot to discuss. Do you have time to chat with me tonight?"

Caelum's hand stilled on my back. He gripped me tighter.

But like a true prince, he led us effortlessly back into the dance, easing back into the choreography again like we hadn't missed a single step.

"Of course, we'll talk. But for now, try to enjoy this with me?" He grinned, a shy imitation of his usually broad smile. "I know you're not sentimental, per se, but I am. I only plan on being wed once. I'd like it to be special."

Shadows relaxed their grip on my heart, the reminder melting away the ice that'd snared me.

I wasn't the only one making a vow tomorrow. And for all the ways he was still growing, Caelum Borealis was a man of his word. A man of sentimental honor and fastidious virtue.

If he made a promise, I had no doubt he'd keep it.

And if I failed, it would not be my mess alone. Not anymore.

No one told me how heavy my father's crown would be. But perhaps I didn't have to carry it on my head alone. Perhaps I could share the weight with my betrothed.

My future husband.

A lump congested my throat. "I don't know that I deserve such an honor, but I will do my best to prove it to you."

Caelum's smile softened. *Sparkled.*

A hand left my waist and settled against my cheek.

We stopped dancing.

"The world has told you that you are a monster, but that is not how I see you." A thumb swept against my skin, and his eyes scanned my face, intense in their honesty. "I see a woman who loves her people, and who is maybe afraid of being loved in return."

Soft as his words were, they still struck hard, stinging vulnerable, uncalloused parts.

I fought the urge to step away. To withdraw and hide behind my shadows. "You will be easy to love, Caelum. I am not."

Caelum's pupils dilated, violet bruised indigo. His other palm cradled my face, holding me steady.

"I don't need *easy*." The corner of his mouth danced upward. "I'm not afraid of a challenge anymore, thanks to you."

And in front of the entire banquet, in front of his father and the gossiping, venomous courtiers, in front of all the people that wished me dead or had plotted against us both . . .

Caelum kissed me.

Much like Luxian dances, it was somehow both chaste and fluid, our lips sweeping together quickly before dashing off again.

But it was more than a kiss. More than a moment of attraction or passion.

It was a declaration.

A vow.

Wolves circled us both, criminals hid in the shadows, and corruption lined Kato's fancy sleeves.

We would not face them alone. Together, we'd protect each other and our people, no matter what we had to sacrifice.

I took a step back from him—but I didn't let go of his hand.

Together. "You are going to be a great king."

Blush darkened his cheeks. "You already are."

"What a beautiful couple," a voice interrupted, cleaving through the moment like a sword through soft flesh.

I whipped around faster than I'd have liked—the urgency too close to a startle. I was barely hanging onto my control today, still shaken from all that'd passed.

Freckles crinkled as Lord Pollux smiled, dipping his head in a bow.

My fear abated.

Caelum's jaw clenched, and he forced a smile. "Thank you, Lord Pollux."

Florian Pollux stood straighter, his handsome green suit less decorated than many of the others, but still fine enough to accent his similarly colored eyes.

They flicked to me.

"If it's not too intrusive, may I cut in?" He held out a bold hand —another declaration to those watching. Pollux was not afraid to risk his reputation either, it seemed. "Since we hadn't had time for our meeting?"

His stare and posture were nothing but polite, but something about his voice set me on edge—something in its rough, cold dip— like he tried to get me to hear the words he wasn't saying.

Curiosity scraped against the back of my neck with dark claws.

Caelum stiffened. His hand fit through mine. His ring—Amma's ring—imprinted against my palm. "Oh, that's—"

"I'd be happy to." I squeezed Caelum's hand once for reassurance, hoping he'd understand. "Why don't you go find the captain? She should be present for our discussion later."

We did need to talk—all of us—before Caelum and I said our vows.

And before more of our peoples ended up dead.

Caelum sucked in a breath. He looked between Pollux and I several times before blowing it back out again.

Raising my hand to his mouth, he pressed a possessive kiss across my knuckles. "I'll be back shortly."

Then he wove through the crowd, dodging other courtiers' attempts at conversation with tact.

I watched him go—longer than I should have—until a throat cleared.

Pollux held out his hand again. This time I took it.

This dance was immediately different from the first, even though the music was the same; Pollux held me further away, which was a boon for my toes, based on how uncoordinated some of his steps were.

He didn't dance often, then.

I brandished my favorite smile, carefully avoiding his clunky steps. "What is it you wanted, Lord Pollux, other than to show me your . . . impressive dance background?"

A noncommittal shrug. "You looked like you needed rescuing. Cold feet?"

My gaze narrowed. Had my anxiety been that palpably clear? Had I done something as the prince had kissed me to indicate displeasure?

Or did Pollux know more than he let on?

"I assure you; my toes are warm as the sun your people love so much." A humorless chuckle worked up my throat. "But thanks for the laugh. You're growing on me, Pollux."

Growing like a tumor.

His grip tightened as his expression did. "Yet you've been avoiding me."

My teeth gnashed together, and I almost purposefully stomped on his fucking toes.

Is that what this was about? A dinner I mentioned to him weeks ago? Amidst everything going on?

I'd liked Pollux upon first meeting him, and Kappas' warning had piqued my curiosity, but impressions were not always accurate, and my gut churned with a new disquiet. There was a fine line between bold and arrogant, and he was one stumbling misstep away from crossing it.

"I assure you, it wasn't intentional." I blinked away the red-rage that tinged my vision, wrangling my expression to neutral. "Things have been busy, and I apologize, but I didn't forget my promise. We'll dine soon. I will make it up to you after the wedding tomorrow."

And maybe then I'd finally get answers.

He made a quick glance over his shoulder, and his smile dropped. "That may be too late."

My stomach bottomed out like he'd punched a hole through it. Too late for *what?*

A shadow twirled around my wrist, and I came to a halt. My fingers dug into his shoulder. I punctuated each of my next words. "Why? Do you plan on going somewhere?"

Spinning us in time with the music with a sudden jolt, Pollux tugged me closer. His mouth brushed against my ear.

"Tell your spy to keep a closer eye on the King and the Prince." His whisper sent a shiver of dread chasing down my back. "What happened at the portal was not an accident."

Even as we twirled, my heart stopped. I missed my next step, nearly toppling us both.

Questions slammed into me, one after another, so quickly, they all crashed and jumbled together.

How did he know about the portal? About Nyxia spying? How involved did he assume the king was?

And what did *the Prince* have anything to do with it?

But all I managed was a hissed, *"What?"*

"I cannot say much here." Pollux's hushed speech was a hurried, urgent current against my skull. "But be aware. I am not certain the attack was isolated. I still suspect foul play with the prisoner."

He pulled away again, just as abruptly as he'd gotten close.

My shadows screamed inside of me. I fought to find reason, dread a stone through my toes.

"Is everything all right?" a stern but warm voice asked, both feminine and feral.

My heart knocked a vicious beat against my breastbone, and I whirled.

Rory stood next to Caelum, matching him in the same fine-made navy-blue dress uniform she wore during the welcome dinner at the Summer Palace. But instead of the glower she'd accessorized with that first day, concern wrinkled her face as she scanned me—not assessing if I *was* the problem, but if I had one.

"Of course." Pollux laughed as if nothing had happened, patting my shoulder like we'd been friends for ages. "Her Majesty was just telling me how I pale as a dance partner compared to the Prince, so I'll leave you all to enjoy the rest of this exquisite evening before I embarrass myself further."

"Goodnight then, Lord Pollux." Caelum dismissed him with a smile.

The Minister struck away without further protest, bowing and taking his leave before I could discipline my tongue back under my control.

Caelum watched him go, a shade between suspicion and envy shadowing his expression.

Rory's gaze didn't leave mine, somehow interrogating and subduing all at once. "You wanted to talk?"

My fists clenched at my side.

Wars were always fought on two fronts; what one had to protect, and what one would sacrifice to do it.

But as I looked between Caelum and Rory, looked between both people who I'd sacrificed little pieces of my trust to, between the two elves who'd somehow stolen bits of my shredded, tattered heart . . .

Pollux's words echoed through me on repeat.

What happened at the portal was not an accident.

And I realized that in all my efforts to save my people, I had forgotten to protect myself.

CHAPTER
TWENTY-NINE

CAELUM

When I was maybe nine or ten, I found a stray kitten out in the gardens, rail-thin with hunger and sick with fleas. As soon as I'd laid eyes on the little tabby-coated wretch, I felt connected to it. Like I was destined to be its best friend.

But when I'd tried to reach out and grab it—to bring it inside and feed it, to give it a home—it swiped its tiny claws at me, hissing and spitting with a viciousness far larger than something so small should've possessed.

I had tried to help it. To save it. I sat and waited and cooed for hours, but it never relaxed. Never let me get closer, too scared to accept my outstretched hand.

And I'd been too scared of getting hurt by its little claws that I did nothing.

It died like that—alone and afraid of the very person who might have saved it.

I'd cried for a week, barely eating or sleeping, my gut folded in on itself with the pain of my first heartache. From the guilt of my inaction.

Thera had yet to hiss, but the way she trembled as Lord Pollux walked away had my stomach in the same knots.

I couldn't imagine what someone as powerful as her might be afraid of. I'd never seen her so much as ruffled, her confidence normally unwavering, even in the face of rebel attackers and Shadowborne claws.

But there it was—in the dark clouds in her gaze, in the quivering fingers at her side.

Fear.

And this time, no matter how she hissed or scratched, I would not let her suffer alone.

"Goodnight then, Lord Pollux." I clipped out as the man fled, a protective, predatory part of me rearing its hackles.

Whatever he had said to her—*done* to her—would be discovered and punished.

Rory was tense as a board at my side, though she'd been like that since I found her prowling the outskirts of the party.

But it was her that reached out a hand first, patting Thera's arm, even as her eyes narrowed to slits. "You wanted to talk?"

Thera blinked, and her shoulders slumped. The shadows—a constant accessory as of late—quieted, withdrawing back toward her.

"We should go somewhere private." Her fists clenched at her sides. "Now."

I nodded, rubbing the back of my neck, and made a quick

glance at my father, still seated at the table with Lord Pall and a few other dignitaries. I'd have to make an excuse—perhaps some lie about Erebus wedding night traditions—but it was worth it if it helped Thera feel safer. "I'll say my farewells."

"*Now*," she spat, fangs bared, and I stepped back.

Rory's gaze flicked to me—a silent warning in their midst—her scar somehow more prominent.

Thera acted out of fear. Out of desperation.

But she was no little kitten with itsy bitsy claws.

The *Sykagos* was not a creature one risked backing into a corner. Her talons not easily survived.

"Okay." I raised my hands in surrender. "Rory, lead the way."

My guard nodded, but I didn't miss how her hand lingered on the hilt of her sword while she pointed us in the right direction.

Nor did I miss the way Thera's shadows writhed beneath her every step while she followed, her expression the same impenetrable dark.

Rory navigated us out of the ballroom without a scene, a miracle in itself, turning us left from the double doors and guiding us down the hall toward the servants' stations. She waved a hand to the guards we passed—a silent order to stand down—affording us the privacy we needed, until she opened a small wooden door at the end of the hall and ushered us inside.

A click echoed as Rory flicked the switch. *Zo'is* lanterns buzzing as they set the small space aflame with a blue glow.

A storeroom, towering white ash-wood shelves filled with creme linen tablecloths, spare silver candelabras, and enough periwinkle napkins to dress a large army of tiny pixies if ever the need arose.

The door shut behind us, the lock shifting into place with a dull tick.

Thera exhaled.

My heartbeat sped, so loud I knew that both could hear it in the quiet.

Rory gnawed at her bottom lip, and she looked at Thera, rocking back on her heels.

"Is this about last night?" Rory spoke first—the bravest among us, yet again.

Thera's attention snapped to her with the force of someone slamming a book shut.

I raised a brow. "What about last night?"

Last night, I'd been with my father, and Rory hadn't been at my door for her shift, but I'd thought nothing of it. She'd been so busy, and I'd gotten back late, Syrax and the other midnight guard already manning the post.

Had something happened? Had they fought again?

Rory's expression crashed. She opened her mouth to speak—

"Did he tell you about what happened at the portal?" Thera trounced whatever Rory had been about to say and stepped closer to me. Her mismatched eyes narrowed. "Did he tell you?"

I pursed my lips as I fought—and failed—to make sense of a single word. "What?"

Thera flinched. Tears gathered against her dark lashes. "Your father. Did he tell you what happened to my people?"

Confusion and compassion battered my skull like the rain slapping against the small, square windows. I reached for Thera's hand. "Please, I—I can see you're upset, but I have no idea what you're talking about."

Thera smacked my hand away. Straightened her back, blinking back the suspended tears. Her eyes went cold and lightless.

"Twenty of my people are dead, and there are reports that your father's escorts never showed." Her throat bobbed as her voice broke out of her. "That *your* people didn't show, Captain." She poked a manicured finger at Rory, a flash of unexpected hurt streaking across her face like lightning.

A similar rumble of unease rolled through me, my gut clenching as her words sank down.

The Erebushi faction wasn't dead. They couldn't be.

405

They hadn't arrived today, though I'd assumed it was due to the storm. Or that perhaps they would attend the wedding itself, but not the party, our celebratory customs far different by Thera's accounts.

But dead? Abandoned?

My hands went numb, and I spun to Rory, waiting for her to deny it. Waiting for her to give me an answer that would set it all right.

"That can't be." But even as she protested, her brow drew tight, something dark and disappointed crashing over her face. "Or at least, I've heard no reports."

That made no sense. Rory was the captain of my guard, but this had been her side project. If there had been such a serious threat and loss of life, Erebushi or not, Rory would have known.

I would have known.

I shook my head, freeing myself of the itch creeping its way up my back. "My father would have—"

"Your father would have lied to your face if given the chance," Thera snarled, and though she was shorter than me, I'd never felt so small. "We intercepted his messages. The Shadowborne attack we witnessed was not the first to happen within Solis, just like in the Summer Palace. And he's hiding all of it."

Rory went still. She sucked in a sharp breath. "The King's personal messages, not the reports addressed to me or Tiberius?"

Thera's jaw clenched and unclenched. "Correct."

I stumbled back from her, bumping into a shelf, the wood nipping my back.

I'd trusted Thera. Had given her access to my mother's library, access to parts of myself I'd let no one else see. That I hadn't even let Rory or my *father* see.

And despite her frequent criticisms of his transparency, she hadn't been honest with me, either. She'd withheld, just as she accused my father of the same. She'd lurked in the shadows, dabbling in her espionage, while proclaiming her moral superiority.

"You've been spying on my father?" Anger surged through my veins, licking my face hot. My hands fisted at my sides.

How much more did Thera know than I did? How much had she kept from me, all whilst using me and my mother's library to get more information? Whilst justifying it all by telling me she was the only one who wouldn't hide from me?

She flinched like I'd slapped her, and my stomach soured.

"Of course, we've been spying! I'm alone in enemy territory, Caelum." Her voice quivered, a vulnerable part shaking her form. Mismatched eyes blazed with hot tears. "I've been *alone* this whole time, risking my life and my throne for a chance at peace with people that all want me dead. You said it yourself—they all see me as a monster. And you'd blame me for keeping myself safe?"

My emotions tangled together, each one indecipherable from the next. "No, Thera. I don't blame you for having your guard up, I'm just hurt that you lied about it!"

Hurt, yes, that was it. Hurt that she'd left me out, just as she'd promised not to. That she'd protected me from the truth, instead of letting me in.

Thera stilled. Her tears dried, like they'd been recalled back behind her walls.

A single trace of regret didn't exist in her upright stance, not even a glimmer of remorse. Just icy rage. Just darkness. "My people are *dead*, Caelum. Your hurt is the least of my worries."

Hot, metallic tears gathered in the back of my throat, stinging as my words pushed past them. "They were supposed to be *our* people."

My heartbeat defeated my ears, pulsing in a sickening repetition. That's what she'd promised. That we'd manage together. That we'd be honest and would push each other to be better.

"Thera is right, Cae." Rory laid a hand on my arm. "If these messages are true, this is a big problem for all of us."

I swallowed the lump.

Not just us.

All of Erebus and Lux. The future of the continent and the downlands.

I ran a hand over my face. I had to calm down, had to get my heart rate back under control, otherwise I might faint again.

This didn't make sense, which meant we missed something. My father was a good king. He'd never gone back on any of his promises, and he'd promised Thera guests at the wedding. Promised to send escorts. Plus, if there *were* Shadowborne attacks, he'd have tightened security around us—me specifically —before anything else. This wedding would've been a private, quiet affair.

I blew out a regulating breath. "I hear what you're saying, but there has to be a mistake. My father might not be entirely forth-coming, but he would never lie about *this*."

Thera didn't snap again. But her shadows tucked closer, not like snakes ready to strike, but like a blanket pulling around her shoulders. A *shield*.

"Ask him then, Caelum. Ask him if I'm lying." There was no more bite to her tone, a hollowness instead cracking through her words like thunder without rain. "And then we can have a real talk."

I didn't try and stop her as she turned to leave. Didn't ratio-nalize or argue, my fire spent.

But Rory chased after, latching on to her elbow. "Thera, *please*. We need to—"

Thera jerked away. Her face fell. "You haven't even seen my thorns, Captain."

Rory flinched back like Thera had punched her.

No one halted her again as she threw the door open and slammed it after herself, another click reverberating through the overstocked space.

Maybe it was a trick of the blue *Zo'is* lamps, but Rory's face paled, and she stared at the door like she was hoping it would open again.

Neither of us spoke for a long, excruciating clip.

I had no idea what to say. No idea what to feel, what to *think*. Everything emptied like Thera had sucked out my soul with a look.

"I'll check in with Julius and Commander Tiberius. There must be other accounts of this information somewhere," Rory tried first, finally tearing her gaze from the door to meet mine. Lips pursed. "And then, I promise, we'll sort this out. All of it."

And in another moment, she was gone, the door shutting with a quiet, punctuated pop this time.

I stood alone for several breaths, numb and paralyzed by my inadequacy and ignorance.

Ask him then, Caelum. Ask him if I'm lying.

My father would have the answers, just like he always did whenever I needed him to.

I just had to hope that he'd—no, I had to *make* him tell me the truth.

I barreled back into the ballroom, the lilting music a stark contrast to my percussive steps. Chatter died around me, and I marched toward my father, the crowd parting like a curtain.

There was no sign of Rory or Thera, which I supposed was a blessing rather than a curse. I didn't know if I had the strength to follow through, and I didn't need them here to see me fail yet again.

My father had moved to his throne, lounging atop it without a care in the world. One foot dangled over the edge as he sipped at his goblet of wine, his cheeks rosy this late into the festivities. He chatted with Lord Pall, Lord Diras, and Lady Mirena, all three of them doting on him like the sun rose and set in his smile.

He was so casual—so *confident*—that I faltered for a second. He wouldn't be this relaxed if something were truly wrong.

Maybe he really didn't know about what was going on, and if so, I had to inform him.

Before Thera took that upon herself.

"Come with me," I blurted as I stood at the foot of the dais, not bothering to kneel. "We need to talk."

Four heads snapped my way, eyes narrowing like I'd just told them all they smelled of manure.

My father didn't shift, his seat still relaxed, but his jaw clenched. His grip around his goblet tightened, just as his smile did. "You'll have to excuse my son's poor behavior, tonight is a very important night, and he's been anxious—"

"*Now,*" I interrupted before I could lose my nerve. I cut a quick glance to his courtiers, their mouths already hanging open in shock. Quickly, I added a quiet, "Please."

Lady Mirena's brows shot up to her ornately braided hairline. This would make for the gossip of the century, the vultures ready to pick me clean.

My father understood politics better than anyone. Understood what such gossip could mean in the court of public opinion. With a practiced, careful laziness, he set down his wine, stretching his arms above his head as he rose.

"All right, all right, it's late anyway." He winked at his admirers. "If you'll excuse me, it seems my son needs some fatherly advice before his wedding day."

The courtiers chuckled, but they'd still talk the second we left the room.

My father knew it, too. He jerked his head for me to follow, setting an easy, unbothered pace as he led me away, their beady eyes following us.

My father's genial facade lasted until we made it to the emergency meeting chambers behind the dais, the gold door slamming shut. The room was plain; a meeting table, a giant map of the continent, a few shelves with parchment and ink, a lazy *Zo'is* lamp that offered a meek haze to see by.

Even though I'd never been to the dungeons, the cold that crept through me was the same as I imagined crawled through the bowels of Stellaris.

Before the Shadowborne attack, I'd never really known true fear—not as it lived in my body. I'd seen it on others, had witnessed it in the hollow expressions of the soldiers that returned from the war, in my guards' and doctors' faces whenever my blood assessments came back poor.

My father turned to me, shoulders rigid and his face a dark mask of thinly veiled anger, fear prickled against my spine almost as vividly as it had before the Shadowborne.

"What in the Sun's bright rays do you think you're doing?" he growled, low and ominous. "Speaking to me like that in front of courtiers? Have you gone *mad?*"

"Maybe I have." I gulped around the words, shoving that fear away, embracing the madness instead. "What happened to the Erebushi delegates?"

My father's anger dispersed, like a single drop of blood in a river. He walked toward the large map of Lux that hung high on the wall, the vague outline of the Great Bridge of Sidus just a blot of dark ink at the bottom.

"I have no idea. They didn't show." He shrugged, rubbing a finger over the spot like it was a stain that could be wiped away. "Maybe they're shy."

Thera's face flashed through my mind—the horror, the rage—and my fear died entirely.

I crossed to the map, putting myself between my father and the depiction of the kingdom. Between the current king and the people I was sworn to serve. "Don't lie to me."

Lightning flashed outside, searing the low-lit room in vicious, bright light, emphasizing the shadows beneath my father's eyes as he went still. "*What?*"

I'm not afraid of a challenge anymore, thanks to you.

I hadn't lied. I'd *promised.*

"What about the Shadowborne attacks?"

His brows chased to his hairline before they knotted again in concern. He reached for my cheek, and I flinched at the sudden change in demeanor. His hand stopped midair before he dropped it, his face falling in tandem. "Caelum, we've been over this. I'm so sorry for what you witnessed in the markets. I'm sure it was terrifying after what happening to your friend at the Summer Palace, but—"

The reminder of Quinton stung, and I hissed. "No, the other attacks *in* Solis, Papa. In the inner city. Why haven't you told me about *anything*?"

A frown tugged his mouth, like it used to when I'd argue that I was old enough to play outside without a chaperone. Like it used to when he'd catch me staying up past my bedtime. "You speak nonsense."

"Stop treating me like a kid!" Rage spewed up from the darkest parts of me, and I smacked a hand across the map—right over the miniature of Stellaris. "I know you've been hiding things from me!"

The pity and compassion disappeared from my father's expression. He stepped closer, acidic, wine-scented breath heating against my face as his glare smoldered. "Where are you getting these *ridiculous* ideas?"

"Thera told me—"

"So, the *Sykagos* has poisoned you against me? And you *believed* her?"

"My *future wife* has intercepted some of *your* messages."

"Then how was I supposed to receive these supposed threats? Should I have read her mind?" he asked, knowing that I couldn't answer. Seeing the same trap of logic I had when Thera had first introduced the idea. When I had no immediate response—our back and forth over and him the clear victor—he threw his hands in the air. "How do you know they're even legitimate claims? Were they from trusted sources? Were they falsified by rebels? They are barely more than pests to us, but this is exactly the kind of misinformation they want you to believe. I thought you had better deductive skills, Caelum."

Doubt itched beneath my skin, my tunic too tight, my boots too heavy. "I—"

My father blew out a long breath, resting against the map as the fight expelled out of him. Gone was the anger and contempt— the last glimmers of the warrior king—instead replaced again by the aging monarch I knew best. Fatigue claimed his shoulders, and his frame drooped. "I am disappointed by your lack of faith in me, son."

Tears burned the back of my eyes, my throat prickling, but I refused to let them fall.

It was the first time he named it aloud; that festering, ugly thing that I knew always lurked between us. The wound that always bled in the most hidden parts of my heart, the voice that whispered terrible things in the back of my mind.

Disappointed.

He was disappointed in the man I was. In the hobbies I kept, and in the weak body I wore. I wasn't the warrior prince he'd always dreamed of, the strong, fearless elf that bore his courage along with his coloring.

He loved me.

Yet I'd never measure up to the fantasy of what I could've been instead if I was born different. If I was less like Mama, and more like him.

But I was my mother's son, even long after her parting. Her blood ran through my veins, her too-large heart beat in my chest. And if she believed in me—believed I could be the king Lux needed —I would make him believe, too.

I stood straighter. "I have every reason to be suspicious. Especially after what I found in Mama's library about Grandfather. Or do you think she was unreliable, too?"

I realized my mistake too late.

Everything went silent, not a single breath between the both of us.

"What library?" he asked, just above a whisper.

A stone sank to my toes. "I didn't—"

My father shot forward, his hands gripped my shoulder, their strength punishing as they bit into my skin. My father shook me, madness devouring his face. "What library, Caelum?"

"Her study! The books . . . " I hesitated, torn between betraying my secret with Mama and quelling my living parent's distress. "She had a collection."

My father stopped the shaking. His hands fell to his sides as his face went utterly blank. "Show me."

"Papa, I—"

"*Now.*"

The world moved too fast.

We walked all the way from the meeting chamber to Mama's quarters, my father summoning Tiberius along the way as we then reassembled in her private wing. My heart sped in time with my father's hurried march, in time with the buzzing in my ears and the blistering thoughts swirling in my head.

It might have been hours or minutes by the time Father had searched through every title in Mama's collection, piling the books on the table until it bowed in the middle, sagging under the weighty stacks.

I was just as heavy, ready to break under the gravity of my father's grim stare as he waited for an explanation.

My throat was thick with dust and shame. "I don't know how she got them, but she used to say they'd help make me a good king."

Father gripped a book so fiercely I suspected the spine would snap if he held onto it a moment longer. He threw it at the stack; the tower tumbling to the ground, pages flying open as the books toppled over each other in dull thuds.

My stomach flipped. Crashing to my knees, I scattered to pick them up—to right them back on the table.

"Do you have any idea what these books *are*? The kinds of treasonous elves that wrote them?" The ice in my father's voice froze me in place.

I hung my head, hiding the tears that bit my eyes. Treasonous elves, like Arturus, betraying his country for an Erebushi General. Like me, for reading his book and stowing it among my personal effects without handing it over to my father.

I latched onto the book nearest me—*Medicinal Herbs of The Deadlands.*

Was that so treasonous? Medicine? Resources, for a world that had so little ever since my people cast them out? For an entire society trying to survive in utter darkness?

My voice shook as I tugged the book—and my mother's belief —close to my chest. "They aren't all that way. Some just offer a different perspective."

"Commander Tiberius?" My father ignored me, kicking books out of the way as he crossed to his top command. I winced at each beat, as if he were kicking me instead.

Commander Tiberius's sword clacked at his side as he bowed, a hand flattened across his breastbone in salute. "Yes, Your Majesty?"

My father halted. Turned back toward the room, eyes raking over the space with no emotion. "Burn these books immediately."

A breath. A pause.

Tiberius nodded. "Yes, Your Majesty."

"No." My protest was just above a murmur, my tongue lame with shock, but my arms flew out, and I put myself between the books and the commander. I pleaded with my father, tears spilling down my cheeks. "Please, *no.*"

The commander shoved me aside unapologetically, collecting the books for their grave.

I spun to the king, my head whirring at a dizzying speed. "You can't, this was Mama's, you can't!"

My father said nothing.

The commander didn't stop.

I rushed forward, trying to grab as many of the books as I could, snatching them out of the way.

Tiberius sighed. Like I was a nuisance, not the prince. Not the next king.

My father's hand snagged my wrist. He twisted—and I recoiled, dropping the books, each precious piece clattering to the ground as my heart shattered.

"Caelum, that's enough." The king ground through his teeth.

For the first time in twenty-five years, I found my breaking point.

I'd had *enough*.

"No, I won't let you do this." I tore myself from his grasp, using a disarming technique I'd learned from Thera, before pushing at his chest.

He stumbled back, surprise catching him off his balance as he knocked into Mama's favorite chair.

Mama's chair. Mama's study.

Mama's books.

I didn't care if they were all lies and slander. Didn't care if they were dangerous or treasonous.

They were hers.

Mine, now. The last I had of her.

My limbs trembled, and I shouted, spit and rage flying from my viper's tongue as I stood over the king—my father. "Mama would hate you for this. She'd fucking hate you."

He surged back to standing, marching forward until he was a breath away. "Your mother was deeply, deeply disturbed, and I don't give a fuck what she might have thought."

I staggered back. Panic squeezed my lungs, a single breath escaping. "*What?*"

The haze cleared from my father's eyes. He blinked. His mouth fell open, then slammed shut again.

"Her mind was just as foul and corrupted as these pages," he said through a clenched jaw. "And by the end, she wasn't herself. I didn't know it ran this deep, I see now that I made a mistake in shielding you from the truth."

My skin burned, and my blood boiled beneath it.

My mother was shade on a too-sunny day. A quiet space to escape from the noise. A soft place to rest in this hard as marble-and-gemstone world of Stellaris.

She was reserved. Withdrawn, even.

But if she was foul, the rest of this fucking place was utterly rotted.

"You're lying." I hissed back at my father—at the King of Rot and Ruin. At the mimicry of the man I once admired and *adored*. "She was sick, she was—"

"She didn't die of the illness you share, Caelum. Her heart didn't give out. She gave up, and she *killed* herself," the King of Lux shouted, his voice booming like an oncoming storm. Like lightning striking me down. "*Because* she dabbled in these books and in the shadows. She was so desperate for a cure, for power, she tempted fate and played with forces beyond her control. And if you're not careful, son, you might find yourself in the same position."

All my protests died as my father's truth stabbed through my heart, murdering my will on impact. As his stare—a match for mine in color, but opposite in contempt—slashed through me just as brutally.

My mother loved life. Loved me.

There was no way she'd ever . . .

But there was no sign of deception on his face. No tell of a lie. Only a widower's grief and that dawning disappointment. The first, for the love he lost—the second, for the son she left behind.

"I expect you in the gardens at dawn." My father smoothed the wrinkles from his tunic, schooling his face into the same placid nothingness. "You have a duty to uphold."

The unspoken command blared through the room, even as he careened out of it.

Don't disappoint me again.

I should've heeded his order. Should've marched back to my room to cry myself to sleep, should've tried to push this entire affair from my mind.

Should've followed him and begged for his forgiveness, or punched him straight in his fucking face.

Instead, through the last hours before the day of my wedding, I watched as Tiberius stole every book from my mother's room. As he tallied and added each and every one to the pyre.

And as he set my world on fire, the blaze consuming and crackling and destroying each book, as the perfect image of my father burned away with them . . .

I understood, for a moment, why my mother might have craved the same end.

CHAPTER
THIRTY

"My vows belong to no man, but to my people. I am wed to Elysia, and no portal could ever divorce me from my true love." —An excerpt from Queen Glorianna's letter to the Elysian people, circa 2 A.G.W. (After the Great War).

THERA

The sun prowled over the city as dawn descended, devouring the evidence of yesterday's rains and warming the earth.

The sun had left me in awe, at first. Mesmerized by its beauty. Enchanted by its life-giving heat.

But I'd learned my lesson. Learned that the sun dazzled and blinded. Learned how it *burned*.

The gardens of Stellaris didn't seem as ill-affected. Day flowers stretched open, shaking sleep off their petals. They sucked up the first rays, their colors decorating the castle grounds like they, too, were ready to celebrate.

A beautiful morning for a wedding.

And everything was wrong.

Neither Caelum nor Aurora had found me in my chambers after our discussion, but I hadn't expected them to. Even if they didn't know about what happened at the portal, they were complicit in this. They'd both done nothing to help. Nothing to save my people. The Prince was content to be a pawn, The Puppet Prince, as they called him, and the captain prioritized fawning over Caelum before her promises to anyone else. It stabbed through my chest, their squandered potential a knife in my side.

I'd been a fool to put any faith in them, just as I'd been naive to think Lux would hold up its side of the bargain in the slightest.

My people still had no *Zo'is*. No resources or food. No time.

We cut through the expansive gardens to the sacred grove at the very edge of Stellaris' grounds. My eyes snagged on each colorful petal, like they mocked me silently. The flowers here had never known hardship, never known starvation.

But I was not a pretty flower that needed pampering. I was a weed. I infiltrated and took what I needed without remorse.

I'd be married in an hour, and if Lux didn't pay its dues, I'd take what I was owed from the King's flesh.

No more bargaining or compromising. No more waiting and starving and dying.

Kings bowed to no one.

"I urge you one last time, *Mi Vassilla*." Nyxia trailed after me. Her boots squelched through the dewy grass, each echoing the sick feeling roiling through my stomach. "Call the wedding off."

"For once, I agree with Mistress Drakos," Commander Kappas said, his voice gruff with sleep and stress. They both wore their starched black dress uniforms today—the same they'd worn to my father's funeral—like this, too, deserved such solemn reverence. "There is something wrong here, and I worry about safety."

The shadows around my heart faltered.

I slowed my steps, eyeing him warily, trying to discern if Kappas' loyalties were truly aligned with mine. Or if he had played against Lux, using this trip to further my father's war.

But he did mourn for our dead comrades; he carried the twenty dead Erebushi lives in his dark heart, just as I did mine. Now he, Nyxia, and I were all each other had in this sun-bleached plane.

And there were thousands more back home, still waiting in the dark. Still desperate.

"My safety is not my priority," I slowed for a moment, blades of wet graze tickling my ankles like the worry crawling beneath my skin. "My people are. And I need to marry Caelum to enforce the treaty, so I will. Once that is done, if they deny me what's rightfully mine, I will have a legal claim to continue the war."

War, my father's favorite pastime. His most practiced art.

Mine too, though I took no joy in it. Not even as a last resort.

Kappas hung his head.

Nyxia gnawed at her lip. "We can find another way."

I'd hoped so, too. Planned for it, even. Stavros and I schemed for years before my father's death. I'd done things, had sacrificed so much to ensure that another way existed.

The lump in my throat burned as I swallowed it down.

Any Erebushi farmer would tell you that if even one wheel was stuck in the mud, the plow could not move. It'd only churn in place, eating itself into a deeper hole.

Despite all my efforts, despite the late nights and early mornings bonding with my betrothed, despite me biting my tongue and sheathing my claws in front of the King, Lux was still mud-ridden and stagnant. And I was getting nowhere.

Today, that would change.

"Is my Mistress of Spies going soft?" I teased, but my humor missed its mark, falling flat into the ground between us. With a sigh, I rubbed Nyxia's arm. "I will be fine. But I must see this through. That's the last I'll speak on it."

Her throat bobbed, her teeth grinding as she held a funeral for all the protests she wanted to say but wouldn't. "Yes, *Mi Vassilla*."

I shifted my focus to Kappas. To the commander that would need to be my sword if it came to blows. "Can I count on you both to stand with me?"

Kappas grimaced, but nodded along.

With the first rays of sun in my eyes and my shadows at my back, I marched forward, hiking up my too-long skirts, ready to say my vows and change history.

Grass fed into stone once more, a geometric marble path patching through the clover leading us toward the grove. My heels clacked against it, Nyxia's boots squeaking from the transition from wet to dry. Bushes became sparse trees, then lush, weeping willows, branches decorated with tear-like pearl strands.

I wondered if they mourned for me.

I rounded the corner, facing the makeshift altar and the crowd gathered in front of it. The sun was gentler here—the willows waited in a small valley at the base of the largest hillside, protecting it from the unkind dawn. But even without such brightness, everything sparkled.

The altar was the only plain thing in the clearing, a slab of gray stone decorated only by a single gold goblet and a silver dagger. In front of it, several rows of metallic chairs crested in semi-circles, the seated courtiers in increasingly ostentatious dresses and suits a rainbow of overstimulation. Only Lord Pollux dressed reasonably—his suit a dull, soft gray. I nodded to him—a thank-you for the warning last night—but he cast his gaze downward, ignoring me.

Fine then. I didn't need allies or strange, veiled messages, anyway.

Behind the altar, a row of guards in their platinum armor and dress uniforms stood sentry like they were planted with the willows. Aurora, Julius, and Tiberius were centered among them, staring forward in rapt, orderly attention.

The captain's gaze flicked to me once, then away. Her focus hardened again, she sank back into her given role.

It stung more than I wanted it to, the brief memory of strawberries and wine gathering at the back of my throat.

My stomach flipped, not with bridal nerves or wistful regret, but with disgust.

My people should've been here. Should've worn the soft, flowing black of comforting shade to offset the cacophony of color. Should've been sporting encouraging, tear-stained smiles instead of the vicious, beady glares of those waiting for me to trip and fall.

When King Kato emerged from behind a willow, dressed from head to toe in a gold that rivaled the blinding, glittering sun, my disgust grew teeth and named itself hatred.

He raised his hands, and the courtiers stood. His mouth ticked upward. "King Thera Umbrus of Erebus, please come forward."

"What, no fanfare?" I tsked, noting the lack of flair. For a kingdom that loved its riches, this wedding was still just another insult to me—another half-done slight meant to embarrass me into fealty.

But kings would not be leashed by shame.

My head high, steps slow and steady, my grass-stained dress kissed the floor, and my shadows created a train of night behind me. They circled my arms, my waist, my skirts, blotting out the silly white dress I'd shoved myself into, creating instead an ethereal, flowing gown that moved and breathed with me.

Gasps echoed in time with my steps, and they fueled my shadows more, feeding their appetite for gossip with the reminder of the power resting in my veins.

I could be my own fanfare.

But when Caelum stood from his seat in the front row and found his spot before the altar, I faltered, my shadows winking out for a moment.

He wore a stunning white tunic, high neck and dangling sleeves somehow both regal and delicate, and it might have suited him beautifully if it weren't for the utter exhaustion that captured his features. Deep plum bruises lived beneath his dull eyes. Shoulders hunched; his white hair hung limp around his ears.

Captain Bellatore watched him too, her stance shifting and angling toward him, like she was ready to spring forward and catch him at any moment.

"Good morning," I murmured as I neared. It wasn't the vitriolic, accusatory speech I'd rehearsed in my mirror all morning—nor the confession of hope and budding romance I'd imagined in the weeks before my delegates went missing—but it was a ceasefire, concern winning out above all else.

I didn't want to hate him, and I certainly didn't want to see him look so unwell.

And I didn't know if he could break free from the chains of his upbringing.

Parts of me—silly, romantic parts—wanted him to. Wanted his kiss last night to mean something. Wanted my mother's ring on his finger to inspire change.

Caelum's jaw ticked. He didn't so much as look at me. "Hmm."

The single syllable speared me through, chasing away concern. My fingertips went numb, leadening as reality sank to my extremities. So much for wanting.

I turned back toward the King, sending all my malice and fury his way. Wishing that he'd catch fire from the heat of my stare. Caelum and Rory had both wounded me, but they were only weapons, not the wielder. Tools that the King had used against me.

He smiled and lifted the chalice high. Sunlight glinted off its face, blinding me.

"We gather here to unify not just two people, but two kingdoms," His voice boomed through the open space. "Two mighty civilizations, both ready to lay down their arms and instead offer their hands."

I withheld a scoff at the hypocrisy, biting down on the inside of my cheek.

The King tipped the goblet, revealing the burgundy liquid sloshing within. A small patch covered the back of his hand.

Blood. His, an offering to the Aether beyond. "The blood of our forefathers initiates this pact."

Focusing on us again, the King brandished the small, silver knife.

Caelum wobbled next to me, and my stomach clenched.

"You don't look well," I whispered, so low only he could hear.

"This is supposed to be the quiet portion of the ceremony." My betrothed clenched his jaw.

I winced at the icy sting in his voice.

Caelum stuck his hand out over the altar, glaring at his father with the same glacial sharpness. It wasn't just toward me, then.

A quick swipe of the knife, and Caelum's blood dripped into the goblet. Three drops, thick and sluggish. Dehydrated.

King Kato quickly produced another patch, splaying it over his son's hand and staunching the wound.

I shoved my worry down, deep into the darkness where my shadows lived.

The King frowned at his son, but said nothing. He looked at me, waiting.

I shoved my hand forward—palm up. It would hurt more this way, but I wanted to feel that. Wanted my sacrifice for my people to be enough.

Wanted to let Kato—and all the courtiers know—that pain did not deter me. That instead, it *made* me. Disciplined me.

The king cut deep enough to scar, a cruel tick at the side of his mouth displaying his enjoyment.

I refused to flinch as I tilted my hand, my bright crimson blood spattering against the metal cup in heavy thuds.

The King didn't offer me a staunch.

My shadows shifted, and I wiped my bleeding palm across my white bodice, staining it instead. Another shadow tied itself around the wound, thick enough to slow the bleeding.

Kato's lips pursed, but he didn't say anything about it. With the knife, he swirled the contents of the goblet, mixing the sanguineous stain into one deep palate.

He held the cup to Caelum's lips first, reciting the next bit. "At this dawn, may the sun shine upon us all."

Caelum paused for a moment; the cup suspended as his eyes narrowed. He took a gulp, throat bobbing. Red painted his mouth to cherry, standing out even more against his graying skin.

"May its rays brighten our lives," the crowd chanted.

The goblet lowered, and red dripped from the prince's lips onto his fine white clothes.

The King hurried his next line, shifting the goblet to me. "In this light, may our gardens grow and flourish."

I grabbed the goblet from him, lifting it to my mouth. Iron and salt stung my tongue as I took a deep dreg of the thick liquid, licking the last from my lips.

"May the planted seeds reach toward the sky," the crowd chanted again.

We'd gone over the ceremony during a meeting a few days back, and I'd read the customs over and over to better understand my role. But even knowing what came next didn't prepare me for the dread that sloshed through me.

Caelum turned, eyes sunken and glazed over like he'd somehow escaped his own head. Like he'd left his body entirely, slipping out through a secret back door, rather than be present for this moment together.

With a sway forward, his lips brushed over mine in a quick, disinterested peck, sealing our fate.

It wasn't like the other kisses we'd shared—sweet, promising, even if brief. Full of affection and excitement.

No, this was cold. Aloof.

And for the first time since meeting the prince, I had a sinking fear our marriage would be the same.

Caelum stepped away—the wedding was over just as quickly as it began.

Kato smirked, satisfied, and spilled the last of the goblet across the altar, proclaiming us wed. "And now two lives are joined as one, growing together beneath the sun's observation. Dum Vivet!"

Long Live.

That was it. The end. It was over, the most important moment in my life and in my kingdom's history, finished with a few curt words and a loveless kiss.

I was married, and the future consort of Lux. Of a people that still hated and feared me. And Caelum now was the consort of Erebus, a land he'd never seen.

My husband.

Head hanging, white strands of silken hair curtaining his eyes like the willow branches around us, he turned to go.

Something surged up from my middle, something I thought fear and rage had killed. Something I was equal parts surprised by and scared of, as I caught his wrist.

Hollow eyes seared my knuckles, and then my face, as they swept over me, still distant and dark.

"In Erebus, we make promises to each other at the end of the ceremony," I declared loud enough for all the guests to hear—but my words were only for him. For the boy who loved books and had once been willing to read mine. "Caelum *Arturus* Borealis, I, Thera Dymitria Umbrus, promise this to you; that my strength will be your strength. That my passion will be yours, too. And that the good of *our* people will be the only thing I hold reverent above you."

I thought they were our people.

They were now.

He blinked, the rest of the crowd fading away.

Someone—Lady Mirena, perhaps—might have scoffed, but I didn't care. Not when his eyes glimmered, a brief flash of something *alive* that sparked hope in my chest.

War waged in the small space between his brows as they pulled close together. "I ... I promise ... "

A shadow cast him in black, and the rest of his sentence fell off. The darkness crept over the congregation, the low-hanging sunlight swallowed up, like the great hand of some higher being had turned back the wheel of time, thrusting the world into night once more.

Kato spun to me, accusations cocked and ready on the tip of his tongue.

But these were not my shadows.

Backing up to see over the willow tops, I tilted my head as far as I could, squinting toward the towering hillside to see what had shrouded us in darkness.

Screams shattered the air, piercing through my ears just as I spotted them.

All feeling fled my body, replaced with the cold, distant numb I'd learned in the Pool of Souls.

Shadowborne.

Not one. Not a dozen.

Hundreds, standing on the peak of the hill in rows so thick, they shielded the entire clearing from the sunlight, spit dripping from their growling, curved maws.

Hungry. Ravenous.

Smiling.

They charged.

CHAPTER
THIRTY-ONE

"A Shadowborne's senses are far superior to ours, but their cognition is their weakness. In all observations, they are driven by hunger, not thought, which is both comforting and horrifying." —A Study of the Effects of Shadow Magic, Minister Kristos Agyros, 2079 A.G.W.

RORY

In the tension-wrought moments before my premier battle with the First Legion, my commanding officer had reminded me and the rest of my rookie platoon of most important rules of war:

Rule one: Everyone pisses themselves the first time. If you're pissing, you're still alive. Wear the stain with pride if you survive.

Rule two: Shadowborne can detect you before you can detect them. Our only defense is to always be ready and hope that the bastard that forged your armor wasn't drunk that day.

Rule three: Instinct is just as powerful as training. If you panic and forget what you've been taught, let your body do the work. It will lead you to safety if you don't fight it.

But as the scent of piss and fear flooded the clearing, as the courtiers screamed and scrambled and wet themselves, as the Shadowborne's heavy footfalls roared when they careened down the hill, too fast to flee from . . .

My instinct did not lead me to safety. Didn't prioritize my survival first.

I did not hesitate.

I drew my sword and slashed at the first beast's neck before it could get to Caelum, cleaving it from its leathery shoulders in a single, decisive swoop. Black, pus-like blood soiled his fine white clothes, covering any other stain he might have made as he ducked behind me.

No hesitation as I spun myself between Thera and the next monster's outstretched claws. It was too close for a melee. A familiar lightning burn rocketed up my arms as my bracelets flared, blue light running up my veins as the *Zo'is* euphoric power rushed through me. And in a burst, power flashed from my palms, burning the Shadowborne's grotesque face to ash.

The beast fell dead at my feet, the smell of its singed flesh tickling my nose.

Thera's shadows cleared. She looked at me, mouth parted and eyes watering. "Thank you."

I nodded, my heartbeat clanging so loudly, it nearly drowned out the chaos. There was no time for discussion, not with more of the hoard rushing through the willows, branches cracking beneath their weight as they launched off them, toward my guards and the nobles.

It was a total ambush.

War.

"Get the King!" Tiberius hollered from deeper in the treeline, cutting through another Shadowborne, splattering black across the greenery with his great sword. His *Zo'is* gauntlets flared hot, his blade burning with its electric heat. His smoldering gaze met mine for a brief flash. "Captain, the King, *now.*"

The king.

Right, Kato.

I swiveled, searching . . .

And found him sheathed behind the altar to my right, only a few paces from Thera, Caelum, and I.

But he didn't watch the oncoming hoard, didn't look for a way out or for a weapon to defend himself.

He stared at *me.* Eyes narrowed, flicking between Thera and I.

The King I was tasked to kill—the one he'd just watched me save.

Dread sank through me, a chill running down my spine even as adrenaline blasted my veins.

An itch across my tattooed arm pulled me back to the moment, right as Julius bounded up to us, gold hair streaked with black blood. Worry knotted his brow, and he made a quick scan of me. I didn't have time for him to fuss.

"Julius, take the King," I ordered.

My *Vinculum* nodded, patting me on the cheek before rushing to the monarch's side.

King Kato tore his gaze from me as my giant friend enveloped him, shielding him with his body. They scurried out of the clearing, Julius's bracelets flaring, and his sword raised.

I'd deal with that later. Jules would keep him safe.

Breathe in, Rory.

Focus.

Caelum and Thera needed to get out, but we couldn't abandon the rest of the guests as fodder. I tracked to see who was closest to them, relief pooling in my middle as my gaze snagged on Syrax and Dama, fighting back-to-back only three trees away. "Syrax, Dama, get the courtiers out of the fucking way!"

"On it!" Syrax tore through two Shadowborne at once with his twin swords, his long strides almost a match for theirs. More snapped and growled on his heels, but he danced away. Dama gave him cover, and he raced toward the courtiers that were still alive, screaming and sobbing among their half-eaten friends.

Friends that would soon start their own transformations if we didn't behead them.

As if she could read my thoughts and feelings as easily as Julius did, Thera's shoulders rolled back when she looked to the courtiers, shadows swimming forward. Determination set her jaw. "I've got this. Go with Caelum."

I grabbed her wrist before she could run toward them. "No, you're coming with us."

"I can handle myself." She jerked out of my grip, shadows devouring more of her form. Soon, they'd swarm her like an exoskeleton, sheathing her wiry frame from view, only the dark, imposing silhouette remaining. Only the *Sykagos*.

There was a fourth truth told to new conscripts during their first battle. One I'd forgotten then, and it nearly cost me my right eye and my *life*.

Rule four: If you see the *Sykagos*, say a prayer.

She could more than *handle* herself. Thera of Erebus was war incarnate. Not just Erebus's greatest weapon, but a master of the very killing power that birthed the Shadowborne monsters closing in on us. A conduit of the same death magic that turned elves into pure, hungry animals, that tore us from our senses and mangled our bodies into pure, beastly strength.

But she was a king, too. One that needed her new people to see the girl in the journal more than she needed to show them her strength.

Fear lingers.

"No. Not with those." I jabbed a finger at the snake pit of angry ink at her feet, then at the cowering courtiers. "They will never look at you the same way again."

Thera blinked, darkness clearing from her gaze.

"I'll keep it low profile." Her armor of darkness receded, before one of her shadows sharpened to a blade-like point and whizzed past my ear. "Watch out."

I spun. The shadow sliced the Shadowborne's head off faster than lightning could ignite a dry forest.

I'd forgotten rule two.

Always be ready.

The Shadowborne's head rolled in front of my feet, its mouth hanging open like it still tried to swallow me whole, even in death.

Thera stared at it impassively, that same muscle in her jaw ticking. She lifted her head to Cae. "Believe me now?"

Caelum doubled over and heaved, watery yellow vomit bright against the black. He wiped his mouth with a pristine sleeve, his face ashen. "How the fuck did they get in here?" His voice shook out of him.

Bile stirred in my gut. The mountains behind us hadn't been breached *ever*. Stellaris was a palace, but it was also a fortress, built to protect and outlast.

This was an inside job. There was no more denying it.

We had a traitor in our midst.

I fought the urge to scan the courtiers again, to rack my head over who hadn't shown, or who looked anxious. My investigation would have to wait until after I had my future king and consort *safe*. "I have no idea, but we have to move."

Easier said than done. Two more Shadowborne leapt from the other side of the altar. The larger one jumped on me, knocking me back onto the ground. Wind rushed from my lungs in painful scrapes as I slammed back, the world spinning. Instinct and training took over, my gauntlet-braced arms coming up just in time to block the beast's teeth. Its fangs clanged against the metal bracket, and with a thought, the *Zo'is* channeled and flared again, pummeling straight down the ugly fuck's throat.

With an ear-splitting cry, the monster convulsed, the power of

433

light burning through its insides, and then it collapsed on top of me.

My muscles cried beneath the weight, but I shoved it off, rolling onto my knees. Air finally rushed back down my lungs, the *Zo'is* in my veins helping me heal quickly. I turned, looking for the second beast—

Thera had it trapped in bindings of shadows, strung up like cattle to be slaughtered and separated for parts.

"*No.*"

The word cracked from Thera, her arms dropping at her side, her jaw slackening. Her hands trembled, unsteady in a way I'd never noticed from her before.

"What's wrong?" I shuffled to her and looked closer. My eyes widened. This Shadowborne wasn't even fully formed. The long fangs and gray, leathery skin were there, but its head hadn't expanded and balded yet, little tufts of black hair still gathering at the top of its skull, and its ears were still the same size as ours, not yet the bat-like protrusions most of the Shadowborne sported.

Its face was still person-like enough to be Elven. To be recognizable.

Thera stopped trembling. Stopped *breathing.*

Her fists clenched instead, red from the wound on her hand dripping through her knuckles.

"Stavros." A tear ran down her pale cheek, sorrow replacing any fear or urgency in her expression. "Stavros, *no.*"

The name registered, several passages from Thera's journal springing to mind.

Stavros, Thera's most trusted advisor, who the King doted on. Whose guidance had taken on a fatherly quality in many of their years together. Who'd helped her plan every detail of her ascent to the throne, and who'd always offered a shoulder to lean on when she needed it most.

Stavros, whose name was first on my list of the invited Erebushi delegation.

Caelum tucked closer to my side, his brow furrowing. "Who—"

"The Minister of Laws," I answered before Thera had to.

Her head snapped to me, realization splintering across her face.

The Erebushi hadn't just been killed then, but *infected.* Used to purposefully get under Thera's skin.

A flick of Thera's fingers, and the Shadowborne's head fell, blood surging from the wound as tears poured from her. "Goodbye."

We had no time to give Stavros the proper funeral he deserved, not while shouts and blood-curdling roars still echoed through the willows as more of them sought their prey. His body would be burned later with all the others, the collection team sent out and ordered to dispose of the bodies indiscriminately.

Now, we had to act, before any of Stav—no, the Shadowborne's —pack mates could catch us.

Before Thera had to face any of her other fallen subjects.

I didn't give her or Caelum a choice this time.

"Follow me." I grabbed their wrists, tugging them away from the altar and toward the castle. If we could get out of the grove, we'd have better sightlines—and a better chance at survival.

It was an effort not to look at the damage already done to the grove. At willow branches collapsed, their green bathed in black and red blood. At the body parts strewn about, Shadowborne and Elven alike, jutting up from the earth like grotesque statues. At the bodies drained of blood, lifeless eyes staring into the ether, their corpses dried, shriveled husks too withered now to fill out their fine clothes.

In a spurt, Caelum stumbling to keep up, we shot for the tree-line. The Shadowborne had the advantage there—the trees giving them plenty of space to sneak up on their prey—but we had little choice if we would make it back to the castle. And at least out of the clearing, Thera could use more of her *Skia* magic without the nobles witnessing her if she had to transform.

We hit the first few willows, ducking behind them to let Caelum catch his breath.

My heart thundered in my ears, drowning out the not-so-distant screaming. If everyone would shut up, we'd hear the Shadowborne coming, but war was a noisy business.

Flattening myself against the tree bark, I peered around the tree, eyes scanning for any movement, any sign of—

A black clad shape jumped down from the branches.

I drew my sword, ready to strike, but the ambassador ducked just as I swung.

"Miss me?" Nyxia grinned, but it was shallow, her eyes just as wide with fear as the rest of us as she assessed her king.

I lowered my weapon, and Thera pulled her into a quick, bruising hug. "Thank the moon and mist." She pulled back, a frown tugging at her mouth. "Where is Kappas?"

Nyxia's lips pursed, and she flipped her daggers in her hands. "Helping the guards with the no—"

Another body dropped from the trees, a snarling mass crushing into her.

"Nyxia!" Thera's shadows shot toward the Shadowborne, clamping around its neck, but Nyxia was faster, rolling from under the beast and flipping over it so she was on its back, a dark creature on an even more sinister mount. Her daggers dug into its back, holding her in place.

The monster whimpered like a kicked dog.

"Get them the fuck out of here," she snarled—not at her king, but at me, one weapon to another.

I looked at Caelum, who paled as he nodded. My prince was used to being protected and knew when to surrender. Knew when it was better to hide and wait.

King Thera had never had to protect herself. And Nyxia was right.

I had a duty to my kingdom. To the people I cared about.

"Let me go! I can't leave her, I can't lose her too."

I wrapped my arms around her middle, she thrashed against my hold. I held her tight and hauled her over my shoulder. She shot a kick to my stomach, but I let *Zo'is* ripple through my hands, shocking her system. She convulsed and screamed for her friend, shadows hissing and spitting at me as they closed around us.

But they didn't hurt me. Didn't so much as slow me down.

They wouldn't. *She* wouldn't.

Because she cared, too.

And I wouldn't stop running. Not even as I glanced back to see two more Shadowborne close in on Nyxia, leaping at her, one of them sinking its claws into her flank. Not as she screamed, hurtling two more daggers from wherever she had hidden them into its eyes so it freed her.

Thera's cries turned to roars, and the shadows tightened, her fingers shifting to claw-like daggers that bit into my skin.

I tore right. Whether Nyxia survived or not, I had to get Caelum and Thera to safety.

Even if neither of them forgave me for it.

"Follow me," Caelum panted and veered left—not toward the castle, but deeper into the expansive willow grove.

"No, Caelum!" I skidded to a halt, calling after him.

"Trust me, Rory," he pleaded. "I know this place better than anyone. There is an old garden shed not far from here."

I swallowed down the lump of fear, my instincts blaring at me to run away. To find the shelter of the castle and blockade us in a sturdy room far from any Shadowborne claws.

But rule five of war, according to our commander, had always been to trust your comrades. We were safer in numbers, and mutual obedience was the tenant we lived by.

Despite the tingle of fear in my gut, I obeyed and pushed left, following the Prince of Lux deeper into the shady gullet of the Willow Grove, carrying the sobbing, screaming Sykagos in my arms like she was a small, broken child.

CHAPTER
THIRTY-TWO

CAELUM

If you ever need sanctuary from the sun, my love, know that it is okay to seek shade.

Mama used to repeat it on the days the sickness kept me weakest. The sleepless nights where my pulse wouldn't slow and my skin felt too tight, the endless afternoons where the sun zapped my strength through the salty brine that licked my face and neck.

But it wasn't just a sweet saying to give me hope.

It was an *instruction*.

Her library had been my last connection to her mind—to her soul, each book a reminder of the person she was. The person I might've become if she'd stuck around.

But it hadn't been Mama's only hiding place.

And whether my father was right about her descent into madness, I was glad for her forward thinking as we ran from the Shadowborne, my chest heaving with every labored, stumbling step.

Having barely slept, I was already exhausted, and the stress had made every limb ache, my stomach clenched in knots around itself. I hated that this body could not cope, but I had no choice but to obey its commands. There was no way I'd make it back to the castle, even with Rory and Thera protecting me, not unless I wanted to let them drag my limp form all the way there.

The small garden shed behind the largest trees on the southern border of the grove had sat abandoned in the last few years, since I hadn't the heart to attend to it without her. Ivy clung to its frame, obscuring it from view, trees shadowing it in a small cocoon of darkness. Shrubs shielded the door, overgrown and in the way, but it took little time and only a few splinters to clear them enough.

The hinges of the door were rusted, red blotches eating away at the metal, but they'd hold for today. I cracked it open, the stench of must and mildew rose, churning my stomach yet again. The mouth to the shed was a dim, gaping hole, just as hungry as the Shadow-borne jaws we sought to escape.

I'd rather be swallowed up by some stuffy hothouse than torn to shreds by a monster, so inside I went, my heart racing as the claustrophobia devoured us.

"Shit." Rory shut the door behind us, dousing us in utter darkness.

"Give me a second." My hands fumbled against the wall, blindly seeking the *Zo'is* switch I knew was there somewhere. It'd been ages, and I was much taller now, my sense memory faulty as I scraped against the half-rotted wood over and over to no avail.

"Excuse me." Thera's hoarse voice brushed against my neck, and she pressed around me, her feet clapping against the wooden floor.

"Thera, hold on," I cried, panic twisting my throat.

I couldn't remember exactly what tools remained, but last I was here, this place had been crowded with backhoes and scythes and sheers. I'd tripped over a rake once and twisted my ankle so badly, Mama had to carry me out.

Thera's humorless chuckle sounded from deeper into the shed. "I'm not afraid of the dark, Caelum. My eyes are used to it."

A second later, and the click sounded. *Zo'is* lamps flickered and buzzed to life, thick cobwebs muting their shine, but not enough to dull them entirely.

"Much better." Rory squinted.

A single bed, a tiny cabinet of non-perishable food, and a little stack of books were the only hospitable decorations in the damp room. Along the walls, sharp, mismatched tools hung from rafters and shelves, rusted blades and spikes and empty planters menacing the space. *Zo'is* lamps lit the cramped quarters in blue, everything pale and ghostly with no windows to offer sunlight—or to ventilate the stale air.

Sanctuary had a different definition in different contexts.

Stellaris was supposed to be my sanctuary, not some mold-infested shed. But here we were.

I shuffled to the bed against the wall, falling back onto it. A cloud of dust enveloped me, but I held my breath, ignoring the itch that squirmed over my skin. I was too drained to fuss, my heart rate still running like a Shadowborne chased it as I stared at the ceiling.

Outside, the monsters were loose upon my home. Tearing into my people, ruining my mother's fucking willow garden. Tears stung my lash line.

This was supposed to be a day of celebration. A union to stop the bloodshed and war. But now it had come to my doorstep, undeniable and unavoidable. I did not know who to trust, and now people were dead because of it. I covered my eyes with my arm, ignoring the stains on my sleeve.

We stayed that way, for a while, silent aside from the gentle crying from both myself and Thera and the gentle hiss of Rory sharpening her sword with a stone. Like none of us knew what to say, what to do, with everything that had been taken today.

It was hours later when weight shifted the mattress next to me.

I peeked around my arm to find Thera sitting on the edge of the mattress. Her blood-spattered dress was a collage of gore and pain, a painting of the horrors we'd endured that would never be fully cleaned. A reminder that our wedding day would always be remembered as a tragedy.

Our wedding day.

"Are you—are you okay?" Thera—my *wife*—spoke through a frown. "You didn't seem to be feeling well before."

Before. When I'd been nothing but cold to her, too wrapped up in my sadness and confusion to follow through on any of the promises I'd made to her. When I'd been content to make today a tragedy with my sour mood alone, my anger and hurt toward my father impeding being a partner to her.

To my wife.

"I'm so sorry, Thera." I shot up, emotion clogging my throat, and reached for her hands. Sorry wasn't good enough, but I had to try, had to make her understand. "I should have listened to you last night. Everything has just been so—"

"Fucked?" She smiled softly, absolving me of the guilt I should've been sentenced to life with.

I let my head fall forward, crashing into her shoulder. "Absolutely fucked."

"I'm sorry I assumed the worst of you as well." Her gentle hand stroked the back of my neck tenderly—so opposite to the way she'd been hours before; a thrashing, screaming, vicious thing. Her voice now was raw and battered but feather soft as it caressed my cheek. "Trust is another rare resource where I'm from."

It was rare in Lux, too, if today was any indication.

Rare, but not gone.

"You trusted the friend you lost."

441

Thera's eyes misted. "He was not a friend. He was family."

I sat straight as the mattress creaked again, Rory sitting just behind Thera.

"We need to start talking to each other." She slumped against the metal bed frame like all her strength had been sucked out. It had been incredible to watch her fight—incredible, and horrifying—but now her eyes screamed of hollowness, her exhaustion palpable. Each sighed word was a surrender. "All of us. In the training core, the only way we function is through communication and mutual obedience."

Thera nodded, a hand on Rory's shoulder, a gentle stroke of her thumb across the small strip of bare skin beneath Rory's armor. "Thank you for saving us, Captain. I—I was not in my right mind."

"I understand. In my experience, grief is just a step away from madness." Rory leaned into the touch. Her throat bobbed. "I know you would have done the same. And I'm sure Nyxia will be fine."

Thera grinned, but it didn't reach her eyes. "She's a hard fucker to kill."

My eyes narrowed at the point of contact between them. Something not *unpleasant*, but unexpected wriggled in my gut. "When did you two start getting along?"

Rory's face went blank. Like it did when she tried to hide something. "Are you against it?"

Thera dropped her hand, but didn't scoot away. She nudged Rory's side, mischief simmering in her stare.

"We can go back to bickering, if you prefer. I'm sure the captain could use a good tongue-lashing." Her voice pitched, husky, the first hint of normalcy returning.

Blush tinted Rory's cheeks. "This room is too small for any kind of *lashing*."

I blinked. Maybe it was the shade, the light so dim in here, it was hard to make out details. Or maybe, after the trauma and stress of the last twenty-four hours, I'd just gone completely insane and started imagining things.

Maybe Mother's madness was contagious, and the infection had spread to me.

But there, in Rory's eyes, in her awkward, lopsided smile that made her scar crinkle . . . *affection*. The same brand I often enjoyed the warmth of, like a hearth crackling on a winter's day, or the first rays of sunlight on a dew-soaked morning.

For the Soul Eater.

For my new wife.

Hope blossomed in my chest, something I didn't think possible after the death and destruction I'd witnessed today. But even if it wasn't real, even if it was just a panic-born fantasy or the lowlight, I didn't want to risk shattering the illusion.

I did what any coward would do and changed the subject. My hands fisted in the dust-ridden, moth bitten bed sheets. "Any theories on how the Shadowborne got in?"

That got their attention. Any trace of potential affection fleeing from their expressions like a deer would a wolf.

Like we had the Shadowborne, leaving the others to fend them off.

"Someone in your father's ranks, or perhaps the King himself, has plotted against this union from the beginning." A growl built in Thera's throat. Her jaw clenched as she stared at the hatch. "We should be out there helping and finding the bastards responsible."

Rory shifted, angling herself to block Thera's view. To shield her, instead of fighting her. "No, we need you two safe. If this is all to stop you both from unifying, it makes it even more essential that we take care of you. The First Legion will have been deployed by now, and they will handle the Shadowborne. In Lux, it is an honor to protect our nobles."

Thera turned to me. Lifted her chin. "In Erebus, the noble and powerful protect their people instead."

It was a statement, but it was pitched as a question, like she sought my permission. Me, her husband—the new consort of Erebus.

443

I wanted to be the man she needed. The king Elvenkind needed.

But I wanted to be smart, too. Prepared, if paranoid, like my mother had been when she'd hid her library.

If you ever need sanctuary from the sun, my love, know that it is okay to seek shade.

There was a time for blazing into battle, and a time for hiding. For planning.

I fit my hand through Thera's, like I should have on our wedding altar. Like I should have last night, when she first came to me with her concerns. "We need to find a middle ground. Learn to protect each other, and to plan instead of just reacting to what's thrown at us."

"You're right." Thera's fingers wrapped around mine, her other hand rested on Rory's knee. She squeezed us both, grasp both firm and reassuring. *Uniting.* "We deserve more."

More.

More than hiding in a shed, scared and trembling. More than waiting for my father to tell me what to do, for him to puppet my decisions and placate my every worry. More than having to choose between my duty and my heart, more than having balance between my kingdom and my safety.

More than fighting amongst ourselves rather than focusing on our true enemy.

More than survival, but success. Joy.

Love.

Rory didn't look as against that as I'd imagined she would. Instead, she covered Thera's hand with hers, fingers filling between the gaps, just as her strengths supported my weaknesses. "When we get out of here, we'll discuss that."

The moment shattered as a banging echoed through the room, someone or something pounding against the door.

Rory jumped up, snagging her sword, as the darkness in the room seemed to move—no, *breathe.*

Thera stilled.

Three bangs again.

"Open up! The coast is clear!" a muted, familiar voice said.

Rory lowered her weapon, shoulders dipping as she ran to the stairs. "Syrax?"

A knot formed in my gut. "How did you find us?"

"We tracked your footprints through the grove," Syrax answered, warm light invading the doorway as Rory opened it.

Syrax and Rory clamored inside, while a third form hobbled unevenly behind.

Thera collapsed to her knees, a sob of relief echoing out of her. "Nyxia, thank *fuck.*"

The ambassador limped to the King, one leg bandaged and bleeding, a cut across her eyebrow, but very much alive. Alive, and *frowning.* "Don't thank anyone yet, this is bad."

The room quieted, and fear crept along my spine. The only noise was my slamming heartbeat, banging against my ribs. "What's wrong?"

Syrax stared at the ground, weight shifting. His hands shook at his sides, a rare display of fear from the overconfident, assertive male.

"Captain, Your Highness, Your Majesty," he addressed each of us separately, a hitch to his speech that sent a shiver of fear down my back. "You have all been summoned to the throne room immediately."

CHAPTER
THIRTY-THREE

"The only death offered to a traitor is a bloody cut with a dull sword."—Rule Eight of the Luxian Soldier's Codex, written by King Alixsander the 1st, 3 A.G.W, Updated by Commander General Atlas Tiberius, 1989 A.G.W.

RORY

T he fear hit me first.

Just outside of King Kato's office, it thrummed through my chest, an aching, gasping thing that stole the breath from my lungs.

I knew this fear. Knew it well. The cold, silent dread that settled between bones, the atom-deep chill that froze the edges of the mind.

Fear of death. Of oblivion.

But this was not *my* fear. Not my mortality on the line, not as I walked briskly with Syrax, Nyxia, Caelum, and Thera. This didn't

446

live in my marrow, but itched just beneath my skin, writhing and warning as we got closer and closer.

Realization hit me second, just as we crossed into the meeting room.

This wasn't *my* fear.

I saw *him* first, before anything else came into focus. Before I noted King Kato behind his desk, or Tiberius with his hand on the hilt of his sword.

In front of the picturesque window, silhouetted in dying sunlight, his arms were bound tightly behind his back. The *Zo'is*-laced chains chafed his bronze skin to raw, his armor and gauntlets discarded to the side. Only his torn undershirt remained, barely covering his tattooed chest. Gold hair streaked with black Shadow-borne blood, muddled by the vibrant red seeping from the deep gash across his forehead. A cloth gag protruded from his mouth, his jaw misaligned and swollen around it.

Our eyes locked, tears welling in his eyes. My *Vinculum's* fear smashed into me like an anvil.

Everything blurred crimson.

"What the *fuck*?"

I moved first, not thinking, but an arm jutted out in front of me, blockading me from reaching him.

Tiberius glared, a silent warning not to take another step. With a press of the button, the *Zo'is* chains surged, and Julius trembled. The shock sweeping over him, the whites of his eyes flashed before they focused on me again, pain and fear written in every bloodshot vein.

I felt the pain with him, the itch so unbearable I wanted to scrape my skin off with my fingernails.

Breathe, Rory. Promise me.

"Second Lieutenant Argentis, shut the door." King Kato spoke from his chair, his hands steepled in front of him. Tension radiated from his straight back; those light eyes frosted over with a dark rage I'd only seen in his glory years on the battlefield.

Tiberius lowered his arm, knowing that I wouldn't take another step.

"Yes, Your Majesty." Syrax's voice was strained, and the door clicked shut.

Fear froze me to my spot.

Silence rippled through the room like a shiver down its back. I scanned everyone's faces, unable to puck a focal point, searching for anything that made sense. Anything that could stop the fear, the *pain.*

Then Caelum stepped closer, a steady hand on my arm. His jaw clenched as he looked at Julius, skin paling. "Father, what's going on?"

King Kato's gaze raked over his son, over his torn and blood-stained clothes, before it darkened. "I am glad to see you alive, my son. So many others are not as fortunate. We lost Lord Dinas, Lady Mirena, and several other valuable allies. Lieutenant Fortis, what do you have to say for yourself?"

Tiberius yanked the gag out of Jules' mouth. My *Vinculum* spat a thick wad of blood, eyes blown wide and trained on me. "I swear, Rory, I didn't know. I would never have done any of this if I knew —"

The gag jammed back, my *Vinculum's* cries muffled by it. King Kato's knuckles blanched white as his hands pressed together, barely containing his rage. "I will not sit and listen to such *lies.*"

"You're not even letting him speak!" I thundered, feeling the oppressive mass of the gag like it was in my mouth.

"Explain, now." Thera had been quiet since we entered, but her voice cut through Jules' groans like a knife, cold and sharp.

King Kato flexed his hands and let them fall to the desk.

Tiberius took that as a signal, retrieving a stack of papers from the drawer and placing them in front of the King.

Kato looked at me, then at Julius. "I couldn't tell you for obvious reasons, Captain Bellatore, but the Lieutenant has been a suspect in our investigation of the Summer Palace Shadowborne attack." He sifted through the documents as he spoke. "We have reason to believe he's been colluding with the rebels as well, and today's egregious treachery confirms it."

Each word pinged against my skull like a pebble against armor, demanding attention, but denied access, none of them registering.

Breathe, Rory.

Julius wasn't a traitor. He couldn't have been, or I'd have known. I'd have felt it, through our bond. His anxiety, his upset, his fear . . .

But I hadn't seen much of him lately; consumed by my confusion and frustration, that I could've easily missed the signs of his.

If something is going on . . . if something was really wrong, you'd tell me, right?

Julius would've come to me if something had been wrong. He would've told me, our trust bone-deep, with or without our stupid tattoos.

"He would never—" I stammered, breath coming up short. "There has to be a mistake."

The King shook his head, mouth opening to spew more of those vile, odious accusations

"Father, let's slow down, please. Lieutenant Fortis has been covering most of the guard rotations with me. It's hard to believe he'd have had the time to betray us on such a grand scale."

My heart grew wings and took flight, gratitude choking me, and I looked to Caelum. A prince, who didn't protect with swords or shields, but with his kindness and compassion. Whose power drew from something deeper than strength.

Kato pushed back from his seat, parchment in hand.

"Which gave him the access he needed to orchestrate your friend Quinton's death, as well as the attack in the market. Tell me, was he within your sight at all times, Caelum?"

Kato shot down any fleeting hope before it could soar.

Caelum winced when Kato shoved the paper—a letter, by the

looks of it—toward his son, then another at Thera. She grasped it with two fingers, like it had been dipped in piss.

"The deaths of the Erebushi faction were also his doing. We found evidence of his correspondence with the rebels, and he used his knowledge and station to let the Shadowborne in today."

Julius jerked against his chains, cries turning a painful hoarse. The next shock that reverberated through his body rippled through mine as well, a moan yanking up from the pits of my stomach.

No, this couldn't be happening. Not Jules. Not the elf that dragged my body to the medics on the battlefield, using his own torn clothes to staunch my would-be life-threatening wounds. The friend that willingly offered his own life source to heal me, that entered a *Vinculum* bond with me not because he wanted to, but because I would've died otherwise. Not the man that'd stood by my side through everything since, his loyalty stalwart and his heart true.

Not the soldier who loved Lux above all else. The guard that would give anything, *anything*, to see it safe from harm. The boy whose sister and mother died by the very monsters he supposedly helped.

My knees trembled, threatening to give out. "Your Majesty, you said Quinton let the Shadowborne into the Summer Palace."

"What?" Caelum's eyes blew wide, then narrowed at me with accusation. "How long have you known—"

"It was a misdirect." King Kato answered, staring at his wall of books and scrolls. "We needed time to figure out the real culprit."

"How was this evidence acquired?" Thera crumpled the letter in her hands into a small ball before she tossed it to the shadows.

"I intercepted many of the correspondences myself," Tiberius answered. "The rebels have been purposefully planting false reports and letters through our normal channels, so I'd made it a priority to have all the messengers followed and tracked. We caught the Lieutenant in the act."

Another beat of silence deafened. Jules stopped thrashing, a coldness capturing him in stone. A similar severity hardened through my chest, a dead-eyed clarity surging up from the part of me that was a soldier first. The part that fell back into logic when all else failed.

This couldn't be true. There had to be proof to absolve him, or an explanation that made sense. Someone had to have framed him or tampered with the evidence somehow to get Tiberius off their tail.

And I'd find them and kill them myself.

Thera sucked in a breath. "And will you oversee the trial, Kato? Will you make sure he is brought to justice for every Erebushi life lost?"

The room chilled, swirling, hungry shadows blanching the heat from the air.

My stomach knotted.

Thera's back was straight as an arrow, her red-painted nails biting into her palms as she clenched her fists.

She was grieving. Hurt. Looking for someone to blame for what happened to her advisor. Sharpening her thorns to protect her heart.

I'd have to find evidence to support Jules before the trial, had to find something that might absolve him of such wild, woeful accusations. Had to give the *Sykagos* another soul to devour.

She couldn't have Julius'.

Kato's boots knocked heavy against the floor like a death knell. He returned to his seat, folding his hands in his lap again.

"This meeting is not to discuss a trial, but a sentencing." He nodded to Tiberius. "And by our customs, the only sentence for such treason is immediate death."

Death.

"Father, that's an old custom." Caelum made one last attempt, but it was flimsy, his voice devoid of urgency. "Surely we can hold a proper trial. We know Julius. He's a friend."

"Which makes his betrayal even more nefarious, son. There is no mercy for that level of treason."

His words darkened the room, and I flinched.

My throat closed.

There was no trial. No hope. Whether Julius was guilty, it didn't matter. Noble blood had been spilled and wasted today, and the monarchs on both sides wanted their vengeance. Wanted their pound of flesh, even if it was carved from the wrong hide. Carved from my very soul.

Everything screeched to a halt, including my heartbeat.

I didn't know which happened first—if Tiberius drew his sword, or if I lunged.

Syrax caught my middle, giant arms bracketing me tightly before I could reach Jules. Before I could jump in front of him, like he would for me. Like he always had.

Breathe, Rory.

"No!" My scream echoed against the walls as they closed in. My fists battered Syrax's hold, but he didn't budge, a noose wringing tighter the more I thrashed. "No, please—"

"Shh, Captain, or they'll charge you with him," Syrax murmured against my ear, an ache in his own voice. But his grip didn't falter.

My *Vinculum* bond seethed at the placation. I should be with him. Should be by his side, now and always. In life and death.

Breathe, Rory.

But I couldn't, each breath short and jagged at the very thought of doing so without him, without Jules . . .

"Please, he has to be innocent!" My shouts broke apart into messy, tear-stained pleas. My nails dug into Syrax's arms hard enough to draw blood. "Caelum, Thera, *please*—"

Tiberius tore the gag from Julius' mouth, his sword angled against his throat. His brows knotted. He'd trained us both himself —had nurtured us from seedlings into sycamores. Now he would be the one to cut us down. "Any last words?"

Gold eyes—warm like sunlight, soft like summer—fell on me.

Jules shook his head once. Grinned, like he always did when he tried to ease my worry. "Sorry, Sunshine. I had to take the deal, and I would do it again if it meant protecting you." He swallowed, throat bobbing against Tiberius' blade. Gold stare watered with silver tears. "Aurora Bellatore, I love—"

I should've followed Caelum's lead and turned my face. Or I should have mimicked Thera and closed my eyes, escaping the sight.

I watched.

The pain hit me first. The searing, agonizing sting of Tiberius' sword slashing across Julius's throat—not an honorable beheading or hanging, but a secret-spiller's death.

Fear slammed into me. Panic rising as he choked on his own blood, the end of Julius's sentence silenced forever.

The thud reverberated up my bones when my *Vinculum's* body collapsed to the ground, one last echo of our connection.

Something inside of me *snapped*, my own tattoos fading.

Then there was nothing, *nothing* at all.

Syrax finally let go of me, and I crashed to my knees. Crawled through Jules' blood to his body. I wretched his massive, muscular form—too heavy, without his enormous life force to power it—to my chest.

"I loved you, too," I murmured, over and over again between kissing Jules' forehead, cold already beneath my lips. "I loved you, too."

Loved, because with his heart stopped, mine was dead, too.

A hand grasped my shoulder, pulling me back.

"Let this be a reminder of what happens when you fail me. When you protect the *Sykagos* instead of your homeland," Kato's dark voice whispered in my ear, so low that not even those with superior might catch it, his grip hard enough to bruise. "Next time, it'll be *your* head, or perhaps someone else *precious* to you, even if it means I have to end the Shadowbitch myself."

453

CHAPTER
THIRTY-FOUR

"Beware a woman's softer art; it'll warm your bed, then tear you apart."—From "A Divorcee to his ex-wife," by Luxian Poet Obilos Hammon, 899 A.G.W

CAELUM

As a boy, the doctors told me that there is a point of failure that the body could not return from. That if I didn't take my condition seriously, if I pushed my organs and nervous system, there would be no recovery. That my heart would give out, or my veins would collapse irreparably.

The moment her blue *Zo'is* tattoo faded to black, the moment Julius's soul left his body, I knew there was no coming back for Rory. No rehabilitating, no healing for what had broken inside of her.

My father whispered something in her ear, grip tight on her shoulder.

My eyes narrowed.

He stormed out, Tiberius on his heels, leaving Syrax behind to clean up the mess. To gather the shattered pieces that could never be fused together again.

Rory trembled, her body heaving with weighty sobs, but she didn't leave. Didn't let go, clinging to Julius' body with all her strength, knuckles white and eyes blurred red.

Anger fumed in my belly, hot and electric like *Zo'is*. If this was true—which I still was not convinced—how could Julius do this to us? To *Rory*? She needed him more than anyone, and this was how he responded? How could he betray Lux and leave her behind? He'd always been so kind, so strong, but perhaps I'd been wrong all this time.

I doused the flames before they could eat my mind alive. Julius was gone, and I wouldn't get the answers to those questions by standing here and watching Rory break.

We had to get out of here. Had to pick up whatever shards we could salvage and go, before death settled too deep in her, too. I'd heard stories from older soldiers—those bonded during the second wave of the war—that said the death of a *Vinculum* was a pain so intense, their bonded partners could pass on, too. That the grief alone could kill them.

Julius might have betrayed his kingdom, his partner, but I wouldn't. I wouldn't let her suffer for his mistakes.

"Rory?" I placed my hand on her shoulder. "Please, we should go."

"No. I won't leave him." She shrugged me off.

Thera made eye contact with me, a frown wrinkling her lips. She knelt beside Rory, her already-saturated wedding dress soaking up Julius' blood. "Let's go talk elsewhere. He's gone, Captain."

Rory bared her teeth, a feral dog snapping at anyone that got too close.

"You must be thrilled." Her rage sharpened to a point and

seeked Thera as her first target. "Are you happy now that he's dead? Is your *justice* served?"

Thera winced as the hit landed, but she did not snap back or scurry away, like I might have. Her bright eyes watered with genuine tears. "There is no justice in Lux, it would seem."

Syrax shot Thera a warning glare before his eyes darted around the room like he was being watched.

My palms clammed up and my breath drew short. We were still in my father's office—he had to have security systems in place here.

It could not have been a coincidence before that Syrax found us so quickly. That he and Nyxia knew where to look in the grove's expansiveness.

We were being tracked, somehow. Maybe a *Zo'is* glamour or some other surveillance magic.

The rebels might've had eyes in the castle, but so did my father. Eyes and ears.

I had to get Rory out before she said something treasonous. Before her grief grew fangs and lodged itself in her own jugular. She'd always protected me, and it was my duty to see her well, to take care of her now that her *Vinculum* couldn't do the job. She needed time, and likely a long bath, but then we could talk. Could figure this out, the three of us together.

I knelt on her other side, opposite Thera, my voice soft. "Aurora, please. Let someone clean this up."

"Fuck off."

"I'm not leaving you behind." I wrapped my hand around her wrist, the *Zo'is* bracelets tingling beneath my fingertips. "When it blows up in our faces, we can burn together, right?"

She'd offered me the same truce, back in my quarters, weeks ago, and I'd never given her an answer. I'd told her I'd think about it, my duty and misplaced sensibility getting in my way yet again.

There was no more thinking. Thera was my wife, but this marriage was political, even if pleasurable. My bond with Rory was more. Built with time and trust, with steel and sentimentality. I wouldn't forsake her when she needed me most. Wouldn't leave her behind like Jules did.

But Rory did not leap into my arms like I hoped she would. Didn't soften or let go of her grip on her *Vinculum's* body.

Rory's expression hardened into stone.

"No, Caelum." She spat my name instead of my title, and that was somehow worse. "When it blew up in my face, you turned away. You couldn't even fucking *watch*."

A sharp intake of breath; Syrax, Nyxia, and Thera gasping in unison. Bracing.

There was a threshold of pain that most bodies could withstand, and though chronic pain was my long-term acquaintance, the acute, searing agony of those words burned through me like fire.

I heard the words she didn't say.

Coward.

"I know I'm a coward." Tears blurred my vision, and I rose, towering over her even as my legs swayed beneath me. "But at least I'm not a traitor. Julius made that choice for himself."

The moment I said it, I wished I could take it back. It was true, and it was also cruel, Jules' body still cooling in her arms. Her heartbreak still throbbing in her chest.

But there was no sucking the words back down, no apologizing or explaining, when Rory *laughed,* a broken, distorted chuckle jutting up out of her in jagged spokes. "And I just made mine."

There was a point that no relationship could return from. Where the fractures splintered into full breaks. Where the puncture wounds burst open to gaping, hemorrhaging lacerations.

Rory plunged us both over the edge. With one last kiss across the traitor's brow, Rory finally let go and stood. "Syrax, I'm promoting you to Lieutenant. The prince is your charge."

She stormed from the room without a look back, her haunting laugh still ringing in my ears.

Syrax's mouth fell open, his gaze darting between me and Julius' body.

Between his fallen brother-turned-betrayer, and his newly promoted charge.

"Don't worry, I've got him." Thera linked her arm through mine, steadying me back into my body. Back to the new, debilitating pain cracking its way through my chest. "Please make sure the Lieutenant's body is given proper rights, Lieutenant Argentis."

Syrax's throat bobbed. Tears misted his eyes. Then he bowed low, saluting Thera with a hand across the chest. "Yes, Your Majesty. It would be my honor."

Thera led me out of the room before I insisted Syrax burn my body, too.

"We both need to get cleaned up," Thera sighed. She entered my chambers, tugging at the abused, ruined fabric of her dress.

I froze in the doorway, unsure of my own feet.

The room had all the same furniture it had this morning; my large, white-blanketed bed, my favorite creme-colored reading chair, stacked with fuzzy, plush pillows, my rich curtains drawn to block out the morning sun.

But now, it was foreign, without Rory here to guard me. Or Julius, the two constants in my life, abandoning me with different excuses.

But Thera *was* here, making herself comfortable, her shade a welcome respite.

She crossed into the washroom, hands on her hips, commanding the space like it was her personal suite. I supposed it was now—what's mine was hers, after all. "I'll draw a bath. You can wash first."

I stumbled in, desperate not to be left outside alone. I never wanted to feel this alone ever again. "We could . . . we could do that together."

Thera blinked, appraising me with narrowed eyes. "You don't have to."

I took another step into the room, closing the door behind me. Shutting the rest of the world—my father, Rory, all of Lux—out. "I don't want to be alone."

Green and blue softened. She loosed a sigh, her hand extended. "I'm right here."

I reached out, taking her hand, letting her lead me again.

Thera had the bath ready in moments, steamy tendrils of smoke rising from the tub in delicious, cardamom-and-amber scented plumes. Rory always hated that bath oil. Complaining it made me smell like I lived in Madame Seraphina's perfume shoppe, but I'd secretly loved it. I inhaled deeply, savoring the rebellion in each puff.

She made her choice. I could make mine.

Julius had deceived us. And Rory chased his memory, too consumed by grief to see how he'd betrayed her most of all.

But I was still a prince, and now the consort to Erebus as well. I had a bride who hadn't left my side, who'd protected me despite how it negatively impacted her.

Who sat now on the ledge of the large tub, immense dress hitched up to her thighs, her hand skimming the surface to check the temperature. I'd never seen a creature so dangerous look so domestic. Dark strands of her long hair fell forward, silken and unmatted despite the dirt and blood caked against her scalp. Her smile was as warm as the hot bathwater steaming the mirrors.

"Get in, the water's perfect." She pivoted, facing the far wall. "Don't worry, I won't look."

Not waiting, I shucked out of my marred suit, throwing it in the wash bin at the other end of the room. Then, dipping a cloth into the water, I quickly scrubbed away the evidence of what had happened.

I wanted no reminder of today, other than my bride. Other than the future we would build together.

I kept my eyes away from the cloth's changing color. I didn't want to know what happened to cotton when Shadowborne and Betrayer's blood mixed.

When I was done, I threw the towel away and sank into the bath. A groan escaped my mouth as the water unknotted and unmade me, washing away the weight of the day.

"I don't hate that sound," Thera chuckled.

I sank deeper, gaze fixed on the fresco ceiling. But my ears strained to the symphony of subtle sounds; the scrape of silk over skin as Thera discarded her dress, followed by the scrub of a towel. The brush of a body through water as she joined me in the tub, ripples nipping at my chest while she settled.

I swallowed, heat rising in my middle that had nothing to do with the temperature of the bath. "Comfortable?"

A satisfied hum answered. I lowered my head, meeting her stare.

Her hair cascaded in front of her, the dark veil and the murky, soapy water obscuring the details of her body that hid beneath the waterline. There was no shyness in her stance—her arms open and resting back against the ledge, her head tilted as her gaze swept over me once . . . twice.

"What's on your mind?"

I snorted. A million warring things buzzed through my head, demanding attention.

Rory's pain and resistance. What was she doing now? Would she quit the guard? Had I lost her forever? Was I making a grave mistake by not chasing after her?

Julius' sentence. Was it true? Did he do this alone? When had he started betraying us? How long had he been lying for?

The scent of death, and the sound of the nobles screaming as Shadowborne tore into them. How many had we lost? How was my father supposed to put out this fire? What would it take to reestablish security, now that one of our own had given away so much intel?

What had he said to Rory when he left? What other secrets could he be hiding?

My wife's power and protectiveness. Her stalwart vows and softer promises.

The immeasurably small distinction between green and blue . . . and the fact I'd never be able to prefer one color over the other again.

All other thoughts flickered and died like gnats that flew too close to a *Zo'is* lamp, my mind solely transfixed on her. On the impossibly thin gap between us in the bath, our legs just inches from brushing against one another.

"Tell me about you?" I asked, needing to know. Needing a tether to this world now that all my puppet strings had been cut.

Thera smiled. "What do you want to know?"

"Everything."

So she told me.

She told me of the man she'd lost today. The advisor that had always protected her from her overbearing father's scrutiny and taught her of loyalty. She spoke of her people, of the struggles they faced back in Erebus, the plights that our union would one day be the remedy for.

She talked of her joy and her grief. Of the soft, salty food she'd craved since arriving at Lux, and the fresh fruit she'd learned to love and would miss whenever she went back to Erebus.

And in return, I told her about my mother. About the countless hours in her library, and of the horrifying truths my father had revealed about her untimely end. I told her about Rory . . . about the friendship we'd crafted for years, and the attraction that'd grown out of it.

I whispered my fears to her, too. That I'd never be enough. That everyone would leave me behind. That she, too, would grow tired of me one day and discard me like the rest.

461

We shared until the bathwater went cold, until the *Zo'is* lamps flicked on automatically, until our fingertips wrinkled to prunes and our eyelids grew heavy.

Still, I wanted more. Like each word out of my mouth only emptied me further, a groaning pit of insatiable hunger opening inside of me. Like the only remedy to the utter lack inside of me was more of her in return. I wanted to devour her truths, her fears, her wants and needs, wanted to taste each of them on my tongue and savor their unique flavor.

I must have been staring, because Thera's head tilted, a smirk playing on her full lips. "What's on your mind now?"

"I'm thinking we should consummate our marriage. Our kingdoms need our union now more than ever."

It came out far less seductive than I wanted it too, the reminder of our shared duty and disjointed kingdoms, not the aphrodisiac I'd hoped it would be.

Understandably, Thera's lips pursed. A sigh poured out of her, and she sank deeper into the tub.

"Caelum, fuck what you *should* do. I wouldn't expect that of you after everything you've been through today. We can wait." A hand found my knee beneath the surface of the water, a single, gentle stroke of her thumb meant to placate and soothe.

It had the opposite effect, that vicious, gnawing craving sinking its teeth deeper into my soul.

"I don't want to wait." I caught her hand before she could withdraw, holding her close. Wanting her *closer*. "Not anymore. Not when you never know what . . . what could happen."

Not when monsters no longer lived in storybooks, but prowled through willow gardens, bloodthirsty and brutal.

Not when traitors lived among us, smiling at us day in and day out, pretending to be our strongest allies.

Not when friends could become strangers in moments of heartbreak, and former enemies could become lovers in times of need.

Thera kneaded her lower lip between her teeth, conflict striking across her expression. Her fingers threaded through mine. "I understand. But I want you to enjoy your first time, not regret it because it was used as a tool to numb the pain."

"Stop protecting me." I tsked, a feral part of me unwilling to go back into that cage. I would not be left behind, not again. If she didn't want me, I'd accept. I'd let her go, not a complaint or contradiction in my words or actions. But I would not be told what I *should* want or feel. Would not deny my will any longer for the sake of protecting myself.

Thera didn't respond, curious eyes watching me. Waiting for me to prove it to her . . . and myself.

I waded closer, my knees brushing between hers, ripples shimmering the surface of the now chilly water, goosebumps shivering in their wake. "I want you, Thera. I've wanted you since I saw you in that clearing. Since I saw you tilt back your head and soak up the sun like it was pure ecstasy. I've imagined you and me in every book I've read since. I don't want to numb anything; I want to *feel* something."

Something unlocked in her gaze, a question answered as her pupils blew wide.

"I want you, too." Her knuckles swept across my chin, shivers trailing after them. "But I also know you want other things . . . and I'm willing to be patient."

Things like Rory. Things I'd told her about tonight, things I'd imagined since I was old enough to know what attraction was.

Things that were not here right now, not in this bath with me. Not in this room, even, their choices a chasm between us.

Things that were much, *much* less important than the force of nature splayed naked in front of me.

My *bride*, the Soul Eater, who I'd gladly offer myself up to on a silver platter, overjoyed with the honor of being devoured by her.

"I don't want your patience. I want your darkness." My arms bracketed her head on either side, and I leaned closer, breathing her in—cardamom and amber, *my scent*, mixed with a tinge of her.

463

The ravenous yearning burned lower still. "I want your wilderness. I want the king that conquered her shadows and knows her own desire."

Thera's breath hitched. "Cae—"

"Yes or no, *Dymi*?"

Her eyes made a single, fleeting brush over me before finding mine again.

I shifted closer, a silent question.

A chance for her to say no, to walk away from this. For me to do the same. For us both to fall back into the roles we *should* play right now. Back into the grief and mourning and waiting.

A hesitant breath, as neither of us withdrew.

"Yes."

My mouth claimed hers, insistent and consuming.

Thera moaned, and she rose to the occasion, her tongue swiping against my bottom lip, her teeth grazing as her hands wound around my back, tugging me closer. Pressing herself into me, her skin smoother than the water lapping around us.

It was not one of the shy, teasing kisses we'd shared before. And it was certainly not the awkward, guarded peck I'd bumbled on the altar.

It was *need*, insistent and hungry, our mouths fighting for more of each other. Rage and fear and sorrow and pleasure, rejoicing in an outlet as tongues clashed and teeth scraped.

Pure, unfettered desire.

And I wanted to lose myself to it.

My hands gripped the ledge tighter for purchase, for anything that would hold me to this world, this body, my mind begging to transcend into the Ether.

Thera broke our kiss first, gasping for a breath as she writhed against me . . .

I came undone.

My hand flew to her hair, tangling in the long, damp strands. "I want to see more of you."

But her hand stayed my chest, a small ask for space.

I wrenched back, letting go of her, disappointment crashing through me. This was it, then. My wife had seen the truth of me, seen the dark, wanting parts I kept veiled. And she'd walk away, just like everyone else had. Like Julius and Rory. Like my mother, who'd chosen to take her life rather than stay with me.

Thera pushed out of the water—ready to flee, to abandon . . .

Instead of racing out the door, she settled on the ledge, bare body dripping onto the stone. Legs crossed, she flipped her hair over her shoulder, revealing the swells and dips of her breasts, the vast lengths of unblemished, moon-pale skin.

A finger beckoned closer.

"You're in charge." Her voice dipped, and she trailed a hand down her front, a slow, deliberate tease I couldn't help but track with predatory focus. "Whatever you want to try, if you want to *stop*, the control is in your hands, Caelum."

Every hair on my body rose to attention, basest parts of me hot and rigid as I drank her in. She was shade and danger, sharp and wild. But she was also soft and nourishing, an oasis from heat and light, like the cold, refreshing darkness at the bottom of a well.

What did I want?

I'd had a thousand fantasies of this moment. Hundreds of scenarios that I'd played in the shelter of my mind, more delicious and daring than the next, things that even my books could not imagine.

I wanted her trembling in pleasure beneath me, before me. I wanted to make her face tilt up like it had that morning in the sun, enraptured by *my* heat and light.

I wanted to taste every inch of her, to watch as she moved and breathed and lived.

I managed a single word. "Bedroom."

"Yes, My Prince." That wicked grin widened. She pushed out of the bath, splashing me in cool water, but nothing could temper the heat that jolted down my core.

She wrapped a towel around herself, throwing one at me.

I caught it, stumbling after her, a hungry dog following its master.

Drying hastily, I relished the sway of her hips as she trod into my bedroom, a stream of soapy footprints behind her.

She'd named me in charge, but she was truly in control, her aura commanding even in its feigned submission. She hopped onto the edge of my bed like it had always belonged to her, her gaze raking over me as I stood at the edge.

My heart throbbed against my ribs, every part of me aching for more. I barely recognized my voice as it cleaved from my throat, hoarse and wanting. "Lay back."

Her dark, wet hair splayed across my bedspread, soaking the fabric, but I didn't care. Hardly noticed, captivated instead by the lithe stretch of her body, her long, slim arms reaching above her head to grasp the headboard.

"Like this?" She cocked her head to the side, waiting for my direction. For me to stop imagining and watching and start *living*.

I stroked myself once, my cock whining for attention.

More.

I wanted more. "Wider."

Her legs fell open, revealing the whole of her. Every pale inch, every smooth dip and pink blush.

One hand dipped between her legs, painted nails dancing over the spot I wanted to claim for myself. The only sustenance that would ever feed the famished beast in my core. Thera's gaze locked onto my fist, clenched around myself. "How does it compare to your books?"

"There is no fantasy in this world or the next that compares to the reality of you." I reached out a hand, desperate to not just see, but to *feel* her. It hovered just above her thigh, waiting for her permission. For her to push us both over the edge.

A single syllable was my unraveling. "*Please.*"

Fuck.

There would be time later to taste and savor. To touch and explore and trace.

But in that moment, all that remained was the rough, untamed need that commandeered my body.

And then I was above her, my chest pressed to hers. Tangled with her, her legs wrapped around my back, my hands shackling her slim wrists. *Inside* of her, her slick, sweet heat embracing every inch of me.

There was a pause, and the moment stretched to eternity. We'd crossed the threshold, and here we were, in the most intimate, vulnerable place imaginable. *Together*, nothing separating me from her, my end and her beginning intertwined. Our souls merging as our bodies did.

No book on earth could have described the feeling of the depth and truth it deserved.

Then, I moved with her. Our rhythm started slowly, each drag in and out, sending waves of pleasure through my every cell like a shot of *Zo'is* straight to the fucking soul.

"Oh moons, Caelum." Thera moaned, those wretched, delightful nails carving down my back.

I hesitated, clarity rushing back in a moment of panic. "Are you . . . is this, okay?"

Thera knotted her hand in my hair, forcing my gaze to meet hers. Blue-and-green shifted to pure, shadowed black as the Sykagos let *go*. "Don't fucking stop."

I didn't.

Our pace sped, my heart thundering and my breath short, but it didn't matter. I would not stop, would not slow.

Not until my name shattered through her lips, a prayer and curse in one. Not until I timed each thrust with a brush over that sensitive, heavenly bud between her legs, driving her closer and closer to the edge. Not until her nails scratched so hard at my back, my chest; they drew blood, the same crimson I'd offered at our wedding altar.

Not until my release built and spilled inside of her, her name, my *wife's* name, cresting out of me with a force I didn't know I possessed.

Not until night dragged on, darker and darker still, and I gave into the shadows—into her. Completely.

CHAPTER
THIRTY-FIVE

"It is an act of bravery to care when it is easier to strike. Your darkness is not only a sword, but an embrace." —From the recovered letters of Minister Lucius Stavros to Thera Umbrus, circa 2101 A.G.W.

THERA

T he best way to tell a person's true nature was to bed them, and sleeping with my new husband was revelatory.

Caelum Borealis had starved for so long, he'd forgotten what it was to be hungry. So deprived of power, that he'd convinced himself he had no want for it. No need.

But gentle and kind and satisfying as he was, a delicate balance between attentive and assertive . . .

There was a darkness to the Sunkissed Prince's soul. An angry, vengeful creature that lived in the shadows of lack, a beast licking its lips for just a taste, ready to devour.

It did not scare me.

It *thrilled* me.

And when I woke the next morning with his fingerprints bruised into my hips and *my* scratches over his pretty skin, a small bud of hope rooted in my chest that maybe, maybe things would be all right.

The thought was short-lived as memories flooded back and my grogginess abated.

Erebus without you is like night without darkness.

No, nothing was truly all right.

Not with Stavros gone. Not without the one person I trusted above all else vanished from this world. Life without him would be like the sky without the Sun, cold and dark as Erebus.

The hollow throbbing in my chest had subsided during last night's activities, sex an old friend I'd used time and time again to numb the vicious grief. I'd been projecting when I'd told Caelum he used it as a tool, knowing full well it was a distraction from my despair.

But now, with morning light filtering in single, hazy strands through Caelum's curtains, it was hard to keep the sorrow at bay. Tears slid down my cheeks, splattering on Caelum's silken sheets like rainfall.

I'd succeeded. Despite the obstacles, against the odds, I'd married the Prince of Lux. I would now have the power and resources I needed to save my people, to right the wrongs history had buried beneath ash and bloodshed.

But the visionary that'd helped me plan it all, that'd crowned me himself and raised me from the shadows . . .

He would not be there to witness our decades of planning realized.

A knock at the bedroom door—three direct, distinct raps—roused me from my thoughts.

Caelum sighed, turning over, and nestling deeper into his mountain of pillows. I fought a grin, running my hands through his

470

hair, and kissed his head once. I did not have Stavros, but I wasn't alone, not anymore.

Snagging my robe, I slid from the bed, covering myself, and kept my steps quiet. Shadows kissed my exposed skin, blanketing me in a protective veil.

Last night had been a watery departure from the burning world, one last moment of peace before it all crumbled to ash.

It'd also been a bond, crafted by something thicker than the blood we'd spilled on the altar. Born of mutual desire and passion, forged in heat and connection. Something strong enough to change worlds and transcend the shackles of our pasts.

Today, there would be no avoiding. Our people, our *kingdoms*, needed us to be present and resilient. And I hoped the traitors and rebels were ready for the sharpened darkness my new husband and I would rain down on them.

Stavros would've been proud. I would build the world he wanted to see, brick by brick.

I sucked in a deep breath and thrust open the door, ready for whatever lay on the other side.

Captain Bellatore stood, still in her bloodied armor, eyes blood-shot and bleary, hair a nest of tangles.

"Thera." My name croaked out of her; her gaze unfocused as she took me in.

I'd seen that look before—in my own soldiers, after a harrowing battle. In the eyes of civilians, after a Shadowborne raid decimated their villages. In my mirror, every time the shadows released me from their hold, the memories of what I'd done flooding my mind.

In Erebus, we called it the *Nekros*.

The look of the living dead.

Without anger as a shield, death had sunk its teeth into her head, her heart.

A part of me—the part that grieved, too, the part that knew the frozen fingers of death's grip intimately—wanted to wrap her in a hug, to thaw her limbs from the outside in. Or to banter and bicker, like we had on the training pitch, to warm her blood back to boiling. To get under her skin and inspire life back in her veins.

More rational parts won out.

"Captain," I slowly backed away, opening more of the door for her. My movements were careful, considered, trying not to spook her, and I forced my face into a soft smile. "I'll go wake Caelum."

"No, don't, I . . . " She blinked, some of that hollow haze clearing. "I came here to find *you*. You weren't in your rooms."

My heartbeat sped, panging through me. She'd gone to my rooms first? It had been no secret that my things had been moved here yesterday morning during the wedding, but had she really expected me not to stay with him?

But before I could ask or explain her head shifted toward the next room—to where Caelum still slept—and then back to my robe, piecing the rest together. Her mouth flattened into a thin line.

A surprising tickle of guilt shuddered down my back, like spiders creeping over my skin. I had nothing to say sorry for—sleeping with my new husband was nothing to be ashamed of, and if anything, it was an expectation—even so, a halfhearted apology found its way to my lips. "I'm sorry, but I thought I'd stay with Caelum to give you and your men some space—what happened yesterday was tragic." I pulled my robe closed, jerking my head to invite her in. "Come in, and we can talk."

She staggered backward.

"No, I need—" She shook her head, like she tried to free herself of the mites and fleas of whatever swarming thoughts infested her. Something solidified in her expression, and she rolled her shoulders back. "I need you to come with me. It's urgent."

Shadows rippled around me. "What happened?"

She grabbed my wrist, tugging me toward the door. "I'll explain on the way."

"I should get Caelum." I planted my feet, slowing her. If there was an emergency, I would handle it, but not in my robe. And I would not leave my new, vulnerable husband alone just to follow the captain into whatever madness was urgent enough to break her mourning.

But Rory pulled again, gold eyes wide and bright as the noonday sun. "No, he can't know."

My gut knotted in tight coils. Caelum had been open with me yesterday—sharing his fear of abandonment. Of being left behind. What would he say when he woke to an empty bed? Our marriage had almost been thwarted by our lack of transparency and connection, and I did not want to continue down that thorny path. And as much as I wanted to ease the captain's suffering, I did not want to create further divides. "Then we should wait for someone to attend the post."

Her head shook again—violently. *Insistently.* "Someone will be here shortly."

Something was wrong. Twisted, like the world had gone to bed right side up, and awoken upside down.

"Rory—" I used her name, not her title, hoping it'd get through to her.

"Thera, *please.*" *My* name, and that soft, broken plea, so quiet, yet loud enough to echo through the empty chambers of my heart. Both hands clasped around mine, like a child begging for help. "It's easier if I show you. But I need you to *trust* me."

I should have waited. Insisted.

Should've sent for Nyxia immediately, should've checked with my Mistress of Spies.

I should've called for Caelum, should've honored the bond we'd tied the night before.

Instead, something about that word, that promise of trust, had me abandoning my senses. Something about her panicked, pained expression had me wishing I could make it right.

Quiet enough not to wake my sleeping husband, I shucked on a dress, grabbed a dagger, and took the captain's hand. "Lead the way."

CHAPTER
THIRTY-SIX

"I crave friendship like a fish craves water, and yet I cannot bring myself to swim, for fear of what hurt lurks beneath the surface." – From Thera Dymitria's personal Journal, circa 2088 A.G.W.

RORY

Jules' bunk had been cleared out already by the time I reached it—Tiberius's men confiscating all his belongings as 'evidence' before the trial had even begun.

I had nothing left of him. Not even a tunic or a strand of his honeycomb hair. No mementos to remember him by, no tokens of our friendship for me to treasure. Nothing that captured the deep, booming bass of his laugh, nothing that would remember the way his eyes crinkled in the corners or how his little finger permanently jutted sideways after I'd broken it in a spar.

All I had left were my memories and my rage.

Sorry, Sunshine, but I had to take the deal.

So, I did what I did best.

I fought for nothing.

I slammed my fist against the stone wall, knuckles slicing open. Kicked the bedpost, my toe throbbing in my boot.

But with the well-placed kick, the mattress toppled over, and everything halted.

Taped to the bottom of the bed, a letter with my name on it stared back at me.

Rory.

I snatched it quickly, clutching it to my chest, like someone would steal this, too, if I let them. My heartbeat throbbed an incessant rhythm in my chest. I opened the letter, reading through blurry eyes.

If you're reading this, I'm gone. And I'm sorry, Sunshine.

It took all my strength not to ball it up and throw it away or tear it to shreds. All my strength to keep reading, to swallow down the last words my *Vinculum* had for me.

Kato approached me to infiltrate the rebels weeks ago, after Quintin let the Shadowborne in. He assumes the rebels somehow have access to the beasties, so it's been my job to figure it out. They've never mobilized like this before—so far, they've only just spread lies and propaganda through the city. But this new boldness had me worried, and I complied. I should have told you, but the King advised me not to. If I kept quiet about this mission, he'd reward us both.

My heart stopped. Kato had— I swallowed. Kato had assigned Julius to infiltrate the rebels?

My *Vinculum* wasn't a traitor. He was a victim.

475

Framed.

Seems I'm not in a position to fill that end of the bargain.
I don't know how you're finding this—if the rebels made me and
sent my head back to the palace, or if a Shadowborne finally took
a bite out of my ass.
But either way, if you're looking for an informant, Lord Pollux
has been helpful.
And if . . . if some of my other suspicions are right . . .
Be careful who you report to. This whole thing has been a wild
goose chase, and I'm thinking I've been played. Hence why I'm
writing this letter while Syrax snores in the bunk next door loud
enough to rattle the whole place.
Love you, Sunshine.
-Jules

My head spun, rage burning through me. I tore the paper to shreds.

Julius was framed. He was killed as an example, as a distraction to turn everyone's heads away from Kato.

To remind me of what the King would do if I failed my mission.

I punched again and again until my blood painted the space in angry, garnet streaks. With each outburst, I blotted away more and more of the last few hours, drowning out the sound of my friend's last gargled breaths, fighting to hold on to the lilt of Jules' laugh instead.

Hit after hit, I forgot about the smell of the gore and excrement and the King's stuffy office, hanging on to the leather-and-sandal-wood scent of my *Vinculum's* shampoo. Closed off my senses to the empty pit of sorrow expanding and contracting in my core, begging my mind to remember my friend as he deserved to be.

But when rage burnt out, late into the night, spent with every teardrop and hoarse scream into what used to be Julius' pillow . . .

All I had left was fear.

Fear that Kato would stop at nothing, *nothing,* until whatever dark plans he had were seen to completion. That whatever he was doing—whatever these double-crossed deals bought him—was worth however many honorable lives he had to sacrifice to finish it.

Fear Caelum would be next. That the King would follow through on his whispered promise.

Fear that if I didn't complete the insidious task *I'd* been assigned, that if I failed Kato again, Julius would only be the first to fall.

And as night broke into day, as the envious sun rose again to lay the truth bare in the bright light . . .

My fear took shape, morphing into a half-mad plan of action. Stealing paper and an ink-pen from the barracks store room, I drafted two quick letters; One to the King of Lux, the other to his son.

When I received my promotion to Captain, the commander had warned me about the law of numbers in battle. That there would come a day when I had to choose between sacrificing the few to save the many.

Thera was a good king. A good woman.

More than that. She was a visionary and an artist. A lover and a creator, not just a destroyer of worlds. She was kind; to her people, and to anyone that offered her the same. Protective; of the ones she loved, and over those who didn't deserve it.

But her sacrifice would save those I needed to protect.

And thanks to her journal, I now understood her one weakness.

Her rooms were empty, Nyxia and Kappas both nowhere to be found, but it was better that way. The spy master would see through me in a heartbeat, her silvered stare armored with a truth-telling power Thera did not possess, despite all her magic and prowess.

The little devil didn't care to be loved like her king did.

And it would be that same secret wish I'd have to exploit.

477

Still, as I trailed the familiar path to Caelum's rooms, the first glimmers of doubt gnawed at the edges of my already frayed thoughts.

What if we were caught? What if Thera wouldn't come? What if this plan wasn't enough?

But when she opened the door—her hair sex-tossed, her skin flushed and glowing—and her mismatched gaze brimming with concern, resolution armored my bones and shut off the part of me capable of regret.

Royals would always enjoy themselves while soldiers bled. They did not lose sleep—or satisfaction—over the cooling corpses of the elves that fought for their crowns.

So, I would not lose heart just because mine fluttered whenever I was with her. Would not fail again, if it meant keeping Caelum and all my other guards safe. She was an artist, but poetry would not buy us peace. And her hands were not just bloodied by those she'd devoured, but by every elf she'd failed to protect. By every low-born soldier that had died in her name or fighting against her legions.

By Julius's blood.

My decision was made. There was no turning back.

It was time I put an end to the *Sykagos*.

Even if it meant killing the girl it held hostage.

My hands shook at my sides, and I led her down the hall, bloodied knuckles throbbing in time with my too-fast pulse.

We entered the back stairwell—servants' passages—she fell into step next to me, mouth pursed. "Where are we going, Captain?"

Zo'is lamps burned on low, flickering against the cobwebbed stone, and I ducked my head, hiding my face in their wide shadows. This was the dark, disused underbelly of Stellaris, and like the rat I was, I'd scurry away from the light. My throat closed on its own accord, parched, and choking on half-assed explanations that I couldn't spit out.

A hand closed around my arm, stopping me mid-step.

She was so strong, for someone so thin.

So *breakable.*

"Aurora?" My name wasn't an accusation or an insult, but treated with care and reverence, like it meant something to her. Like it wasn't a curse upon anyone who spoke it. "What is going on?"

In the First Legion, orders were always given on a need-to-know-basis. It kept sensitive information private, but it spared the lower ranks' morale from the crushing weight of grim reality.

Guilt ravaged my insides like a thousand razor blades. I swallowed down the harsher picture, instead forcing my lips around the sweeter half-truths that would have to placate her.

"There is something in the dungeons I should show you." I gripped her hand again. "It's . . . it's where the First Legion keeps the Shadowborne they capture instead of kill."

Eyes narrowed to slits, whether by suspicion or scrutiny, I couldn't tell. I had to give her this small truth to get her to ignore the rest, and I knew how much this meant to her. How desperate she'd been to study the Shadowborne now that they'd changed their tactics.

As I'd guessed, she didn't turn around. Didn't flee or attack me striking me down with her limitless shadows.

She followed.

Love leaves.

Thera's didn't. It propelled her forward, down the last set of stone steps, to where the mouth of the hallway narrowed into a dark, single corridor. Below the surface of the world, where the oppressive sun could not reach us, a damp chill licked at our exposed necks and hands, Thera shivering in her too-thin dress. The darkness hugged the gray slabs of stone. Strange, hollow sounds echoing from the world above like this was the belly of some great beast that'd swallowed us whole.

But at the end of the hall, a haze softened the dark to ashy gray, emitting from the thick metal door, a lock buzzing with cerulean streaks of *Zo'is*.

As planned, the guards stationed in this area had been redirected, an order from Tiberius himself granting me the access I'd needed. When I'd sent him my request, he'd approved it immediately, King Kato himself signing off on the missive.

They would expose *some* secrets, it seemed, if it meant the *Sykagos's* head on a platter.

It turned my stomach to think that I furthered Kato's agenda. Boiled my blood, that I was about to fulfill part of the hidden prophecy my *Vinculum* died to keep secret.

But if I didn't play my role, if I didn't enact King Kato's story, more would fall.

My honor was worth less than the lives I'd protect.

I fit the key into the lock, the metal crunching and humming as the mechanism shifted and popped. A stench slammed into us, musty and rotted, fitting for the lowest level of hell.

The door swung open on screeching hinges; the last warning Thera had to run. To leave before it was too late.

She didn't. Instead, she strode inside first, her chin lifted with its signature, overconfident air.

Cobalt lamps flicked on, and I shut the door behind us. The lock clicked as it sounded, a similar thud repeating in my gut as the guilt and dread consumed me.

But Thera didn't notice. Didn't even flinch, too occupied with the horrors in front of us.

The room was purposefully bare, the smooth stone floor interrupted only by the metal sewage grates on the sides, the clay walls empty aside from the deep scratches that decorated their faces and a single lever next to the door.

All except for the fourth wall; the one furthest from the door. There, behind the thick, rusted bars of a giant cage, twenty-or-so Shadowborne stared back at us with unseeing, electric blue eyes. Their fanged mouths hung open, clawed hands drooping at their sides. They waited, utterly motionless aside from the flare of their wide nostrils at the end of their wrinkled snouts as they breathed. More of the same unnatural blue ran in rivets through their veins, dark gray skin discolored to translucent, ugly green, pulsing with each heartbeat.

"This is—" Thera's voice rattled. She clutched her fists at her sides, rage and abject horror contorting her face. "I've never seen Shadowborne act like this."

If I had any hope or care for myself left, I might've been afraid or upset, too.

But looking into their empty eyes, I only saw my reflection.

Monstrous pawns, blank-minded and subdued, awaiting slaughter. Creatures to be used and manipulated and bonded by magic, just to be torn to shreds, all in sacrifice to Kato's whim.

Just like me. Like Julius.

"That's because they all have been given *Zo'is*."

Thera pivoted, teeth bared. "What?"

Focusing on my bracelets, letting my power ripple up my arms, I raised a hand.

The Shadowborne mimicked my movement in perfect synchronization, distended, too-long limbs flying skyward. Their faces remained impassive, unseeing. "Turns out, already turned Shadowborne are good conduits. The *Zo'is* makes them . . . "

"Controllable." Thera gasped, tears whetting the corners of her eyes as she stepped closer to the cage. Ghostly pale fingers brushed across the bars. "Puppets."

"It doesn't last long enough to employ as a military strategy. Not yet, at least," I explained, buying myself time as I burrowed deeper into the well of power in my bracelets. It was so much less now, so much shallower, without my *Vinculum's* energy to amplify. "But it can be effective in small attacks."

"How long have you known?"

"Two days? I followed Tiberius here the night before the

wedding," I whispered, finally letting one of my secrets go. Then, one last truth. "I should have told you in the garden shed."

If I had, maybe she would have figured it all out. Maybe she would have swept Caelum away, would have protected him in Erebus from Kato. Maybe the three of us could have figured something else out. Could have chosen more.

Maybe my *Vinculum* would've survived.

But the maybes died when he did.

"Did Julius know about this? Could he have—could he have told the reb—" Thera slammed her mouth shut. She stilled in front of one of the Shadowborne, back rigid, knees shaking.

One whose transformation was still half-formed, his snout still closer to his face, his cropped hair still hanging to his head. Whose black clothes hung in tatters around his shoulders, the material sturdier than most Luxian garb—meant to keep out the sunless cold.

A shiver rattled through her. She lurched forward, hand reaching out to touch the beast's cheek. "Commander Kappas?"

That was my opening.

I ran to the wall, yanking down the lever that controlled the cage's locks. They all fizzled as the *Zo'is* cracked through them, the tumblers sliding out of their sheaths. The bars groaned, and the doors swung open.

Thera whirled on me, eyes wide.

I raised my arms again, power shaking through me. The Shadowborne followed—the late Commander Kappas included.

"I'm sorry." I unleased the restraints I had on the *Zo'is*. "This was the only way I could keep him safe."

Thera's gaze—blurred with hot, angry tears—didn't leave mine as the Shadowborne attacked.

CHAPTER
THIRTY-SEVEN

"When does a story become a tragedy? When the tellers give up before the end." –Quote from "A Tale of Forgotten Love," A Luxian Epic Romance written by Madea Thisbe, circa 1867 A.G.W

CAELUM

I woke to an empty bed.

To sheets, pulled back and discarded.

To silence, my breath the only one in the room.

To a disquiet that seeped through every pore of my skin, a sticky, rotten feeling that permeated any comfort the night before and the dreamworld had brought.

I flung back my blankets, snatching a pair of loose-fitting trousers from my closet and shuffling into them, scanning my room for signs of life.

Or a sign of *her*. A sign that last night hadn't been a dream, a fantasy conjured from stress and sleeplessness.

I peeked into the bathroom first—toward the tub that'd been our sanctuary. Her dress was still a discarded pile of gore and gossamer stuffed in the corner, and something eased in my chest. So not a dream then, the harsh reality of stained silk proof that she'd been here.

But where had she gone?

Had she woken and decided it was all a mistake? Had she fled before the sun could rouse me, hoping to forget about this?

Or had something else demanded her attention? Had one of her people—Nyxia or Kappas—found something about her dead convoy or the attack?

I padded into the greeting room, hoping to find her sitting quietly in front of the fireplace, a book in her lap—

Empty. The hearth long gone cold.

But a note, laying on my entryway table, with familiar hand-writing scrawled on the back, caught my eye.

Cae.

Not Thera's writing, but Rory's. My heart thudded through my chest, each beat louder and more demanding than the last. I picked up the small slip of paper, questions assaulting my mind. When had she been here?

Had she reconsidered her choices?

I unfurled the note with shaking fingers.

And my heart stopped.

To my Sunkissed Prince,
I'm sorry. For what I said, and for pushing you away. I'm sorry
for not telling you the truth, either.
I know you will never forgive me for what I have done, or for
what I'm about to do.

Panic blurred my vision, tears misting. A thousand scenarios flashed through my mind, each more vivid and gruesome than the last, my imagination betraying me with dark horrors.

None of them compared to reality as I forced myself to keep reading, a knot in my stomach and a lump in my throat.

But fear not—when it is done, I will punish myself accordingly and join her and Julius. Thera and Erebus did not deserve this, and I am sorry for it. But if I hadn't agreed to kill her, they would've hurt you instead, and as your guard, I could not choose that.

I don't know what deal Julius took, but I do know this of my own: I'd do it again, a thousand times, if it kept you safe.

I don't know if that's what your father truly intended. But it has been my sole priority—and honor—since the day we met.

I will always be there, step for step, even if you can't see me.

I love you.

-Rory

"No." The word shattered out of me. I crashed to my knees, the tear-stained letter crumpling in my fist. My breath came short and sharp, like a panicked, wild animal was stuck in my lungs and trying to escape. "Rory, what have you done?"

My heart thudded in angry, too-fast beats, the normally pitiful organ urging me to go, to *do* something, before it was too late.

I will always be there, step for step, even if you can't see me.

If I didn't, everything I ever loved would die.

Head spinning, legs trembling, I *ran*.

Step for fucking step.

I couldn't save them on my own, and I knew that. Even if I found them in time, there was no way I'd be able to stop whatever Rory had planned, and even if Thera could still fight her off, I could not come between them without hurting myself—and them.

But there was someone who could.

Servants and guards stared at me with wide eyes as I ran through the halls of Stellaris, wearing mismatched boots and an untucked tunic, panic surging me forward. It would be fodder for the gossip mill tomorrow, even with all that'd transpired in the last few days. But I didn't care.

I had no time.

Instead of running to my father or Tiberius, my gut and my feet led me to the one person currently in Lux that might be able to do something. To the one person who might just be willing to believe me and help, and the one elf that Thera would trust with this task.

My fist was an anvil against her door as I bellowed, "Open up, Nyxia, I know you're in there!"

I probably should've employed more stealth. More secrecy. But I didn't have time for that.

Thera didn't have time.

I pounded again, doubt tying itself around my throat in knots.

Was Nyxia gone, too? Had I miscalculated? She was so slippery; she easily could have disappeared somewhere with no one knowing.

The door flung open on the eighth knock, revealing Nyxia standing behind it, clad in a much-too-large tunic. "Your Highness, what—"

"Where is Thera?" I demanded, ignoring her disheveled state.

Her face darkened. She took in my half-dressed, half-mad attire, brows furrowing together. "I don't—I don't know."

I slammed my hand against the doorframe, misplaced rage and panic burning through me. "Find out."

Another form appeared behind her, shirtless and covered in love bites, his long brown hair a tangled mess as he fastened his trousers.

Syrax's eyes narrowed. "What's going on?"

Surprise slashed through my panic for a moment. Argentis was the last person I'd ever imagine finding with Nyxia, but I didn't care. I could use his strength right now, and he'd been one of the few soldiers to ever stand against Rory on the sparring pitch and hold his own.

"Thera is . . . " I started to explain, but the sentence fell off, my tongue tangling over its rotten taste. "Rory is with her, and something is wrong. If we don't get there soon, they both might die."

They gasped in unison, Syrax cursing under his breath.

Then he retreated, fast steps storming back into the room.

He returned in less than a moment, shirt and sword both on, handing Nyxia a pair of her trousers.

"Follow me," he commanded.

Nyxia slipped into her clothes and shoved her feet into the pair of boots by the door.

Syrax pushed out of the room first, steps sure and purposeful, and he turned right down the hall, but I hesitated, relief soured by a suspicious question nagging at the back of my mind. "How do you know where to go?"

Syrax paused. Frowned.

"Her gauntlets." The *Zo'is* in his own flared in confirmation as he tapped the metal. "I have—the King made sure I could track her with them. As a precaution after . . ."

His sentence trailed off, the rest of it floating unsaid in the air between us.

After Julius.

I nodded, thinking of how my father would react when he found out about Rory's attack on the new consort of Lux. Would he make an example of her, too?

I swallowed the lump in my throat, pushing that fear from my mind. That would be a problem for after. "This stays between us."

"Yes, Your Highness." Syrax crossed his hand over his heart in a salute. "The captain's safety is my only objective."

"And Thera's," I added.

487

I wouldn't lose either of them.

Nyxia's gaze flicked to me for a second before tracking back to Syrax. She strapped her daggers to her hip, her jaw set and her stance square. "Lead the way, pretty boy."

CHAPTER
THIRTY-EIGHT

> *"The betrayal has been forgiven, but not forgotten. It will live in the bones of every elf born to darkness. And they are not responsible for the shadows they will learn to wield against you." –An excerpt from Queen Glorianna's letter to the Elysian people, circa 2 A.G.W.*

THERA

At the bottom of the Pool of Souls, there was a quiet darkness, so complete it consumed the senses. A buffer to all outside noise, all I could hear was the beat of my heart, the slosh of my gut, the grind of my *bones*. With no light, my eyes could not tell if they were opened or closed, playing tricks on me in the shadows, envisioning phantoms that were not there.

It was maddening. Calm didn't exist in such deprivation, no rest in such solitude.

Just endless, horrifying nothingness.

But when the *Zo'is*-drugged Shadowborne—Kappas at the helm—surged, slaves to the captain's command, I wished for a moment that I could sink back into the Pit. That I could find solace in that never-ending darkness once more.

Because here, with the sun's constant surveillance, with *Zo'is* burning and flickering even in the bowels of the castle, there was no escape from the light.

Because *there*, with no one to betray me, perhaps I could finally be at peace.

My shadows lashed out, slicing through the first round of Shadowborne with ease.

Body parts severed into thick chunks that thudded to the ground, spews of ebony blood painting the gray slab walls in shadows.

Kappas' disfigured head cleaved from his shoulders, rolling to my feet.

I did not mourn.

Couldn't. Not when another of the beasts attacked, fangs gnashing for my throat.

I knocked the creature away with a burst of shadows, but it whirled, and its claws sliced at my back, opening old lash scars my father had given me.

Pain rippled through my spine, boiling my flesh, but I grit my teeth. Pain was not a stranger, but a friend. One that'd kept me company in the darkness. One that would never betray me, a constant companion.

My shadows tore the creature limb from limb.

The remaining beasts hesitated. Jaws slackened, hands falling to their sides again.

"You're bleeding." Captain Bellator blurted, her stance matching theirs, like it hadn't been her who'd piloted these flesh-bound tanks. Like she hadn't planned it all from the moment she'd met me, getting closer to me to find my weak points. To craft her strategy.

It'd worked.

I'd given her everything she needed to end me. My attraction for her, my journal, my trust, my respect.

All she'd need to follow her orders.

"Who put you up to this?" The last parts of me that wanted to hold on to her—the last *good* parts—asked, my voice ringing hollow.

I already knew the answer, the captain's missive coming from one elf, and one elf alone. A man that'd proven untrustworthy and secretive. A man that'd been too easy to convince into a contract.

King Kato had played me from the start, and his precious captain his favorite chess piece.

Aurora opened her mouth, tears budding in the corners of her eyes, and then shut it again. Fists clenched at her sides—the reminder of her master enough to reinvigorate her purpose here. "I'm not who you should worry about."

Zo'is lit paths of lightning strikes up her arms, the dim lamps in the room flickering as her power surged. Amber eyes tinted electric blue, a shudder running up her back as the euphoric substance took over.

Low, throaty growls sounded behind me. Heavy footfalls shook the concrete floor, the Shadowborne shifting their weight. Ready to pounce.

Only one escape in this hellish room—the door we'd come through—or I'd have to retreat into the wall of built-in cages. But with Shadowborne at my back and the captain stalwart in front of the exit, I had no choice.

There was no running from this one.

My shadows pulled closer, a shield of darkness. A shield I never should have lowered. "I trusted you. I *cared*—"

"I know." Rory hung her head, her glowing arms straining toward the low, molded stone ceiling. "I'm sorry. But it always must be him. He's all I have left."

491

I braced for impact, shadows unfurling from my fingertips, murmuring through my veins in anticipation.

Rory raised her palms.

The Shadowborne snarled.

A clanging at the door halted everything.

"Rory!" a voice cried—strained with tears and panic. "Let me in!"

Like a candle blowing out, blue doused from the captain's skin, her arms dropping with her jaw. She swiveled to the door—putting her back to me and the Shadowborne. "Caelum?"

I could've attacked; could've ended her there.

My father's favorite weapon did not concede battles.

But my shadows paused, too, like they held their breath for my husband's next words. Like they waited, *hoped*, with me, that another way existed. That this wasn't all over.

"Please Rory." His voice muffled through the thick metal door, but the care and desperation in his tone was unmistakable, *love* fortifying every syllable. "Don't do this. I can't lose you."

Of course, he'd come for her.

For his best friend. The girl he'd wanted to be with last night, using me instead as a relief from the pain.

For the elf that would kill his bride.

The woman he truly *loved*.

It always must be him.

He'd forgive her, too. He might have already, if he hadn't been in on the plan from the start, this charade his father's doing, after all.

Something broke inside of me. The bars to the cage I'd kept around my most monstrous parts cleaved open, my benevolence severed from my soul.

At the bottom of the Pool of Souls, I'd known what it was to be utterly alone. To only have myself and the darkness to rely on.

But in the blackness, I'd found something else, a leviathan that did not trouble itself with weak concepts like mercy or kindness. A titan, chaos incarnate, that devoured desire and churned it into pure, lethal power.

My shadows grew teeth and sank into my heart, consuming what was left of it entirely.

The *Sykagos* unleashed itself.

CHAPTER
THIRTY-NINE

RORY

My regret came a moment too late, Caelum's voice ripping back the veil my grief had shrouded me in, exposing me to the harsh truth of my mistakes.

I had no time for remorse. No time to recalculate my failure, to beg for mercy.

"Move away!" a gruff voice shouted from the other side of the door.

The hinges cried open, cerulean *Zo'is* crackling through the locking mechanism. My ears rang with the blast when Syrax stepped through, gauntlets blazing, chest heaving with the effort.

Nyxia and Caelum scurried inside behind him, the first clasping her daggers with eyes narrowed, the latter's hands covering his face, his pupils blown wide in fear. Neither looking at me, but past me, transfixed by the Shadowborne growling behind me.

No, that wasn't a Shadowborne call. The snarl was deeper. *Hollower.* Like a million shadowy voices combined in one, all echoing and rumbling together in a storm cloud of fury and vengeance, skittering over my skin like the charge before a lightning strike.

A chill crept up my spine, hairs raising to attention.

"*Mi Vassilla,* no!" Nyxia reached out her hand, her scream tearing from her throat.

"Thera!" Caelum cried, wincing backward.

Something slithered across my neck, cold and demanding. And all air cut off as shadows wrapped around my throat.

My nails frantically scraped at the obsidian limbs to no avail, unable to find purchase in their strange substance. The *Sykagos* dragged me to her, my lungs aching with lack of air, panic seizing my muscles.

She drew me to her face, and my heart stopped.

Gone were the beautiful, gemstone-colored eyes, the whites and pupils an impenetrable black instead. Gone was the pale, milky flesh, covered in ebony shadows that armored her entire body like dragon scales, pulsing with sick, dark power. Gone was the luscious, silken hair, masked by tendrils of darkness that protruded from her head in a crown of horns, sharp and imposing.

Gone was King Thera.

The creature staring back was the same that'd haunted my nightmares. The same that'd sliced me open on the battlefield and left me for dead. The same that'd single-handedly ended legions of my fellow soldiers.

The *Sykagos* had returned.

And I'd summoned her.

I choked on the scream that crested from the deepest chambers of my belly, the shadows pulling tighter around my throat. But I did not have time for fear. I had to move, to *survive*. I kicked and thrashed, but each movement made my lungs pinch and scrape harder, the air thin and heavy.

The *Sykagos* grinned wide, exposing a row of finger-length, shadowy teeth.

My vision blurred. My head spun.

This was the end.

I was going to die.

Breathe, Rory.

I couldn't.

Something silver flashed—a dagger—lodging itself into the *Sykagos'* shoulder. Blood rained from the wound, and the beast cried out—an inhuman, screeching wail that shook the room.

She dropped me, and my stomach punched up my throat. I smacked the floor with a sick thud, my head cracking against the concrete and the wind knocking from my ribs. Vomit crested at the back of my mouth, and I rolled to my side just in time to unleash it.

Blackness flickered at the corners of my eyes, a hammer throbbing against my skull.

"Get back!" Nyxia unsheathed another dagger. She dropped in front of me—between me and the *Sykagos*. "The Tygian iron just distracts her, and while it can pierce the shadows, it doesn't slow her down."

Something jolted through my body, hot and piercing.

Zo'is, from my gauntlets. Redirecting to try to heal my wounds.

Fear lanced through my side.

"Fuck," Syrax hissed before I could get the same word out, staggering in front of Caelum. His eyes latched onto the beasts behind us. "She lost control of the Shadowborne."

Limbs reanimated as the blue hue in their eyes flickered out. The beasts shook their heads, dispelling the last of the magic holding them at bay.

Angry, hungry eyes blinked red, focusing on the bodies in the room. Wrinkled, gray lips pulled back, fangs dripping with saliva.

Just as the *Sykagos* hunched forward again, the bleeding staunched and her claws lengthened.

I didn't need to sound the command.

Run.

Strong hands hefted me up—Syrax—and we bolted.

Caelum clattered into the hall first on wobbling legs, then Syrax and I, the Lieutenant pitching me forward; I crashed to my knees, palms stinging. Then Nyxia hopped through just as Syrax pulled the door shut with a groan.

A second later, something big slammed into it, clanging against the metal. Syrax braced, the veins in his forearms popping with the strain.

Howls and snarls and snapping teeth sounded on the other side, reverberating through the cracks. Shadows peeked from beneath the door, slithering through the gap in probing, ghostly fingers.

"This isn't good," Syrax grit through a clenched jaw, *Zo'is* pulsing in his gauntlets as more of the Shadowborne threw themselves against the door.

He couldn't hold them for long.

My bracelets flared again, the last reserves of my *Zo'is* flickering as I directed my hand to the lock. If I could repair it, maybe then we could wait for reinforcements.

A zap hissed through my fingers, and my gauntlets went dead, the silver and blue dulling to slate gray.

Fuck.

"What's happening?" Caelum's voice trembled, his arms wrapped around himself. "We can't just leave Thera in there . . ."

"We have to." Nyxia cursed under her breath. Lips pursed. "I've only seen her lose control like this once. She's—it's not really her, right now."

My stomach heaved again, though it had nothing left to spend.

Once, after her mother passed.

She dreamed of that day often, detailing the recurring night-

497

mares in her journal in several accounts. The day she gave into that dark force, into the pit of misery she'd worked so hard to hold off.

The day she slaughtered a whole Luxian fleet.

It was her first kill. First *massacre*.

Snarls and howls morphed into yelps and throaty screams, ear-splitting and mind-numbing and bone-rattling.

And then, all at once, silence.

Black blood oozed from under the door, the shadows caressing at our ankles.

A shudder ran down Nyxia's back. She stumbled backward, out of the shadows' reach, like even the little devil knew to fear the darkness. "We have to stop her."

"Do you have any ideas?" Syrax shifted his weight to avoid the viperous tendrils.

Nyxia shook her head.

No, there was no stopping the *Sykagos*. No controlling that immense, all-consuming power.

Rule four: If you see the Sykagos, say a prayer.

The only path forward was to run as fast as we could or pray that she was in a merciful mood.

Silence blanketed the hall like mist.

Something scratched from behind the door. Once. Twice. *Three* times.

Beckoning.

"Shit." Syrax planted his feet firmer, adjusting his grip on the door handle, readying for the attack.

But realization washed over me in a chilly wave. Thera didn't attack because she didn't want to. If the *Sykagos* wanted us dead, this door would not have stopped her. Would not have even made her break a sweat.

I'd seen her tear through metal armor like it was paper. Seen her crumple tanks with those shadows like they were made of glass.

After all, love leaves. Fear lingers.

But it doesn't stop me from trying to remember what love felt like. From trying to find it again—to no avail.

The *Sykagos* had returned.

But the little girl was still in there. Still trying to remember.

I couldn't leave her. I shouldn't have ever tried.

"This is my fault," I whispered. "I should fix it."

Nyxia's expression dropped. "Don't be an idiot—"

Caelum paled, realizing what I was about to do. Knowing me better than I did myself. He reached for my hand. "Rory, no!"

My knuckles grazed Syrax's temple, the punch knocking him down. I ignored his grunt. I swiveled around Nyxia, pushing her into Caelum, keeping them both out of the way. I ignored her surprised expression. I hurtled through the door, slamming it shut behind me. Ignoring Caelum's cries.

I ignored the pools of black blood that puddled on the floor, my careful footsteps splashing through them. Ignored the scattered, shredded body parts, stepping over each as I got closer.

The *Sykagos* stood tall, still cloaked in darkness, one dark claw scraping against the stone wall, over and over again. Black eyes fixed on me; her teeth bared.

But she did not move. Didn't attack.

"Thera?" I called her name, and a growl rippled through her. I sucked in a breath, holding my hands up—in surrender—as I approached. Then, softer, "Dymitria?"

The *Sykagos* blinked. Her mouth slammed shut, her head tilting ever so slightly.

Breathe, Rory.

I exhaled, stepping closer, lowering my hands—and extended them toward her.

"Rory, stop it!" Caelum whispered from the doorway, knuckles white where they clung to the frame.

"This does not end well," Nyxia cautioned, but I ignored her yet again.

I stared directly at Thera, into the blackness, trying to find the

499

green and blue in the darkness. Trying to uncover the girl behind the thorns. To find the king behind the beast.

I racked my brain for anything that would call her out again, for any tidbit from the bursting pages of her journal that might lead her back to her senses.

Back to me.

My mind snagged on a memory, not one of mine, but hers. One she'd written about just before her father's death—a mantra she'd wanted to use to craft her new world.

"Your Amma used to say your mercy was your greatest strength, right?" I kept my voice low and steady, despite the furious beat of my heart. Despite the pounding in my head. I stepped closer. Reached further. "I'm so sorry for what I did. I deserve your rage. I deserve to die for what I've done. But they don't, right?"

I jerked my head to Caelum and Nyxia in the doorway. To the innocents I'd dragged into this.

"Captain, back away," Syrax clipped out, concern tying his voice in knots.

But I wouldn't. Not until I made this right.

Closer, again, and my palm grazed the pulsing shadows of her chest, right above where her heart dwelled. Where I knew it still beat, for Caelum, for her people, for the world she wanted to build. "Kill me and let them go."

She stilled beneath my touch. The scraping halted.

Another blink, and I swear, the faintest glimmer of blue-and-green flashed beneath the shadows.

But then something made a banging sound. Syrax's gauntlets against the door, perhaps, or Nyxia's boot—

Thera's head snapped toward it.

And the shadows lunged.

"No!" Nyxia shouted.

I braced, waiting for the stinging, slashing agony.

Someone knocked into my side, tackling me to the ground. Wrapping their arms around me.

His smell, cardamom and amber, my least favorite of his soaps, filled my nose. The white and bronze and violet blue of his face flooded my vision.

Then, everything went black and *red*.

A scream catapulted out of him, a soul-deep pain I knew too well. A cry that echoed through my own memories, born of a pain I'd felt myself, on a dusky battlefield, and in every nightmare since.

He slumped off me and went quiet, falling face down into the black blood, his own crimson life source pouring from the gash that stretched across his back.

He did not breathe.

CHAPTER
FORTY

"What have I done?" –Excerpt from a letter from King Theron Umbrus of Erebus to General Danae, circa 2074 A.G.W.

THERA

Shhhh. The shadows whispered, gentle as they dragged me under. *Deeper.*

Into the blackness. Into the end.

Into the void.

Into the rage and regret. Into the chaos and despair. Into the pleasure and power.

Darkness took shape—a familiar outline that haunted my earliest memories.

"Please stop," I begged, flinching away, rubbing at my sore muscles.

A disappointed sigh. My father threw down the riding crop, running a hand over his face.

Emotion choked my throat. I took a hesitant step forward, my knees nearly giving out. "Are you angry at me?"

The oppressive emerald, green gaze flicked to me. "I'm never angry at you, Thera." *A hand reached out. I braced for another slap, but fingers stroked my cheek instead.* "I only seek to make you better. Endurance is survival."

Tears welled in my eyes—I'd be punished for them later, but I couldn't help it. "I don't want to be a monster."

A breath.

"Monsters do not exist." *A sturdy grip lifted my chin, forcing me to meet that gemstone stare again. Forcing me to face my future as his heir.* "Only weak people that cannot understand power, so they fear it."

I wiped my tears. Sheathed my heart. Swallowed my fear. "Yes, Mi Vassilo."

"Mi *Vassilla*!"

A flash of gold sunlight pierced the dark, fleeting and fast. No, not sunlight—but a wisp of sun-touched hair.

"Caelum, please." A bronzed hand stroked white locks away from his face—staining it red. "*Please* hold on."

A shadow blocked my view, small and edged with silver. "Syrax, get *Zo'is*. I'll hold her off."

"Mi *Vassilina*," *Stavros cooed, hunched over his chair. This shadowed memory was clearer—less faded with time. So clear, I could make out each wrinkle that crowned his furrowed forehead.* "We can't wait any longer. Erebus needs you to take the helm."

Shadows knotted in my gut with a fear I thought I'd outgrown. "They will see me as a monster if they know what I plan."

His monster, unleashed upon its master.

A firm, reassuring grip on my arm. "You do what you must to endure." Stavros' warm voice, gentle and steady like moonlight.

I shook my head. "I can't."

"Caelum, you can't leave me." Her voice was so, *so* soft. Like dawn's first rays, warm and inviting. Inviting him to stay. "You *can't*."

"Pressure on the wound!" A more urgent call, shrill and slicing. "Thera, please, come back!"

"Dymi, come out." My mother crouched beside the bed I hid under, her long hair—just like mine—falling forward. A chuckle lilted. "You can't hide down there forever."

I pulled my knees tighter to my chest, shadows hugging my frame like a warm blanket. "Yes I can."

A pout pulled down at her mouth. She reached out a hand— unafraid. She'd never been afraid of what I could do. "If you stay here, I'll miss you too much."

My heart ached. I'd miss her too. I always missed her when she wasn't around. When she'd go off to battle, leaving me with him. With the darkness.

My voice quivered. "It hurts out there."

"I know." My mother sighed, grabbing my hand. Squeezing once. "But we can endure."

"Thera Dymitria!" The scream shook me.

No, *hands* did, gripping my face, desperate. Tears streaked down her pale skin.

Nyxia.

Shadows fought to drag me down again, but I batted them away, gasping for breath. Like I always did when I emerged from the Pool of Souls, I coughed the darkness from my lungs, furiously blinking to clear my vision. A chill rattled my bones, my head throbbing.

But blood dripped down Nyxia's forehead, a gash opened above her brow. Another across her shoulder, her left arm going slack, her jaw dropping. "You're back."

Back?

I'd been gone?

Shhhh, the shadows coaxed again, offering the same respite, caressing my neck.

But stark, vivid clarity rocked my center when my eyes finally focused. When my vision spattered not with black, but angry, gut-churning red.

The captain knelt beside the prince, a bloodied shirt pressed against him. Against a long, muscle-deep gash that split the plain of his back into two, a river of red running from him.

I don't want to be a monster.

What had I done?

"What—" I croaked, my mouth dry and chapped, pushing past Nyxia and stumbling toward them. "*Caelum.*"

Rory leaned over his body, covering him. Snarling like a tiger protecting its cub.

"Don't hurt him," she begged between sobs, her shoulders shaking. "This is my fault, but please don't hurt him again."

I winced back. Panic clogged my throat. I scanned Caelum again, horror bludgeoning my ribs with every heartbeat.

His chest didn't move.

He wasn't breathing.

But he still bled, his heart pumping.

He wasn't dead.

But he was dying. My husband was *dying.*

And it was all my fault.

Footsteps thundered and Syrax crashed through the door, eyes blazing, a syringe in his hand. He halted as he looked at me, fear glazing over his expression. But with a sharp inhale, he nudged his way next to Caelum.

"Move." He growled and lined the needle with Caelum's neck. Blue liquid sloshed against the sides, Zo'is glowing in the dim room. Beveling the needle into the prince's skin, he shoved the plunger down, a small bud of blood blooming from the entrance site. "Come on, Your Highness, you're stronger than this."

We all waited, still except for shaking hands and too-quick hearts.

Nothing.

"He needs the bond." Rory's voice came out hoarse, but her expression was set with sheer determination. The Lieutenant's jaw dropped, but the captain shook her head, holding out her own arm. "The *Zo'is* isn't enough, Syrax. It wasn't for me. I wouldn't have survived without it. He needs to *bond.*"

The Lieutenant didn't wait. Didn't question it.

He drove his next syringe into the captain's arm first, drawing out her blood and contaminating it with the blue substance inside. She hissed, but didn't flinch, not until azure tinted purple. Then, again, in a swift, decisive strike, he plunged the mixture into the prince.

A beat passed, breaths held. Fists clenched at sides, no one moving a muscle.

Not until *he* did.

My *fault.*

A gasp. Caelum's eyes flew open. Followed by a pained moan, the *Zo'is* shuddered through him, working its way to his lungs, his wound. It ran through his bloodstream like ink, a dark blue tattoo marking his exposed back as skin knit itself together again.

Rory crashed back onto her heels, a fresh wave of tears running down her cheeks. Her skin paled, like the life had been sucked from her veins. But she stroked the Prince's face with reverence. "Caelum, oh thank the Sun."

"Rory?" Caelum groaned again, shivering as the bleeding

slowed. He twisted, laying on his side instead of face down, clutching his middle.

"I'm here." Rory shifted so his head could rest in her lap. Taking the saturated shirt, she held the staunch in place against the wound. Her jaw clenched, the captain in her commanding the situation once more. "You're going to be okay."

Relief slammed into my chest, stealing my breath. But it was mixed and muddled with guilt, my legs numb and my hands shaking.

This is my fault.

All eyes in the room snapped to me.

Even Caelum's, the violet bloodshot and watery.

I winced. I must've said it aloud this time.

I took a trembling step. "I'm sorry—"

Caelum scrambled closer to Rory, eyes widening in fear. A whisper shivered on his lips. "*Get away from me.*"

Black clouded the edges of my vision.

"*Get away from me!*" *the soldiers cried, trousers darkening, the smell of piss and shit wafting over the battlefield.* "*Please, get away!*"

"*Don't hurt them!*" *the civilians shouted, huddled in the corner, shielding their children behind them, faces blanched.* "*Spare us, please!*"

"*Monster!*" *my father hissed, covering his face. Hiding like he'd never allowed me to.* "*Betrayer.*"

"*Mi Vassilla, please.*" Nyxia tugged at my sleeve, pulling me toward the door. Panic sparked across her face, all the lines wrong, distorted. "Reinforcements are coming. We have to get out."

Had to *get away*, before the soldiers could come for me. Before the armies could attack, their wounded prince all the justification they'd ever need to begin the persecution.

The hunt for the *Sykagos*.

507

Everyone's favorite monster.

Get away from me!

Monster.

"*Mi Vassilla,* I need *orders.*" Nyxia clutched her shredded shoulder, her gaze jerking back toward the door, our last window of escape closing.

I looked, one last time, at Caelum. At my husband, his head cradled in Rory's lap, her hand tenderly embracing his cheek.

One last look, at the future I'd dreamed of. At the Sunkissed prince and the fire-hearted soldier who might have, in another world, another *life,* helped me bring about peace. Who might have cared for the girl beneath the thorns.

But there was no peace in Lux. Not for monsters like me.

Get away from me.

So, it'd be war, then.

"Let's go." I stalked toward the door, Nyxia trailing behind me.

"Wait!" Rory called, one last attempt to lure me in. One final, desperate act of trickery. "I'm sorry, please wait—"

I stilled.

"I'm sparing you all as a mercy this time." My voice carried on the back of my shadows, dark and brimming with all of my rage and hurt. All my pain and misplaced guilt. "Next time, I will not be so generous."

I wiped my tears. Sheathed my heart. Swallowed my fear.

I didn't look back.

CHAPTER
FORTY-ONE

"All I ever wanted was for you to know joy. I am sorry to be a source of your sorrow. And I am sorry I was too blinded by his light to see his shadows." –Queen Dellia's recovered letters to her son, Prince Caelum, circa 2096, A.G.W

RORY

M y knees kissed the marble floor of the throne room, my head hung low, my gut a wreck of knots, and I bowed before King Kato.

I'd delayed this meeting long enough. I'd spent the first few days after the dungeon incident at Caelum's medical bay bedside, attending to him as the doctors stitched his wound and helped his heartbeat settle again. He hadn't woken yet, but they assured he would, and when he did, I'd be there.

His new *Vinculum*.

But when the nurses shooed me from the room, insisting I was

509

only in the way and that my emotions would be too overwhelming when he woke, I'd spent the last week trying to 'help' Tiberius and the First Legion track Thera—which mostly meant sending them on false leads in hopes they'd exhaust themselves while I crafted a better plan.

Not that it mattered. She was long gone, her trail nothing more than mist and shadow.

I'd been too out of my mind to say goodbye. To say *sorry*.

But it would have to be added to the long list of regrets I'd take with me to the grave, my treatment of Thera since I met her top among them.

The girl in the journal was gone, and I'd been the one to chase her out.

And my time was up.

It was nearly two weeks after the incident that King Kato finally put me out of my misery and summoned me. He sat atop the Sunkissed Throne, his attire simple but imposing as it revealed the honed muscles he often hid.

His sword—unused in years but sharpened and recently buffed again—leaned against his knee, a beacon of strength.

"You surprised me, Bellatore." His fingers thrummed against the armrest in impatient beats. "I didn't think you would follow through, but you almost had her."

I bowed lower, my face prostrated to the cold stone. Hoping it could armor my heart for what came next.

"I am sorry I failed you." The lie fled easily from my lips, my recent practice in the art of deceiving people straight to their faces improving my competence. "I accept whatever punishment you give me."

Boots clicked against stone, three times, the tip of his sword scraping as he dragged it with him.

He stopped, a shadow darkening the white floor before me.

I held my breath, waiting for the end. I'd known from the moment that I led Thera down the steps that someone would have to be made the villain. Someone would take the fall for restarting this war, for sullying the peace agreement. Someone would be framed and blamed, just as Julius had been, for the King's scheming. The last two weeks had only offered mercy because Tiberius and Kato had more important matters to attend to first, the aftermath of the Shadowborne attack and word of Thera's rampage stoking enough unrest to keep their hands full.

I should've used the time to run.

But I wouldn't leave Caelum, not even if he wanted me to. Not again. He should never have been mixed up in this, and in my attempt to protect him, I'd been the one to put him in the most danger.

I closed my eyes, adding his name to my list of regrets, too.

A low chuckle reverberated through my bones.

I dared a peek up, to find King Kato smiling down at me.

"Relax, Bellatore. Your task isn't done." He waved his hand, motioning for me to rise. "War is on the horizon once more, and we need all of our strongest soldiers ready for the fight."

I sat back on my heels, but didn't stand, frozen in confusion and rage. Of course—my execution hadn't been canceled, simply rescheduled. "You're sending me back to the Legion? Back to the front lines?"

Back to the bloodshed and darkness. Back to the screams of the dying and the mind-numbing fear.

Kato wanted me dead. He just didn't feel bothered enough to do it himself.

"Of course not." A scoff challenged the dark thoughts whirling in my head. "I will need you here to protect Caelum more than ever. You are his *Vinculum*, after all."

I blinked, trying to make sense of the ever-shifting ground beneath me.

Of course, King Kato's threat to Caelum after Jules' death had just been a bluff. A game, to get me to do his bidding. A deal, like he'd made with Julius, with *me*, to leverage my protective instincts against my grief, and see which drove me deeper into madness.

But now that insanity had fully taken its toll, now that chaos had sunk its claws deep into my heart, I would not be fooled again.

I ventured a dangerous, rebellious question, my mask slipping. "Protect him from who exactly, *Your Majesty*? Ther—the *Sykagos* has fled. There are no monsters left in Lux."

None but the one standing in front of me.

A grin flickered across his mouth, his head cocking to the side.

"Oh, she will be back." He circled back to the throne, lowering himself into it slowly. Fingers rapped again at the armrest, the dark expression falling over his face a contrast to the glittering gold of his seat. "I'm sure she'll want to visit her husband . . . or perhaps his lovely guard."

Fury and fear fought in my middle, clashing like great beasts, snarling and snapping at each other.

King Kato was still unconvinced; not just of my loyalty, but of his son's. Of the boy he'd used as bait for Thera, and then as a dagger to twist in my side. And if I didn't convince Kato of both, perhaps the next threat would not be a bluff, but another *example* of what he was capable of. "Your Majesty, I—"

"No more *almosts*, Captain." He clasped the edge of his armrests so tightly, his knuckles paled. "She must die."

I nodded, pushing to my feet once more, rolling my shoulders back.

I would protect the heart and soul of Lux with every last breath. I would end this war to keep my prince safe, and see my country safe once more. It was the oath I'd taken the day I joined the core, and an oath I'd keep until my final moments.

Now, my opponent was all that existed. My enemy. The sting of my knuckles and the fury of my fists.

My blade, and the end of the *true* monster that threatened my home.

"Yes, Your Majesty." I lifted my chin high, my voice resounding through the throne room with unshakable confidence. "I swear on my life that the King will die by my hands."

I meant it. This vow was one I would not break, no matter the cost. A promise etched into my being, a contract with the sun and stars above, that I would sooner rip my soul from my body before defying this bond.

The King will die by my hands.

King Kato should have executed me when he had the chance.

One day, somehow, *his* blood would feed my sword.

The shadows did not flee Lux with Thera's absence, nor did they arrive with her.

They had always existed, whispering in dark corners, slipping between the cracks in the marble floors and rotting the foundation. Lurking in the wrinkles that framed greedy smiles. Hiding behind flowery words in their edged voices.

I'd ignored them too long—too caught up in my own eclipsed heart to pay the murmurings any heed.

But now, I listened.

And as night stretched above Stellaris, the shadows growing and creeping down the long halls, I let them lead me.

If I would keep my promise, I would need allies. Powerful ones.

And though my *Vinculum* had died with nothing to his name, with no inheritance to pass on, he'd left me with something far greater.

Somewhere to start.

Florian Pollux had a single suite in the east wing where most of the courtiers dwelled during the high season. Rumor had it he was rarely here—instead spending most of his time in his own housing out in the main city, closer to the public—but as luck would have it, much like the rest of the nobility, he'd stay in Stellaris until the Shadowborne problem was better resolved.

So, riding the high of surviving my would-be-beheading, with my sword clutched tightly at my side and the tattered shreds of Julius' note tucked against my chest, I marched to Lord Pollux's rooms, ready to strike.

My fist battered his door, echoing in the wide hallway.

The door swung open, a freckle-peppered face appearing before me. "I am both surprised and glad to see you still have your head, Captain Bellatore."

His expression remained flat, no trace of said surprise on his features as he remained in the doorway—barring my entrance.

My fists clenched at my sides, nails biting into my palms. "My *Vinculum* was not so lucky."

At that, Florian blinked, long lashes batting away some unsavory emotion—guilt, perhaps.

"I heard. Lieutenant Fortis was a good elf." His voice dipped to a low whisper, something hoarse coating its edges. The door opened wider, and Pollux stepped back; an invitation inside. "I'm sorry for your immeasurable loss. But I hear you have already nominated his replacement."

I shoved through the threshold, shutting the heavy door behind me. The nobleman's receiving room was plain—just a collection of a few armchairs and an unattended desk—evidence that he truly spent little time here. But there were little touches—a vase with a single, orange tiger-lily flower, a wood-carved mug—that spoke instead to his time outside of the palace, natural-looking trinkets that reflected the style of the outer city and stood in aggressive contrast to the gilded, sharp aesthetic of Stellaris.

Stellaris was not this man's home.

And I had to hope that it meant his loyalty did not lie in its bejeweled crown.

My words ground out through clenched teeth. "Are you sorry because you feel bad for me, or sorry because you're complicit?"

Words I didn't say echoed through the half-empty room. *Did you betray him?*

Florian's expression dropped again, the cracks sealing over and cementing me out. His arms crossed. "Captain, while your company is . . . most welcome . . ." His voice was clipped, careful. "I'm afraid I need to know what this visit is about. I'm very busy these days."

My hand clasped around the hilt of my sword, and Pollux's bright green stare tracked the movement.

But I was not here as a soldier. Not as a friend, either, or a mourner, despite the ever-present knife of grief between my ribs.

I was here as a spy. An assassin, just as Kato had made me to be.

"Ju—the Lieutenant left me a letter," I spoke low, though there was no one else nearby. Stellaris had ears, and I was not keen on returning to Kato's chopping block today. "And I suspect you might have some answers to help me clarify."

Pollux remained neutral. Unbothered. *Unhelpful.* "I don't know —"

"I'm going to kill Kato."

Pollux gaped. "What?"

Well, maybe I didn't possess the tact of a spy, after all. But war was won by initiative just as much as it was won through battle, and I had spent too long letting everyone else beat me to the punch. I straightened, my fingers unclasping the captain's medal that rested on my uniform.

And I tossed it on the ground, the metallic sun clattering against the floor like a warning bell.

"I'm going to end Kato for what he's done. And I believe you have the means to help me."

Pollux watched me for a long moment, candlelight—not *Zo'is* —flickering across his face. The promise of power—or ruin— taunted him. "I could have you killed for that statement."

Or worse.

He could have everything I've ever loved taken from me. He could see me tortured, could turn me over to Kato and use me as a bargaining chip for his own advancement.

515

He could betray me, perhaps like he had Julius, and make me an example. Could frame me for his own crimes.

And all I had to protect myself was a hunch and a vague letter from a dead man.

I was stupid. Reckless.

And I was too fucking angry to care.

"Go ahead, Florian." A smile broke across my face, a half-delirious laugh cleaving from my hollow chest. Wars were won with initiative and sacrifice, and though I had nothing left to give, there were so many dark, unspeakable things I would *do*.

Florian walked around the empty desk—eyes never leaving mine—and exhaled a sharp, pointed breath. "You're serious."

"Deadly."

A grin flashed, and his stare cleared. Sharpened, like a veil had been lifted, one layer of his many masks slipping away.

"Fine then. I must admit, knowing someone in your unique position might have its benefits," he said as casually as one might comment on the weather. He popped open the top drawer of the desk and produced a stack of letters, spreading them across the bare desktop, the warm glow of the candles illuminating the contents.

I scanned them quickly, my heartbeat ticking up a notch with each impossible word.

The missing communications, all with official, *classified* Luxian seals.

Florian's grin widened, and somehow, the knife stuck in my ribs eased. "Welcome to the rebellion, Captain Bellatore."

FORTY-TWO

> "If a body has survived breaking, it can, in theory, contain the shadows. But though it is not a scientifically observable factor, I do believe the nature of a person's soul determines their ability to withstand the madness." –A Study of the Effects of Shadow Magic, Minister Kristos Agyros, 2079 A.G.W.

CAELUM

At the brink of death, only darkness existed.

Peaceful black, a serenity in the oblivion that beckoned and coaxed.

Shhh. Come here. Be free.

Free of the pain. Free of the worry. The doubt.

But something wrenched me back from the edge—something equal parts dark and light, something wretched and holy and cold and vibrant all at once. It dragged me back to my body, rewiring my essence, stitching itself along my bones, through my veins, into every muscle and cell.

Life, it seemed, had not finished toying with me yet. Had plans and plots left to put me through, my story unfinished.

When I woke, and in the weeks later, my body felt better than it had in ages thanks to the doctors, the *Zo'is,* and the new blue tattoo that marred my back, intertwining the giant pink scars, pulsing with energy from a source I didn't want to think about.

My muscles and joints ached less, my heartbeat had been steady and well-paced even when exercising, and I greeted each morning without the weight of that eternal fatigue on my shoulders. For the first time in my life, I felt normal. *Powerful,* something newfound and delirious surging through my veins with every strong heartbeat. It was not a cure, just the aftereffects of that much medicine and magic at once. But it was delicious, a sensation I could easily get lost in.

My soul, however, had not made it out unscathed.

I barely remembered the moment Thera attacked, just a flash of shadow and the pounding of my heart. No memory of what I'd said to her when Syrax administered the first syringe, nor did I recall how he and Rory carried me all the way to the medical bay after. I only knew of both instances, thanks to Syrax, who'd filled me in when he escorted me back to my proper rooms.

When he told me about my new bond.

But I did remember a few painful truths, the memories of what happened *before* inflicting a more gruesome scar than the line down my back.

One; Rory had betrayed me. She'd made a deal to kill Thera long before I'd said my vows on the altar and had kept me in the dark. Her letter had revealed as much.

Two; Thera was not in control of herself, her power far less mastered than she'd let on, and unless I put a stop to her, both of our kingdoms were at perilous risk.

Three; my father wasn't innocent either. His behavior the night before the wedding and his quickness to kill Julius were suspicious. He hid something—and silenced anyone that might have a clue.

And four; I had no one left in the world I could trust.

It was that last truth that led me back to Arturus' journal. Back to the passages about the second wave of the war, about Danae, seeking answers. Seeking anything that would help me navigate through this realm of secrets and sabotage.

I found what I looked for in an entry halfway through. One I'd skimmed over before, too tired and distracted for proper translations that night.

1776 A.G.W. Inferni, Erebus. Fort Tygian rebel camp.

Danae has informed me that she received a message from my king, striking a deal of ~~peace~~ ceasefire. Offering to marry Danae to his young son, making her the new Luxian consort. The prince is just a boy, so the marriage would not take effect for long after, but it would be the start of negotiations, according to the report. Danae is considering the option, excited by the promise of peace.
I do not know if I can tell her it's a lie.
I do not know if I have the heart to break hers, knowing what I know of the young prince and my daughter.
He offered me the same deal when I agreed to this mission. My wife's family was thrilled—a chance to make a name out of a lesser-known house.
But perhaps this is a clerical error. I doubt the king himself would send such a letter. Or this could be a test for me, for Danae to evaluate my knowledge or candor.

I slammed the book shut, my hands gripping the leather so roughly my nails tore at the surface.

I didn't look at the date last time. Didn't pay attention to the details, or the content, instead assuming, like Arturus had, that it was a mistake or a lie, since it hadn't been mentioned again—the next entry stating Danae had never met with the king.

My father was only eight years old in 1776. Of course, he hadn't been aware of this offer, or any attempted double arrangements his father had made for him. And Arturus' wife must have still made good on the original deal, even if Arturus defected to Erebus—my mother's marriage to my father evidence enough.

But King Kato had learned everything from my grandfather. He modeled his every trick after him, reading his journals nightly even now for inspiration.

And the story sounded familiar. The tropes reused; a marriage to broker peace. A spy with a hidden agenda, posing as a guard.

Mama used to warn me that history repeated itself until someone got the message.

Time I started listening.

I felt her first.

My thoughts were interrupted when the door to my rooms burst open, footsteps hurtling toward me—a wave of emotion crashing against my back with enough force to make me nauseous. I had just enough time to stuff the book under my pillow and step away from the bed before Rory slammed into me, wrapping her arms tightly around my neck.

"You're awake!" Her face nestled into my shoulder, body pressing into mine, and her feelings—*love, relief, shame*—pulsing through my veins. Enveloping me in warmth I didn't know I'd ever get to experience again. "Oh, sun and stars, I was so *worried.*"

I stiffened, setting my jaw. Fortifying my courage. "Please let go of me, Captain Bellatore."

Rory immediately fell back, letting go of me, scanning for injuries.

When she found none, her expression changed, worry morphing into dread, the knots in her brow retying in a different arrangement. "Caelum? What's wrong?"

I took another step back—sucking down a deep breath to steady the surge of her feelings against mine—a necessary boundary if I would keep myself safe. If I would fix this mess.

"My father has decided to not dismiss you from your post, and as my king, I will have to respect his decision." My voice was cold, a mimicry of my father's icy tone. I'd need it to finish this sentence, to freeze over my heart. "But you and I have no more personal business together."

I fought a wince as something in her face shattered, hazel eyes welling with tears. She reached a hand out and dropped it again. "I'm sorry, Caelum. I made a terrible, terrible mistake. And I know you can feel how sorry I am, because I can feel how hurt you are. But we must protect each other. Things are still not safe."

No, they weren't. Not with Thera's power unleashed upon the world. Not with the Shadowborne and the rebels still at large. Not with my father's lies muddying the water.

But I wasn't safe with Aurora, either. I'd given her my trust freely my whole life, and she'd betrayed it. I'd always flocked to her when I was sad, always exposed my vulnerability and heart to her whenever she was near, unable to resist her warmth and strength. Unable to see past the protective girl I loved and instead see the soldier, violent and *ambitious*. The trained warrior, capable of warfare and deceit, just like Arturus had been.

I clasped my hands behind my back to keep them from shaking. "Who did you make a deal with?"

A sharp inhale—and a tingle of fear. "*What?*"

"In your letter, you said you'd make the deal again," I pressed, wishing she'd just say it. Giving her one last chance to be honest with me, one last way to earn my trust again. "That if you didn't kill Thera, they'd hurt me. Who put you up to it?"

She stilled, every battle-honed muscle in her form going taught, like it always did before a fight. Before a *lie*. "I can't—"

I surged forward, that new, unrestrained thing snapping in my chest. I clutched her face, fingers squeezing her cheeks, and her

521

eyes widened in fear, the end of her sentence muted. "Tell me, or I'll have you beheaded for treason, just like Julius was. I don't care if it fucking kills me."

Fear gave way to rage. Rory spat, "That won't happen."

I dropped my hold, and she staggered back, glaring at me like she'd never seen me before. Like I was a threat, something new and dangerous she'd yet to encounter.

Perhaps I was.

But my fight wasn't with her, not today, at least.

Another person had lied to my face for years. One man who had the power and influence to shield me from the truth and keep me powerless. To turn Julius and Rory into spies, double crossing his deals just like his father had taught him to.

"It was my father, then."

The strike of grief and guilt through our bond was the only confirmation I'd ever need. "I—"

I brushed past her without a look back, my attention needed elsewhere. "Don't come back into these rooms without my permission."

―――――

The Sunkissed Throne was more giving than it looked from afar, the jagged gold metal well-cushioned to accommodate the sitter.

No wonder why my father had gotten so comfortable in it. So complacent.

When he opened the doors to stride into the room, I modeled his easy, lounging posture, a taunt in my voice I'd learned from him, too. "You took your time, didn't you?"

My father paused, gaze sweeping over me. His mouth pressed into a line. "You look good on the throne, Son."

Son.

I bit my tongue, the pain staying my composure.

"Hmm." I tsked, put out and condescending, like Grotchkin used to be when I'd challenge her. "Is that all you have to say?"

My father's tongue poked at his cheek, a quick flash of annoyance, before he pressed on a smile.

"I'm sorry, Caelum." He sighed, walking up the dais at a comfortable pace. He clapped a hand over his heart. "For everything happened. For putting you in danger. If I'd known the *Sykagos* would betray our treaty like that—"

"I do like sitting here." I patted the cushion with my own fake grin. Easing deeper into the seat, I let every muscle relax and adapt to the shape and size of it. "It makes me feel powerful. Do you feel powerful, Father, when you lie to me?"

Frost hardened his gaze. "I don't know what you're getting at."

Another lie. Another predictable miscalculation.

"You have lost your edge, old man." I laughed, the sound throaty and hollow. I tapped a finger against the armrest like he often did—a habit that drove me crazy.

It had a similar effect on my father. His jaw clenched. "Is that so?"

"Mm. You underestimated your opponent and overestimated your leverage. Rory would never have killed the *Sykagos*."

No, Rory had tried, but she wouldn't have succeeded. Thera was too powerful, and Rory . . .

Rory cared too much. It would be her undoing.

The King's stare darkened, but he said nothing, his silence just as imposing. Intimidating, a tactic he used frequently to keep me in line.

But now, I'd tasted death. Now, I was limitless. *Lawless.*

"I will make you a deal myself." I sat forward, resting my hands on my knees. At this angle, he towered over me, an obelisk of marble and might. But my ass was on his throne, and that gave me everything I needed. "You tell me everything. I want every detail of what you've been up to. Everything that is happening in Lux and Erebus, I want to know."

He crossed his arms, scoffing. "And what does it get me?"

I sat back. "I won't usurp you."

His smile morphed into a grimace, teeth flashing. "You couldn't even if you wanted to, boy."

Boy.

Son.

Nothing.

That's what he saw me as; nothing. A child, unable to fend for myself. A doll, incapable of moving without my master's puppeteering.

I had been once.

Not anymore.

My laugh tumbled out of me like a curse, a *prophecy* I'd taken back with me from the brink. "Didn't you hear me before? Don't underestimate me again, Father. I'm now the consort of Erebus. If I wanted to, I could go join Thera right now and take this palace by force."

His eyes rolled. "Enough playing. Get up."

He reached for my arm, ready to wrench me from my seat like he used to when I was little, playing pretend where I wasn't supposed to.

But his hand stopped. Suspended, midair, by a single rope of darkness that clasped around his wrist.

"What?" His eyes went wide, staring at the shadow, following it back to where it connected. Back to my fingertips, sheathed in the same blackness.

Glowing blue lines rippled down my forearm, stark against the shadows. Against the other gift I'd stolen from the brink, the other bond I made. The *Zo'is* hummed beneath my skin while the shadows whispered in my ear, both in perfect countermelody. "Oh, this? A side effect, I suppose, of whatever happened to me in the dungeon. One I hope to use well."

With a flick of my hand, I released my father, and he stumbled back, rubbing his wrist. But his gaze did not leave mine, not even to blink, transfixed.

Hungry.

His beaming smile surprised me, real and *proud*. The King of Lux puffed out his chest like I'd just handed him the keys to everything he'd ever wanted. "Fine, then. If this is what you want, I suppose it's time. Let's talk."

CHAPTER

FORTY-THREE

"The portal is the only defense we have against the onslaught of the diavolos. But fear not; I have taken measures to ensure it can never be undone." –The Commandments of King Alixsander Bore- alis the 1st, 1 A.G.W.

THERA

No one told me how heavy my father's crown would be. How the weight of his monstrous choices—and my own—would crane my neck. Bend my back.

But kings bowed to no one, no matter the burden they carried.

No matter the parts of themselves they had to sacrifice to stay standing.

Sitting atop Asteris, my face tilted upward toward the sun, I soaked in the last rays of Luxian warmth I'd get for a while. It kissed my cheeks to burnt, watered my eyes to bleary.

It was time to go back to the darkness. Back to where the sun could not shine. Back to where I was not just a monster, but still a king, with a people to serve.

"Are you sure you want to do this, *Mi Vassilla?*" Nyxia's hands fisted tightly in her mount's reins. Like it was an extension of her, her *Skialogo* chuffed, hoofing the ground with anxiety.

She'd been uneasy since I'd lost myself to the shadows. Ill-tempered and worried, our entire two-week journey back through the Polus Mountains peppered with her complaints and frequent questions. *How are you feeling, Mi Vassilla? What now, Mi Vassilla? Have you eaten enough, Mi Vassilla?*

I bit my cheek to keep from snapping at her.

She only worried because she couldn't yet see.

But thanks to the darkness, I didn't need light to forge a path forward. My eyes had never seen clearer.

I straightened in my saddle, staring down at the portal in front of me. The Great Bridge of Sidus hummed and hissed and wheezed, the magic barrier taunting me to take a shot. King Alixsander's legacy practically begging me to undo it.

I grinned. "I've spent my whole adult life trying to undo my father's teachings. Trying to surpass him, and to change his vision for the world," I said aloud, not just for Nyxia, but for myself. "But all along, he was right."

Head high, Thera.

Nyxia's silver, no-bullshit stare cut to me. "I don't know that Stavros would agree."

His name was a punch to the gut, the first taste of doubt souring at the back of my tongue with the reminder.

Stavros had wanted more for Erebus. More for Lux. Wanted the Elysian empire to unite once more, to have all elves love beneath the sun's warmth and dance beneath the moon's glorious smile.

"Stavros is dead for his ideals." I patted Asteris' neck, soothing my mount and myself. "Erebus needs me to be strong, or this will be the end of us all. Kato will make sure of it."

It hadn't taken me long to figure out who'd put the captain up

527

to her assassination attempt. Who'd made a deal with Fortis, and then made him the scapegoat to silence. Who'd captured Kappas and Stavros, just to taunt me with their grotesque, disfigured corpses.

Who'd waged war this whole time, under the guise of peace talks.

The answers had been there from the start, but I'd been blinded by the sunlight and the promise of a glittering future.

Stavros wanted better. But Kato had sentenced his people and mine to endless darkness long before I took the crown.

It was my job to put an end to it. An end to *him.*

Nyxia blew out a breath, leaning back into her saddle. She smiled, the first genuine one she'd managed in over a week. "I stand with you no matter what."

Her support fueled me, bolstered my resolve.

"Then stand back."

With a click of her tongue, Nyxia and her horse trotted backward, far out of my shadows' reach.

Then, I dove.

Deeper, deeper.

Into the pit of discipline and disillusionment. Into every ounce of chaos and control I possessed. Into the love and loss, into the hatred and heartbreak, into the joy and jealousy.

Into the bottom-most depths of darkness and power.

Head high, Thera.

Tossing my head back to the sun, throwing my arms open, I let it all go; the shadows blackening the sky.

The closed portal between worlds, Alixsander's last cruel trick, exploded.

Like a dying star, it shimmered and boomed, laying waste to the plains around it. The blast shook the world, so loud and ferocious, I'm sure they could hear it all the way from Stellaris.

And when the smoke cleared, when the debris stopped raining

from the heavens, when I could finally peer through to the other side . . .

Erebus stood, waiting for its king to return.

END BOOK ONE

ACKNOWLEDGMENTS

Kings might rule alone, but writers do not, and I am privileged to have the best team in all of the worlds. This book was terrifying to write; the scope and scale was unlike anything I'd ever undertaken before. But I did not have to walk a single step alone, and for that, I am eternally grateful to the following incredible people.

To my dear Cass, for always being the sounding board I bounce ideas off of, and for seeing my vision like you're somehow in my head. If writers had Vinculums, you'd be mine. Thank you for challenging me and celebrating each triumph.

To Kellie and Jen, my marvelous critique partners, who saw this beast at its worst and still managed to point out the potential. Thank you for the enthusiasm and insight that helped shape this mess into something meaningful.

To my Beta Readers, Meaghan, Rebecca, Kelly, Cayla, Julia, Lauren, Kim, Lucy, Alessia, Jenny, Maddie, Katie, Camilla, and Natalie; thank you for being the first people to experience this book in its entirety, and for giving me the amazing feedback that helped me truly finish it. The perfect blend of constructive criticism and excitement, this was one of my favorite beta experiences, and yes, I will be inviting you all back for book two.

To Brit my outstanding editor, for your expertise and artistry. Thank you for gentle-parenting me to do better, and for offering me the tools to not just refine this story, but to elevate my craft overall. Your passion and talent is next to none, and I am honored to work with you.

To Cassidy, my wonderful proofreader. Thank you for catching the typos and researching when King should be capitalized, and for doing the job I hate the most with integrity and enthusiasm. I especially thank you for the reaction gifs that never fail to make me laugh.

To Julia Rohwedder, for creating the face of this book with talent and integrity, and for dealing with my many edits on the hands. You have somehow captured the idea that took me 155k words to convey in a single stunning image, and I am blown away.

To my ARC Team for taking a chance on a new series. This book felt like a risk from the start, but your support and love has made it all so worth it.

To my family, for always taking an interest in my work even when its not your cup of tea, and for always offering to buy dinner whenever I hit a milestone. Our village has always been the foundation for my creativity, and I continue to thrive thanks to your unending love.

To Armand, my amazing husband, for being my partner in all things. For holding my hand through every creative block, and for always being the one to drive whenever I need a brainstorming ride. Thank you for loving stories with me, and being the best part of mine.

And to you, dear reader, thank you for venturing into the dark with me. For embracing the shadows and not turning away. Magic will always exist in the world as long as there are people like you out there, willing to believe in it.

ABOUT THE AUTHOR

Growing up on the east coast in small-town New Jersey, Lina spent her early days playing pretend and making up stories for her friends and family. Little did they know, that pastime would soon turn into a lifelong passion for storytelling in all of its forms. While she's a family therapist by profession, she's a writer at heart. When she's not scribbling ideas about fictional worlds into the margins of her notebooks, Lina spends her time reading anything she can get her hands on, driving her Husband crazy with her wild daydreams, and snuggling her adorable pup.

ALSO BY LINA C. AMAREGO

THE CHILDREN OF LYR SERIES

Daughter of the Deep

Sister of the Stars

Mother of the Moon

OTHER WORKS

Of Fate & Fury, A Deadly Sin Anthology

Wind Flowers; A Babylon Novel

THE ELYSIAN SAGA

This Eclipsed Crown

These Broken Thrones (2025)

Milton Keynes UK
Ingram Content Group UK Ltd.
UKHW010758130624
444148UK00013B/114/J